R E G E N T

The Coelacanth Project
Book III

Sarah Newland

*For my mother, who always let me read at the dinner table.
And for my father, Captain Deano.
Thank you for teaching me to question things. Even you.
Especially when you say there are snacks on the boat.*

"You're mad, bonkers, completely off your
head. But I'll tell you a secret.
All the best people are."

Lewis Carroll
Alice's Adventures in Wonderland

REGENT

United Kingdom, DAILY MAIL

The attack on the Chesapeake Bay Bridge-Tunnel has pushed global politics to a precipice. The Royal Navy assists in shielding the United States' eastern coast while fellow NATO countries bolster their own forces.

High profile members of the peacemaking coalition Nautilus remind us that the path to peace isn't always peaceful and have volunteered their own troops to the effort.

War is no longer a question.

It is imminent.

CHAPTER 1

When one is lost, stand still.

That's what Natalie's mother taught her. In the park. At the market. If you don't know where you're going, stay where you are. Someone will find you.

Beneath the craggy shores of Iceland grew a forest. Cloaked in manufactured moonlight, iridescent buildings peeked through the treetops. Squirrels stretched in their nests, fireflies winked, and the earliest birds perched on the highest branches to meet the coming dawn. And in the distance, beyond the tree-dotted blocks of a sprawling city, a black lake reflected a ceiling of artificial stars, all trapped in a bubble of earth within a tectonically divided island.

Natalie had never felt more lost in her life. The entire scene was impossible. Not only that she could be there, but that it could exist at all.

Atlantis.

Rumor, legend, fantasy, fate. Natalie had no idea where she was going, but she would have no issue staying put.

"Nat."

Scrutinous black eyes watched her. She straightened her shirt, self-consciously folding her arms. More often than she liked, Edwin perceived too much.

"Sorry." Natalie tore her gaze from the horizon and refocused on him. "I'm listening."

"Alright then." Edwin fidgeted with the three silver hoops capping his right ear. "Do we need to hear it again? Or are we square?"

"Objective is clear." Tawney raked her wild curls into a knot that framed her head like a starburst. She knelt over a blue and silver metal sheet, thin legs nimble and ready.

"Target understood." Leo winked at Natalie and her stomach flipped. He passed her a floppy rectangle of metal the length of her torso before settling into the cement culvert beside Tawney's. "Remember," he peered sideways at her, "no one likes a sore loser."

Tawney smirked. "Oh, you'll be sore, alright."

"Obnoxious."

"Arrogant."

Behind Natalie, Owen poked the material suspiciously. Ripples raced from the center and disappeared over its edge.

"Are we certain this is a good idea?" he asked. "Do you even know what it's made of?"

"It's a friction-free polycarbonate with a glycerin-fluid coating over a cobalt center for ease of handling and durability," Edwin pompously picked invisible lint from his jacket. "It's called a DartFrog."

"A DartFrog?" Leo's eyebrows drew together with the question, but his smile never dropped, creating a delightfully confused expression.

"DartFrog," Edwin confirmed.

Tawney wrinkled her nose. "Because they're blue and slippery?"

"Precisely."

Owen was not convinced. "Are you sure this is entirely–"

"Safe?" Edwin wiggled a hand in the air between them. "Nothing is entirely safe my friend, though 97 percent is certainly enough to ensure minimal likelihood of bodily harm."

Natalie bit back a smile. Though only a few years older than them, Edwin often sounded like a textbook, and he was speaking Owen's language.

"97 percent?" Owen frowned. "Where exactly did you–"

"Of the past 100 participants, three have suffered injuries, only two of which were permanent and one of which was fatal."

As captivated as he may have been by the inventive semi-liquid DartFrog, Owen held it out at arm's length. "Fatal? Maybe we should–"

"Get on your bloody sheet before I put you on it." Tawney served the warning with a flash of teeth.

Owen grumbled something under his breath but complied, climbing begrudgingly into the retired-aqueduct-turned-slide next to hers.

Natalie adjusted her own DartFrog on the worn stone half-pipe. Whatever water once ran the channels had left the masonry smooth and polished. Stabilizing her sneakers on either side of the ancient concrete, she settled the heavy bag of books on her back.

Thousands of miles away, she was certain Christopher turned in his grave. No doubt he'd disapprove. He'd shout and scold and explain, in great detail, the irresponsible stupidity of what she was about to do. And he'd fight back a smile through every word.

Edwin assumed his position atop the long-empty aqueduct on her left and all five of them crouched. Heart pounding, head pointed forward, Natalie felt a grin tug at the corners of her mouth.

"Go!" Edwin shouted.

Natalie kicked off the wall and landed hard on the DartFrog. It rippled around her, absorbing the force of her impact as it launched forward. Her stomach floated into her throat as the aqueduct arced towards the city and *dropped*.

Friction-free felt fast.

A delighted scream tore from her chest, dissolving into giggles as the slide leveled out. She had no idea how fast she was going but between her laughter bubbling up and the breeze speeding by it was near impossible to draw a full breath. The wind wrenched at her clothes and whipped back her hair, pulling tears from her eyes as she forced them open. She didn't want to miss a second.

And Atlantis did not disappoint.

The city molded itself to the landscape. Intricate façades alluded to massive buildings carved into the basalt walls. A sea-green dome capped a marble rotunda. An ornate iron and glass clock towered over a parapet. The architecture stood conical and square, hexagonal, and rhomboid, and every inch as beautiful as the impossible spread of nature around them. Glass-paneled buildings shone in sage and silver, in iridescent blue. Most hardly breached the highest boughs while others stretched so tall she craned her neck to find their peaks.

Even in the darkest part of the city, starlight reflected off the paths, making Atlantis appear to glow from within. Green and blue mosaic streets glittered with patterns of wave-cresting tile. Natalie watched them flick by until Edwin's makeshift coaster curved abruptly, and she dropped again.

Her eyes squeezed shut on instinct, but she forced them open, and what she saw sent tingles of anticipation all the way to her toes.

They sped headfirst towards the lake.

Unable to stop, Natalie gulped mouthfuls of air, preparing to be propelled into the water with such force she'd–

The DartFrog slowed. A gentle tug coaxed the sheet from breakneck speed to a lazy float and, as usual, only Edwin appeared unsurprised. He leapt out of his aqueduct before the DartFrogs had fully stopped, offering a not-so-modest bow.

"Again!" Tawney popped to her feet, a fist in the air as she surfed out her DartFrog's momentum. "That was better than any rollercoaster at any park ever!"

"No." Owen poured himself over the edge of his slide, flopping onto the rocks like something dredged from the lake. His complexion was more than a little green as he muttered, "Nope. No thanks. Never again."

"The brakes," Leo swung his legs over the stone wall. "Magnets?"

Edwin beamed. "Installed them myself."

For good reason, too. As Natalie's DartFrog stopped she tiptoed to the edge, discovering the aqueduct didn't just drop, it *ended*. The pipe terminated on a sheer cliff-face. Anyone daft enough to DartFrog over the edge would become a flattened byproduct of velocity, gravity, and the surface tension of water.

Natalie had a good guess how the one racer died.

The height should have been unnerving, yet she inched forward. Wiggling her sandaled toes over open air, Natalie balanced on the precipice of existence until all she could see were the constellations in the sky above reflected in the water below.

All those stars, they're surrounded by an abyss of darkness, but they burn anyway. Imagine the courage that takes.

Had it only been weeks since Christopher uttered those words to her?

"Is it real?" Natalie had meant the question to come out differently. She knew it wasn't *real*. They were underground; everything that appeared in the Atlantean sky of stone was a combination of projections and holograms. Yet, again, Edwin keenly perceived exactly what she meant.

He cocked his head. "What a curious thing to ask."

"Impossible," Owen joined them on the edge, his motion-sickness retreating at the presentation of a puzzle. "This can't be the real night sky. There are too many stars."

"What you see is what truly exists overhead, minus the interferences of atmosphere and pollution." Though his voice dripped with pride, Edwin dismissed the sight with a wave, as though the ingenuity itself was more beautiful than the result. "You'll never see this many stars anywhere else on Earth. You'd have to go to space." He gazed at the city instead. "Isn't it incredible?"

Even blurred by the fastest tour known to man, Atlantis was one of the most marvelous things Natalie had ever seen. Despite the forced quarantine since they'd arrived, glimpses stolen through open windows and cracked doors had left her breathless. Not to mention insatiably curious.

Which is probably why it had been so easy for Edwin to convince her to slip out after curfew.

"Your ten days of quarantine are up at dawn anyway," he'd stated with perfect rationale.

And that was all the encouragement Natalie needed. The first few days of rest had been welcomed, something she'd needed more than she realized.

After barely escaping Nautilus on the Chesapeake Bay Bridge-Tunnel, she slept an entire day. Her wounds were tended; healed disturbingly fast with the aid of Atlantean medicine. She ate better than she had since the start of the summer. And, perhaps most importantly, she mourned.

Her rooms offered more privacy than she'd known in weeks. She could cry as loud as she needed, let her sobs rock her well into the night and never worry about waking a soul.

Oh, how she had needed to cry.

When the tears finally ebbed and her body was spent, she'd let a DreamEater Tab dissolve on her tongue. Not even Atlantis had evolved beyond revolting grape-flavored medication, however the gagging proved worth the dreamless sleep that followed.

The vial of purple tablets had appeared on Natalie's bedside table after her first night in the city. After she'd suffered nightmare after nightmare reliving her parents' deaths. After she'd felt the bulletless gun ripped from her grip twenty times over. After her father fired the unloaded weapon again, and again, and again, to always end the same. She'd woken hoarse from her own screaming.

She hadn't asked for the medicine, but she was grateful for it. She hadn't dreamed a single night since.

A breeze billowed off the lake and Natalie wavered on the edge of the cliff. Leo's arms twined around her waist, planting her back on solid ground.

"Really though," Tawney rocked on her heels, her DartFrog tucked under one arm. "Let's go again."

"Not yet," Edwin clapped. "There's more. Are you ready for some real fun?"

"You're joking," Tawney's face lit up. "There's more?"

"About 20 feet more," Edwin wiggled his eyebrows towards the cliff's edge where land gave way to air.

Natalie felt as though she'd swallowed a rock.

"I'm sorry," Owen blanched. "Are you suggesting…are you saying," he pointed out at the lake. "Do you want us to *jump*?"

"No. I'm saying *you* want you to jump."

Owen squinted. "Are you trying to Jedi me?"

"Not exactly," Leo chuckled. "That's gaslighting. For those who lack the Force."

"Ah," Owen nodded seriously. "You mean plebeians."

"Anyway," Edwin's heels hung over the edge where Natalie had just stood. "Who's first?"

"As though that's even a question." Tawney stepped confidently beside him, prepared to leap into oblivion when Edwin put out his arm.

"Not so fast," he warned. "There's a cost."

"You have an addiction to dramatics," Leo scolded him. "You should get help. Quickly. Before it manifests in song and dance."

Edwin ignored the jab, though Natalie caught him swallowing his laughter.

"First," Edwin held out his hand. "You must surrender your sparks."

CHAPTER 2

Edwin might as well have asked for the moon.

No one moved. Natalie could have sworn the leather-wrapped stone grew heavier on her wrist. She rolled it with her thumb, feeling each of its five sides glide over her skin as she traced the Coelacanth symbol etched into it.

Her spark was an extension of herself. As familiar as her own arm or foot and infinitely more capable of saving her neck. Edwin couldn't possibly believe she'd willingly allow the stone to slip out of her control and into someone else's.

No. That wasn't about to happen.

That Edwin would even ask made the hair on Natalie's neck stand on end. He knew what the sparks meant to them. He knew how many people had died so they could keep their power their own.

So, what is he playing at?

"Edwin," Leo turned serious. "Why are you doing this?"

Edwin opened his palm expectantly between them. "What?" he asked innocently. "Don't you trust me?"

A chill turned Natalie's veins to ice. That's what scared her the most. She did trust Edwin.

"Will you give them back?" Owen pushed his glasses up the bridge of his nose.

"No, I'm going to hoard five chunks of aurichalcum that are entirely useless to me," Edwin rolled his eyes. "I can't tack, Owen. Obviously, I'll give them back."

Natalie huffed. Edwin was a lot of things; *obvious* wasn't one of them.

"Challenge accepted." Tawney dropped her spark unceremoniously into his hand. Her gaze lingered there, as though instinct told her to snatch it back, but she resisted. "Wow. That feels…good."

Owen fidgeted with his jacket, his expression pinched. In one rushed motion, he lunged forward and passed off his spark like a hot potato. Puffing out his cheeks, he grinned.

"That *does* feel good."

Tawney attempted to pull Leo towards them until Edwin stopped her.

"No," he cautioned. "They have to do it on their own."

"You say that like it's hard." Though Leo's tone was mocking, Natalie saw the sweat glinting on his brow, felt the nervous twitch of his fingers as his arms unwound from her waist. "This," he said slowly, "is only because you didn't shoot me in Paris."

Edwin cocked an eyebrow. "I'm still not convinced I shouldn't have."

Leo snorted, though the comment must have comforted him because he relinquished the spark with apparent ease.

Then everyone stared at Natalie.

She slipped the stone into her fist, squeezing the pointed edges against her palm. Removing the spark felt like putting on chains. As though Natalie was landlocking herself to the city.

Not that I'm allowed to leave anyway.

She pushed that selfish thought away. Atlantis was the worst kept secret that no one ever found. She understood why the Regent enforced a quarantine. Why only certain people were allowed to go to the surface. She was protecting her people. Natalie just didn't like it. And she liked giving up her spark even less.

Her family had sacrificed their lives in more ways than one to get Natalie to Atlantis. She had no idea who they were before they'd entered the Coelacanth Project. She didn't know where they'd lived, where they'd worked, or who they'd loved. Maybe they had pets. Maybe they'd had a family. Maybe they had nothing.

Yet they gave up everything to help Christopher safeguard their future, to protect a city they only knew from legend. They'd taken history's greatest blind leap of faith.

Maybe Natalie wanted to take one of her own.

The expansive lake glinted temptingly in the dark and suddenly she couldn't let go of the spark fast enough.

It dropped into Edwin's palm and she was *light*. Her shoulders lifted as one worry after another shed from her skin, leaving her raw and new. The weight of her parents, of Nautilus, of time-travel, of a world on the brink of war all dropped away because it wasn't hers to carry anymore.

That's what Atlantis was for. That's what the Regent was for. That's why her family fought so hard to get her home.

Home.

She stepped around Edwin, prepared to jump from the cliff when he stopped her. The touch was subtle, firm enough to halt her steps but gentle enough to avoid notice from the others.

"Woohoo!" Tawney's curls spiraled as she threw herself over the edge. The moment she splashed down, Owen leapt off behind her, glasses clutched in his fist.

Leo paused only long enough to kiss her hand. "See you at the bottom."

Natalie bit her lip. She wished Leo had waited, because now that she was alone with Edwin, she could tell it was exactly what he'd wanted.

The lighthearted glee of their escapades vanished and seriousness scrunched his scowl. "You'll want to give me that," he nodded to her pack.

"Oh. Right." She slipped the backpack from her shoulders, rubbing the red marks it left behind as she tried not to think about the treasures tucked inside. *The Sceptical Chymist. Jurassic Park. Oh! The Places You'll Go!.* Chef Lehana's damning Coelacanth documents outlining their adoptions. Their last remaining family photograph. Admittedly, the contents were more burdensome to her soul than her back.

Natalie had lived in more places that summer than she had her entire life. Now, robbed of her childhood home and four Ancora's, she found it difficult to unpack. It hardly mattered that Atlantis was the safest place on Earth. Her entire life had been reduced to that backpack. Where she went, it went.

"Be careful not to lose yourself down here," Edwin warned, slinging everything she owned over his shoulder.

"You mean down there," Natalie pointed at the lake.

"Dive too deep and up turns to down. Before you know it, the tide sweeps you away. If I were you, I'd find an anchor."

His words lacked the shadow of a threat, yet she shivered. He looked like he wanted to stop there. Like he should have stopped there. As though he teetered on the edge of another cliff she couldn't see. But instead of backing away, he leaned in.

"Should you ever need to surface, here's the door."

Before Natalie could ask for any hint of what he meant, Edwin backed away, leaving her with her toes dangling deliciously over the cliff's edge.

Freedom is a powerful and terrifying thing. An enigma that taunted her since the day she graduated high school. The world was larger than she'd imagined. Her future lurked ahead of her as opaque and mysterious as the fathoms far below. She was scared to the point of trembling, yet she wanted to know, *needed* to know what waited for her.

The unknown beckoned.

And falling felt like freedom.

Natalie stepped forward and the ground slipped away. Not suddenly or weightlessly as it did with tacking, but slow enough for her to feel every grit of rock stutter against the sole of her shoes. Then gravity stretched its greedy claws and hooked her from the sky.

Her stomach turned, her heart leapt into her throat, and laughter emptied the air from her lungs until she was hollow, heaving in the oxygen that blurred by.

Natalie dropped into the water. The impact stung her skin as bubbles tickled past, bound for the surface as she sank. Her hair fanned into rivers of caramel and she was weightless. Alone. It was only when her lungs burned and writhed in her chest that she finally surfaced with a gasp.

Salt.

Natalie nearly forgot to tread water. The mineral burned her lips and dissolved on her tongue.

Edwin had called the lake a door.

Because it's not a lake at all, she realized. *It's a* sea.

That's why Edwin had asked for the sparks. So they couldn't tack. So they could just swim.

When was the last time she'd enjoyed the sea for what it was?

When was the last time she *swam*? Certainly not this summer.

Natalie floated on her back, riding each rolling wave up and over and down. The water lapped over her ears, drowning out the quiet sounds of its impossible city. All she could hear was her pulse and the waves and the quiet rush of turbulent water against the cliff and adjacent beach.

It was perfect.

Atlantis was perfect.

Natalie floated to shore, beaching herself as the water chased her up the sand before thinning and receding behind her. She dropped onto her back beside Tawney and welcomed the warmth of the sand. It stuck to her sopping wet clothes while the wind wicked water off her body, leaving salt sparkling on her skin.

Tawney edged away from her. The motion was subtle. Not enough for Natalie to say something, but plenty to remind her of the tension between them.

Natalie had lied to her best friend. And Tawney was not about to let her forget it.

"One more stop on our tour, folks," Edwin jogged down a narrow path from the cliff, tossing them each a spark as he approached. Natalie's landed like a boulder on her chest, swiftly followed by her backpack. Both heavy and unavoidable. "Who wants breakfast?"

Tawney actually moaned.

Edwin was already making his way off the beach as Leo pulled Natalie up. He smiled, all green eyes and jollity, as he plucked the spark from her fist and put it into her pocket.

"You don't have to wear it." The statement came out as though it was obvious, yet the concept shifted her world. "Not anymore. Not here." He kissed her, so featherlight and swift she could have imagined it. "There's more to life than tacking and time-travel."

Natalie knew he was right. In fact, her life had become steadily emptier since the discovery of either. Homeless. Adopted. Orphaned. *Lost.*

Her thoughts must have reflected on her face because Leo cupped her chin, tilting it up to him and shamelessly kissing her full on the mouth. He tasted like summer. Like warm breezes and salt and a stifling heat that made it hard to catch her breath.

"I'll do this every day," his smile pressed against hers, "for the rest of my life."

"Cliff jump?"

"Kiss you."

"Get breakfast or get a room," Tawney yelled across the sand. "You're ruining my appetite." It was a lie; nothing ruined Tawney's appetite. Not that Natalie was in any position to say so.

"Come on," Leo stole one more kiss before taking her bag, swinging it easily onto his back as they trailed after the others.

With one hand in his, Natalie slipped the other into her pocket. She locked the spark back onto her wrist. It was heavy, certainly heavier than it looked, but it was still part of her.

Following Edwin's lead into the city, Natalie stared so intently at his back it was a marvel he didn't feel it. She licked her lips, tasting what little salt Leo had left behind, and rolled the spark reassuringly against her wrist.

Her mother died to get her to Atlantis. Her father and Chris, Chef and Angie. The Johnson's, and Mr. Davis, and Mrs. Merrick had all perished to see them make it to the lost city.

Even Edwin risked his life to get us here, Natalie thought grimly, recalling his morbid promise to the Regent should their stay go awry.

So why show me how to escape it?

CHAPTER 3

The rising sun poured over Atlantis like molten gold: red hot and glimmeringly gilded. Treetops punctuated the skyline, interlaced so seamlessly with the architecture Natalie wondered more than once why Atlantis hadn't been famed as the Lost Forest instead. Groves lined every street and pocket gardens framed every corner. Even the city's basalt walls were strung with venturing ivy and ferns.

"Real sun or not, I'd advise against staring at it," Edwin fell in lockstep beside her.

Natalie blinked away spots dotting her vision. "Does the projection mimic the Sun exactly?"

"Not at all." He nodded at the orb of light rising on the horizon. "The Atlantean sun is unique; far more than a projection."

"There is not a real sun down here."

"Not *yet*," he flashed a lopsided grin. "But it's the next best thing. Archimedes designed it."

Natalie tripped. "Archimedes? As in *the* Archimedes?"

"Greek inventor, physicist, astronomer–"

"I know who Archimedes was."

"Great," Edwin pointed at the Sun. "That's his death ray."

Natalie stopped altogether.

"Kidding, kidding." He trotted ahead to join the others. "Mostly."

Death ray or not, its effect was stunning. Light glinted off the hide-and-seek sheen of infrastructure between the trees and, as her friends drifted ahead, Natalie followed the sunbeams through one of the city's countless gardens.

Blue and green tiles paved her path, swirled in an interlocking pattern parallel to the main walkway. It could have been as normal as any garden, with tree-shaded benches and exotic flowers, if not for the fountains. One marked the center of every garden, a simple stone triquetra locked in concentric aurichalcum rings. Natalie let the fountain's spray trail over her skin, flashing brilliantly white as the tacking energy dissipated.

Seawater coursed through Atlantis like blood through veins. The closed system of streams and outlets reminded Natalie of metro-lines, only there were never any delays and the stations were always clean. For those who could, tacking was the fastest way to get from one Tertian of the city to another. Mail, medical services, the most epic game of tag; anything going anywhere fast used the gardens.

Which was precisely why Natalie backed away from the fountain. One tack would only take her as far as a few blocks, but even that was too much. She didn't want to miss a pebble.

For what must have been the hundredth time since her arrival, Natalie imagined what it would have been like growing up on those streets. She'd once thought the worn pavestones of Williamsburg ancient, their bricks laid sometime in the 17th century, but the Atlantean streets were *thousands* of years old. They'd survived the unfolding of history itself. She wondered what they thought of her, if every tile weighed her significance with the measure of her steps.

A high-pitched bark snapped her head up and Natalie darted out of the garden, tripping over her own feet in her haste. She'd know that bark anywhere.

"Enzi!"

The dog ran so fast he skidded past her. Nails scraping the abalone street, he doubled back and jumped up in excitement. Yipping and slathering her neck with slobber, Enzi planted two heavy paws on her.

"Hi! Hello." Natalie laughed, easing Enzi down as he continued his production of pathetic abandonment. It was an elaborate performance, full of whining and head tossing. "I know," Natalie scratched under his muzzle. "I missed you too. That hour apart was unbearable."

The white German Shepherd brushed her knees in obvious agreement before twining himself amongst the others.

"Told you he'd be fine," Edwin said pointedly, scratching Enzi's rump. "Andrei's a fair guy, even if he is a little overzeal-"

"Edvin!" A portly man with a rosy face burst out of a pastry shop, squeezing Edwin tight around the middle. "So long it has been!"

"Andrei," Edwin squeaked. "You're squishing me. Again."

"Oh-ho!" Andrei released him with an invigorating slap to the back and Edwin stumbled several steps before regaining composure. "So fragile with youth still!" he chortled. "Come, sit, eat!"

Enzi's ears perked at the three words he knew best and followed after Andrei, his white tail high and swinging.

Still wincing, Edwin motioned them to a café off the path: Andrei's Appétit.

"We can't stay long, friend," Edwin cautioned.

"Bah!" Andrei scoffed. "You stay, you eat! Least you can do for having me watch that bottomless pit, eh?" He jabbed a flour-coated thumb in Enzi's direction. "Ate an entire batch of croissants, he did."

Natalie's face burned hot. "I am so sorry, Mr. Andrei. I'll pay for those."

"Pay?" He patted her shoulder with such force she dropped into the nearest seat. "There's no currency in Atlantis," Andrei reminded her, a devilish twinkle in his eye. "Though I must admit I'm a bit of a collector, hm? What have ye? Out of curiosity, of course."

Natalie swung her backpack around and rifled through its pockets, scrounging up exactly five dollars and seventy-six cents. She blinked at the crinkled bill and smudged change. It was all the money she had to her name. And it certainly wasn't enough to cover an entire batch of pastries.

"I can try to find more–"

"Bah!" Andrei's massive mitt lingered delicately over the offering. He flicked away the paper note with unfiltered distaste and sorted the coins, shining them and organizing them deftly by date. Finally, he settled on two quarters and two dimes.

"That's it?" Natalie marveled.

"I thank you kindly, miss," his hand engulfed hers as he shook it. "And I was jokin' before, of course," he winked. "The pup only ate half a batch."

Natalie flashed Enzi a glare he determinedly ignored and Tawney pocketed the five dollar note with a grin.

"I'd better hang on to this. For security purposes."

Natalie put away the meager change that remained. She'd been drafting a mental note to fully repay Andrei when a new thought interrupted the first.

"This is your Contribution then?" she gestured to the café. "Your job?"

"Oh, no," he explained politely. "Baking is my passion. I serve Atlantean Contributions through horticulture, mostly," he let out another one of his contagious grins. "Planting is nature's own baking, eh?"

Owen frowned, surveying Andrei like a puzzle missing a corner. "Then why open the café?"

Andrei paused as he arranged a menagerie of delicacies over the table, blinking in surprise at Owen's question. "Pastries are delightful."

Natalie's attention scattered between chocolate dipped croissants, whipped grey pudding, and miniature waffles no bigger than her thumb. And those were just the foods she recognized. Brightly colored and oddly shaped tarts filled the table, all sheltered in the cool shade of the corner garden.

"Woah," Tawney picked up what looked like a curled tentacle swathed in golden batter. "Is this octopi?" she asked eagerly.

"Atlas no!" Andrei balked. "Tentalily stalks! Atlantis specialty."

"Oh."

"Octopi are too intelligent to inhabit a menu," he scolded her, filling a tray of stemless glasses with blue-green liquid. "They're nature's most genius puzzle solvers. Atlantis uses them to test Archives and securities. Cephalopod tested, Regent approved," Andrei said with a chuckle.

"They are incredible creatures," Owen agreed around a mouthful of something orange.

"Doesn't make them any less delicious," Tawney nibbled on a tentalily. "Though I'll admit," she popped the entire piece into her mouth with a satisfied groan. "These are fantastic."

Edwin clinked his glass against Leo's before draining it and requesting a refill. "Coffee is good and wine is fine, but ch'a is what the Atlas dine." He nursed his second cup slowly. "Man, it's good to be home."

"Ch'a?" Leo asked.

"It's tea, more or less," Edwin practically purred, sinking deeper into his seat. "Original and pure. And one of the best things about Atlantis." He smiled into the swirling contents of his glass. "Ch'a is a blend of electrolytes, vitamins, and a hint of flavor, minus the sabotaging effects of sugar on the body and coffee beans on the planet."

Leo's eyes widened as he sipped. "Woah," he nudged her. "Natalie, you have to try this."

Natalie swirled her glass, watching the blue and green stripes of liquid dance an elaborate waltz. Leo was in his element, intoxicated by a new city with strangers to meet and streets to get lost in. Bringing the cup to her lips, a bizarre tingle tickled the back of her mind.

The drink was exquisite. It ran glacier fresh down her throat, zapped to life with citrus, coconut, and a splash of vanilla. She drank deeply and the tingling dripped out of her brain and down her spine.

"Is there alcohol in this?"

Edwin raised an eyebrow. She knew the rules, but he recited them anyway. "Atlantis operates on a strict two drink a day limit. And certainly not before noon."

Then Natalie couldn't explain the tingling in her shoulders. Nor the fact that her mind remained unblurred by bubbly fermentation. "It feels strange."

"Yeah?" Edwin leaned towards her, dropping his voice below the hum of surrounding conversation. "I bet it feels familiar."

Even as Natalie dismissed him, her heart hammered. As far as she could tell there was no imminent danger. The birds sang. The breeze shifted. The streets swelled with every day Atlanteans starting every day Atlantean tasks. It wasn't until Leo draped his arm across her back that she realized it wasn't fear or adrenaline she was feeling.

It was *joy*.

Edwin, as usual, was right. She might have no tangible recollection of ch'a, but her body did. And her taste buds spread the

news far and wide. *We are home*, they cried.
   I am home.

CHAPTER 4

Natalie sipped her ch'a and watched the passersby, half listening while the others debated local tacking sports. There was the Tertian Tourney, where three teams scoured the Ancient City for a flag. There was the Tertian Triathlon, which Natalie understood to be quite similar to the traditional triathlon, only it was with a partner, and a series of tacking obstacles replaced the cycling leg. And then there were the emeritus Tacking Trials, which sounded all in all barbaric and had been rightfully suspended. But by this time Natalie's mind had wandered far afield from the trivialities of games.

A flash of white dragged her attention to the garden. She could just spy the fountain through the trees, and from it emerged a man in blue robes deftly balancing a stack of packages that towered over his head. Natalie couldn't help but stare. It was still bizarre that the Moirai could tack, watching strangers do it was even more disconcerting.

It had been made apparent since their arrival that only a few natural born Atlanteans could tack. Edwin couldn't, but she'd heard the Regent, Aislinn, could. And while her friends accepted that fact with grace, it stuck out in Natalie's mind like a crab pot buoy: something to navigate carefully.

When Christopher gave them their sparks, he had suggested the Coelacanth Project was special because they could tack. But maybe that had only been her assumption. Maybe he'd meant something else. The obvious was time-travel. But if that was the case, why involve the others at all? Why go through the trouble of protecting five people when you only really needed to look after one? Why risk the lives of ten parental guardians instead of two? It didn't make sense. And the most important thing to Christopher was sense.

The incongruities nagged her, a mental itch she couldn't scratch.

Natalie's gaze slid lazily back to the crowded street. None of the Atlanteans seemed to care who could tack and who couldn't. Maybe because it wasn't something you could see from the outside. Like herself, every Atlantean appeared so incredibly *ordinary*. The population was a kaleidoscope of color and dialect that inspired her to sit up and watch with earnest.

"Looking for someone?"

Natalie spilled her ch'a and she flushed. Less from the fact Andrei had snuck up on her and more from the realization that she *had* been looking for someone. Searching for her mother in every passing face proved a hard habit to break. That she would never again see her father appear around the corner in his suit and tie–

"No," Natalie forced a painful smile. "No, I'm not looking for anyone. The Atlanteans are just so–"

She stiffened as the fountain flashed white again and three extraordinary young women parted the crowd like a river. Every Atlantean snuck a second glance at the trio of so-called sisters, many going so far as to stroke Lache's silver hair or feel Clo and Atro's robes.

Natalie swallowed her irritation with what little remained of her ch'a. It wasn't the Moirai's fault that the council waived their quarantine. It wasn't their fault the Atlanteans fawned over them while Natalie and her friends were eyed with questioning suspicion. And, if she was being honest, it wasn't their fault Leo's smile widened when they were around.

Even as she thought it, Lache slid into the seat beside him, her blue-white eyes as bright as the morning sky. Leo's touch dropped away as he passed the Moirai her own cup of ch'a and Natalie pursed her lips. She wasn't sure if she wanted to leave so she didn't have to watch or stay so she didn't have to wonder.

"Morning Moirai," Edwin said cheerily, sharing ch'a with Clo and Atro.

"Morning," Clo's pixie spiked hair shone nearly as translucent as her skin. "Did you see the sunrise blossoms?"

"Afraid we missed it," Owen patted her arm, though the news did little to dampen her delight.

"Only Clo wakes early enough for such things." Atro shared a smile with Tawney and they both quickly turned away.

Natalie watched her, uncertain if Atro's small humor was genuine. Of the three Moirai, Atro remained the most difficult for her to read. Lache was as comfortable as sandpaper and as trustworthy as a wasp, while Clo couldn't care less if the world imploded so long as it spared her precious eucalyptus. Yet their sister remained a mystery.

Atro's skin was as dark as the cattails that lined the banks of Christopher's marina: a rich brown crisscrossed with silver scars; the pattern of light refracted underwater. They emphasized every expression, every gesture, and for the first time, Natalie wondered if Atro became unreadable on purpose.

She thumbed her own identical scar, a fraction of the size though made by the same Nautilus weapon. Maybe if she'd been conditioned to torture, she'd not give her emotions away for free either.

"After the Curia ends your quarantine," Lache's silky tone sifted Natalie from her thoughts. "I can give you a tour of the athletics complex." The Moirai all but batted her silver eyelashes at Leo.

"Athletics complex?" he and Tawney repeated together.

"What?" Edwin crossed his boots on the table. "Did you think we read books and did math all day?"

"Pretty much," Tawney stuck out her tongue.

"But we *can*, right?" Owen refilled his ch'a. "If we want to?"

"Of course. Once the Curia clears us."

Natalie opened her mouth, but Edwin was already pointing a pastry at her.

"Which will happen whenever they're ready," he said firmly. "We do things differently here. No rushed job is done well, and multitasking makes mistakes. Don't worry," he assured her. "They're working on it."

"I still don't understand why the Moirai are exempt," Tawney pouted.

Edwin tugged at the back of his neck. "The Moirai's situation is…complex. They've been on the Curia's radar for years, not to mention what they represent to the scientific community. The ability to tack is rare enough, and it manifesting beyond Atlantean lineage is unfounded. But you," he frowned, "you lot were unexpected. And Atlantis does not care for the unexpected."

"It's not our fault they dropped the ball," Leo countered.

"Perhaps not," Edwin poked the table. "But to slip beneath the Curia's radar is a skill few people possess, and the Regent doesn't like to be duped." He smiled ruefully, and Natalie suspected he spoke from personal experience. "It's dangerous," his grin shifted to a grimace. "Deadly if you aren't careful. Honestly," he drummed his fingers, "it's likely better that your uncle died when he did."

Natalie choked on her ch'a. It was as though she'd plunged again beneath the frigid waves outside of Nautilus's cells, towing Uncle Chris behind her, the cold stealing her breath as it sapped his life.

"What did you say?" Natalie breathed.

"You heard me."

Leo and Tawney leapt from their seats. Owen's face turned splotchy, his knuckles white around his cup. And out of habit, Natalie reached over her shoulder for her bolt only to clasp empty air. Atlantis had confiscated the weapon on her arrival, and though part of her had always hated the electric baton, it was better than nothing. Especially when Edwin was determined to be so deliberately obtuse.

"Come *on*!" Edwin groaned. "How are you going to behave before the Curia if you can't even pretend to keep it together with me? They're going to try and rile you, to test your intentions. It's like you *want* to be angry."

Natalie bit her cheek. She *was* angry. And Edwin pointing it out only fueled her fire. Neither of which would help their case before the Atlantean Curia.

She dropped her head back. The projected blue sky was streaked with gilded clouds and a manufactured wind tousled her hair. Logic told her those things should not exist in a cave beneath the earth.

And yet.

"Greetings, guests."

Natalie scrambled to her feet. Regent Aislinn stood with the poise and beauty of a Renaissance painting. Her dark hair rested perfectly plaited over one shoulder and her green robes just dusted the mosaic path beneath her sandals.

In the brief time she'd known her, the Regent had changed Natalie's life. As the head of the city's council, she held sway over everything from Atlantean infrastructure to global politics. But most important to Natalie, she took care of them. Regent Aislinn was the reason their parents and Christopher had been so desperate to get them to Atlantis. She held the responsibility of ending Nautilus in her capable, regal hands. She removed the weight of the world from Natalie's shoulders. She looked after them. She *cared.*

It was more than Natalie had dared to hope for, a relief she'd needed more than she realized. Aislinn meant no more guessing, no more questions, no more running. For the first time since Christopher died, Natalie had someone to look after her. Someone to lean on. Someone who already had all of the answers.

"The Atlantean Curia requests an audience with you," Aislinn announced softly. "Shall we?"

They each muttered their gratitude, Natalie more passionately than the others. Though none were quite sure how to behave around Atlantean leadership. Owen absorbed himself in cleaning his glasses. Tawney bowed. Leo looked as though he might try to shake her hand, then thought better of it. Only Edwin and Andrei appeared at ease, greeting the Regent with a polite nod.

"Perfect timing, Aislinn, as is your forte," Edwin gave a small salute.

The Regent's eyes narrowed, a movement so subtle and restrained Natalie wasn't certain it had happened at all.

"Well met Andrei. Lachesis. Clotho. Atropos," Aislinn acknowledged them each in turn, then gestured for Natalie and her friends to follow, leaving the Moirai with Andrei to enjoy their ch'a and pastries.

Enzi trotted so close to Natalie's side his fur brushed her knees. She stopped, motioning for him to sit.

"Stay here," she told him. "The Moirai will watch you until I get back." Natalie could have sworn Clo actually got paler. "Or Andrei," she modified.

Enzi sniffed the breeze, but otherwise didn't move.

"Enzi," she pleaded. "You can't come today."

"Nonsense," Regent Aislinn snapped her fingers. "Come, shepherd. The Curia will adore you."

Enzi paraded proudly after her, lifting his nose to boop Aislinn's regal palm.

Perfect, Natalie smiled to herself. *Atlantis is perfect.*

The Russian Federation, MOSCOW TIMES

A series of mass shootings have put the United States' capitol of Washington D.C. under a state of martial law. While their government seeks to swiftly subdue this state of terror, they are withdrawing international aid from Europe.

Global tension is rising.

Keep ready.

CHAPTER 5

The Atlantean Curia felt more like a cathedral than a courtroom. Held within the rotunda Natalie spied from Edwin's DartFrog, a seafoam dome capped towering marble columns, filtering Archimedes' sun into ribbons of turquoise. A knee-high wall cut the diameter of the room, separating desks from rows of white lacquered pews. It was the kind of place that seeped history from the mortar. The kind of place that promised sanctuary.

Natalie watched with rapt attention as the council trickled in. The steady march of robed officials emerged from a central stairwell, and it was only once the entire chamber settled that Regent Aislinn joined them.

"Good day, council," Aislinn greeted them from her podium. "Let us begin."

They discussed everything from Contribution requirements to the failed wheat crop in the northern Tertian. They celebrated the opening of Einstein's Eats and heartily debated not one or two, but four proposed countermeasures to the evolving state of climate change.

A gathered audience observed the proceedings, voicing their opinions when prompted by the Regent. And despite the constant murmuring of those in the assembly, Natalie could perfectly hear the Curia. She wondered if there was some unseen Atlantean technology at play or simply the natural acoustics of the turquoise dome.

After two failed attempts to wander, Enzi sat trapped between Natalie's knees. He pouted, ears flat against his head as she frayed the braided leather of his collar.

Now that it was finally time to tell her story, nerves tapered Natalie's excitement. Still damp and sandy, she was hardly fit to address any council, let alone this one. These people were leading *Atlantis*. They were responsible for funneling ingenuity to the world above and she had to waste their time with a plea for permanent residence. Underdressed and underprepared, Natalie wiped her palms on her jacket, replacing sweat with brine.

"The aqueducts have been retired for centuries," one bald councilman explained. "I see no reason to implement them now. Not with the fountains fulfilling our needs."

"Their absence has always been more of a hindrance than a benefit," a woman in violet countered. "And we've evolved since their detachment."

"Besides," another backed her up, "it was a decision rooted in fear made over two millennia ago. Why not trial them for a decade and see what becomes of it?"

Edwin leaned around Natalie to whisper at the others. "Ah, but how else would we DartFrog through the city?"

She thought of the massive aqueducts they'd slid down that very morning. Even if the linked garden fountains were all the Atlanteans required for tacking about the city, rivers above the streets would have been beautiful if nothing else.

She cupped her palm around Edwin's ear. "Why were they turned off?"

"Betrayed." His voice was so low she knew she must have misheard him, yet he offered no further explanation.

Admiring the stained-glass overhead, Natalie tried again to focus on her speech, mouthing lines she'd rehearsed on a loop for days. This was her chance to sway the Curia in their favor. Atlantis had been accommodating but that wasn't enough. She needed acceptance. She needed them to believe her. And if a decision was reached for the aqueducts, she missed it.

"What of the southern cave extension?"

"It is too near the surface cities," a man with a beard to his belly coughed. "At present we lack sufficient quake activity to cover the work."

How long had they been talking? Ten minutes? An hour? How long would it take to convince them to let her and her friends stay? How long would it take to recount all the evil Nautilus had done to them?

"Council members," the Regent's authority carried her voice to every edge of the room. "What of the surface threat: Nautilus?"

A murmuring rippled through them until a black robed councilwoman projected, "Nautilus has been reduced to a secondary threat. No additional action is required at this time."

No additional action... Natalie choked back a sob of relief.

Without access to global news or radio, she'd heard nothing of the outside world since stumbling down the rabbit hole of Atlantis. Arguing for a stand against the Ward had comprised over half of her speech. She should have known Regent Aislinn would already have things under control. She should have known the Curia would never allow something so sinister to go unchecked. It was why her parents had wanted her there, why Christopher wanted her there. Regent

Aislinn could offer something they never could.

Protection. And this was better than Natalie ever dared to hope for.

"Very well," Aislinn nodded. "Then the final matter for today concerns our refugees."

"Edwin." A squat man in red pursed his lips. "We see you have found your way home," he cleared his throat. "Again."

Edwin acknowledged the Curia with an exaggerated bow. "With the Curia's blessing," he began, "I move to reinstate my residency. Upon your approval you will never see my face in these hallowed chambers again."

"Drama king," Leo muttered.

Edwin's mouth twitched though his lips remained tightly closed. His gaze locked on the Curia, many of whom noticeably perked at his offer. After an extended debate, the Regent turned to Edwin, her pleasant smile strained.

"Residency restored," she said evenly. "Contingent, of course, on the terms agreed to upon your arrival."

Edwin thanked her, yet when Natalie turned to congratulate him, she found his forehead shimmering with sweat and a vein pulsing in his neck. She'd been there when Edwin vowed to pay with his life if they brought Atlantis any trouble, but with the threat of Nautilus negligible, hadn't the noose around his neck loosened, if not disappeared entirely? Hadn't he just gotten everything he wanted?

"Leonidas Merrick," the Regent called. "You are capable of tacking. Do you confirm?"

Leo stood to answer. "Yes."

"And how did you come by the spark on your wrist?"

"It was a gift from our late uncle."

"Deepest sympathies for your loss," Aislinn offered a respectful moment of silence and inclined her head. "Did he share with you how he came by our technology?"

"No," Leo frowned. "Honestly, ma'am, for a man who loved to talk, I'm not certain he ever really shared anything. I don't think we knew him as well as we thought we did," he paused. "I'm not sure we knew him at all."

"Hmm," Aislinn tapped the podium. "Do you believe he meant our city any harm?"

"No." Leo's firm response dislodged the lump in Natalie's throat. "No way."

They might not have known who Christopher was, but they certainly knew who he wasn't. He gave his life to keep Nautilus away from Atlantis, and Natalie knew he'd do it again a hundred times over.

Naturally, the Council was less certain. They didn't know Uncle Chris and they didn't know Leo. They weighed not only Leo's words but the way he said them, how much he believed them.

"And do you, Leonidas?" the Regent's stare pierced him. "Do you mean us harm?"

"Of course not," Leo opened his palms. "We came here desperate for sanctuary. We have nowhere else to go," he huffed. "We want to stay. We want to help you fight back."

The Atlantean Curia shifted, muttering in too many voices all too low to hear.

Natalie leaned closer to Edwin. "Are they not used to outsiders offering to fight for them?"

"No." That vein in his neck ticked again. "They aren't used to fighting at all."

Regent Aislinn repeated the same questions for Tawney and Owen before finally calling on Natalie. She mimicked their answers, trying to resonate with as many council members as possible.

"And I would like to confirm, for the Curia's sake, your name please," Regent Aislinn smiled sweetly, but Natalie's tongue felt thick and heavy.

Her thoughts tripped over the Coelacanth document stashed in the backpack between her ankles. The one that reduced her name to a single letter. A question.

Natalie A.

Natalie Anonymous.

Natalie Anyone.

Natalie Alone.

Natalie didn't want to be any of those things. She wanted to stay herself, the person she'd always been. She wanted to carry the legacy her parents had died for, even if Morrigan was just a name Christopher picked out of a hat.

Natalie A. She supposed she should be grateful; at least the Coelacanth document had prescribed her a letter. Her friends hadn't been so fortunate.

"Natalie?" Regent Aislinn coaxed again. "You name, please, for the Curia."

"Morrigan," she strained. "Natalie Morrigan."

Beside her, Edwin hissed between his teeth.

"And I must ask, how did you come to find our city?"

The question seemed fair enough. After all, Atlantis was called the lost city for a reason. But there was an edge to it, as though their stay balanced precariously on Natalie's answer.

"Edwin brought us to the gate," Natalie answered, ignoring the sweat tickling the back of her neck.

"Yes," Aislinn's eyes cut briefly to Edwin before softening on Natalie again. "And how did you get inside?"

Natalie exchanged glances with her friends, her own confusion mirrored on their faces. "I…I don't understand the question," her throat felt like sandpaper. "We spoke with the Curia through the hologram. You…you were there."

"Forgive me," Aislinn waved a hand. "I mean to inquire as to how you came by the answer to the gate's riddle."

Natalie's mind reeled. When they'd found the locked door to Atlantis, they'd been confronted with a single question: *what have you learned?* To gain entry to the city, one had to admit ignorance. Atlantis treasured the eternal pursuit of knowledge above all else. And they might have never found the answer if it hadn't been for Christopher.

"I only know that I know nothing," Natalie repeated the riddle's answer. "It was written in a book my uncle left for me."

"*The Sceptical Chymist?*"

"Yes."

"And this is the same uncle who gave you your sparks?"

Natalie wetted her lips. "Yes."

Aislinn folded her hands on the podium. "Given the circumstances, I realize Boyle's book must be very dear to you." She gave Natalie a sympathetic look. "However, it is also quite dear to this city. It belongs here, in our Temple of Thoughts. I must ask that you return it."

Natalie instinctively shifted her backpack further beneath the bench. *The Sceptical Chymist* was the last gift Christopher ever gave her. She couldn't bear to part with it. But she couldn't exactly defy the Regent of Atlantis either.

"I…I can't."

The Regent arched a brow. "I remind you that your stay here is contingent upon your cooperation. I should not think–"

"She doesn't have it," Edwin cut in.

Natalie bit her cheek to hide her surprise.

Aislinn blinked. "You do not have it?"

"She doesn't have it."

Natalie bit her cheek harder.

"Nautilus took it." Edwin leaned casually against the seat as though what he said was of no consequence. As though he wasn't lying to the entire Atlantean Curia. "During that little incident on the Chesapeake Bay Bridge-Tunnel."

Aislinn gripped her podium with both hands. "I see."

Staying silent, Natalie reminded herself to breathe. She didn't want to draw any attention to herself, or the sweat on her brow, or the pack on the floor that most definitely held Boyle's book.

To her relief, Aislinn moved on.

"Very well." She addressed the Curia. "Our guests have suffered greatly to reach sanctuary here. Neither rumors nor delusions should deny them their peace. I implore you grant them permanent residence upon the standard conditions of Contributions and Counseling, and rest assured that the action they took in Virginia will suffice for Nautilus. No further intervention is necessary at this time."

"*What?*" Natalie's protest died with a strangled cry as Edwin yanked her down onto the bench.

There had been a mistake. She must have misheard. After all, the Regent was supposed to take care of her. Of all of them. She was supposed to dispose of Natalie's demons, not shove them under the bed and pretend they didn't exist. Fighting to free herself from Edwin, Natalie wound up clinging to him instead, his words replaying in her mind.

They aren't used to fighting at all.

How could the Curia believe delaying the Ward would be enough? Even if he couldn't take Atlantis, the Ward would certainly take everything else. So how could they possibly reason it? How could they do *nothing?*

Aislinn nodded at her council. "Are we agreed?"

"Aye." The room echoed with the finality of a tomb.

"Very well." The Regent bowed her braided crown and the

Atlantean Curia rose, dismissed.

"No," Natalie wriggled out of Edwin's arms and leaned forward over the wall. "No. Wait!"

The assembly dissolved with notably more speed than they'd entered with, and Natalie flushed as Regent Aislinn approached.

"Miss Morrigan," she said gently. "I know it is not what you expected, but trust that the Nautilus threat has been assessed by the greatest minds in our city. We are safe here. *You* are safe here."

The genuine concern in the Regent's eyes crumbled Natalie's anger. She'd been through hell and back in the past few months. Her emotions were wrecked. Her brain was a minefield of painful memories and snapped synapses.

Meanwhile, the Regent had faced challenges Natalie could only dream of. She saw the whole picture while Natalie struggled to see beyond her own fear. Aislinn was right. Aislinn had to be right. Her parents had trusted her. Christopher had trusted her. Atlantis had survived wars and natural disasters and, most impressively, the relentless passing of time. They knew how to handle Nautilus. They had to.

Because Natalie didn't.

"You are safe," Aislinn reached over the knee-wall between them and fixed a strand of Natalie's hair. It was the kind of thing a mother would do. It was the comforting touch Natalie needed.

"New concept." It was the most she could muster in way of an apology. Thankfully, it proved sufficient.

Regent Aislinn smiled. "Ah, well, you will fit right in. Atlantis is full of those." She rubbed Natalie's arms. "The Curia decides when and where to act, but know I have my eye on things. Atlantis keeps watch all over the globe. Nothing happens that we don't know about."

Except us. Natalie buried that seed of doubt and forced in a breath so deep her lungs ached.

Her name was not the problem at hand; the Ward was. And the Ward was no longer her problem at all. He was Aislinn's. Every impossible responsibility that had been dropped into Natalie's lap was now neatly stacked on the Regent's desk. Exactly as her family had intended.

The woman led a secret city and their every endeavor to advance humankind. Aislinn knew what she was doing. The Ward was nothing she couldn't handle. That's why she was Regent. That's why Natalie needed her.

Aislinn stroked Enzi's pointed ears. "Your Contributions begin tomorrow, along with your Counseling summons. In the meantime, I presume Edwin will have no problem escorting you home."

"Home," Natalie whispered. The word rolled over her like a wave, lifting her up and pulling her under all at once.

CHAPTER 6

There was a crack in Natalie's ceiling. It fractured the alabaster tile, carving an indigo line that forked and curved.

She scowled at it. The crack hadn't been there the night before. At least she didn't *think* it had, though the longer she wondered the less certain she became. Perhaps it had always been there. Maybe she'd seen the crack a hundred times and never recognized it for what it was. Like Christopher. Like her parents. How often had her mind glossed over their imperfections, showing them not as they were but as she wanted them to be?

The vial of DreamEater tablets trembled on her chest, surfing the swell of her breath. Natalie's parents were far from perfect. It had taken losing them to realize that and finding them to love them anyway. Not being perfect didn't mean they weren't enough.

And Atlantis's imperfections hardly seemed to matter at all.

The city was beautiful. The food was delicious, the architecture flawless. The people themselves were intellectual impossibilities arranged in a mosaic of culture and thought. The Regent might not prioritize problems the way Natalie wanted her to, but what did that matter when Natalie didn't want to lead? Aislinn chose to put Nautilus in the background, and despite the dark clouds of doubt churning her stomach, it wasn't Natalie's call anymore.

Leo's legs tangled with hers as he shifted next to her, sighing in his sleep. Natalie loved that sound. It made her heart stutter and the tension in her belly uncoil. And when she blinked the crack in the ceiling was gone. She dug her thumbs into her temples.

No, Atlantis wasn't perfect. But it was certainly close.

She moved closer to Leo, wrapping his warmth around her like a cloak. She was exhausted, the kind of tired that leaded her bones. The kind of spent that should claim her swiftly. For once, she didn't want to take the DreamEater tabs. Not unless she had to.

Yet sleep proved elusive.

She traced the constellation of scars on Leo's forearm. They healed as well as Christopher had promised, though her guilt still burned fresh. It had been Enzi that bit him. And the pink and white ridge on his stomach was her fault, too, though she hadn't been the one to shoot him.

As Christopher would say, she'd made a bloody mess of things. So much so that she needed the Regent to clean it up, to shove Nautilus back under whatever rock it came from and put the Ward and his son somewhere Natalie would never see them again.

"Ugh," she groaned.

Brant.

He didn't leave scars on their friendship; he obliterated it. When Brant went with Nautilus, he left the rest of them behind. He made his choice and at the end of the day it wasn't her. Not even close.

Natalie popped open the DreamEater tabs.

Bang.

She froze. Other than the steady rise and fall of Leo's chest and her own racing heart, the room was quiet. Not even Enzi moved. He slept sprawled on his back, his paws tucked against him, curved so his snout snuggled the crook of Leo's arm.

Still, Natalie didn't budge.

How long did gunfire echo in the mind? Days? Weeks? What would she have to do to rid herself of the memory of her parents on that bridge?

Natalie cursed under her breath. She should have taken the sleeping tablets hours ago.

BANG.

Enzi leapt over her like a furry white whale. Landing with hackles raised and teeth bared, he growled with all the reckless courage of a wolf.

Nautilus isn't here, Natalie reminded herself firmly. *I am safe. We are safe. Nautilus isn't here. Nautilus can't be here.*

BANG.

Leo dropped out of bed and crouched at Enzi's side in nothing but his soccer ball boxers. He lifted clenched fists towards the door.

"Nat?" Tawney's voice filtered through the wall, but whatever relief Natalie felt was brief.

Leo straightened, excavating his hoodie from the sheets and yanking it over his head. "Closet or wardrobe?" he hissed.

"Closet," Natalie answered, already shoving him inside.

Bang-bang-bang, Tawney's fist pounded the door.

"Alright," Natalie tip-toed barefoot over the basalt floor. "I'm coming!"

The door swung wide as Tawney, Owen, and Edwin rushed out of the shadows and straight into her. Enzi's ears perked, all ferociousness gone.

"What are you doing here?" Natalie feigned exhaustion. "It's still dark out."

"Edwin said it couldn't wait," Owen yawned and pushed up his glasses, rubbing away sleep.

Meanwhile, Tawney was anything but tired. Her gaze lingered too long on the disheveled bed.

"You're in *Atlantis*," Edwin brimmed with excitement. "Are you seriously going to let a little darkness stop you? Besides," he winked, "you really think I'd let us get caught?"

They'd agreed to behave themselves, to keep their heads down and lay low, and to conform to Contributions and Counseling, whatever that meant. They'd already tested curfew once and, remembering how Edwin reacted to Aislinn's declaration in the Council, Natalie was surprised he toed the line at all.

Still…he wasn't wrong. Natalie's entry to Atlantis had been bought and paid with blood.

She deserved to see every inch of it.

"Let's go."

As though he'd known her answer, Edwin already lingered by the door. "Just need to collect Lev – I mean *Leo* – and we're off."

Natalie halted. "Right," she rocked on her heels. "You know what…I'll meet you down the hall. I need to get something first."

"Let me guess," Tawney kicked open the closet door. "It's tall, dark, and arrogant?"

Leo poked his head out. "Says the short, salty, and belligerent."

"You really want to start the day with your nose in the dirt?"

"I'd consider it an honor." Having already found a pair of jeans, Leo tied his hair back, preparing for battle until Owen stepped between them.

"Can we be civil for five minutes? Just five minutes?"

They looked at each other, bewildered.

"What's he saying?" Leo asked Tawney.

"No idea," she watched Owen warily. "It's gibberish. Nonsense."

Owen wiped his glasses on his shirt. "Real mature."

"Come on," Edwin checked the hallway. "You're going to love this."

The apartment corridors were almost perfectly round, reminding Natalie of a giant rabbit warren or, perhaps more fittingly, a Hobbit hole. Much of Atlantis extended beyond the boundaries of the stone dome and projected sky, spreading deep into Iceland's foundation.

Natalie traced the smooth basalt wall of the dormant lava tunnel. It leaked a chill that condensed in her chest. The cold was familiar. The walls were familiar. Hugging herself, Natalie smiled. Familiar felt good.

Tawney sauntered alongside her, stepping between puddles of light cast by glowing sconces. "I remember when I was your only sleepover buddy," she teased.

Tawney hadn't spoken to her directly in two weeks. Not since the beach outside Atlantis. Not since Natalie admitted she'd known about their adoption. If Leo sneaking into her bed was all it took to spark conversation, she would have let it slip to Tawney days ago.

"Listen," she started slowly, adjusting the bookbag on her back. "About the Coelacanth document—"

Tawney's expression clouded over. A wicked storm brewed behind her eyes and she marched away, leaving Natalie gritting her teeth. She should have been faster. Or perhaps started with *I'm sorry* and worked backwards to an explanation. How was she supposed to fix what she'd broken if Tawney refused to hear her out?

She was still shrugging off the sting of rejection when Leo doubled back to her.

"She'll talk when she's ready."

"It's Tawney," Natalie countered. "She'll never be ready. She doesn't want to talk. And sweeping it under the rug is what created this mess in the first place." She sighed. "I just have to keep trying."

Ascending a narrow flight of stairs, she climbed backwards to face him. "How did I get you to forgive me?"

"Who says I have?"

Natalie nudged him and he pulled her to a stop, letting the others go ahead in the dark. A step above him, she nearly matched his height. And she knew what he wanted without him having to say it.

Their foreheads touched, noses brushed, until finally his lips parted hers. His hands locked around her waist as she traced the muscles of his shoulders, his back, his neck. There was no need to run, no demons coming to drown them. For Natalie, that was the best part about Atlantis. There was no need to rush.

Parting, she frowned. "That won't work on her."

"It might," Leo laughed. "Stop trying to force it," he coaxed her up the stairs. "She knows you love her. Give it time."

Time. The four-letter word tasted sour. She wanted to talk about something else. Something that hadn't turned her life completely around and upside down.

Naturally, Edwin had other plans.

"That's where we're going." He thumbed towards a massive door, the lacework of metal and wood out of place in the tunnel.

"It's locked," Owen squinted at the thick beams barring the handle.

"Indeed. This way," Edwin funneled them into a narrow tunnel and up yet another set of stairs. The passages wound like servants' routes in a castle, narrow and full of shadows, with uneven stones reaching up to trip their feet.

Reaching no destination Natalie could see, Edwin suddenly turned to her. "Your name isn't Morrigan," he said quietly. "You *lied* to the Curia of *Atlantis.*"

Natalie crossed her arms. She'd known her name wasn't Morrigan since Chef smuggled her the Coelacanth documents in

Nautilus's sunless cell. No more than a note on a page, she'd kept the issue tucked away while more important ones were dealt with. Like finding her parents. Like staying alive.

And frankly it was none of Edwin's business.

"I gave the only name I have," Natalie replied curtly. "The only name I want. And what about *you*?" She shook her pack in his face. "Why did you tell Aislinn I don't have Boyle's book?"

Edwin shrugged. "Maybe because I didn't want you losing any more than you already have. Besides," his voice dropped to a whisper, "it doesn't belong to them anymore. It belongs to you."

Natalie's pulse thrummed in her ears. Christopher had left the book for her in Paris. It saved her life. It was a foundational element of modern science. And it was hers.

But how had it ever been his? If the book and the sparks had once belonged in Atlantis, did that mean Christopher did, too? Did that mean he stole them?

Edwin watched her. Irritated, Natalie brushed past him in a single step.

And the world dropped away.

Her fingers scraped the walls as she fell into nothingness. Wind rushed past her ears, her stomach lodged in her throat, and a squeak escaped her clamped jaw as she fought the urge to scream. She braced for impact, softening her knees to dampen the landing as Tawney taught her. And it might have worked if land had risen from below.

Instead, solid stone slammed into Natalie's side. The world shifted, or perhaps she shifted, venturing somewhere new where down was sideways and sideways was up and she belonged somewhere or nowhere in between.

Curiouser and curiouser.

Oh, how she hated Wonderland.

With renewed force, gravity grounded her. Sliding down a funnel of stone, Natalie crumpled to a stop at the bottom. She had all of ten seconds to catch her breath before another body smashed into her. The momentum threw them both painfully forward and, untangling herself from gangly arms and legs, she groaned.

"When did you get so heavy?" Natalie helped Owen up.

"Guess Tawney's workouts are finally doing something," he answered, inspecting a scraped elbow. Blood leeched up his sleeve, a black stain in the dark. "No less fragile though."

Leo appeared next to them, running down the end of the slope while Tawney followed and flipped at the bottom.

"That was awesome," she stretched a toothy grin from ear to ear.

"That was nothing." Edwin walked down the slide behind her, carrying Enzi like a giant furry toddler on his hip. Putting the dog down, he crossed the narrow room and paused. As he leaned against the wall, his outline softened and faded, and Natalie thought the sconces had dimmed until he smiled.

She blinked. Nothing was wrong with the lights at all; something was wrong with Edwin. His legs, his chest, his arms all dissolved until the last glint of his Cheshire grin chased him into oblivion.

One moment he was there, the next he was gone.

CHAPTER 7

Natalie stopped so suddenly Leo stumbled into her.

Edwin's hand jutted out from the stone wall where he'd disappeared. It floated midair, beckoning them forward before vanishing again.

Owen whistled. "Hologram."

The hair on Natalie's neck stood on end. For a moment, she was back in Ancora I, watching Enzi's tail swish through a solid wall that wasn't. She was back in her parents' office, holding her breath as Amir Amani's polished shoes passed inches from their protective veil.

"Déjà vu," Tawney whispered.

"Yeah," Leo agreed grimly. "Déjà vu."

Unphased by the trickery of light or the memories it dredged, Enzi padded through the hologram, tail wagging out of sight. Natalie followed, moving through the false wall into a corridor so dark she couldn't see her hand in front of her nose. The stone pressed roughly against her shoulders, but she inched on, pivoting sideways, navigating sharp turns that zigged and zagged.

When one is lost, stand still.

Someone will find you.

And that was the problem, wasn't it? Nautilus had found her. Not once or twice, but again and again. In her parents' home in Williamsburg. In Ancora. In the dark.

Natalie quickened her pace. A jutted rock struck her shoulder. Her breath caught. Her blood thudded in her veins. She moved faster and steps smacked the floor behind her.

They were catching up.

A lifetime of Tawney's training couldn't help her outrun Nautilus, but Natalie wasn't about to stop. She burst out of the tunnel, arms pumping, and a quick survey of the moonlit room proved it offered nowhere to hide. In the wide and barren hall, all she could do was sprint.

Where are the others? Natalie's thoughts punctuated the rhythmic thud of her shoes. *And my parents? Where's Mom?*

Instinctively reaching over her shoulder, her stomach plummeted. No bolt. Fear raced a drop of sweat down her spine. She wasn't armed. Why wasn't she armed?

I missed something.

Natalie ran harder, as though she'd find the answer with the next breath. Or the next one. Or the one after that.

Desperate, her gaze skipped over the cavern, finding nothing familiar but the shadows.

"Nat!"

The edge of a crack caught her eye. It sprouted from the floor up to the ceiling. And as Natalie watched, it *spread.*

Bang.

She tried to stop.

Bang.

Momentum claimed her.

BANG.

She tripped and suddenly Natalie knew exactly where she was. She was back on the bridge. That's why Mom wasn't there.

Mom was dead.

BANG.

Dad was dead.

BANG.

She was next.

"Stop!" They were closer. Five paces behind her. Ten at most. "Nat, stop!"

Natalie had never been good at running, but if her family had taught her anything, it was how to stand her ground. It was how to die on her feet.

Mortem ante cladem.

Natalie turned to fight only to be knocked to the ground with a face full of slobber. Pinned and breathless, she squirmed and struggled and froze. A mouth of white teeth glinted back at her as Enzi's hot breath panted across her cheeks.

The bridge was gone. The crack in the wall was sealed. And though Natalie still wasn't sure where she was, she at least knew where she wasn't.

A figure hovered over Enzi, staring down at her with a sickening concoction of concern and fear.

"Edwin…" Adrenaline leaked out of Natalie's veins. Its absence made her head throb.

He made no move to help her up. Instead, Edwin stood immobilized in a way Natalie had never seen him. As though for the first time in his life he didn't know what to do. It made her head hurt worse.

"What did you see?"

Natalie didn't answer. She craned her neck to peer around him, hoping that maybe the others hadn't noticed. That maybe she wouldn't need to explain what had happened, since she wasn't sure she could.

"Nat–" Edwin clamped his mouth shut, swallowing the thought.

"Hey," Leo jogged over to them. "You alright?" He knelt beside her, redirecting Enzi towards Tawney and Owen who followed close behind.

"Of course," Natalie lied. "Let me up."

She managed to prop herself on her elbows before Enzi pounced on her again. Flat on the floor, a blur of white paws and pink tongue smothered her. She let it happen, resigned to her furry fate until thin arms locked under hers, swinging her to her feet.

"Thanks," she murmured to Tawney, though her friend didn't stick around to hear it. She moved on to scratch Enzi's exposed belly.

"What happened?" Natalie asked.

Owen's eyebrows shot up over his glasses. "You tell us," he gestured around them. "Edwin was taking us," he paused, scowling. "Well, he hasn't said yet, but you kind of checked out and took off and…" He trailed off and waited.

They all did.

Natalie's head swam. She wished she hadn't followed Edwin out of her room. Sometimes, she wished she hadn't followed him anywhere at all. It was a long moment before something reflective of the truth wiggled out of her mouth.

"I slipped."

"Slipped," Edwin repeated, his voice hollow.

Leo and Tawney exchanged a loaded glance. Owen cleared his throat. And Natalie deployed her only escape rope out of the conversation.

"Where are we?" she asked.

No longer running for her life, Natalie properly studied the room. Two paths of glass divided the floor, emitting a cold light that vanished in the ceiling's rugged crevices. Low silver tables lit by mercury-plated lanterns sat surrounded by plush cushions. And all around Natalie, the room hummed. It was as though an orchestra played beyond the chamber, their echoes just out of reach.

Approaching the nearest glowing stretch of floor, Natalie stopped short when the surface *rippled.*

"Is that…water?" Owen crouched at her feet, squinting into the stagnant river that looped and spiraled across the surrounding tile.

"Woah." Natalie knelt at the water's edge and the humming deepened, reverberating in the marrow of her bones.

Saltwater. She could feel it. Taking care not to disturb the reservoir that rested perfectly flush with the floor, Natalie hovered over the first river.

As far as she could see, hundreds of items waited submerged beneath the surface. Shiny titanium gadgets, a spiraled double helix of DNA, screens of code, and dozens of others Natalie couldn't recognize let alone name. They floated, turning on an invisible axis, illuminated by pinpoint silver lights that lined the water like fireflies.

"This is the Temple of Thoughts," Edwin explained. "Every advancement humankind has ever made, all of human history, is preserved within this room."

Owen folded his arms behind his back as though physically stopping himself from touching anything. "Everything?" he gaped.

"Everything," Edwin confirmed. "The wheel. The arrow. Glass. Parchment. Nuclear fission. Even languages, extinct and extant. It's all here."

He led them deeper into the Temple, pointing out inventions and records of revolutionary thought. Stepping around a loop of water that held a scale model of the first locomotive, Natalie's sneakers snagged a crevice in the polished floor: two lines of etched text.

TEMPLE OF THOUGHTS
THE PAST IS PROLOGUE

"Shakespeare."

"Sort of," Edwin tapped the quote with his shoe. "That one he took from us."

A gust of wind could have blown Natalie over. "Shakespeare was here?" She pointed at the floor. "Right here? In this room?"

"Shakespeare. Zhang Heng," Edwin's grin widened the further her mouth fell. "Galileo. Yi Xing."

"Yi Xing?" She had no recollection of the name.

A few paces over, Owen cleared his throat. "Buddhist. Invented a form of the clock. Powered by water, if I'm not mistaken," he added off-hand.

Tick-tock. Natalie shivered. She had more than a few choice words for Yi Xing.

"All forms of genius have graced this hall," Edwin went on. "Atlantis monitors for new patterns of thought, for individuals pushing the boundaries of what's possible, and invites them here to the city. We give them support: financial, technological, emotional. And in exchange they make history. They redefine the world as we know it. And I wanted you to see it." His spine stacked, his chin lifted, and his smile morphed into something that resembled pride. "I wanted you to see why Atlantis is here.

"The city stands to protect these creations and all those that come next. Information is collected, genius is cultivated, and when bold, new thoughts are freed to the rest of humanity, we celebrate. We honor them here."

"How often does that happen?" Owen asked.

Edwin's prideful stare turned steely. "Probably not as often as it should."

"It's beautiful," Tawney turned in a circle, taking in the scope of the room.

"Of course it is. It's progress. This way," Edwin led them deeper into the hall. They passed invention after invention, admiring everything from modern day syringes to the recorded sequencing of vaccines.

A familiar cut of stone snagged her attention down river. Natalie drifted towards it and found herself standing before the very first spark.

It was identical to the one on her wrist, save for the leather straps and Coelacanth symbol etched along one side. And the question Edwin asked only minutes before floated to the forefront of her mind.

What did you see?

Without having to discuss it, they hovered around the same stretch of tile, waiting until their friends had wandered far enough to grasp a semblance of privacy. Leo took the longest, requiring many assured smiles before venturing more than a pace or two away. Finally, when Edwin did try to speak, Natalie cut him off.

"You didn't ask me what happened," she said bluntly. "When I…slipped." She shook her head, recounting how easily reality fell away. "You didn't ask me what happened…because you already knew."

His silence was confirmation enough.

"Ever since that night on the bridge you've been watching me like I'm an explosive kitten."

Edwin's seriousness fractured with a grin. "That's incredibly specific."

"You aren't sure if I'm helpless or dangerous."

"Well, you're certainly perceptive."

"I learned from the best," Natalie replied curtly and when he appeared smug, added, "Not you."

"Answer me then," he shifted to admire a sunken glass model of the Earth. "What did you see?"

She waited an entire breath and then another. It wasn't until Leo began winding his way back to them that her confession tumbled out.

"The bridge."

Edwin stiffened.

"Was it–" Natalie's teeth skimmed her lower lip. "I mean, I couldn't have actually–"

"It wasn't real," Edwin finished for her. "You never left the Temple. Whatever you saw, whatever shards of the past you carry, it was all in your head."

None of what he said made her feel any better.

He watched her, fidgeting with the silver hoops on his right ear. She knew he wanted to say something else, but by the time Leo loped his arm around her, Edwin's expression was flawlessly placid.

"Edwin was just telling me why the city's aqueducts were turned off," Natalie changed the subject. "He mentioned in the Atlantean Curia it was because of a betrayal."

"Really?" Owen peeked up like a red-haired meerkat. "Betrayed by who?"

"Ah, who else?" Edwin swept back towards the cramped passage, embellishing his walk with exaggerated gestures. "He spread the legend of Atlantis as far as the written word would carry it, across continents and time, until his notes were bound and housed," he stooped low, scooping Natalie's fingers to brush a featherlight kiss over her knuckles, "in your very pack."

Leo toed the back of Edwin's knee, making him wobble. "Are you up for an Academy Award we don't know about?"

"No guesses then?"

Tawney shrugged. "Jules Verne?"

They all turned to stare at her. Owen looked like he might propose.

"Don't go throwing an aneurism," she scoffed. "I am a literate human being, just like the rest of you."

"Excellent guess," Edwin conceded. "But no. Care to wager a second?"

"P-Plato?" Owen stuttered out of his stupor.

"Indeed! *Critias.* The ending of which was rather conveniently lost. Much like our beautiful city, hm? If you think that's a coincidence, think again." Leading them back through the passages, Edwin revealed a perfectly sensible set of stairs alongside the slide they'd descended on.

Natalie hesitated, her attention snagging on the ornate iron door that guarded the Temple.

"Why is it locked?"

"It didn't used to be," Edwin answered without breaking stride. "But things didn't used to get out, either." He ascended the stairwell quickly, tossing advice back to them over his shoulder. "Remember, a house isn't a home in a day. It has to be lived in, explored and made your own. Take advantage of every opportunity Atlantis has to offer." That wicked grin curled up his cheeks. "I promise you won't be disappointed." The stairs emptied them in a familiar shadowed hall. "Contributions start at dawn. Tardiness is frowned upon."

"Noted. Super important." Tawney stifled a genuine yawn, dragging a handful of curls over her face. "Goodnight loved ones and sworn enemies."

"Night." Natalie waved, knowing perfectly well where she fell on that spectrum. She caught Edwin glance back at her twice before Leo turned them down her hall.

"You slipped?" Leo repeated her words back to her. Dimmed sconces cast hard lines over his face, darkening the scratch of stubble along his jaw.

Natalie leaned against him as they walked. "I…I forgot where I was. Just for a second." There was no other way to put it.

Alone, she always waited for his confidence to collapse. For him to decide that her ability to time-travel and all the chaos that came with it was too much or too strange to deal with. Yet Leo never faltered. His hold on her hand was fast and sure as his stare stretched beyond the corridors, searching for answers to questions they didn't know how to ask.

"We're all exhausted," Leo decided, the knot of hair at the nape of his neck bobbing. "You especially."

Turning down the well-lit, well-traveled arrangement of the Atlantean Apartments, Natalie relaxed. She knew exactly where she was. She was tucked beneath a mountain of Icelandic rock, taking refuge in a city the world refused to forget.

So how had she forgotten?

Enzi trotted ahead of them, yet as she made to follow him inside, Leo tugged her back.

"Hey," he lifted her chin, his gaze dropping to her mouth. "What are you thinking about?"

"The Curia." It wasn't exactly a lie, and anything was easier than the subject of herself. "What's happening outside the city."

"Nautilus."

"Yeah." She watched the dark, as though merely speaking the name would summon them.

"Do you want to talk to Aislinn? I can go with you. Maybe there's more going on than–"

"No." Natalie rested her palm on his chest. Nautilus and its Ward were the Regent's problem now, and Natalie wanted to let them go.

She wanted to feel like herself again. She wanted to heal. She wanted him. She wanted him in a way that required no words at all.

Natalie backed into the room, pulling Leo in after her.

Counselor's Notes
Subject: Owen Johnson

OWEN: "Why do we have to do this?"

AJ: "Contributions are how you serve the city. Counseling is how you serve yourself. Here we will find your passion and your purpose."

OWEN: *Appears uncomfortable. Fidgets with his coat and glasses.*

AJ: "Edwin briefly told me of your trauma. You may use this time in whatever way you feel you need. You may talk or cry. You may speak or question. The road to healing is not a straight one."

OWEN: "I don't want to talk." *Subject sits back.* "Tell me something."

AJ: "What would you like to hear? Inspiration? Comfort?"

OWEN: "You can't comfort me." *Subject closes his eyes.* "Just…tell me something I don't know. And explain it for as long as you can stand to speak."

CHAPTER 8

"Contributions are currency." The willowy councilman circled a chest-high stage with reverence, though there was nothing on it Natalie could see. Even the structure itself lacked adornment, offering no hint of its purpose or function.

"As your daily trade and role within our community, Contributions are essentially what modern surface civilizations consider employment." As the man went on, the podium began to rotate. "While Counseling will aspire to harness your interests and establish personal goals, I still recommend choosing a Contribution that speaks to you." He paused, the monotony of rehearsed speech giving way to inspired thought. "We are most fulfilled when all facets of our lives embody both purpose and passion."

His teal robe rippled as he directed Natalie and her friends around the dais. In a blink, three miniature holograms flickered to life in front of Natalie's platform: a grooming cat, a pooling pothos plant, and a newspaper. The fine gossamer images winked and, instinctively, she tapped the newspaper.

"Ah!" The man let out a tiny hop of excitement. "This way, dear."

Though she bubbled with intrigue, Natalie hesitated. Her friends still stood before the podium, debating their own choices. Only Leo stared straight through the shimmering lights, his attention locked on her. A knot coiled in her chest. Atlantis was separating them.

"I'll see you later," Leo promised her aloud. He blinked at her once, slowly. A silent vow that set steel in her spine.

She *would* see him later because Atlantis was not Nautilus. Their separation would be temporary. Hell, it would be normal. Yet her hands still trembled as she buried them into her pockets. She marched after the proctor, Enzi's fur brushing her legs with every stride.

"Your Contributions will begin straight away," the man explained pleasantly. "An escort is waiting to impress upon you our expectations and lead you to the newsroom." Depositing her outside the quaint chamber, he bid his farewell with a light pat on Enzi's head.

"Sir," Natalie blurted before he could depart. "What if," she bunched the fabric lining her pockets. "What if I chose wrong?"

To her surprise, he smiled. He adjusted her jacket, smoothing the creases and flattening her hood. "Ah," he chuckled, making the lines of his face deepen. "Contributions are merely a service. If you do not like your choice, in a few months' time you may choose again. Over and over until you are satisfied. Though if you chose with your heart, there will not be a need."

Embarrassed by her relief, Natalie studied her scuffed sandals. She should have known better. Atlantis really wasn't Nautilus. She wasn't vowing to serve for life as a Curtana, or a Dove, or an Artisan. She wasn't sealing herself into an inescapable cell. She was taking a job.

And being incredibly overdramatic about it.

"Thank you."

He waved her gratitude away and gestured beyond the door. "Your escort waits at the base of the stairs. Good luck."

Natalie waited until he disappeared into the Choosing Chamber before resuming her journey down the stairs. Enzi circled her, discontented with her pace and ready to run.

"We'll hit the beach later, hmm?" She brushed his fur as he lapped her again. "Now that we're out of quarantine you can run off all this ener—"

She caught sight of someone in the stairwell and stopped. The proctor had said there'd be an escort, but this couldn't be right. Surely, she had better things to do than walk Natalie to work.

"Miss Morrigan," Regent Aislinn greeted her brightly. "The *Atlantean Article* is a fine choice." She managed to uphold the epitome of regality even as she scratched Enzi behind his ears.

"*You're* my escort?" The question fell out of Natalie's open mouth before she could catch it.

"I wished for an opportunity to talk without all of the," her slender fingers twirled in the air before settling on the word, "distractions."

Natalie tried not to stare. She'd been in the Regent's presence a handful of times, but never alone. Never with the intention of carrying on a one-on-one conversation.

"Shall we?" Aislinn's robes shone emerald in the morning light as she led them out onto the street. "Tell me, Natalie," she began, setting a leisurely pace. "How are you finding Atlantis?"

Natalie fumbled for a summary of everything she'd experienced. A city enclosed within the earth, an underground sea, the Temple of Thoughts, the DartFrogs. Where was she supposed to start?

"It's…unbelievable."

"And your apartments?"

"Great," Natalie assured her. "Truly."

"I am glad to hear it."

They carried on in comfortable silence for several turns, their path looping into the nearest garden. Aislinn inclined her head towards the bubbling fountain and Natalie stepped back.

"I'd actually prefer to walk," she adjusted the spark on her wrist. "If you don't mind."

Regent Aislinn arched a brow in surprise but led on by foot, keeping them tucked amongst the gardens to avoid curious crowds.

Natalie had questions, hundreds of them. How was the city built? How was the Curia monitoring Nautilus? Were the aqueducts truly turned off because of Plato? What were the latest reports on the Ward's activity? Did she know anything about Brant? But when Natalie finally found the ability to speak again, she didn't ask a question at all.

"Thank you, Aislinn."

"You have nothing to thank me for."

"I do," Natalie was so bold as to stop her. They stood beneath the massive clock tower Natalie spied on the DartFrog. Its façade stretched from the basalt wall that ringed half the city while the bulk of the building extended within the rock. "So many people have helped me," Natalie shrugged one shoulder, "and I've lost them before I could tell them what it meant. What *they* meant."

"Anyone would do what I have done for you."

"That isn't true," Natalie countered. "You took us in when you could have turned us away. You took us in knowing it could bring Nautilus pounding on your door. And I don't think it was only because of Edwin's promises to keep the peace." The Regent's lips pursed at her boldness, but the dam had broken, and Natalie couldn't stop. Every worry she'd been holding in, every nightmare, every memory commandeered her mouth. "I am so grateful for everything you have done for me and my family, for the world. But you have to know…Nautilus will destroy everything unless you intervene."

Natalie braced herself for the reprimand. She'd just questioned the decisions of the Regent of Atlantis and her Curia to her face. But she'd witnessed first-hand what Nautilus could do, how thoroughly and indiscriminately they destroy. So, while logic told her the Regent was infinitely more qualified to handle the situation, Natalie's conscience refused to stay silent.

But instead of riling with anger or contempt, the corners of Aislinn's mouth twitched up in a smile. "Miss Morrigan, do you think I was chosen for Regent because I look nice in these robes?"

Natalie's cheeks burned red with embarrassment. "I–No! No, of course not."

"I say this only because it seems you will have no peace unless I do," Aislinn tucked a stray lock of hair behind Natalie's ear. "There is always a storm on the horizon, yet rarely do they make landfall. Nautilus is not news to the Curia. There are contingencies in place, plans in position." She bent until they were eye to eye. "If, and I do mean *if*, the Ward makes his move, I will make mine."

Natalie flushed with equal parts shame and relief. She didn't agree with the Curia's tactics, but that was as helpful as judging a book by its cover. She didn't have all the facts. She couldn't see the global story because she was still consumed by her own chapter.

The Curia's choice to let Nautilus fizzle out on its own felt dangerously apathetic. But Natalie had to wonder if that judgment was based on reason or fear. Because she couldn't deny that fear had carved a home in her. She saw demons in the dark. She dreamed of bolts and bullets and heard screams echo in silence. Her own experience with Nautilus was an intimate one. The Ward had personally undermined every pillar Natalie was built on.

He burned her home. He stole her family. He made her question herself.

No matter where he positioned his pawns on the global chessboard, the Ward's vendetta against her was personal. Natalie had been focused on protecting her own pieces in the game while the Regent saw the entire board.

Aislinn was trained to lead. Natalie had barely managed to survive.

She knew nothing of running a city, let alone one that molded the technological processes of the entire world. Her own parents, even Christopher, had sacrificed everything to get her into the Regent's care. They trusted Aislinn. They trusted her enough to die knowing Natalie would be safe in Atlantis.

She needed to stop questioning the Regent and let her do her job.

Accepting Natalie's silence as understanding, Aislinn inclined her head towards the ancient building before them. "You will find the *Atlantean Article* down the hall on your left." She gave Natalie a sympathetic look. "Give it time. Atlantis will feel like home before you know it."

Home.

The truth was, Atlantis did feel like home. The fresh scents of citrus and mint on the breeze, the mosaic blue and green tiles underfoot, even the hush of the streets and rustle of passing robes soothed her frayed nerves. The idea Natalie could have lived there before her parents, before Williamsburg, seemed outlandishly impossible until she stopped thinking and simply *felt*. Her feet knew the streets as well as her lungs knew the air.

As though hearing her thoughts, Aislinn squeezed Natalie's shoulder. "I suggest you take every advantage your coming Counseling has to offer," she urged, her voice dropping low. "Time-travel poisons the mind. Thankfully your abilities are minor; fully gifted travelers are not as fortunate."

What the Regent offered as comfort hit Natalie like a blow to the chest. She recoiled. Her heart lurched.

"What?"

But Aislinn's green robes already swished away, leaving Natalie to resonate in her echoes.

Fully gifted travelers are not as fortunate.

That meant there were others who could tack through time. There were others like *her.*

Natalie could have sworn the Earth shifted under her feet.

Did Christopher know? Surely Edwin did.

And he'd never said a word.

Emotions warred within her. Aislinn was watching Nautilus…but if Natalie wasn't the only time-traveler, did the Ward know? Were the others safe within the walls of Atlantis or were they spattered about the globe within Nautilus's greedy reach?

And if Natalie's own power was *minor*, what could a fully gifted time-traveler do? Why hadn't the Coelacanth Project protected them instead?

Question everything.

Christopher's advice made her head spin. Again and again, she was brought back to the same question that had haunted her since the day her parents went missing.

Why me?

But for the first time since their disappearance, she felt close to the truth.

CHAPTER 9

When one is lost, stand still.

Natalie had no idea how long she stood in the clock tower's shadow, but eventually someone came looking for her.

"Miss Morrigan?"

"Hmm?"

"You are late."

Natalie considered leaving. She needed answers. She needed to talk to Edwin. But answers from Edwin did not come easily. If she burst into his apartment demanding something, he'd be more likely not to give her anything. Not in the depth she needed him to. It was likely the centuries of information stored in the Atlantean newsroom would be more forthcoming and less enigmatic.

So when Enzi bounded up the stairs to greet his newest friend, Natalie followed. The man was older, his shoulders hunched forward with his gait. Unlike most of the other Atlanteans she'd seen, he forwent the traditional robes in favor of slacks and a baby-blue button down. He warily let Enzi sniff his hand, relaxing when the dog fully leaned against him.

"Tardiness is the eighth cardinal sin, you know."

Natalie considered giving the excuse she'd been with the Regent, but the tension in his jaw made her think he wouldn't care if she'd been with Queen Victoria in 1855.

"It won't happen again," she promised.

He nodded curtly, turning on his heel and marching beneath the edifice of sparkling marble. Doing her best to ignore his frigid countenance, Natalie admired the towering halls of arches and columns. Beyond the clock tower, the building was several times larger than it had appeared from outside. Every footfall echoed down the chasmal halls, stretching deep into the basalt crucible of Atlantis.

Lined with closed doors and wide windows, the passage reminded Natalie of the covered streets of Paris. Peeking through one of the massive panes, she half expected an assortment of boutiques and patisseries, yet they weren't shops at all.

They were classrooms.

She hurried on to the next and the next, and in every room she found children sitting at desks, reading or playing with toys. Infants, toddlers, and teens, many nearly as old as herself and already as tall.

"Atlantis has a school?" Natalie blurted.

Her chaperone bobbed his head, appearing more amused than annoyed, and Natalie couldn't help feeling shortsighted.

Of course Atlantis would have a school. She'd spotted groups of children around the parks and playing soccer in the streets. It made perfect sense. Yet the concept of a place as impossible as Atlantis having something as common as a school remained difficult to swallow.

"What are they taught?"

"Oh goodness child, what aren't they taught? The Academy covers languages, mathematics, culture, art," he counted the subjects on his fingers. "History, both reported and obscured. Astronomy. Biology. Logic!" His abrupt clap made her jump. "But mostly," he turned solemn, "they are taught to question."

Natalie watched the little man curiously. Christopher would have liked him.

Down two narrow halls and around several sharp turns, they finally stopped beneath a cursive metal *A* suspended from the ceiling.

"The *Atlantean Article*."

The man disappeared through a fogged projection flawlessly mimicking a glass door and, following close behind, all Natalie managed to say was, "Wow."

The *Atlantean Article* redefined what it meant to be a newsroom. Glass screens stretched from floor to ceiling, sparkling like crystal as they filled and refilled with text. There were no ink-scribbled notepads or bulletin boards, no arrangement of newspaper clippings. In their place, holograms flashed and flickered, each displaying headlines and breaking stories. And most jarring of all, there were no people. The *Atlantean Article* had usurped the iron pen to rule with a digital fist.

Natalie skirted projections of sprouting trees and a distant sunrise. She found a three-dimensional rendering for the grand opening of Einstein's Eats, an immersive depiction of the coming Floriade in Almere, and an entire wall dedicated to the much-anticipated Grand Egypt Museum. The images were so lifelike they appeared to breathe, and every time Natalie turned, the stories changed. Developments, achievements, *progress* from all over the world funneled past her in a blur.

Captivated by a modular display of what was soon to be the world's largest wildlife crossing, Natalie beamed. If Christopher was rolling over in his grave from all the chaos of the world, then Johannes Gutenberg was having a party in his. The very purpose of the room she stood in would not have been possible without him.

"Gutenberg would swoon," she said.

"We certainly like to think so." Her companion darted away, and Natalie followed his shining bald head to the back corner of the room. "Though we never forget our origins."

Beyond the last of the projections, Natalie resisted the urge to lean against one of the few things in the room that wasn't a hologram. She had only ever seen the contraption in drawings and photographs, but she had no doubt she stood before a genuine 15th century printing press.

"Is that truly Gutenberg's design?"

"That, child, is the original." Nudging her, he added, "Who do you think funded his research?"

Natalie gaped. "That," she pointed at the arrangement of wooden levers and planks. "That's…"

The old man chuckled. "Incredible, isn't it? There are intellectual geodes cached all over this city, in the Temple of Thoughts and beyond."

Natalie could only stare. She stood less than a foot away from one of the greatest inventions in human history. Not a hologram or a replica. *The* printing press. *Gutenberg's* printing press.

Natalie's disbelief soon outweighed her reverence. Reaching out to touch the nearest leaver, her fingertips brushed a clear barrier. She yanked her hand back, silently scolding herself for having attempted at all.

"How is this here?" she asked.

The man looked at her quizzically. "It never left."

It hit her then, the gravity of what Edwin had said in the Temple of Thoughts.

All forms of genius have graced this hall.

Gutenberg himself had at once walked the same streets she did now. His printing press had been perfected in one of those very halls. The concept made her dizzy.

Returning to the front of the newsroom, Natalie glanced back at the printing press as though it might vanish. "Have you ever touched it?"

"Oh, no." He clicked his tongue and added with a sly smile, "Not yet. I'm Hugo, by the way."

"Natalie."

"I know." Hugo gestured to one of the frosted panels where that morning's *Atlantean Article* projected. Natalie groaned.

A screen-long report displayed a picture of her and her friends at Andre's Appétit. She sipped her ch'a while the others rocked with laughter. Only Atro found the camera, her icy-blue eyes unblinking.

As though her face on the front page wasn't bad enough, a twinge of unease made Natalie's toes curl. The photograph reminded her of another, of one tucked away in the pack on her back amongst the other questions that kept her up at night.

Chef had given her more than a bolt the day she'd lost her life freeing Natalie from Nautilus's cells. The Coelacanth Project adoption documents and a photo of a Formal Friday long past weighed heavily in Natalie's bag. A picture no one in their makeshift family could have taken.

"Who took this?" Natalie croaked, her throat dry.

"An Atlantean reporter," Hugo shrugged. "The very notion of reporting was born right here, you know. Atlantis sends observers out into the world and they record what they see. Fascinating, no?"

"Fascinating…" Natalie's thoughts raced on a circular track. Who had taken their photograph? Who had known about them when all of Atlantis seemed oblivious? It was the same problem over and over: all questions and no answers.

"Well, let's get started," Hugo rubbed his palms together. "I'm to run you through the basics before I head out."

Natalie's attention snapped back to the present. "Head out?" Her spirits lifted. "I'm going to be working here...alone?"

"Yes, yes. The workload is light, so we'll split days. I'll run the morning. You take the evening and head home at sunset." Without waiting for her answer, Hugo showed her where the finished articles came in, what should be featured on the first page over the fifth, and where the ch'a press was located for breaks.

"That's it?" Natalie confirmed when he'd finished. "We don't do any actual writing? We just," she fished for the words, "organize and print?"

"Not even that much." Hugo waved at a frosted pane, summoning images of the next morning's *Atlantean Article*. "Distribution is digital. No printing necessary."

"Right. I knew that." Natalie's shoulders relaxed down her spine. A little mindless organization might be exactly what she needed. Perhaps it would put her own thoughts in order. "Thank you."

Hugo slung a pack over his curved back. "If you get stuck or confused, we can figure it out tomorrow." He made to depart and turned sharply in the doorway. "One more thing," Hugo dug a folded note from his pocket. It was by far the most archaic thing in the room. "Your Counseling summons. Tonight, after Contributions."

He waved farewell and, for the first time since entering Atlantis, Natalie was truly alone. Aside from Enzi, who pointedly nosed his way under her arm.

"Don't worry," she assured him. "We'll be fine."

Hours passed and Natalie sorted through incoming articles, arranging them in whatever way she saw fit while familiarizing herself with the platform. She'd been right: the silence was welcomed. Her mind wandered to the places in the pictures, around the world and back again until it settled on memories of home.

Oh, how her father would have loved that room. He could have spent hours devouring every report, so consumed by his research he would forget to consume anything else. Mom would undoubtedly show up with something sweet and make faces at Natalie as he prattled on about every advancement from Hong Kong to San Diego. The image made Natalie smile despite the stabbing ache in her chest.

She missed them. She missed their late-night hot chocolates in midsummer and day trips to the beach. She missed having someone there when she had questions, even if they couldn't, or wouldn't, answer them. They'd known so much more than they shared. Maybe they knew about other time-travelers, too.

Maybe they knew who took that Formal Friday photograph.

"Natalie."

She jumped, a crystal tablet bouncing from palm to palm until Leo snatched it from the air.

"Sorry," he flashed her half a grin. "I forget that Natalie Morrigan isn't always where she appears to be."

His thumb grazed her collarbone and heat singed under Natalie's skin.

Your name isn't Morrigan. Edwin's reminder pierced her thoughts and she flinched.

Only Leo took it as something else. He stiffened. A question hovered behind his eyes but instead of asking it, he pulled her in. He smelled like a forest at the edge of the sea, like pine and salt and earth.

She wanted to tell him everything then. About Edwin keeping secrets and the other travelers and the crack and the photograph. About her name. But doubt seized her throat. She could feel the constellation of scars on his arm, she could trace the raised remnants of every puncture without looking. She wouldn't drag him down another rabbit hole without knowing what waited on the other side.

She couldn't.

The last time she did, she lost him for months.

"What Contribution did you pick?" she asked.

"The Athletics Complex," he huffed out a laugh. "Most of the sports are strange, even the workout systems are bizarre. Did you know they have weighted holograms?" Natalie shook her head against his chest. "Me neither. Anyway, thankfully soccer seems universal. It's nice seeing something familiar for once."

"I can imagine." She felt him tense again, his shoulders shifting as he adjusted his arms around her.

"Listen," he cleared his throat. "I'm having dinner tonight…with my dad." The words strained out of his mouth, as difficult for him to say as they were for her to hear.

She wondered what it was like for Leo, rebuilding bridges with someone so familiar that had always truly been a stranger. If her own parents had survived Nautilus's attack on the bridge, she guessed she'd feel the same mix of emotions. That she'd be treading in the same tonic of relief and anger that made Leo's smile forced.

"Will you come with me?"

Natalie was grateful he couldn't see her face. She hadn't spoken to Mr. Merrick or Mrs. Davis since they'd arrived in the city. Not since they'd seen their friends and family slaughtered. Since they'd learned of Brant and his father's betrayal. And she wasn't ready to start now.

"I can't."

Leo unwrapped himself from around her. The cool air wicked away the remnants of his touch as the inches between them settled into miles.

"I get it. They're ready when you—"

"I have Counseling," Natalie presented the summons.

"Oh," Leo's voice lifted though his frown remained fixed. "Okay, well…good. That's good. I'll see you tonight, then?" He backed off, scratching Enzi in farewell as he paused in the doorway.

"Yeah," Natalie nodded. "Tonight."

He left her alone then, with words unspoken and kisses not taken.

She'd been walking a perilous plank with Leo since they'd arrived. Having spent so long trying to get back to each other, every moment together was treasured. If they avoided the hard topics of parents and last names, of Brant, then a relationship felt almost normal. Yet every time they teetered near something real, something painful, walls went up, guarding the pieces of themselves that still hurt.

Her heart flopped in her chest, frustrated and pained.

Natalie turned off the *Atlantean Article* interface and, on her way out the door, dropped her Counseling summons in the trash.

French Republic. LE MONDE.

Car bombings in the heart of Paris have Parliament divided, halting preparations to join global NATO efforts. Until the violence in the Capitol is managed, all foreign aid programs are to be suspended.

But the movement for peace is not without support. Nautilus forces gather off the northern coast of the United Kingdom, sailing under a blue and silver flag.

CHAPTER 10

Natalie did not go to Counseling.

She let Enzi take the long route back to their apartment, winding beneath ancient stone archways and around twenty-first century architecture. Her reflection morphed in the passing windows, the fading light playing with the shadows of her face. A hush crept through the streets like a fog, the silence a fitting companion to the gathering dusk. But despite the detour, Enzi nosed his way into the apartment far sooner than she would have liked.

Slate floors and cream curtains reflected a taste of Iceland far above their heads. An illusory window projected the Atlantis skyline on the basalt wall and, though she could have picked any image she liked, Natalie preferred being able to see where she was. Even if it was just a trick of the light.

The only thing out of place was the note on her desk.

Staying with Dad. See you tomorrow.

-Leo

Natalie's stomach knotted. In spite of the pain of losing his Mom, of the awkwardness of rebuilding a relationship with the man who was always his Dad but never his father, Leo was making Atlantis as much of a home as he could. Natalie twisted the strap of her backpack over her knuckles.

Shouldn't she do the same?

Tucking his message into her nightstand drawer, she unloaded the contents of her pack alongside it. The bloodstained cover of *Oh! The Places You'll Go!*. The creased spines of *Jurassic Park* and *Plato's Complete Works*. The worn envelope of adoption papers with the obscure Formal Friday photograph. And, finally, *The Sceptical Chymist*.

Natalie propped the picture against the wall. The corners were torn, the paper rippled with water damage, but the details endured. It was the last night they'd all been together before Brant's Mom got sick. She glazed over the figures that hurt the most: her mother and father on either side of her, Chris seated at the head of the table. In truth, she could hardly stand to look at any of them save the one who'd condemned the rest.

Mr. Smith, the Ward, sat suspended in time. Locked forever in a conversation with Natalie's father, the smile on his face spread so wide it crinkled the corners of his eyes. Was Nautilus already in motion when the photo was taken? Was betrayal on the tip of his tongue or was he truly as innocent as he appeared, another father at dinner with his family?

Natalie dropped the picture in the drawer, rubbing the echo of the image from her eyes.

If what Edwin said was true, and the Curia hadn't known about Natalie and her friends, then who took the photo? It didn't make sense. *Someone* must have known. Which meant Edwin was wrong.

Or, more likely, he lied.

Something shuffled outside. The floor creaked. Slinking off the bed, Enzi sniffed at the shifting shadow beneath the door. Natalie lifted the thickest book from the drawer, squeezing the spine so hard her knuckles blanched.

Enzi whined.

"Shh!"

Natalie yanked the door open and a petite figure tumbled in, all arms and legs and curls.

"Tawney?" Natalie helped her friend to her feet, where she promptly swayed and crumbled again, letting out a lone hiccup. "Tawney are you…*drunk?*"

Leaning back on one elbow, Tawney gave a thumbs up.

"What happened to the Atlantean two drink limit?" Natalie asked as she settled beside her. She wondered if she should fetch a bucket before realizing she wasn't even certain Atlantis had buckets.

"Andrei," Tawney hiccupped again. "Andrei happened."

"Ah."

She eyed the book Natalie had grabbed to defend herself. "What were you gonna do?" she snickered. "Give me a papercut?"

Natalie tucked *The Sceptical Chymist* back into the drawer. "I was thinking more blunt force Boyle."

"Hmpf."

Enzi reclaimed his spot on the bed as a heavy silence bloomed. Full of all the apologies Natalie had tried to give and all the cold shoulders Tawney had met them with.

The space between them was supposed to be safe. One where secrets were shared and dreams ran wild, where each protected the other at all costs. But Natalie hadn't held up her part of the bargain. She'd hidden the truth about their parents, about their adoption. She withheld information for weeks. It didn't matter that she only wanted to protect Tawney. It mattered that she lied.

Natalie had known Tawney her entire life. She hated as fiercely as she loved. She'd be lucky if Tawney still–

"Nat, I'm sorry."

"Don't," Natalie cut her off. "Drunk apologies don't count." She pulled her knees up to her chest. "And you're right to be angry with me. I should have told you about the adoption. I should have told you about everything."

Tawney squinted at her. "Why don't drunk apologies count?"

"Because they aren't meant half as often as they're remembered," Natalie sagged against the bed. "And you aren't likely to remember any of this."

"Hmm." Tawney sank lower, resting her head in Natalie's lap. "What is Nautilus doing out there?"

Natalie toyed with her friend's curls, tugging a spiral until it snapped stubbornly back into place. "I don't know."

"What do you mean you don't know?" Tawney challenged. "You spent all day in the newsroom. Don't *lie*."

"It's not that kind of news," Natalie insisted. "It's mostly Atlantean. And stuff from the surface…" she paused. "Well, it wasn't about Nautilus, or conflict, or politics. It wasn't about war at all."

Tawney frowned. "How is that possible?"

Natalie chewed her cheek. There wasn't a single report in the *Atlantean Article* that covered anything remotely despairing. Not one. And for a city vowed to serve the world, a world wrecked with strife and deception, it didn't make sense.

It didn't make sense at all.

Projected moonlight painted beams of silver through the window, spilling into Natalie's thoughts.

"Can I tell you a secret?" she whispered.

"Duh."

"I was summoned to Counseling today. I skipped."

Tawney rolled onto her back, a wicked smile on her mouth. "I was summoned to Counseling today. I went."

They stared at each other for a full breath before breaking with laughter. It felt good. It felt normal.

Tawney's giggles faded first. "It's sad, cause it's not even that funny." She tugged at a loose thread on Natalie's shirt. "Brant would have made it funny."

His name made Natalie's stomach ache. They didn't talk about Brant. Leo flat out refused. Edwin barely knew him. And as for Tawney and Owen, there simply wasn't much to say.

He betrayed them. That's all there was to it.

"I wish I could see him," Natalie confessed. "If only to ask him why."

"You know why," Tawney scoffed. "The Ward is his Dad."

"I can't believe he'd go through all of this, shooting Leo, setting the fire in Ancora III, just because Mr. Smith said so. If I could just talk to him…" Natalie trailed off.

What was she really after? An explanation or a change of heart? Would either satisfy her? Would either truly matter?

"Honestly, I've thought of little else since Edwin took us to the sea."

"You mean the lake."

"No," Natalie tugged another curl. "I mean the sea."

Tawney sat up, the haze of alcohol usurped by adrenaline. "As in *ocean?*"

"Why did you think Edwin took our sparks?"

She snorted. "That boy has a flair for the dramatic; I thought it was some hella elaborate trust fall. Nat," Tawney's voice dropped to a traitorous whisper. "If the lake is an ocean, do you think…do you think we could leave?"

It was crazy. To even consider leaving Atlantis, the place so many had died to get them to, the city that illuminated the world, *home*, was irrational. Illogical. Selfish.

Which is why Natalie would have never told Tawney the truth if she was sober.

"Yeah," Natalie whispered back. "I do."

Tawney's arms slid out from under her. She fell back into Natalie's lap, yawning.

"If we left," she mumbled against Natalie's thigh, "we could find him…talk to him." Tawney yawned again. "Punch him in his stupid face."

Her breathing found a steady rhythm and Natalie sank against the bed. It wasn't the most comfortable position, but with the DreamEater tabs out of reach, she'd never sleep anyway.

She wasn't entirely sure how long she sat there. Long enough to earn a cramp in her side, for the stripes of silver moonlight to creep up the floor to the wall. Her body relaxed. Her thoughts wandered. Though when her apartment door creaked open, both snapped to attention.

Her heart leapt. Leo had changed his mind. He'd come back after all, he'd—

Edwin popped around the door frame, his jeans and sweatshirt as dark as the night itself. He lifted a finger to his lips and, pointing at Tawney, cocked his head.

Natalie did her best to swallow her disappointment. "Trust me, she's out." She stood and Tawney slipped to the floor, limp and snoring.

"Apologies for the late hour."

"I was up."

Edwin hesitated between the bed and the door, watching Enzi's paws twitch in his sleep.

"I need to ask you something," he began slowly, "and the more

I thought about it, the less it could wait."

"Are there others like me?" Natalie blurted without ceremony. "Here, in Atlantis. Is that why you say I belong here?"

If her question surprised him, he didn't show it. "Why do you ask?"

"I'm right, then."

"Not at all," he said flatly. Edwin rummaged through her nightstand drawer, skimming the cover of *Plato's Complete Works* before pushing it aside, digging deeper.

"What are you doing?" Natalie asked, too disturbed to be angry.

"Do you have any candy?"

"You can't be serious."

"Please."

Natalie stared at him.

"This will be a lot faster if you just tell me where it is."

She sighed. "Bottom drawer."

Edwin flicked the drawer open with his shoe and stuffed his pockets with brightly colored taffy.

"My turn," he said, slipping a green candy into his cheek. "How do you know I'm real?"

Her breath hitched. "What?"

"On the cliff, before you jumped you asked if it was real. Which suggests you're having trouble telling the difference. No?"

Natalie clamped her mouth shut. The only thing worse than doubting everything around her was admitting it out loud.

Edwin frowned. "Your symptoms are progressing."

Natalie leaned on the wall to steady herself, letting the cool stone leech away the heat from her neck. Edwin said something similar on the beach when they'd arrived in Iceland. Something about the effects of her so-called *gift* being cumulative.

"Time-travel." The words were rough as gravel in her throat.

"This is the cost."

"This," Edwin stepped over Tawney to stand beside her, "is the beginning."

"It gets worse?"

He passed her a candy.

"There have been others like you," Edwin explained. "When the need arises. When events turn tense and history in the making may need to be altered, a time-traveler is born to Atlantis. Make no mistake, Natalie, you're here for a reason.

"We don't understand it all, not even close, but it's clear that in this universe, change costs. Clo's plants spend energy to grow. Stars implode to shine. Changing anything costs something. Changing time costs more." He pressed his shoulder against hers, lifting and grounding her all at once. "Time-travel degrades the synapses in your mind. It's been known to cause madness, and…well," Edwin unwrapped another candy. "Travelers aren't known for their longevity."

Death did not frighten Natalie as badly as it once did. Whatever lurked beyond that veil, she had friends there now. Family. And if it turned out to be nothing, if death meant an abyss of emptiness void of feeling, of sense, of pain? Then perhaps she'd finally have a decent night's sleep.

But madness? Losing one's *self*? Not knowing truth from fiction? She shuddered at the thought. If it came down to a choice, she'd rather die.

"You're certain?" Natalie asked.

"It's history," Edwin looked sideways at her. "So, tell me: how do you know I'm real?"

It took her several heartbeats to answer. "I suppose I don't."

Edwin dragged a hand through his hair, making black tufts stick out at odd angles. "I told you on the cliff and I'll tell you again. Find an anchor."

She knew he was right. She needed something stable and concrete, something that was real in every sense of the word. Something she didn't need to question. But Christopher had told her to question everything. What could be exempt from that? What if nothing was?

Natalie felt some part of her had already known the cost. Why else would she bleed after traveling through time if not for damage? If not for—

A sharp nudge on Natalie's shin jolted her awake. Edwin was gone, and the longer she stared at the place he had been, the less certain she was he had ever come at all. The notion was far from comforting.

Find an anchor.

Another nudge and Tawney loomed over her, sunglasses on despite the window's inky pre-dawn glow.

"Ugh," Tawney held her forehead. "Come on," she groaned. "It's nearly sunrise."

"Where are we going?" Natalie stretched, exhaustion heavy on her limbs.

"To talk to Brant."

Natalie froze, her mouth dry. "We're leaving Atlantis?"

Tawney grinned. "We're leaving Atlantis."

CHAPTER 11

The Atlantean Sea was an abyss. Black waves rolled against the cliff, launching dark droplets skyward as Natalie and Tawney snuck towards the beach. It was the path Edwin had taken only days before, and it was perilously narrow. More so with Enzi acting as a furry 60-pound trip hazard between them. As most Atlanteans rose with their manufactured sun, the hidden city was practically dead before dawn, leaving no one but the dog to get in their way. Or overhear their hushed conversation.

"Were you truly drunk?" Natalie asked skeptically.

"More than I should have been," the corner of Tawney's mouth twitched. "But less than you thought."

The uneven path abruptly spit them out on the beach, and Natalie's sandals sank into cool sand. Inhaling crisp salt air, her pulse quickened.

This is madness.

Tawney stopped inches from the surf. "Your sleepover buddy wouldn't be too fond of this," she side-eyed her.

Natalie's heart wrenched with guilt. She wished more than anything that Leo was there with her. That he would have been willing to hear her out. But this was about Brant. Leo wouldn't stand to hear a word of it, only try to change her mind. Whether or not he'd meant to, Leo had backed her into a corner.

And the only way out is through.

Natalie toed the line where the waves rolled up the sand.

"Ready?" Tawney bounced on the balls of her feet.

Nodding, Natalie held Enzi's scruff. She didn't expect to find Brant. Not in real time, not face to face. Joined with Nautilus, he could be anywhere in the world: leading riots in Germany, starting a coup in France, even training recruits in the Helix. But Natalie didn't need to know where Brant was, just where he'd go. Where she'd be able to leave a message.

"Ready."

A bank of hills rose in her mind, their manicured fields hugged by an iron gate and dotted with polished granite.

There. Natalie stepped into the sea and Atlantis disappeared. Static rippled over her skin as a blinding white flash enveloped them. There was no ocean, no sound, no gravity to hold her. She drifted, weightless, and before she could wonder where she was, the world returned, or she returned to it.

A breeze blew off the incoming tide, carrying scents of seaweed and driftwood with a subtle note of pine. It was home in a different way than Atlantis. It was the comfort of falling asleep in your own bed. Of childhood memories and familiar earth underfoot. Contented, Natalie opened her eyes.

Virginia was cloaked in darkness. Thick clouds blotted the sky, leaving the cemetery puddled with lamplight. As Enzi darted off to scour the shore for crabs, Natalie felt lighter. The night wrapped its warmth around her shoulders and drained the world of color, leaving it less stimulating. Less chaotic.

"Anyone looking will have seen that flash," Tawney scowled at the open sky.

Natalie nodded. It wasn't passerby or security guards Tawney worried about; it was satellites. It was Nautilus. It was anyone searching for tacking signatures that shouldn't be.

"Good," Natalie adjusted the spark on her wrist. "I'm counting on it."

A summer wind whipped at them as they approached the gate, tousling Tawney's curls.

"A real breeze," she spread her arms wide.

"There's wind in the city."

"Fake wind," Tawney's expression soured. "Fake wind and fake trees and fake freedom."

Natalie didn't respond right away. It was true they weren't exactly free in Atlantis. No more than they had been free in the Helix, or Ancora, or, as it turned out, a single day of their lives. But that's not what she said to Tawney.

"I think the trees are real."

"No," her curls shook. "The trees are only there because the fake sun is there. All trapped under a giant *rock*." Tawney kicked a pebble for good measure. "I grew up and became Patrick Star."

The dagger cloaked in her words brought Natalie to a halt. "You don't like–" The city's name lodged in her throat, setting siege to her mouth. For anyone who had set foot there, the synapse block kept the rumor of Atlantis's existence exactly that: a rumor. A myth. It was incredibly effective. And annoying.

She tried again. "You don't like the city?"

"That's not what I said."

"Tawney."

"It's just…it's not what I expected."

Natalie snorted. "Let me know the next time something turns out the way we expected."

Tawney scaled the fence with ease, unlatching the gate from the inside for Natalie and Enzi to follow. "You don't like it either," she said pointedly. "I can tell."

"That's not true." And it wasn't. Natalie loved the city. She loved how the air tasted on her tongue. She loved the maze of mosaic streets, the bits of history tucked into every corner. She loved ch'a and Gutenberg's press. But she couldn't deny something felt…off. Perhaps it was the Atlantean Curia's rainbow veneer, or, more likely, her own lack of sleep.

"Uh huh," Tawney wandered, squinting at grave markers in the dark. "Mrs. Smith is around here somewhere."

Natalie studied every headstone, muttering their names aloud. It had been years since the funeral. She remembered the hill, if not the row or the plot. But she knew Brant would remember it all. Despite the lies. Despite the deception. Despite the adoption. Mom was Mom. He'd know exactly where she was laid to rest.

Her head swiveled in the steps between plots, scanning the cemetery's silhouette for anything that didn't belong. The darkness taunted her. Its inky shadows feigned navy blue. A glimmer of moonlight mimicked the flash of a bolt. Natalie shivered, clinging to the nearest headstone until her knuckles shone as white as the marble.

The demons after her weren't ghosts or ghouls or cemetery haunts. They were worse. They were *human*. Flesh and bone, armed and dangerous, and out for blood.

In the distance, Tawney's silhouette stopped. "Over here."

Natalie hurried to her, straining to make out the headstone's inscription in the dark.

Jennifer Smith

Wife, Mother, Physicist
Fearless Fighter
Until we meet again...

Whatever force of will or fate that had been keeping Natalie upright since the night on the bridge finally gave out. She dropped to her knees, clinging to the fragile blades of grass that stuck between her fingers. How had she not seen it sooner?

Until we meet again.

"This is it."

"Duh. That's why I stopped–"

"No." Natalie couldn't look away from the sparkling marble slab. "This is it, Tawney. *This* is why Brant went with the Ward. This is why they're after time-travel." She traced the ridges of the inscription, her mind replaying every move Nautilus had made. "The political game is a front. Global influence, international power; it's a ruse so they can get to me, so they can get me to manipulate time." Natalie met her friend's wide eyes. "Tawney…they're trying to get his mom back."

She let out a low whistle. "Is that even possible?"

Natalie thought of her own mother. Her father. Christopher, Angie, Chef, Eleanor. She thought of what she'd give to have her past back. Her family.

Change costs, Edwin's warning reminded her.

But what if she was willing to pay?

"Nat?" Tawney sounded far away. "We lit up this place like a flare. Unless you're waiting for an escort back to the Helix, we've already stayed too long."

The foreboding in her voice woke Natalie up. She had wanted Nautilus to see their tacking signature because she wanted Brant to come looking for something. However, Nautilus wasn't what it once was. Nautilus *had* Brant now, which meant they had tacking too.

Their window had closed the moment they set foot on the beach.

She yanked the paper and pen from her pocket, tapping the headstone anxiously. Whatever she wrote would have to be read by anyone, but only understood by Brant.

What would Christopher write? she wondered.

"Want me to lead you off?" Tawney leaned against the adjacent headstone, appearing almost casual save for the nervous twitch of her fingers. "Dearest Brant, kindly explain yourself, you filthy, lying, backstabbing…"

Natalie stopped listening and scratched down the first thing that came to mind. It was far from brilliant. Owen could have been more enigmatic. Leo would have crafted something more personal. Even Tawney's taunts might draw more of a response. But Natalie wanted Brant to know it was *her* reaching out for him in the dark, that beneath his jokes and his choices, she saw the pain he carried. She saw what he wanted.

And she wanted him to come home.

Tawney leaned over her shoulder. "*Knock, knock?*" she scowled at Natalie. "Is that…a joke?"

"Better," she tucked the note against the headstone. "It's an opening."

"To what?"

"Everything."

They made their way back down the path and Enzi bounded to Natalie's side as she met the water. In spite of everything they'd been through, she was convinced that if she could repair their friendship, repair their *family*, then the fissures in her life would fade. She would have scars, but she could feel whole again. They all could.

The ocean rushed up to meet her. A white flash, weightlessness, and it was done. Stone turned to sand, shifting to accommodate her weight. The air felt damp and the silhouette of Atlantis rose up ahead of her, welcoming her return. She set out for it as Tawney tacked in beside her, though she'd hardly taken a step before her friend grabbed her jacket.

"Wait," she scanned the beach, brown eyes black in the night. "What if...what if we went somewhere?"

"Went somewhere?"

"Yeah." Tawney watched the ocean. "Anywhere."

"Are you suggesting we leave...*permanently?*"

Tawney fiddled with her sleeve. Uncomfortable. Anxious. Entirely unlike herself. "What if we did?"

Natalie resisted the urge to shout, to scold her for proposing they throw away everything they'd worked for, everything their parents had worked for. Because when she met Tawney's gaze, her friend looked like the fish they used to reel into Christopher's boat.

Uncomfortable. Anxious. *Afraid.*

"What if we did?" Natalie put the question back on Tawney.

"We could go wherever we wanted—"

"And hide from Nautilus."

"Do whatever we wanted—"

"While the Ward pushes the world to war."

"Forget this place—"

"And leave them to face Nautilus on their own."

Tawney deflated. "It was a stupid idea."

"It isn't," Natalie assured her. "I've considered it more times than I can count, and I guarantee the others have, too." She turned to face her head on. "But Tawney, what if we stay?"

Tawney sighed. "We'll get fat on ch'a and tentalilies."

"We learn to be whole again. And when all of this is over, when Nautilus fizzles out and dies and it's safe—"

Tawney's eyebrows shot up. "We leave?"

"If you still want to, yes," Natalie hugged her. "We'll leave."

"Promise?"

Natalie's ribs tightened like a vice around her chest. If she failed her again, that would be it. There would be so many cracks in the foundation of their friendship a chasm would open between them. She'd lose Tawney forever. And she couldn't even remember the last promise she'd managed to keep.

Natalie caught Tawney's pinky with her own. "I promise."

REGENT

Counselor's Notes
Subject: Leonidas Merrick

Leo: *Subject sits silently. Observes the room.*

AJ: "Edwin told me what you lost to get here—"

Leo: "I'm not talking about Brant."

AJ: "Loss is no small thing to carry—"

Leo: "If that's why I'm here, then we're wasting time. I can't mourn anymore. I'm—" *Subject smacks his fist on his knee.*

AJ: "It is only by acknowledging where we are that we can move forward."

Leo: *Subject leans in.* "I'm stuck in this incredible city with nothing to do but wonder where the Ward is and if the Curia is going to do something about him."

AJ: "Ah, you need purpose. May I make a suggestion?"

Leo: *Subject raises a brow.* "What do you have in mind?"

CHAPTER 12

At Contributions the next afternoon, Natalie's fists clenched as she stared at the crystal screen.

Her entire life, stories had been an escape. A retreat when school was stressful, or the news was terrifying, or when she was simply alone. They were a way to test boundaries, to feel adventure and heartache from the safety of her couch. But as she arranged stories for the *Atlantean Article,* Natalie did not feel safe or comforted.

She felt angry.

How could she have been so blind?

An entire afternoon of searching and she couldn't find a single article on anything remotely unfavorable beyond Atlantis's rocky sanctuary. There was nothing on the attempted bombing of the Chesapeake Bay Bridge-Tunnel. Not a word on politics, or crime, or even natural disasters. None of the bleak but unavoidable topics that filled every other newspaper in the world.

And Nautilus?

Nautilus was a *ghost.*

Before coming to Atlantis, Natalie had learned to sense Nautilus lurking beneath the headlines. That roadside bombing in London? Nautilus. That record stock market dip? Nautilus. The burning of Notre-freaking-Dame? Nautilus.

It was the same gaslighting game they'd played when her parents went missing. The Ward manipulated the media and misinformed the public, turning Natalie and her friends into the walking dead and Christopher into America's Most Wanted.

Sneaking into the Helix as a Nautilus recruit only illuminated how deep their deception went. That night on the bridge was more than a last-ditch effort to seize control over Natalie's ability to time-travel. Nautilus shed its shell of stealth and played the political hero, giving insurgents posted in every major government on the planet leverage and credibility.

And the *Atlantean Article* covered none of it.

It left out anything not sparkling with ingenuity and progress, leading the people of Atlantis to view the world through rose-stained glasses or not at all. It made Natalie's blood churn.

She scoured every record on every crystal tablet she could find. She circled the newsroom once, twice, three times searching for something, anything, to make sense of what she was seeing. Of what she *wasn't* seeing.

It was then the triquetra caught her eye. Unlike most everything else in the room it was solid. Frosted into a massive glass pane stretched across one wall, they were the same interlocking loops she'd seen on Christopher's logic puzzle and the key it held. The same symbol she'd seen in his hidden office in Ancora I.

Only now it wasn't just a symbol.

There was one loop for every Tertian of the city. Beyond one edge were the faint etchings of waves and the rugged cut of cliffs. Within the loops themselves were streets and buildings with swaths of gardens laced between. And in the center, where the three loops overlapped, was the wood.

The triquetra wasn't just a symbol for Atlantis. It was the shape of it.

It was a *map*.

And Uncle Chris had known. He'd drawn the triquetra on his own map not as a marker or a message, but as an architectural amendment.

Natalie leaned against the nearest counter with a huff. Detecting her presence, its surface rippled and the latest *Atlantean Article* appeared in a shimmer of light and air. A rip slithered in from one corner and Natalie silently urged it on. The articles weren't outright lies but they skewed focus. Museums, world fairs, and bakeries were all things to be celebrated, but the darker plights of humanity could not be ignored, swept beneath the bed like an imagined monster. Her frustration swelled and the rip grew and fissured, tearing the news in two.

Not a tear, Natalie realized. The *Atlantean Article* couldn't tear. It wasn't paper; it was pixels and projections. It wasn't capable of being torn apart.

But she was.

The tear wasn't a rip at all. It was a crack.

It's cumulative. Edwin's voice echoed. *Your symptoms are progressing.*

The floor creaked and Natalie spun, reaching for the bolt that wasn't at her back.

"Easy." Leo lifted his arms in mock surrender. "You don't need to live on edge here."

Natalie exhaled, glancing sheepishly at Enzi still asleep in the corner. She wasn't living on edge; she *was* the edge. And how could she tell him that? How did he manage to shed the fear Nautilus beat into them? The questions crowded her mouth only to dissolve entirely as his arms wrapped around her waist and his chin found the crook of her neck.

The embrace was awkward, as though her secrets wedged between them, but it also felt warm and safe and *real*.

"I thought you'd love the newsroom." His breath brushed her jaw and the impossible tear in the screen vanished.

"Yeah," Natalie sighed. "Me too."

She wanted to tell him everything. Everything the *Atlantean Article* left out. The persistent crack she'd seen on the page and the floor and the ceiling. But she held her tongue. She didn't want to sound broken, like something he needed to fix. And she wasn't even sure that was possible.

Travelers aren't known for their longevity.

"Natalie," Leo's tone changed, tension knitting the syllables together. "Where were you this morning?"

"The apartment." Natalie cringed. The lie came out too fast, too insistent.

"No," Leo retreated. "You weren't." It was a single step that stretched into a chasm. She caught a glimpse of the strategies unfolding in his mind, calculating the best way around her defenses. "Where were you?"

"Breakfast." But even as she waved the question away, Natalie's stomach grumbled. She folded her arms over it.

"Look, if this is about," he stopped. A muscle in his jaw twitched and he tried again. "If this is about *him*," Leo grated out the word, "I know you two were…close while I was gone. I get it if you miss him or–"

"Don't you?" Natalie blurted. "He was our friend. Our *best* friend. Brant–"

"Don't."

Silenced, her words festered, and her mind drifted back to the message she'd left in the lantern lit cemetery. She knew Leo wouldn't approve of reaching out, but she wouldn't have done anything differently. If there was a chance of reaching Brant, she'd take it. If only to have the last word.

"He's not our friend, Natalie," Leo pulled at his hair. "He spied on us for his good-for-nothing father. He shot me trying to kill Christopher. He set fire to Ancora III *with Owen and Tawney inside.*" He trembled, though whether from rage or regret Natalie couldn't tell. Perhaps it was both. "He was a lot of things, but he was never our friend."

"Leo…" She stopped as he picked up the Counseling summons. The new Counseling summons. It had been waiting for her on the tablet when she arrived, the time and place underlined for good measure.

Every line in Leo's face smoothed over, a perfectly crafted mask. "I thought you went yesterday."

"Guess I'm a complicated case."

"No," Leo dropped the summons. "You're not."

Natalie fought the heat flushing her cheeks. She was lying. She was lying to *Leo*. Repeatedly. But there was no way around it. If he knew about the cemetery, he'd try to stop her. And if, even guided by the best of intentions, he told the Regent, he would succeed. It might be well and good for your average Atlantean to frequent the surface, but communicating directly with a known enemy? No, Natalie didn't think the Curia would stand for that.

Absorbed in her thoughts, she almost missed the subtle motion in the hall outside. She didn't dare look at Edwin, not directly. Keeping her attention locked on Leo, she watched his blurred figure wave and veer out of sight. Natalie shifted.

She wanted to follow him.

"I need you to trust me." She didn't want to lose Leo. She couldn't lose Leo. But she couldn't ignore the problems laid at her feet either. She refused to drown while her demons grew stronger.

Leo studied the ceiling for a solid minute. When he finally looked at her, his stare burned. He pulled her hips close and pressed her against the counter, blocking her in with his arms.

Natalie's breath hitched. She forgot about Edwin. She forgot about the rip in the projections and the crack in the ceiling. He had her exactly where she wanted to be. Yet when Leo dropped his forehead to hers, he looked like the one who was trapped.

"I trust you with everything I am," he whispered against her mouth. "But I can't help you if you don't let me in."

Natalie's eyes stung. She didn't know what she was doing reaching out to Brant. She didn't know what she was doing in Atlantis. And until she did, she couldn't risk hurting Leo. Not again. Letting him in was not an option.

"I'm always on your team," Leo reminded her. "Even if I don't like the play. When you need me," he kissed the corner of her mouth. "I'm ready."

"Hello!" Clo floated through the doorway, her silver pixie points framing her smile.

As though the Moirai had her own gravity, Leo's touch receded like a wave pulled by the tide. First his arms from her side, then his hips from her hips, until they stood apart. Separate. He slipped away, smoke through her fingers, out the door and out of sight. A black fissure crept up the door frame behind him.

Clo rocked on the spot, oblivious to the tension she'd disrupted, skirting over its surface like a bug over water. She patted Enzi twice on the head when he came to greet her.

"Have you seen Atro?" Clo asked, still smiling. She was never not smiling. "We were supposed to have midday ch'a with Andrei. She did not show."

"No," Natalie rubbed her eyes. "Sorry." And she was. Of the

three Moirai, she found Clo the most tolerable, if, admittedly, the most naive.

Clo cocked her head, a pale lacework of scars glinting in the light. "Why are you apologizing?"

"I don't know. Habit, I guess."

"Odd habit." Perhaps Clo wasn't as naive as she thought. "If you see her…"

"I'll send her straight to you."

After she left, Natalie managed to wait one rattling breath before darting out of the newsroom. Part of her, an overwhelmingly large part of her, ached to run after Leo. She wanted to chase him down and throw herself into his arms and feel safe again. Feel whole. Feel his.

But how could she be his when she was barely her own? When she was made of cracks, and questions, and the blank space of her name?

As Natalie reached the fork in the hall, she didn't follow Leo. Instead, she chased after Edwin.

After answers.

CHAPTER 13

Natalie rounded the corner so fast she never saw him coming. Edwin slammed into her, or her into him, and they staggered, an awkward tangle of arms and legs until he finally sagged against the wall, glaring.

"You shouldn't barrel through life when you don't know what's waiting for you," he grumbled.

Enzi promptly put his paws on Edwin's shoulders, forcing him all the way to the ground.

"You wanted to see me?" Natalie helped him up.

Edwin brushed off strands of Enzi's fur before offering his arm. "Fancy a walk?"

Ignoring his gesture, Natalie maintained a measure of distance between them, taking note of the easy way he moved through the halls.

Since she'd known him, Edwin had more than earned her trust. He worked against Nautilus from the inside out, freeing the Moirai and gathering intel. He saved all their lives on the bridge the night

Natalie lost her parents. He even put his own neck in the noose to guarantee their entry to Atlantis. So far, his motives had always included keeping her alive, but Natalie had seen firsthand what people would do to get what they wanted. They manipulate. They destroy. They turn on those who had once been friends.

And the way Edwin dealt out information as it suited him made her wary. Unfortunately, he seemed the only one willing to give any answers at all.

Silent, they wandered the tangled hallways, passing locked doors until the classrooms drifted into view. Natalie pressed against the glass partition and a hint of nostalgia ached in her chest. Its substance evaded her; the memories, if they were actually memories, thinned to smoke when she reached for them. Perhaps all schools felt similar. Perhaps she once traced the glass windows of a preschool in Williamsburg. Maybe it too had smelled of vanilla and cedar. She couldn't be sure.

"Do you recognize anything?" Edwin's brow furrowed as he studied her. His question was almost pleading. "The floor? The desks?"

Natalie surveyed the scene again. Children no taller than her hip darted around the classroom. Bright tufted pillows surrounded low circular desks and larger-than-life projections of numbers and runes decorated the walls.

If she stared long enough, Natalie could almost convince herself she remembered the classroom. But she was grasping for shells in a receding wave. She saw flickers of *something* before it was swept away.

"Maybe," she shrugged. "Maybe not."

Edwin's frown deepened. "There's no record of your disappearance from the city. I can't find anything on you or your friends, not even a birth certificate."

Natalie picked at the seam where glass met stone. "I'm guessing that's abnormal."

"It's unheard of. You're certain you don't remember anything?"

Frustrated, her neck flushed with heat. "No, I don't."

"Hmm. Why are you avoiding your Counseling summons?"

"What is it with you lot and Counseling?" Natalie groaned. "I don't want to waste my time laying on a chaise spilling my guts to a stranger."

"It's not like that."

"Oh really?" she folded her arms.

"Okay, there *is* a chaise," he confessed. "But all Atlanteans attend Counseling, even the youth. It's about finding your passion, your purpose. For one, it might help you remember more."

"And for two?"

"For two," he leaned against the classroom window. "An essential part of my homecoming is you keeping your head down and doing as you're told." Edwin smirked as he said it, but he was no Brant. A flicker of fear lined the hardness of his smile. Finally home and free, the last thing Edwin wanted was for Natalie's bullheadedness to get him excommunicated to the surface. Again.

"Fine," Natalie deflated. "I'll go."

Relieved, Edwin nudged her. "The first visit is free. After that you have to pay."

She frowned. Atlanteans had no currency. "Pay? With what?"

"Your soul. Come on," he scooted her forward. "This room," Edwin stopped before another glass window, "is as sacred to us as our Temple of Thoughts. This is what sets Atlantis apart." He paused as she peered in, finding a sterile suite illuminated with high-frequency blue light. "This is where you were born."

Natalie cocked her head. It didn't look like a hospital. There were no beds or gowns, no bassinets. No people.

"I don't understa–" It hit her then. The freezer. The pipettes. The incubators. The calligraphy sign that read *Genesis Room*. Owen would have pieced it together immediately. She pressed against the pane, the warmth of her skin fogging the glass.

She'd worried about meeting her biological parents in Atlantis, that she'd compare them to the Mom and Dad who raised her. Feared she would hate them for giving her up or worse, love them more than the ones she knew. But her worries had been wasted. Natalie's biological parents were donors.

"Love is fallible." Edwin tucked in close, his tone sympathetic. "But science? Genetics? That's tangible. That's trackable."

Natalie was hardly listening. "Did they know?"

"Your Patrons?"

Patrons, Natalie's throat closed. Not parents. She managed to nod.

"No. Patrons never know if their genetics are chosen for Progeny."

Progeny. Not children.

"We don't leave our future or our genome to chance," Edwin went on. "Progeny are raised by the community to be more than the byproduct of a family. Families fail. Instead, they're raised to be Atlantean."

"My family didn't fail," Natalie's argument came out in a whisper. "They died."

"That's failure."

Her vision blurred and Natalie feared the crack was returning, determined to overwhelm her, but they were only tears. She wiped them on her sleeve.

"No," she disagreed. "This is failure. Who cares for them? Who can they rely on? Who loves them?"

"They have more love and respect for one another than you can possibly know," Edwin said sharply. "Those things aren't promised by blood."

"I never said they were. My family has nothing to do with my blood."

"Families are flawed."

"And this isn't?"

"No. It's perfect. It's a science-backed system that yields educated, supported, and well-balanced young adults."

"Then how did it lose me?"

Edwin blinked at her. The tension of debate melted off of him, leaving his shoulders slack and his mouth downturned. He let the argument die, gesturing to the building as a whole.

"This is where you would have grown up," he said softly. "I'm only a few years older than you; we would have known each other. We probably would have even been friends if you hadn't been abducted."

"Abducted," Natalie recoiled from the word. She hated the feel of it against her skin. Hated the implications it put on Christopher.

"So, my ability to time-travel," Natalie threaded the hints together, studying the *Genesis Room* beyond the glass. "That was planned."

"No. But not for lack of trying, believe me," Edwin's mischievous grin curled up his cheeks. "Did you know our city is the only place on the planet you can find the metal aurichalcum? The ability to tack at all is a subtle genetic mutation, a slip we still can't replicate. We think it's tied to the metal. That's why some native Atlanteans can tack and others can't. It causes issues at times, less now than before." His jaw clenched. "But many of the older generations still show favor to those who can tack."

Which, Natalie knew, did not include him. She sensed an old ache in his tone, but he didn't linger on it.

Edwin brushed her elbow, a touch so gentle it teetered on reverent. "And time-travel is a step beyond that. It's something science hasn't fully figured out. A gift only nature has the power to give."

Natalie's fingernails dug crescents into her palms. Why couldn't it be simple? Why couldn't she have someone to blame beyond Patrons who didn't know she existed, let alone her name?

"Why did you bring me here?"

"The unexamined life is not worth living."

"Seriously?" Natalie scoffed. "Plato?"

"No," Edwin turned serious. Calculating. "Socrates."

Natalie stared at him. He was right. She'd known that quote. And yet…

"I told you there would be a cost," Edwin's voice was thick with an emotion Natalie couldn't place. Concern? Regret? "How do you feel?"

The answer was a tree with many branches. She felt broken. Hopeful. Sad. Afraid. Happy.

Alone.

She finally settled for, "I think I'm okay."

"In order to know where you're going, you have to know where you've been. And you don't even know what you're made of. You'd feel better if you went to Counseling."

"I already said–"

"I know," he cut her off. "Just…keep your chin up and your head down. Yeah?"

"Yeah."

He led her away from the Genesis Room and back through the school. Again, Natalie paused. She watched the kids play in a toddler room, chasing and tagging, assuming themselves to be free even while skirting the walls of their cage. Suddenly she remembered why she'd followed him there in the first place.

"Edwin–"

"What do you see?" He interrupted her question with one of his own. "When you get lost? When you slip?"

In the short time they'd known each other, Edwin had seen Natalie at her worst. She faked her own death to prove Leo's allegiance. She imploded when her parents died. Their friendship was built on pain and loss. If she was going to tell anyone the truth, Edwin seemed a decent place to start.

"Cracks," Natalie whispered her confession. "I see cracks."

"Hmm." His brow furrowed. To him, she was a puzzle, an enigma. He was fascinated, but she didn't want to end up like the gutted electronics that littered his quarters in the Helix. She didn't want him to break her down to see what made her tick. She rerouted their conversation.

"Who selects the stories for the *Atlantean Article* that come from the surface?"

"The Regent."

It was what she expected, yet the truth slammed into her like a rogue wave, stealing her air. If the Regent controlled what their people did and didn't see, then it was Aislinn censoring the entire population of the city.

"Why did you bring me here, Edwin?" she asked again.

"I told you," he moved closer until he looked down his nose to her. "Because you belong here. Because I need you to know what you're made of. I need you to know what you are."

He turned to leave, and she grabbed him. She hated the pleading notes in her voice. The weakness. The flat-out desperation.

"But what is the *point?*"

"The point is," he stared down the hall, his expression unreadable. "Fate has already made its choice. Now you have to make yours."

He tried to pry himself away, but Natalie held fast to his

sweatshirt, a wild thought taking root.

"If I can travel through time," she wetted her lips, her own words making her head swim. "Can I see how this ends? What's stopping me from traveling to the future so I can pick the best path?"

Edwin looked at her with surprise. "Are you joking? You've seriously never tried?" He dragged a hand over his face, muttering something inaudible before huffing out a laugh. "Give it a whirl. Let me know what you see. In the meantime," he plucked the fabric of his hoodie from her grasp. "Honor your Counseling summons."

He hurried into the maze of halls and Natalie focused on the ceiling.

She wasn't dense. Edwin had told her there was a cost to time-travel. He told her the consequences would progress. It made sense; a person didn't bleed without injury. But as she watched the crack in the ceiling spread and branch, she felt too destitute to pay the price. Injury, death, was one thing, but her *sanity*? Her reality? Her ability to know what was real and what wasn't?

It was too much.

Natalie turned her back on the fissure and marched to the newsroom with Enzi on her heels. Edwin hadn't brought her to Atlantis because she *belonged there*. He'd never leave the world undefended to the Ward, to be run down and taken over by Nautilus. He had something planned. Edwin always had something planned.

And she'd be damned if he was going to shut her out.

The United States of America. THE NEW YORK TIMES.

The recent spike in domestic violent extremism has many NATO countries, including the United States, turning their peacemaking efforts inward. While this seems a natural response, many analysts argue that a more united effort against these acts would lend a more successful turnaround.

Regardless, the coalition of NATO members assembled for peacemaking talks off the coast of the United Kingdom has disbanded. Political leaders and military forces are making their way home as domestic issues trump the possibility of global fallout.

Even Nautilus appears to have abandoned their efforts. As NATO forces retreat, Nautilus ships sail north towards Iceland.

CHAPTER 14

Natalie stood in the rain at the edge of the world. After nearly two weeks in Atlantis, it was still strange experiencing real weather beneath a manufactured sky. Raindrops soaked her clothes as a wicked wind whipped her hair and tossed waves upon the beach. The only evidence of the sunrise was a faint orange glow where clouds skimmed the sea.

Her latest Counseling summons, drenched and smudged in her pocket, wasn't for hours. They had plenty of time to check for a response from Brant at the cemetery.

That is, if Tawney ever decided to show.

Natalie leaned into the fading storm, blinking the mist from her eyes as she stifled the hope floating in her chest. She could not really expect her note to have made it to Brant; there were too many variables. It could have blown away, or been picked up by a stranger, or not picked up at all. And if, by some miracle, he actually did receive her letter, she couldn't truly think he'd write back.

But what if he *did*? What would he say? Would he apologize? And if so, was that enough? Would it ever be enough?

Certainly not to wash the blood from his hands.

Not to bring back the lives he'd cost or those he'd taken. Not for Natalie to forgive him for the death of her parents. Or Owen's. Or Leo's mom and Tawney's dad. Christopher. Angie.

But maybe…maybe it could be enough to bring him home.

It could be.

Might be.

If he wrote back.

The clouds parted on the horizon, leaking splotches of pink and orange over the crests of the weathered sea. A single jagged line like an inky bolt of lightning splintered the world from sea to sky. A fissure. A crack.

Natalie's heart fluttered against her ribcage. The crack wasn't real. She *knew* it wasn't real. Yet every self-preserving atom of her being screamed to take cover because surely the sky would fall. Surely the immense weight of stone overhead would crumble from such a defect.

She squeezed her eyes shut, blocking out the image.

"Wake up, kid," Christopher jostled her.

Her head lolled over his shoulder. "No." She rubbed bleary eyes with tiny fists.

"Come now, Nat." He tickled her side, and she fixed him with her angriest toddler glare. "75 percent of life is showing up, the rest is just staying awake to see what happens." He winked. "Look there."

Following his direction, Natalie tilted her chin to the starry sky. A round moon lit the beach brighter than any streetlamp. It looked enormous, splattered with grey as though someone had dropped a bucket of paint.

And as she watched, one edge went fuzzy. Soon the edge was gone entirely.

"Uncle Chris…"

"Just watch."

Propped on his hip, her stare locked on the disappearing moon. Her neck ached, her eyes burned from the salty breeze, but after several long minutes, the moon was gone. All that remained was a hole in the sky, a black space void of stars as though the universe was too mournful to fill the gap.

"Where did it go?" Natalie whispered into the dark.

"The moon's still there. If you're patient, it'll come back again."

Long minutes passed. The crickets were silent. Waves lapped against the shore.

And finally, a sliver of silver shone in the sky.

"No matter what happens," Christopher gazed up at the growing moon. "I'm always right here with you. Even if you can't see me. Even if I'm gone."

Natalie blinked her eyes open. He'd warned her. Over and over, he'd warned her.

Question everything.

She hadn't known before what Christopher had really meant. She hadn't realized she needed to question *herself*, her perception of what was real and what wasn't.

Enzi rubbed impatiently against her side, bored and sick of the rain. His ears plastered flat against his head, his pearlescent fur grey and heavy with water. Ignoring the indigo crack still scarring the sky, Natalie scanned the empty beach for Tawney again.

"Well," she gripped Enzi's collar. "While we wait…"

Natalie closed her eyes and tried to envision the future. Without any idea of what to expect, she imagined herself on the same stretch of beach, older and alongside her friends. She glazed over details, leaving space for time to fill. And with that partial image held fast in her mind, she stepped into the sea.

The light leapt up to meet her and enveloped in weightlessness, Natalie relaxed. For a single instant, for less than a second, the entire world stilled. It was her favorite part about tacking. That invincible moment where the universe couldn't touch her, where nothing existed and she could almost forget–

Gravity found her first. And then…rain.

She peeked through soaked lashes to find herself stuck in the same storm, waiting on the same friend who had still neglected to show.

Frustrated, Natalie kicked a lump of waterlogged sand. Edwin had obviously known glimpsing the future would be impossible. She'd expected as much herself. There were too many variables, too many cards in play.

Flexing her fingers, Natalie decided to try again. She focused on something simpler and stepped into the sea with the vision of Tawney finally arriving forced to the forefront of her mind. The light claimed her, swept her up and set her down, until Natalie once again stood holding her breath with her eyes squeezed shut.

Something brushed her hand and she jumped, but it was only Enzi. Natalie turned a full circle before finally accepting they were still alone. It hadn't worked.

A beam of sunlight broke through the clouds to glint off the sea. Morning was fading. And whether choice or circumstance held Tawney up, Natalie couldn't wait any longer.

She held the image of Trinity Cemetery in her mind, adjusted the aurichalcum spark bound to her wrist, and tucked Enzi close as they met the next wave.

Weightlessness. Light. Gravity.

When she inhaled again it wasn't the fresh scent of rain and earth, but the humid night air of late summer. Enzi tugged free from her grasp, startling a fox hunting crabs, and Natalie turned inland. She skirted rivers of moonlight as she approached the cemetery, clearing the fence and dropping silently into the shadows on the other side.

Separated by stakes of iron, Enzi sprinted back to her. He paced and whined, sticking his nose between the bars.

She scratched under his chin. "I'll be right back."

Natalie slunk through the dark to Mrs. Smith's grave. Once upon a time, she had been afraid of the night, but now she knew the dark didn't play favorites. It would hide her as readily as her enemies. So, when she spotted the blood red envelope propped against Mrs. Smith's headstone, Natalie didn't run for it. She froze.

Someone had answered.

Natalie's pulse thundered in her ears. She wanted that letter, and to get it she'd have to cross a wide expanse of open moonlight. She'd be exposed. She'd be seen.

Logically, anyone hiding among the headstones already knew she was there. The tacking flash that dropped Natalie on the beach had shattered the night like a flare. Staying out of sight was the only advantage she had left, and to get the letter she'd have to give it up.

Natalie cursed under her breath.

Tawney should be here.

She was stronger and faster and stood an infinitely better chance of getting them out alive if it came down to a fight.

But Natalie didn't have time to go back and find Tawney. Someone else could take the letter. Or the person who wrote it could take it back. If this was Natalie's only chance to reach Brant, she wasn't about to waste it.

Before she could think better of it, Natalie took off. She looped around Mrs. Smith's grave and snatched the envelope without stopping, never missing a step. And between the stomp of her sneakers, above the rattle of breath in her chest, she *heard* them.

The crack of a bolt.

The thud of boots.

The metallic pop of gunfire.

Bang.

Enzi barked at the fence line.

Bang.

"Get them, Tanaka!" a woman howled.

Natalie launched over the fence. An iron spoke caught her sleeve, slicing into her forearm, but she didn't stop. She dropped hard on the other side and sprinted. The wound didn't hurt. Not yet. And she knew if she didn't make it to the water, she'd never live to feel the pain.

Natalie grabbed Enzi by his scruff and made for the waves.

BANG.

At the edge of the bay, Natalie turned. She wanted to see, *had* to see, if Brant was with them. If it was him who'd snared her olive branch into a trap. If he was everything Leo said he was and nothing she hoped him to be. But Natalie didn't see Brant.

She skidded to a stop in the sand. She didn't breathe. Didn't move.

She didn't see anyone.

Natalie was alone.

CHAPTER 15

Natalie's chest stretched painfully as she gulped down air.

The cemetery was empty. There was no army of Nautilus. No Ward on her heels. No Tanaka. No Max. No Brant. It was only her own ghosts returned to haunt her.

Gossamer. Translucent. *There.*

Across the beach, a hazy image of her mother shuddered and collapsed. Her father's silhouette knelt over her, his gun raised at an invisible enemy. Christopher's gun. Christopher's unloaded gun.

BANG.

Natalie rubbed her eyes. It wasn't real.

Except it was. It was a truth out of place, out of time.

My fault.

Natalie scrunched her brow, gritting her teeth against the memory. Forcing it down. Forcing it out.

We'll help you find peace. Eleanor's promise thrummed through her, clearer than the crash of waves behind her.

Natalie shuffled backward. It wasn't real. She knew it wasn't real, yet the blip wouldn't go away. She wasn't going to win. She couldn't fight back. All she could do was flee.

With Enzi tucked close, Natalie stepped into the sea.

She landed on her hands and knees on the Atlantean beach. No cracks. No shouts. Nothing but the white noise of the ocean.

Natalie let out a temporary sigh of relief. She might have left her demons behind, but they knew their way home. They'd find her again. They always did.

It wasn't until her arm throbbed that Natalie forced herself up. The cut from the fence was shallow, more a scrape than anything, but it stung, and the pain brought clarity.

She knew where she was. She knew when she was.

Natalie trudged through the waking city with the red envelope balled in her fist. She sought the seclusion of the gardens, using their massive canopies and narrow paths for privacy. The rain had mostly ceased, leaving behind a fine mist that condensed on her skin.

She sank onto the first bench she reached. Elbows propped on her knees, head hung low, everything trembled.

Wake up, Natalie.

It hit her then how the madness of time-travel progressed. Losing herself wasn't hard; it was waking up. It was having her mind piece itself together only to rediscover the pain, to relive her losses. It was old wounds cut fresh every time she surfaced. The agony was enough to make her stop searching for clarity. To prefer to stay lost. To make insanity a sanctuary, a luxury of illusion.

"Here you are, dear."

Natalie nearly jumped out of her skin.

Andrei smiled down at her, sliding a steaming cup across the table as pieces of the world snapped rigidly into place. The café. The street. The trees. Her feet had taken her to Andrei's on their own accord.

"Rough night?"

Natalie hid her injured arm beneath the table.

Rough day. Rough week. Rough month.

Rough summer.

"Yeah."

"Mhmm." He moved away, wiping tables as he went, Enzi dutifully on his heels. "Drink. Feel better."

Natalie cradled the cup, letting its warmth uproot the chill in her soul. She sipped and a bitter tang raced down her throat.

"Ugh," Natalie cringed. "Is this ch'a?"

Andrei did not look up. "We can call it ch'a."

Natalie scooted the cup away, not trusting anything that would dull what little sense she had left. Enzi trailed unashamedly after Andrei, inspecting every table for croissants or tentalilies.

"Alright, beastie," the man chortled. "Come on, then. Let's see what we have for ye."

Natalie knew Enzi would make quick work of whatever tasty treasures Andrei foraged for him. So as soon as the man ducked inside the shop, she tore open the envelope. Inside was her message to Brant: *Knock, knock.* An open door. An invitation.

One he'd accepted.

Natalie's heart stuttered. Below her note, in his scribbled handwriting, was not at all the answer she expected. In fact, it wasn't an answer at all. It was a question.

Who is going to keep them safe?

Natalie leaned back in her seat. "Huh."

It didn't make sense. Who was *them*? What counted as *safe*? Maybe it was a code? Brant had never given her a code before but that didn't mean anything. Not now. Not knowing she had never really known him at all.

"Hey, nerd." Owen dropped into the seat beside her, glasses fogged and red hair ablaze in the misty dawn light.

Sliding over to make room, Natalie folded Brant's note in her lap.

His puzzle would have to wait.

Leo positioned himself across from her, offering a half-hearted smile and nothing more. His gaze lingered no longer than a few seconds, but it was enough to twist Natalie's stomach into knots.

Oblivious, Edwin sat next to him, whistling cheerily as Andrei brought out a round of real ch'a. Enzi made his way about the table, still licking his lips, and the boys quickly picked up the middle of some debate.

"No," Owen defogged his glasses with his shirt. "You're looking at it all wrong. It's not about tradition. It's about practicality. The aqueducts can't disrupt the original architecture because they *are* the original architecture!"

"For the hundredth time," Edwin pointed two fingers at him. "It's not me you have to convince. It's the Curia."

Leo snorted. "I've been in this city for five minutes and even I know that's a lie. The Curia does whatever their Regent says."

"That's not how it's supposed to work–"

"Yet it's the way things are," Leo berated him.

Edwin lifted his ch'a. "Toush."

"Toush?" Owen scrunched his nose. "Do you mean touché?"

"Of course not."

Natalie sank into her seat as the blaze of Archimedes' sun dissolved the world away. Without any saltwater or sparks or time-travel, she could have been back at Colonial Custards in Williamsburg, exhausted after a day at Yorktown Beach. She half expected a spoonful of ice cream to shoot its way across the table. This more than anything, more than Ancora or Atlantis, *this* felt like home.

Tawney dropped like a stone into the seat beside her, curls bouncing and grin flashing.

Natalie shoved her. "Where have you been?"

"I know, I know, I missed our ch'a date," Tawney practically shouted over her. "But Lache was just telling me, in great detail," she said through her teeth, "about the Atlantean Library."

Lache and Clo settled beside Edwin, officially packing the benches full.

"It is in the very center of the city and—"

Tawney cut Lache off mid-sentence, holding up a frizzy, knotted lock of Natalie's hair. "What on earth did you get into this morning?"

"I'm sorry, Lache was speaking," Natalie leaned across the table, blocking Tawney with her shoulder. Half joking, half not. "You were saying?"

A smile tugged at Lache's mouth. They might not ever be the best of friends, but they understood each other. And sarcasm.

"It is in the Ancient City," Clo explained before her sister could get out a word. "Have you seen Atro?"

Normally, Clo was a dewy-eyed package of perpetual sunshine, but dark circles hung over her cheeks and her expression was pinched in a scowl. Natalie hadn't thought Clo even knew how to scowl.

"You still haven't found her?" Fear crept up Natalie's spine. Hadn't Clo asked her the same question the day before in the newsroom? What could have kept her for so long? They'd grown too comfortable. They'd grown too comfortable, and now Atro was missing.

"I did find her," Clo's teeth sank into her bottom lip. "But now she is gone again."

"You're controlling, you know that?"

Natalie aimed a swift kick at Tawney beneath the table.

"She is right," Lache's fountain of silver hair flowed into her lap. "We are not in Scotland anymore, Clo. We are safe here. Atro is free to do what she likes when she likes. She need not ask for permission," she sipped her ch'a, cutting a sideways glance at her sister. "Nor company."

Clo's mouth twisted and, battling between anger and tears, she said nothing.

"Toush," Tawney whispered in Natalie's ear.

And Natalie might have responded had Owen not draped his hand over Clo's.

"I don't think you have anything to worry about," he patted her, sympathetic. "The excitement of the city will wear off, and Atro doesn't seem the type to have a wandering heart."

Natalie felt more than saw Tawney go rigid, and beneath the table she stuffed Brant's note into her friend's clenched fist.

"Touché."

Her tension melted like a Colonial Custards' sundae, yet Natalie had no time to savor the appeasement. Leo's stare landed heavily on her.

Eager to avoid that conversation, Natalie climbed over the back of the bench. Enzi followed clumsily after her, insisting on retracing her exact path rather than walking around the table.

"I better go," she waved. "Contributions are calling."

"You mean Chores," Tawney made a face. "And FYI: toddlers *bite*."

"Well, anything with a mouth can bite," Owen commented.

Tawney arched a brow high into her curls. "Is that a request or an offer?"

Owen choked on a tentalily.

"Anyway," Natalie backed away as swiftly as possible. "See you." She made it ten paces before Leo fell in lockstep beside her.

"You're not going to the newsroom."

"No, I'm not."

To her surprise, he didn't press. He didn't argue. As they entered the first garden, their fingers brushed, and she couldn't be certain who pulled away. The distance made her chest ache.

Enzi padded between them, disrupting some of their stagnant silence. Still, Leo didn't say anything else until he realized where she was going. They made it all the way to the quartz stairs before he pieced it together.

"Counseling."

Surprise, she'd expected. Concern, relief, and support had all been on her list of Leo's anticipated reactions.

Anger had not.

And it must have broken the dam, because that one question he'd been holding, the one he'd asked every day without speaking, finally came rushing out.

"Why?"

"It's required."

"No, Natalie." Red blotches crept up his neck to his cheeks. "Why won't you talk to me? You just…" He waved a hand in the air, gesturing at nothing. At everything. "Why did we fight so hard to get back to each other if you're looking for every opportunity to throw the game and jump ship?"

She'd known this was coming. She'd known for days. Yet it still hit her like a blow to the gut. Natalie folded her arms, cringing.

"I'm dealing with something and–"

"And I'm not?" he laughed dryly. "What about Owen and Tawney? Are they exempt from suffering, too?"

"That's not–"

"Just talk to me," his voice broke and the ocean of tension between them froze over. "Please."

She couldn't stand it, the way he looked at her as though she was no longer on his side. As though she'd dropped off his team. She could tell he thought it wasn't fair, but he didn't understand. He couldn't understand. Because she wasn't about to tell him she was broken if she couldn't be fixed.

Travelers aren't known for their longevity.

And Leo deserved more than that. More than her sharp edges and cracks and a love cut short.

She didn't move. Neither did he.

"I love you, Natalie," he sighed. "I can't help you if you don't talk to me."

Natalie wetted her lips, meaning every syllable. "I love you, too."

But.

Though she hadn't said it, he'd felt it. The unspoken word poisoned the air between them. And instead of leaning in, Leo stepped back.

"You keep disappearing." His frustration ebbed and exhaustion filled in the gaps. "Where were you this morning?"

She thought of Brant. Of his note in Tawney's pocket. *Who is going to keep them safe?*

"The beach."

Leo pulled at his hair. "We promised not to lie to each other."

A deal's a deal.

BANG.

Natalie's temples throbbed. "I've promised a lot of things."

"Well, I keep my promises," Leo stared at the ground between them; a foot of stone that stretched an eternity. "And I promise when you go home tonight, I won't be there. But when you're ready..." His touch found her cheek. Featherlight and swift, she savored it. A lifeline. A tether. Gone. The muscle in his jaw twitched. "When you're ready to talk, I'm still here. I'm always right here. I'm always on your team."

A lump lodged in Natalie's throat as he left. Hands in his pockets, head down, Leo never looked back. Not once.

Natalie bit her lip. She needed to keep him at arm's length, away from whatever threatened to undo her reality. Away from the cracks fissuring her life. Away from their shipwrecked friendship with Brant she'd tossed a lifebuoy at, because she wasn't certain Leo would reel him in.

She hoped if they could save Brant, Leo would only be better for it. She hoped if she kept him away, her fate would spare his own. Yet she stood staring at the rift in the world where Leo should have been, doubting her every move.

Natalie A.

Natalie Alone.

"Well, well."

Natalie turned to find a bronze-skinned woman atop the stairs, one ebony eyebrow arched.

"I suppose we have a place to start."

CHAPTER 16

Natalie wanted nothing more than to punch Charles Lutwidge Dodgson in the mouth.

Charles Lutwidge Dodgson, credited with the creation of the logic puzzle. Charles Lutwidge Dodgson, better known by his pen name Lewis Carroll, author of *Alice's Adventures in Wonderland*.

Christopher taught her that.

Natalie despised Carroll and his Wonderland. She hated the mystery of it, the secrets that never made sense. Most of all she hated that Christopher dragged her to Wonderland headfirst, kicking and screaming with nothing but a tattered old book to guide her: *The Sceptical Chymist*.

Yes, she hated Wonderland.

But Natalie loved puzzles.

So, while the Counseling room was a gorgeous frame of marble filled with plush black sofas, Natalie's attention locked on the knotted puzzles between her and the Counselor. The three disentanglement challenges were small, each barely the size of her hand, and nothing like the logic puzzle Christopher once gave her. There were no holograms or fancy technology, no hidden compartments with keys to lost cities. They were wood and metal, solid and tangible. Levers that turned and knobs that twisted.

Natalie sat on her hands to stop herself from touching them.

"I don't want to talk about Leo."

"Very well." The Counselor, an Amazon of a woman, made herself comfortable on the opposite couch, tucking her bare feet beneath her.

A ceiling-high mosaic dominated the wall behind her, a tiled mural of dolphins in a crystal-clear sea. The detail was exquisite, and Natalie followed the swirling tracks of water from dolphin to dolphin as she asked her next question.

"How long do I have to stay?"

"I suppose that depends on why you're here."

Natalie's nerves sparked, feral as live wires. Her eyes snapped back to the Counselor. "I'm here because the Curia is making all of us see you."

And because Edwin refuses to share his secrets otherwise, she added silently.

"Ah," the Counselor nodded. "The Regent will be most upset to hear her Curia dragged you here against your will."

Natalie's pulse ticked up. The Counselor smiled.

"Now, why have you come?"

"I was summoned," she repeated through gritted teeth.

"Thrice, I believe," the Counselor held up three fingers. "Yet only now you decide to show."

Natalie barely suppressed the urge to throw a cushion at her. "Edwin wanted me to come."

"Even though you did not want to?"

"Yes."

"Then you trust Edwin?"

Natalie faltered, her frustration stippled with suspicion. "Yes."

"More than you trust yourself."

It wasn't a question, so Natalie didn't answer. She wasn't entirely sure she could as her heart pounded painfully against her ribs. No, she didn't trust herself. How could she? How many had paid the cost for her misjudgments? For her mistakes?

"Very good," the Counselor clapped. "Now that we know why you're here," she reached forward, "I'm AJ."

Natalie shook her offered hand. It was steady and sure while her own was sweaty and meek. AJ felt strong. Natalie needed strong.

"Natalie," she replied.

"Well met, Natalie." AJ tossed her the first puzzle.

She thumbed over the grooves of the wood, studying the levers, noting what moved and what wouldn't.

"Are these some kind of test?" she asked cautiously, suspicious her every word was being measured.

AJ smiled. It came off more sympathetic than joyful. "I've found people are more comfortable talking when they have something to do with their hands."

"Why do they want me to talk to you?"

"They?"

"The Atlantean Curia. The Regent. Edwin."

"Ah." AJ brushed invisible lint from her impeccably ironed dress. "Perhaps I wanted to speak with you. You were *summoned* to Counseling after all, not sent."

Natalie stopped, the wooden brainteaser already half completed in her hands. She supposed that was a possibility. One she hadn't considered. One that had never even crossed her mind.

She blinked. The crack was there, then it wasn't, as though a spiderweb blew across her vision.

Question everything.

She was slipping.

Enzi propped his muzzle on the sofa next to AJ and she beckoned him up. He circled once, twice, then settled with his head on his paws and his stare locked on Natalie.

She squinted at him. Now it was two against one.

"It is interesting that someone who has overcome so much feels their predicament is an impossible one."

Natalie placed the completed puzzle on the table and picked up the next. Keeping her eyes on the loops of wood and metal, she watched AJ in her peripherals.

Three puzzles.

Wake up, Natalie.

No, not three. There was a fourth puzzle in the room: AJ.

"Tell me, Natalie," AJ leaned forward, her plucked brows pinched. "When did you stop trusting yourself? When your Uncle died? Or your parents?"

Natalie clenched her jaw. She wouldn't answer that.

"Or," the Counselor's voice dropped to a whisper, "when you defied the natural flow of time?"

Natalie's fingers tripped on the puzzle.

"Or, perhaps, when you started seeing things that aren't there?"

The blood drained from her face. As far as she knew, the Regent hadn't told anyone of Natalie's ability to time-travel. As for the hallucinations, the *crack*, she'd only told...

"How do you know about that?" Natalie anchored her heels on the floor. Edwin's betrayal made the room sway. She'd told him about the cracks in confidence. She'd *trusted* him. Natalie dropped the second completed puzzle on the table and fumbled through the third.

"It is my Contribution to know," AJ rested her elbows on her knees, her chin level and mouth set.

Natalie paused in her tinkering long enough to meet AJ's stare. Her eyes matched her honey-bronze skin. "How do I make it stop?"

"I only have research to go on: the records of past Counselors, of past Regents, and…others. Did you know you're the first time-traveler since the second World War?"

Research. Natalie was comfortable with research. She worked the puzzle without looking at it.

"No," she confessed. "And what do the records say?"

"To stop running."

Natalie straightened. "I'm sorry?"

"There are things in your past, in your future, that you cannot escape. You need to stop running away from them, to put your energy back into yourself."

Her words struck a familiar chord. She sounded like a ghost. Like Eleanor.

Conquer your demons, dearie.

AJ inclined her head and Natalie realized she'd voiced Eleanor's words aloud.

"Some demons must be conquered, but not all of the dark parts of ourselves are meant to be vanquished. Some become part of us."

The pain doesn't go away. The memory of Brant felt as real and sharp as a knife. *We just get better at carrying it.*

"Like grief," Natalie breathed.

"And guilt," AJ leaned towards her. "But those shadows only define you if you let them. You need to mourn, Natalie. You need to allow yourself to grieve. You must lean into that suffering, accept it, allow it to run its course because it isn't going to go away. And this life holds so much more for you yet."

Natalie pulled back. "The last time someone told me to lean in, I had to let my family die. I had to leave them behind."

"The way I hear it, you did not have a choice."

"Of course I had a choice!" Enzi's ears flattened as she yelled. "I was with my Mom and Dad, I knew what they were running into, and I chose to let my family die. Just like Christopher. Just like Angie, and Chef, and Eleanor."

"You're fighting it."

"You try it sometime," Natalie spat. She was raw. AJ had brought her live wires to water, and she exploded. "It's agonizing. It's Hell. It's enough to...to…"

"To drive you mad."

Natalie's cheeks were wet. Her lungs burned. The crack was there, splintering AJ's bronze face into shards, and then it was gone, and she was whole, but Natalie was not, as though the crack had turned inward and—

Fear boxed in her thoughts.

"What is wrong with me?" Natalie croaked.

"The more you fight, the more you'll crack." AJ took the two pieces of the puzzle from Natalie's hands. Not solved but broken. "Everyone has something that anchors them. I challenge you to find yours, before you've gone too far to heal."

Edwin had told her the same thing. Again, Natalie wondered why she was there, why Edwin insisted she speak to this stranger instead of just explaining things himself.

"What happens then?" Natalie asked. "When you've gone too far to heal?"

AJ shifted in her seat, appearing, for the first time, uncomfortable. "Edwin led me to believe that you two had discussed–"

"I want to hear it from you."

AJ leveled her gaze. "You will perish by your own insanity. Those you love will suffer having to watch you waste away into madness. And when you die, every chance against Nautilus will die with you.

Our city will race you to the grave."

A chill settled in Natalie's bones, making her shiver.

AJ said *when* not *if.*

Yet it wasn't AJ's words that rocked her, nor their promise of death and the end. It was the small part of herself that longed for it. For rest. For quiet.

For peace.

Natalie jumped to her feet. She needed to move, to outpace her thoughts.

"How long does it normally take your patients to solve all three puzzles?"

"You're not a patient," AJ sat back. "And it's not a competition."

"Hmm, longer then. And the fourth puzzle?" Natalie shoved her shaking hands into her pockets, making it more than clear she was on to AJ and her games even if she hadn't quite figured them out. She wasn't sure who the Counselor stood for, but she was willing to bet it wasn't the Regent or her Curia. And Natalie didn't have time to sit around figuring her out.

Tick-tock.

AJ smiled, not saying a word until Natalie had nearly crossed the threshold.

"Be sure to let me know," AJ called cooly after her, "when you've solved the fifth."

Natalie hesitated, white knuckles shining on the doorknob. Her mind jumped to Brant's clue. Brant's *puzzle.* But AJ couldn't know about that...could she?

Enzi brushed against her, pawing impatiently at the door. Behind them, the sound of AJ's bare feet on the marble softened as she retreated.

"It was an honor to meet you," her honey sweet voice faded. "Natalie Atlas."

The rush of water filled her ears.

Natalie A.

Natalie Anyone.

Natalie *Atlas.*

She threw open the door and sprinted down the street. She needed to think. She needed to research.

She needed a library.

CHAPTER 17

I am sorry," Lache's lips pursed. "You want *my* help?"

"Need," Natalie corrected, the word as comfortable as gravel in her mouth. "I need your help."

Lache moved to fill the doorway, blocking the inside of her quarters, but she was too late. Natalie had already spied the pallet on the floor. The unkempt pile of sheets and blankets. The black sweatshirt draped over the couch.

Leo's sweatshirt.

Natalie swallowed the bile that rose in her throat. She'd been the one to push Leo away; it wasn't fair to get upset over where he sought solace. She refocused on Lache's icy stare, on the luminous white scars refracted across her skin.

"Where's the Library?"

"The Library?"

"Yes, Lache, the Library. Big building. Lots of books."

Lache snapped the door closed behind her, setting a brisk pace across the crowded Atlantean street. "I am not sure you will find what you are looking for."

"Well, I'm not finding answers anywhere else."

"Perhaps you are looking in the wrong places."

"Hence," Natalie said through gritted teeth, "the Library."

They moved easily through the streets, the scents of sage and lavender soothing Natalie's shoulders down her spine. Yet as comfortable as Natalie felt in Atlantis, Lache actually looked it. She carried herself through the city as though she was put on the planet to do nothing else. Her gait never faltered, and uncharacteristically warm smiles at passersby were eagerly met. She looked more at ease than Natalie had ever seen her. She looked happy. Meanwhile Natalie wished they could weave through the gardens to avoid the throngs of people.

Thankfully, wherever Lache was taking her wasn't popular. In the span of a few blocks the crowd dissipated, along with the iridescent sheen Natalie had come to associate with Atlantis. Buildings gave way to towering trees, their interlocking branches occluding the sky. She was certain it was the forest she'd spotted in the newsroom, the one in the very center of the triquetra map that each Tertian branched from. She wanted to confirm the idea with Lache when the world fell eerily quiet.

Natalie stopped. Finches chirped and darted overhead. A breeze fanned the leaves at her back. The forest was far from silent; she wasn't deaf. But something was missing. Something was off. Unease churned her stomach.

Whatever it was bothered neither Lache nor Enzi. They marched steadily ahead, and Natalie forced herself after them, every sense on high alert. She squinted into the emerald shadows between the trees, searching for something to explain the twitch of her fingers against her thigh, that feral instinct that told her to flee. Yet the only shapes in the shade were structural ones.

Crumbling time-worn stone cut hard lines in the landscape. Vine-choked columns stood straight amongst arched tree trunks, their Corinthian caps chipped and faded. Thick sheets of ivy transformed once magnificent boulevards into a secret garden's maze; one that Lache appeared to know well.

Not trusting her own instincts, Natalie minded Enzi closely. His ears were perked, his tail high and waving. He was comfortable. Calm. Wholly unaffected by the void that still pressed against her eardrums, an absence edged with apprehension.

"This is the Ancient City," Lache's voice was a sonic boom in the quiet. "Or what is left of it."

"Do you feel that?" Natalie hugged herself as though she could block out the silence like a chill. How could she explain something that wasn't there? How did one describe an absence?

Lache watched her impartially, the way a god might regard a bug.

"Nevermind," Natalie mumbled.

"The Library is this way."

Natalie tried to walk normally, to stop glancing over her shoulder and checking every alley. But something wasn't right.

Atlantis treasured invention, ingenuity, and history. Natalie had hardly noticed a speck of dust on the breeze or a misplaced tile. So why was the Ancient City so decrepit? Why had the Curia left it abandoned?

"Why is no one else here?" she asked aloud.

"Why should they be?" Lache shrugged her sheet of silver hair over her shoulder. "Atlantis started here but has grown beyond this place."

Natalie frayed the hem of her shirt. She didn't like that answer. She remembered her own ancient life, the one with her mother and father who weren't, the home Nautilus burned to the ground. She knew from personal experience that one did not simply abandon their beginnings, no matter how humble. Not without cause.

"Besides," Lache went on, "to travel here is inconvenient without–" Lache rounded a turn and halted. She spun to Natalie, ashen faced and wide-eyed. "Hide."

Natalie might not call Lache a friend, but when push came to shove, they understood each other. They owed one another their lives. And if Lache said to hide, Natalie was not about to argue.

She motioned Enzi to her side and darted into the wood. The dog pulled ahead, ears down, tongue flapping, and skidded behind a massive, half-crumbled arch.

Natalie sank beside him. Her sweat-slicked palms pressed against the stone and she wished the entire wall was still standing. She wished the forest offered somewhere better to hide. She wished she knew what Lache had seen, but as the Moirai tucked in close, Natalie didn't dare ask her.

Shoes scuffed the pavestones and the rustle of fabric folded over hushed voices. Every breath brought them closer, any second she'd see them through the decayed fortress.

Natalie shifted and slumped awkwardly against the wall, whimpering as a shard of stone reopened the gash on her arm.

For a moment, all sound beyond the archway stopped. That unnatural silence pressed on Natalie's ears, and she was about to make a run for it when a firm grip spun her around.

Natalie's fear stuttered when she came face to face with Aislinn.

She shook her head, but the image didn't go away. Aislinn was really there, helping Natalie up, carefully avoiding the blood seeping into her sleeve. A flurry of grey suits stood behind her, the title *Patrol* embossed on their shoulders in elegant script.

"Miss Morrigan!" The Regent cupped her chin, scanning her efficiently from head to toe. "My dear, are you alright?"

Enzi paced at Natalie's side, firing off intimidating barks

interrupted by long whines. He leaned against the Regent's robes and eyed her Patrol warily. At least he was as confused as Natalie was.

"I…I don't–"

"Regent Aislinn?" Lache stepped out, not restrained but also not free. Flanked by two more of the Regent's Patrol, Lache folded her arms. "What is going on?"

"I am sorry, Lachesis." Aislinn squeezed the Moirai's shoulder. "There has been…a development." The Regent's gaze flicked between the two of them, calculating. "What are you doing out here? The Ancient City is hardly a place for sightseeing, not since the aqueducts were retired."

"*That's* what's missing!" Natalie exclaimed. The hum, the steady rush of water beneath the streets, through the gardens, had gone. It was a sound she hadn't realized was there until it wasn't, an absence she could feel as much as hear. Saltwater was the heart and soul of Atlantis; its blood, its *pulse*. And with the aqueducts turned off, the Ancient City was essentially dead.

Regent Aislinn's brow furrowed. "I'm sorry?"

"Nothing," Natalie waved the realization away. "You were saying?"

"I have a great need to speak with Edwin and have been unable to locate him. If you know of his whereabouts, it would be most helpful."

Natalie looked to Lache, who shrugged.

"We do not know where he is."

"Ah," Aislinn paused, and Natalie caught the nervous flick of her robes through her fingers. "Then I must ask you not to engage him yourselves. He may be…dangerous," she paused again. "To himself and to others."

Natalie felt as though she'd been dropped back into the sea without her spark, left adrift and unsure which way was up. Aislinn wasn't making sense. Edwin wasn't dangerous. He was dramatic, and energetic, and inquisitive to a fault, but not *dangerous*. Not to mention he lived and breathed for their city. He loved Atlantis so much he'd offered his own life as collateral just to get them inside and–

The realization turned her blood to ice. Edwin had vowed that Natalie and her friends would be model citizens. He'd sworn they'd bring no discontent to their city. Instead, she'd snuck out of the city (twice), passed secret messages to sworn enemies, and faulted curfew more often than she cared to admit. She'd broken the rules. Was that all it took to condemn him?

Desperate, Natalie turned to Lache and the Moirai gave the smallest shake of her head. But Natalie couldn't do nothing.

"It's my fault," she blurted. "Edwin didn't do anything wrong."

Aislinn frowned, standing so close her plaited hair and violet robe was all Natalie could see. "Miss Morrigan…"

Suddenly, Natalie wanted to tell Aislinn that wasn't her name. She wanted to correct her, like she should have the first time the Regent asked in the Atlantean Curia. *Morrigan* didn't fit anymore. She'd left it behind somewhere on the surface, faded and hollow, shed like a skin. But the name AJ had given her didn't fit right either. Atlas was a coat two sizes too large. It slipped off her shoulders, leaving her simultaneously exposed and concealed.

She wasn't Natalie Morrigan, but she couldn't be Natalie Atlas either. Not until she knew what it meant. Lacking a fitting choice, she said nothing.

Aislinn brushed Natalie's hair from her face, her stare sympathetic but stern. "I beg you not to claim responsibility for crimes you do not yet know. Let us go somewhere we might talk freely. Somewhere more," she glanced at the Patrol, "private."

Crimes, the word buzzed in Natalie's ears. This was about more than curfew and field trips. But Natalie knew the Regent. She knew how Aislinn only showed her people rose-colored truths. Whatever trouble Edwin was in, she wasn't going to learn anything else out in the open.

"I am afraid," Aislinn gestured back towards the main city, "there is something you need to see."

Natalie didn't dare look at Lache, but as they followed Aislinn through the city, she sensed the Moirai tremble. And it wasn't for the Patrol escort or Aislinn's consistently careful countenance. It was what the Regent said that made Natalie's palms sweat. Aislinn was supposed to be strong, she was supposed to be secure, yet she said it all the same.

I am afraid.

Whatever trouble Edwin was in, they were undoubtedly in it with him.

Counselor's Notes
Subject: Tawney Davis

Tawney: *Subject's arms are crossed.*

AJ: *Waits for subject to speak first.*

Tawney: "This is pointless."

AJ: "Counseling is what you make of it."

Tawney: *Subject squints.* "I'm not going to tell you anything. I don't trust you."

AJ: "Fair enough. You don't have to share anything you don't want to. But know that anything you do say stays right here in this room, between you and me."

Tawney: *Subject unfolds her arms. Wrings her hands in her lap.* "No one knows what happens in here?"

AJ: "Not a soul."

Tawney: *Subject nibbles her lip and shifts in her seat. Pulling her knees to her chest, she hugs her shins and weeps.*

CHAPTER 18

Natalie thought she knew what to expect when the Regent escorted her and Lache to the Curia. She expected her friends would already be in custody, which they were. She expected to be questioned for information on Edwin she didn't have, which she was. And she expected Edwin to have the good sense to save his own neck, which he did.

What she didn't expect made her weak in the knees.

Cold sweat slicked her forehead, and between one leaded step and the next a crack in her vision splintered. Its fissures divided and spread like hyphae, stretching out wide to drink her in.

It wasn't real. It couldn't be.

They can't be here. They can't be here, theycan'tbehere, theycan'tbehere—

"Natalie."

No.

"Natalie."

"No!" The word erupted from her chest, bouncing off the domed ceiling to crash back heavily on her ears.

Leo rippled into focus. Forest green eyes. Chestnut hair half pulled back. That worried crease between his brows. Her crease. She'd put that there. Just like the scars on his arm, on his stomach. How many other marks had she left that she couldn't see?

He held her up by her elbows. At some point the Regent's Patrol had become her support, and at another they'd let her go. That didn't make sense either. Why would they let her go? Why would the Regent let any of them go? How was Leo free to hold her when they should be chained against the wall? Executed on the spot.

Leo cradled her palms. Solid. Real. The spider web of cracks receded with every warm touch.

Find an anchor.

"They can't be here," she whispered.

His next words rebuilt the world beneath her feet. "They are."

Natalie inhaled through her nose until oxygen filled her up, cleared her mind, and burned her chest. No matter how impossible it should be, if Leo said the two Nautilus members standing in the center of the Curia were real, then they were.

Nautilus was inside Atlantis.

Which only left one question.

"How?"

"That," Regent Aislinn said slowly, "is exactly what I would like to know."

The unwavering leadership she exhibited in the streets was gone. Her confidence stripped bare. Shoulders hunched, Aislinn studied the two figures clad in navy. "How did this happen?" she asked of everyone. Of herself.

Despite the two captives initially appearing unbound, Natalie's panic ebbed enough for her to catch the glimmer of a force field. With Enzi tight to her side, she approached, splaying sweat-slicked fingers across the nearly invisible surface. She had seen the technology before, from the other side of the cage. At the end of the Earth where the Sun never rose and time slipped and she wondered how different they truly were, Nautilus and Atlantis, Nautilus and Coelacanth—

Leo's arm brushed hers, jolting Natalie's neurons back into place. Though perhaps the madness hadn't been far off. Here she was, trapped again beneath a slab of rock where the Sun was fake and the lies tasted sweet. Even the ones she made herself, the ones she clung to like rafts in a tumultuous sea of synapse slips. And how long would those hold?

"Hello, Raven."

Natalie stiffened. Her gaze skipped over spiked green hair and plump cheeks to settle on toxic green eyes. They burned with the same hunger when she'd tried to kill Natalie in combat training, when they'd fought on the roof of the Helix. A desperation that would never be satisfied.

"Max."

Max wiped the Nautilus shell pinned on her lapel until it shone in the turquoise light of the Curia. She'd entered the Ward's inner circle after all, become the Legate she always wanted to be. And now she stood in the most secret building in the world.

"Tell me," Max leaned in until only the shimmer of the force field separated them, inspiring Enzi to bare his teeth. "Have you found peace?"

Bile stung the back of Natalie's throat. Suddenly, she wished the force field wasn't there. She wished nothing separated her fingers from the thick skin of Max's throat.

Someone slathered a cool ointment over Natalie's scraped arm, distracting her. Regent Aislinn continued with sure movements until the salve warmed and the bleeding stopped.

Nautilus was in Atlantis. Max was in the Atlantean Curia. And the Regent busied herself with superficial scratches.

Aislinn wasn't a bad person. She lacked malice or greed. She appeared neither drunk on her power nor ruthless in it. In fact, lending painstaking attention to Natalie's wound, she seemed the exact opposite. Level-headed and cautious, Aislinn *cared*.

But Natalie wasn't sure caring was enough. The Regent was supposed to guide Atlantis to lead the world. The Regent was supposed to safeguard the constant forward march of humanity. The Regent was supposed to keep her people safe.

Yet Nautilus was in Atlantis and Max was in the Curia.

Natalie pressed her shoulder into Leo's. He steadied her, her anchor.

"You lied to me," Natalie snapped at Aislinn. "You said you had contingencies in place. You said you had a plan."

"I did," Aislinn snapped back just as harshly. "I had plans if Nautilus moved for power on the surface. I had plans for the probable and the possible, but this," a sickly pallor overwhelmed the rosy hue on her cheeks. "This is inconceivable."

Rage, fear, and sheer emotional exhaustion shook Natalie from head to toe. She had needed Aislinn to be what she stood for. For her to explain how Max stood in the Atlantean Curia grinning like a dragon on its horde. But she wasn't doing enough. Not for Natalie, not for her friends, not for their city.

"How?" Natalie parroted the Regent's question back at her.

"The specifics have yet to be determined," she said dryly. "That's why you're here."

"You can't possibly think we did this." Tawney's ringlet curls shook. Owen stood with an arm around her waist, a white-knuckled grasp on her hip.

"She knows that," Atro flanked Tawney's other side as Enzi paced between them.

It surprised Natalie not that the Moirai were there, but that she expected them to be. At some point, perhaps in Ancora IV, or the Helix, or fighting for their lives on the Chesapeake Bay Bridge-Tunnel, their paths tangled so completely that the Moirai and Coelacanth became one endless knot, a jumble of scars and fate. So much so that Atro's dark fist curled protectively over Tawney's.

Clo saw it too. The other Moirai went rigid, a statue of porcelain capped with silver spikes.

"You all know there is no stopping our peace." Max chuckled from her cage, inspiring a smirk from her partner.

Natalie didn't recognize him, but she knew he was a Legate. His arrogance alone would have been telling enough, even without the shell pinned to his jacket.

"Why?" Lache ignored Max, directing her question to Aislinn. "Why do you not suspect us?"

"Because I know who did this, if not how." Tugging the sash from her own robe, Aislinn bandaged the worst of Natalie's arm, the long gash too wide for her salve. "He bears no good will for Atlantis or for me, and you were his ticket back inside. A means to an end." The Regent's mouth twisted. "I warned the Council they trusted the word of a traitor."

Owen pieced it together first. "You think *Edwin* did this?" He scrunched his glasses up the bridge of his nose. "The same Edwin who'd lick every pavestone in this city if it meant he'd never leave?"

"You do not know him as I do," Aislinn warned. "Why else would he not be here now? Why else would he ignore my summons?"

"To save himself a fate he does not deserve," Lache's tone bordered on pleading.

"And because you're fifty shades of crazy," Tawney muttered.

"We mean no disrespect," Leo spoke over her as Owen tucked Tawney behind him. "But what you're suggesting isn't possible."

"Look harder, Leonidas. We live in a universe of impossibilities," Aislinn's arms folded beneath her robes. "Edwin's betrayal is the smallest among them yet shall have the greatest cost. Fate, you will come to know, is a right wicked beastie."

Natalie's stomach turned. Christopher had given her the same warning once.

When they'd arrived in Atlantis, Edwin paid for their sanctuary with the promise of his life in exchange for any grievances. Now Nautilus stood in the Atlantean Curia, two navy blue trophies locked in the Regent's case. It didn't feel right.

It didn't feel real.

And for the first time, Natalie wondered if the most dangerous person in the room did not include those locked away. If the most dangerous person in the room was not one she feared, but one she trusted. Had Natalie been so desperate to trust, to be taken care of, that she'd given the Regent and her rules a pass? That she'd allowed herself to forgive the curfew and quarantine and censorship in exchange for the blessed promise of safety? Of having someone else calling the shots?

She'd never wanted to be the adult in the room. She'd never wanted to have the lives of her family, of her friends, of the strangers in this impossible city in her hands. And even as Enzi rubbed against the back of Aislinn's knees, Natalie knew she wasn't a bad person, she just wasn't the leader they needed. That Atlantis needed.

But Edwin was. He not only loved his city and his people, he'd do what he must to protect them. Whatever the cost. He understood when to use stealth over strength. He understood how crucial Atlantis's role was to the outside world. He understood that apathy was as lethal as a bullet. And if the Curia found him first, he'd not likely live long enough to help anyone. So Natalie did what she did best: she questioned.

"How did Edwin let these Legates in?"

Aislinn pursed her lips. "We are working on that."

"*Why* did he let them in?"

"Resentment. Revenge. Curiosity," the Regent flourished a wave. "As I said, you do not know him as I do."

Natalie fired again quickly, sensing Aislinn's patience burned at both ends. "What is Nautilus after?"

In her periphery, Natalie saw Max go still in her cage. She wanted to know the answer as badly as Natalie did, which made her wish she hadn't asked at all. Why would the Ward send two members of his inner circle into Atlantis without telling them what they were looking for?

None of it made sense.

Though the Regent didn't seem to mind. She shrugged. "Undoubtedly whatever they could get their hands on."

Wrong. Natalie and Leo shared a glance. Max cracked her neck. The Ward was definitely after *something.*

Aislinn's thin mouth disappeared in a line. "Should Edwin make contact, you are to notify myself or the Curia immediately," she shifted away, refusing to entertain Natalie's interrogation any longer. Her voice dropped as she smoothed non-existent wrinkles from her robe. "Failure to do so will force me to align your fate with his," Aislinn paused, either unwilling or unable to meet their stares. "Am I clear?"

"As glass," Owen assured her, already tugging Tawney towards the exit.

Before departing, Natalie squared her shoulders and addressed the two prisoners in their cage. Legates. Leaders. The Ward did not send Doves to negotiate or Curtanas to conquer. Natalie's skin prickled.

"Why did he send you?"

Max appeared preoccupied with her fingernails, while the one with a bruise on his cheek studied the ceiling. But Natalie caught the corners of his mouth lift. They were listening. Intently.

She slammed her fists against the force field. "I don't care," Natalie whispered through the barrier. "I don't care how you got in. I don't care why you're here. But now that you are," she leaned in until the tip of her nose brushed the solid surface. "I hope you savored your last glimpse of freedom."

Both captives turned to look at her and their easy smiles sent chills down her spine as Leo pulled her away.

"Dearest Raven," Max called to their backs. "I'll be sure to drown you myself."

Cool air gusted over Natalie's face as they rushed outside. The afternoon was too bright, the streets too loud. The iron and wood braided door slammed shut and Natalie leaned against it, letting it hold her up as the world fell apart.

It didn't matter that Aislinn put the Legates in a cage.

Nautilus was exactly where they wanted to be.

CHAPTER 19

Leo wasted zero time identifying the next play.

"Aislinn will be keeping tabs on us," he paced outside the Curia, restless and agitated. "In case Edwin makes contact."

Natalie rubbed her neck, wiping off the remnants of Max's stare. "I know."

"We need to find him."

"I know."

"We need to find him before the Curia does."

"Leo, I know!" Natalie stopped him but he stared past her, surveying the streets as though Edwin hid like Waldo in the crowd.

"We cannot talk here," Lache motioned towards the alley. "I know somewhere–"

"No," Natalie cut her off. "No offense, but the last time I followed you, we ended up there," she pointed back at the Curia.

"Oh!" Clo clapped. "I know!" The Moirai plunged into the crowd of Atlanteans so swiftly Natalie lost sight of her pixie hair in seconds.

"This way." Towering over most of them, Owen followed the

Moirai's lead.

It was several turns and two switchbacks before Natalie ducked after him into a low-ceilinged cavern. The path turned steep and slick, and she braced against the walls to keep from sliding. Hot clouds of moisture fogged Natalie's lungs and Enzi panted heavily ahead of her.

"Feels like we're back in bloody Florida," Tawney cursed.

The passage opened and shards of sunlight cut from round skylights in the ceiling, gilding countless bubbling pools. Mosses and ferns lined the walls. Thickets of pothos stretched for the sun.

"It's a hot spring," Owen grinned. He kicked off his shoes and steam sifted up between his toes.

"It is a greenhouse," Clo corrected.

"It's damn crowded is what it is," Tawney frowned, surveying the pockets of bathing Atlanteans. "How do you expect us to talk here?"

"The bubbles from the spring muffle everything," Clo cupped a hand to her ear. "See? You cannot hear them; they cannot hear us."

Leo needed no more convincing than that. "How are we going to find Edwin?"

"Maybe he's down here, too." Owen peered through the fronds, wiggling his naked toes towards the nearest pool.

"If he knows what is good for him," Atro countered, "he has already left the city."

Tawney swatted a pothos vine out of her hair. "When did self-preservation hop to the top of Edwin's to-do list?"

Natalie's stomach knotted. Tawney was right; Edwin didn't care what was good for him. He'd do anything to stay in his city, his home. No matter the risk. No matter the cost.

"He's still in Atlantis," Natalie agreed. "He's too stubborn to be anywhere else."

"We have to find him before Aislinn does," Leo shifted restlessly from foot to foot, his agitation spreading.

Tawney drummed her fingers on her thigh, Owen smeared the fog from his glasses, and Clo nibbled her lip as Atro and Lache stretched anxiously on either side of her. It was then Natalie realized Edwin was more than some guy who'd brought them to Atlantis, who'd helped them escape Nautilus.

He was their *friend*.

And when he needed them most, Natalie had no idea where to start.

She thumbed her temples. "You know him best," Natalie nodded to Leo. "Any ideas?"

"No. Maybe if Atlantis had the equivalent of a junkyard," Leo's brow furrowed in concentration. "He wouldn't go anywhere we know. He's too smart for that. I'm more worried he'll get bored…restless."

"Reckless," Atro amended.

Tawney clicked her tongue. "Maybe we can lure him out with taffy."

"I do not think that will work," Clo frowned.

Leo snorted. "It might."

"Between the Curia and Nautilus, we need to work fast," Owen glanced at his watch. "How ever those Legates got in, more are sure to follow. It's only a matter of time."

Time. Natalie pursed her lips. *Tick-tock.*

"They were too comfortable," Natalie thought back to Max and her partner relaxing in their chamber. "Nautilus isn't even afraid."

"Because unlike some of us," Tawney said bitterly, "they actually want to be here."

"Edwin will know what they're after." Natalie was certain she was right, though it was hard to imagine what Atlantis could be hiding that was more dangerous than herself. If what Edwin said was true, if Natalie was truly the only living time-traveler, the fact the Ward's sights had drifted set her teeth on edge. She had to be missing something, some crucial piece of the Coelacanth-Nautilus-Atlantis puzzle, some hint as to where to begin—

Natalie blinked, the answer suddenly obvious. Even more so because the Regent had beat them to it. "We'll start at the beginning."

"The Ancient City," Leo agreed.

"That must have been why Aislinn was there," Lache's eyes went wide. "She was already looking for him."

"Great. Two groups then. The faster we find him, the sooner I can pummel him. Let's split up, gang!" Tawney hooked her arm through Natalie's as Enzi padded eagerly ahead of them. "Lead on, Scooby."

Leo cleared his throat. "Owen," he called. "Why don't you go with them? I'll stick with the Moirai."

Tawney smiled as Natalie's heart plummeted. She remembered Leo's black sweatshirt on Lache's floor, tangled in the makeshift bed, and she stared up the exit passageway without actually seeing it. This wasn't the time to dwell on whatever brewed between Lache and Leo. And even if it was, she didn't know what to say. As much as Lache had been through, as visible as her cracks were painted across her skin, on the inside she was whole. That's what Leo needed. That's what he deserved.

And that's what Natalie wasn't.

The two groups drifted apart, emerging from the hot spring and breaking off to search the Ancient City from opposite directions. In the silence, Natalie wondered if Leo would hold Lache's hand, if he'd steady her when she stumbled on the pavestones, then she pushed the notion aside. Lache had the grace of a queen; she wouldn't stumble.

Absorbed in her thoughts, Natalie didn't notice Tawney had

stopped walking until it was too late. She collided into her, a wobbling tangle of legs and curls.

"What are you—"

"Knock, knock." Tawney steadied them, but the ground still rocked under Natalie's feet.

It was Brant's clue. They were supposed to be looking for Edwin and she was talking about Brant's clue. In front of Owen. Natalie's cheeks flushed hot. Tawney couldn't keep one secret for one day? But before she could question her, Tawney repeated the words.

"Knock, knock."

"Who is going to keep them safe?" Owen asked.

Natalie rounded on him. His mouth was set in a frown that tugged at his eyes and something swirled beneath Natalie's frustration. The string of a thought she couldn't quite catch.

"Say that again."

"I already did."

He was right. He *had* already said it. The night of Nautilus's first bombing. The night they'd lost their parents. The night they'd gone to find Christopher those exact words had come from Owen as they boarded their uncle's boat.

Hope thrashed like a caged bird in her chest.

Brant hadn't given Natalie a puzzle. He'd given her a memory.

"It's not a riddle," Owen confirmed. "It's a place. He's pointing you back to the marina."

"Are you sure?"

"Of course not," Tawney scoffed. "But we all knew you were sneaking back there from Ancora III."

Owen nodded. "It's where I'd leave a message, too."

"Or a trap," Tawney offered.

Natalie glanced back towards the Ancient City, towards the edge of the forest on the horizon. Edwin had saved their lives in more ways than one. She had to get to him before Aislinn did.

But Edwin would never let a question sit unanswered. He had to know the how and why behind everything. She knew if he was there, he wouldn't hesitate. If he was there, he'd tell her to go.

And how she itched to go.

"We'll be quick," Tawney promised. "Back before Leo's even close to finding Edwin."

"How do you know Leo will find him?" Owen asked.

Tawney rolled her eyes. "He's already lost Brant, and Natalie once. He's not about to lose Edwin, too."

Natalie adjusted the Regent's sash around her arm, the silk flecked with salve and dried blood. Tawney wasn't wrong. Of all of them, Leo was the most likely to find Edwin. And if she could find Brant in the meantime…

"Okay."

Tawney's round brown eyes lit up. "Okay?"

"Yeah," Natalie swallowed the last of her reservations. "Let's go."

Owen paled, suddenly uncertain. "Go?" he repeated. "As in leave? As in, we're leaving Atlantis?"

"Don't worry," Tawney marched towards the beach. "You get used to it."

CHAPTER 20

According to Einstein, time is relative.

To Natalie, a lifetime had passed since she last saw the marina. She had lost Christopher and her parents. She'd gained a home and half a history. A legacy. A name.

Natalie Atlas.

Yet Morning Sun Marina appeared untouched by time. The same planked docks stretched into the same gentle waves. Seagulls perched on every pylon, basking in the summer sun. The bay was quiet and calm, and opposite the water, the boat motel towered over them. Its aluminum walls shone with a painted yellow sun split down the door's seam. In its shadow, Christopher's cottage remained a lone sentinel, guarding the soul put to rest behind it.

Natalie's gaze skipped over the lodge, taking care not to linger on the details. She couldn't allow her mind to stroll up the hill where Christopher was buried. They didn't have time. And it was hard enough standing surrounded by his memory without inviting his ghost to muddy her thoughts.

"Okay." Gravel crunched as Tawney marched to the cottage porch. She cracked her knuckles, prepared to relive Brant's clue. "Let's do this."

Enzi darted around her and pressed his nose to the frame, ready to charge inside. But instead of opening the door, Tawney hovered a fist over it. She stared at the wood.

"Knock, knock," Owen said quietly, sparing her the task.

Tawney focused on her sneakers. "Go away."

"That's not what he actually—"

"It's the abridged version, alright?" She dropped her shoulders back, softening. "Then I knocked again."

"More like tried to break down the door," Natalie corrected.

"And I think you threw some things."

Tawney half shrugged. "Fine. What happened after that?"

"Christopher came out with his stuff," Owen squinted through his glasses, as though seeing it all happen again.

"And Angie," Tawney whispered.

My fault. Natalie's gut wrenched at the dog's name. She folded her arms over her stomach, pushing down the guilt. *No. Brant's fault.*

"And then we boarded the *Learn'd Astronomer*," Owen pointed to the slip where Christopher's boat used to rest. "Where I asked who is going to keep our parents safe."

"No." Natalie's pulse quickened. That wasn't what happened next. Not exactly. "First they put the truck and motorcycle in the boat motel."

Natalie rushed to the marina doors and her breath stuck in her throat.

The lock was broken.

"Nat," Owen stepped between her and the padlock, his stare shifting past her as he scanned the inlet. "This feels like a trap."

She wanted to shove him out of the way. To tell him Nautilus could have taken her in the cemetery. That they could have been swarmed by navy jumpsuits the moment they set foot on the Eastern Shore. But he wasn't wrong. She'd misread Brant for weeks. Possibly years. She couldn't pretend to know what he had planned. And she'd led her friends down the wrong path more than once.

"It might be a trap," she admitted. "You don't need to stay, but I do. I have to know."

Owen didn't even blink. "So do I."

Metal screeched on concrete as the door strained open and Natalie wiped the sweat from her palms. If Nautilus waited in the shadows, they wouldn't stand a chance. Yet as sunlight seared into the warehouse only dust motes spilled out, sparkling in the breeze. No Nautilus. No trap. Anticipation sent goosebumps up Natalie's arms.

Maybe Brant was still with them after all.

Sand scattered over the polished concrete as she stepped inside, turning the ground treacherously slick. Slowly, her sight adjusted to the dim light. Enzi flashed in and out of sight as he investigated every cobwebbed nook. I-beams divided the boat motel into perfect rows, vacant save for the occasional rat in the rafters.

And in the farthest corner, cloaked in the deepest shadow, two vehicles sat dark and dormant.

Tawney patted the black truck, carving a trail through the dust from bumper to bumper. It was Brant's truck. His name stuck in Natalie's throat like glue, as stubborn as the Atlantean synapse block.

"They're like pieces from another life," Tawney marveled.

"The before time," Owen nodded, and Natalie instantly knew what he meant.

Before the bombing at Norfolk Naval Station. Before their parents disappeared. Before their future slipped out from under them, leaving them falling. Constantly falling. Before they'd had to question.

"Every day I still expect Brant to just…come back," Owen picked at the peeling inspection sticker on the truck's front window. "For him to show up at Andrei's Appétit. To play off everything as some elaborate joke." He shook his head. "I still expect him to show up and for everything to go back to normal. Just like Mom and Dad."

"He doesn't deserve to come back." Even as Tawney said it, Natalie caught the tremble of her bottom lip, the glassy sheen in her eyes. "I hate him," Tawney whispered. "But…"

"But it's Brant," Natalie finished for her.

"Yeah," Tawney kicked the nearest tire and sent up a plume of dust. She turned away, rubbing her eyes.

"Why would he lead us here?" Owen stared into the dead headlights of the truck as though speaking to it, as though it knew something he didn't. "It doesn't look like anything's changed."

Natalie shifted away from the vehicle. It inspired questions she wasn't ready to answer. Like when Brant decided to betray them. Or if there'd been anything she could have done to prevent it. She drifted towards the motorcycle instead. Life had been simpler when wrapping her arms around Leo's waist was the most daring thing she had to her name. She tapped the handlebars, tracing over the leather seat and matte black chrome. She made it all the way to the back tire when it hit her.

"It's clean."

"No, darling," Tawney snorted. "This place is filthy."

"No," Natalie circled the bike again. "I mean, yes, everywhere else, but this," she leaned against it. "*This* is spotless."

Tawney scrunched her nose. "You think Brant left us a clue by *cleaning*? No," she shook her curls. "No way."

"Either someone cleaned or this bike magically repels detritus," Owen leaned closer, scrutinizing the motorcycle through glinted frames.

"Really?" Tawney crossed her arms. "That's your line? Tack across oceans, discover the freaking lost city of A–" her lips pursed. "*You-know-where*, and help your fellow nerd travel through time, sure. But a dust-repelling motorcycle is too much?"

Owen wiggled his glasses up the bridge of his nose, not pausing in his inspection to retort, "Smart ass."

A twig snapped outside.

None of them moved. The sunlight beyond the door was dazzling. She saw nothing but light, that blazing line where shadow met sun.

Gravel shifted and Enzi crouched. Hackles up, ears perked, his fur stood on end, making him appear twice as large and a hundred times as fierce.

Natalie's heart hammered. She wished she still had Chef's bolt. Hell, she wished she had a gun, if only to hit someone with it.

Something darted across the marina door, low and furry and–

"It's a freaking otter." Tawney sank against the bike as the creature's wet tail slipped around the corner and out of sight.

Owen squatted, his freckles dark against pale cheeks. "Mutinous Mustelidae," he breathed.

"We can't stay here," Natalie stated the obvious out loud as the wasted adrenaline pooled in her stomach, making her queasy.

"But we haven't found the clue," Tawney protested.

Owen wiped sweat from his forehead. "What if the motorcycle *is* the clue?"

"The entire bike can't be the clue!"

"If there's anything here, we aren't the ones who would know where to look." They stared at Natalie as she wrenched up the kickstand. "We need to ask the owner," she said through gritted teeth. "We need to talk to Leo's dad."

"Here," Owen took the handlebars from her and muscled the bike towards the water.

"I can do it," Natalie protested, and Tawney quieted her with a wave.

"You tacked a *jet*, remember? Let him have this one."

CHAPTER 21

Natalie halted where gleaming tile faded to worn stone. She'd sprinted the entire way back to the Ancient City, hoping to catch up with Leo while Tawney and Owen found somewhere to hide the bike, yet the sprawl of forest stopped her. Heels bouncing, chest heaving, she tried to think of another way. Any other way.

Surely *someone* knew where Mr. Merrick was staying other than his son.

Unfortunately, no one came to mind. Leo was being dragged into her mess whether she liked it or not.

Forcing one brave sneaker forward at a time, she managed to resume a light jog. The absence of seawater that normally hummed beneath the Atlantean streets made her feel vulnerable and alone, though the latter didn't last long.

Enzi barreled up behind her, crashing into Natalie with such force he nearly sent her sprawling. She cut him a look and he cocked his head as they ran, tongue lolling and ears pinned back for maximum speed. His dirt-caked muzzle was the only evidence of whatever distracted him those four or five blocks back. Natalie opened her mouth to scold him for it when, rounding a bend in the path, she saw them.

A half-crumbled tower sprouted from the ground and disappeared into the treetops. Eroded on either end, it was merely the ghost of a wall, a fragmented memory of what the Ancient City had once been. Yet still strong enough to support the couple that leaned against it.

Lache's silver hair rippled on the same breeze that carried Leo's laugh, light and lilting. They sat shoulder to shoulder, studying something stretched between them, bent so close together their arms touched…

Natalie stopped. Caught between a torturous desire to know more and a wish she'd never spied them at all, she couldn't move. A whorl of anger, jealousy, and bitter selfishness churned in her gut. For weeks, she'd tried to keep her imagination in check. She'd not allowed herself to dwell too deeply on the thought of their many weeks alone in that Scottish cottage. Of Lache tending his wounds. Of them plotting against Nautilus together, without her, and being all the better for it.

Because of all the crazed and inexplicable things Natalie had seen that summer, Leo and Lache made sense.

The Moirai was smart, beautiful, and strong. And though she was far from Natalie's favorite person in the world, that had more to do with Leo than anything else. In truth, Natalie would always be indebted to Lache. She saved Leo's life, and as a result they shared something Natalie would never be a part of.

And Natalie couldn't remember the last time she made Leo laugh.

Distracted, she didn't notice Enzi leave her side until it was too late. Cursing under her breath, Natalie darted after him as he nosed himself pointedly between Lache and Leo. Too slow to catch any of their conversation, she at least managed to glimpse a spread of blueprints before Lache smoothly shifted them out of sight.

"Any sign of Edwin?" Natalie asked curtly.

"Not yet," Leo leaned against the wall, holding Enzi's front paws to his chest. "Can't say I'm surprised, though. He knows this city better than any of us. We'll find him."

"Certainly," Lache added.

Natalie ignored her. "Are we still on for dinner with your dad?" In a failed attempt to sound endearing, her tone bordered on aggressive.

Silent, Leo arched a brow.

"I'd love to talk with him." Natalie let her false smile fall and gave him a single slow blink.

Leo straightened. "Yeah. Right, absolutely. He'll be over the moon. Lache," he tapped twice on what remained of the wall. "Catch up later?"

"Anytime." The Moirai tucked a loose lock of hair behind one ear, her voice all honey and silk.

It made Natalie sick.

Leo led her quickly away, and no matter how high she craned her neck she failed to get another glance at the blueprints.

"What's going on?" he asked as soon as they were out of earshot. "You don't have to act like this. Whatever you need to say you can say in front of Lache. I trust her."

Natalie's stomach dropped. That was real. With his hand in her hand, his skin on her skin, she knew it was real. He meant it.

I trust her.

Natalie wrenched out of his hold and walked. She needed to find a corner of the world where she could catch her breath and think.

Marching deeper into the Ancient City, the walls grew taller and sturdier. Once proud avenues were left in disrepair with paver stones that rippled like waves. Towering fountains and labyrinths of aqueducts were dried and caked with dust, their copper coatings worn green with age. Beneath the boughs of the forest, wild shrubs gathered where Atlanteans once stood and eroded sculptures marked every corner: a man, a minotaur, a Fate. The Ancient City may have been forgotten by man but never by nature.

The whole scene reminded Natalie of images she'd once seen of Pompeii. One didn't have to look hard to infer how grand the city must have been. Thousands of years ago this crucible of stone had brimmed with genius and advancement, with purpose. With knowledge.

Suddenly Natalie knew exactly where she was going.

She doubled her pace. She'd come a different way before, and hadn't paid careful attention with Lache leading her, but peeking down the narrow avenues, she eventually spied a familiar corner of half crumbled columns.

Leo followed, close enough he could have touched her. Could have but didn't. And Natalie didn't know if she was grateful or disappointed. She didn't know if he wanted to be there at all.

"Maybe you should go," Natalie offered.

"Is that what you want?"

There was genuine curiosity in the question, and she didn't know how to answer. She wanted him there, but not if he wanted to be somewhere else. Not if he was thinking of someone else. And she suspected he would be once he found out the truth of Brant and the bike and the letter…

Frustrated, Natalie cursed under her breath. It wasn't fair that she'd had to hide Brant's messages from Leo. It wasn't fair that he was so vexed by Brant's existence that her confession would only push him further into Lache's open arms. How had their closest friend, someone who once knitted them together, wrenched them so far apart? One desperate to hold on, the other determined to let go.

Bored, Enzi padded ahead of them and doubled back.

Another turn and the building on the corner caught her eye. She'd seen that structure before with Lache, when the Regent came and–

That way.

While Enzi dashed down every alley, Natalie stayed steadfast on the main path. She scanned what remained of the buildings' archways, deciphering faint whispers of Latin still etched into the stone. It was another three blocks before she found it.

BIBLIOTHECA

Natalie held the glassy lock on the Library's gate with both hands.

"Why would the Regent lock a library?" she muttered.

"You think Aislinn locked it?"

"When Nautilus entered Atlantis, Aislinn came to the Ancient City. She came here. She caught Lache and I maybe five or six blocks back," Natalie shook her head. "She's determined to find Edwin, and she came here first. Then she locked it. Why?"

"You might be right," Leo peered over her shoulder. The heat of his breath tickled her neck. "It wasn't locked before."

"You've been here before?"

"Once. With Lache."

The lock dropped with a sharp smack against the metal. Natalie stared at him, eyes stinging.

Leo's brows knitted together. "What?"

"You came here with Lache?"

"Yeah, she brought me here one night when–"

Natalie shoved past him and stormed around the side of the building. Logically, Lache and Leo made sense, but that didn't mean Natalie wanted to hear about it. That didn't mean she wanted it.

She shook her head, determined to focus on what was important: Nautilus. Edwin. The bike. Her name. Any of which could be the

Counselor's fifth puzzle, could be what the Ward was truly after. All of which could have answers just beyond that locked door.

She scanned the Library for another entrance. Sleuthing down the alley, she inspected every barred window, every crevice that might grant entry. The second-floor balconies might have been possible, but even if Tawney could manage that climb Natalie never would.

Leo followed close behind with his hands in his pockets. "You're upset?"

"Obviously," Natalie pushed her fist against her aching chest. "I can't get inside."

"Don't suppose you want my help then."

Natalie turned to him, surprised. "You can get me inside?"

"No," Leo held her gaze. "I can get *us* inside. This is a team, Natalie. Me and you. Both or bust."

Her heart lanced with every syllable.

Me and you. Both or bust.

Enzi sidled up to her and she bent to pet him, scratching behind both ears. She was grateful for the distraction. For something to focus on that wasn't Leo.

But Leo moved closer, leaning in until they shared the same air.

"As soon as you're ready to talk," his thumb brushed the length of her jaw, making her breath catch. "I'm ready to listen."

Natalie didn't want to talk. Not about what she'd seen between him and Lache. And certainly not about the fragile and fractured state of their team.

She stepped aside so he could pass, so she could breathe. "Lead on."

Leo muscled aside a stack of pallets, exposing a grate with a handle so rusted through, Natalie was certain it would never lift anything. Yet the half-rotted hatch opened with only minor protest, and Leo gestured for her to go first.

Naturally, Enzi beat her to it. He dove inside and out of sight, leaving her hesitating on the surface.

Curiouser and curiouser, she thought bitterly as the dog's white tail swished into shadow. Cool air wafted out of the hole, laced with notes of vanilla and secrets.

Natalie jumped and, as her stomach floated into her throat, she wondered if the rabbit hole of Atlantis would ever end or if she was doomed to fall forever.

CHAPTER 22

Natalie dropped into the Library, brushing cobwebs from her shirt. Leo landed with a grunt behind her.

"What are we looking for?"

"Honestly," she fumbled forward in the dark. "I have no idea. Records, I guess. Anything we can find on time-travel. Or…or Atlas."

"Hmm." Instead of pressing for more, Leo asked, "Do you really want to have dinner with my dad? Or was that just for show?"

Natalie had nearly forgotten the motorcycle. "I do. I need to talk to him."

Gradually, dark turned to dusk and filtered sunlight danced with dust motes in the air. Natalie waved away the debris and every muscle in her body seemed to relax at once. Even in Atlantis, it was a library in every sense of the word, and soon Natalie lost herself in the maze of shelves.

BIOLOGIES, COSMOS, ARCHITECTURE…

"Need to talk to him?" Leo pressed. "Or want to?"

"Need to."

He pulled her to a stop and the silence engulfed them. It was far from the romantic hush between lovers, nor was it a tight-lipped lull of faulted friendship. Their silence was an iron curtain of secrets and lies, and the abandoned library magnified it out to every corner until the quiet was so thick Natalie choked on it.

"Why won't you tell me what's going on?"

Because I don't know.

Because you looked happy.

Because you are healing and I am breaking.

Because I am a shard of glass, as likely to cut you as I am to shatter.

Every answer bubbled up at once and none passed her lips.

Leo's expression turned guarded. "I used to know what went on inside your head."

"Me too."

"What did AJ say when you went to Counseling?"

Uncomfortable, Natalie's gaze drifted up and she straightened. *HISTORY.*

He was leaning on it.

"Nothing." Preferring not to discuss the Counselor and her puzzles, Natalie shifted around him. She thumbed down the rows until she reached the beginning: the A's.

"I doubt that."

Atlas, Atlas, Atlas. The name taunted her. She traced the polished square of shelf where the *A* section of books once lived. It was vacant. They'd been cleared out, and recently, too, judging by the lack of dust.

Natalie thumbed her temples. The crack erupted through her vision, spooling out like spiderwebs. She didn't have answers to anything and the one place she'd hoped to find some had already been pillaged. Frustrated, Natalie's nails dug into her palms, leaving divots for Leo's words to sink into.

AJ, he said. Not *Counselor.*

"You went to Counseling," Natalie realized out loud.

Leo's shrug was confirmation enough.

"What did AJ say to you?"

Head hung low, skimming titles, Leo suddenly looked as tired as Natalie felt. Enzi brushed against his knees, white fur dingy with dust, before setting off again, nose to the ground.

"She suggested I start doing things I used to. That if I could find something that felt normal, eventually everything else would, too." He tried to smile but it didn't take.

Natalie stared at the nearest shelf, the books blurring together as she lost focus. She was a lot of things, but normal wasn't one of them. Not anymore. So where did that leave her? Them? Maybe that's another reason he connected with Lache.

She wondered what they did when they came to the library, and her gut churned until she remembered the blueprints Lache stashed away.

"Leo?"

"Hmm?"

"You're working on something."

The corner of Leo's mouth tilted in a sly grin. "I am."

"What is it?"

His gaze was wicked, like a boy caught with a frog in his pocket. "I'll tell you mine when you tell me yours."

What had AJ told her? Before Atlas? Before she bolted?

Everyone has something that anchors them. I challenge you to find yours, before you've gone too far to heal.

"Do you feel better?" Natalie whispered. "Doing what AJ suggested?"

He wetted his lips. "No," Leo shifted. "Everything still hurts. But…I do feel like myself. I feel like me."

And that was all she wanted.

"AJ told me to find something that anchors me," Natalie confessed. "So, I know—so, I know what's real…and what isn't."

Leo leaned against the opposite bookcase. "Is it hard to tell?"

Not certain she could find her voice any easier than the missing books, Natalie nodded. And that simple motion was like shattering a dam. Her words tumbled out in a rush.

"I see things that aren't there," she blurted. "I hear things that have already happened, or might have happened, and it all *feels* real. It feels as real as a blade at my throat, yet it's smoke and mirrors and fiction and it won't stop, Leo, it won't stop—"

Leo cupped her chin, halting her panicked babbling with his thumb over her lips. "Do I feel real?"

Natalie's pulse stuttered. "Sometimes." She remembered the certainty of his hand in hers, the taste of salt when they kissed on the beach, and the warmth of him in her bed. "Sometimes not." Like when she pictured him with Lache, when she lied to him, when she had to pull back for fear of falling in and dragging him under and—

Leo cleared the distance between them in one step, pushing her shoulders flush against the bookcase.

"I stepped back because you refused to let me in. Because I thought it was what you wanted. That one's on me." He flooded her senses. The smell of cedar, the taste of his breath on her lips, that devastating look in his eyes. He was everywhere. Every line of his body framed hers. A shelter. A fortress. "You can doubt everything else: the air in your lungs, the ground at your feet, but never this. Make no mistake, Natalie, we are as real as it gets."

Foreheads, noses, lips met in a desperate rush. Warmth spilled from his fingertips, carving trails of molten gold across her skin. Shifting, the library shrouded them in a cloud of dust. And Natalie had to admit, he certainly *felt* real.

Leo was solid ground after a life at sea.

She clutched fistfuls of his grey hoodie and yanked it over his head.

Grey.

His mouth slid from hers, trailing down her neck.

Grey.

His hands were a vice on her hips. A lock. An anchor.

Grey.

He drifted back up to her, but she turned, landing his kiss on her jaw.

"Leo–"

"Whatever it is," he breathed, "can wait an hour."

Natalie pinched his chin, forcing him to look at her. His eyes were the color of the Atlantean gardens at night.

"Nothing is this important."

"Your hoodie is grey." She said the facts out loud to test them.

"Yeah," he smoothed her tousled hair. "You like grey."

"I do," she admitted. Even more because the hoodie she'd seen on Lache's floor, the one tangled in the pile of blankets, hadn't been grey.

It had been black.

Leo kissed her again and she savored it for several heartbeats before dropping her head back. Flecks of glass sparkled in the ceiling. They looked like stars. Impossible stars under an impossible sky in an impossible city.

"I know where Edwin is."

Leo stilled. Frozen. Conflicted. Finally, he released her with a groan. "When all this blows over, he's grounded. No taffy for a month."

CHAPTER 23

If hope has feathers, doubt has talons.

Leo pounded on the door to Lache's apartment. Once. Twice. Four times. Not having to go through the trials of quarantine and sanctuary, the Moirai's accommodations weren't carved into the basalt labyrinth of Atlantis like Natalie's and her friends'. Instead, they had a real townhome with real windows that overlooked a real gardened boulevard.

They even had a porch.

Enzi nosed the welcome mat as Leo knocked again, hard enough that the door creaked in protest, and it finally cracked open.

Lache took up most of the doorway, her silver hair blinding in the sun, but Natalie could see well enough behind her. The living room was immaculate: no pile of blankets, no black hoodie, just a spotless space void of stowaways.

"Hello," Lache dragged out the greeting, her icy stare slipping suspiciously from Natalie to Leo. "I was not expecting visitors."

Natalie barged inside. She scoured every surface for some kind of clue, for any evidence Edwin had been there.

But Lache's entire apartment was as flawless as its inhabitant. Doubt dug its talons into Natalie's chest.

Had she imagined it all? What if it hadn't been a hoodie but something else? Maybe it all belonged to Lache? Or her sisters? A black crack lingered on her peripherals and Natalie massaged her forehead, fighting the fissure.

No, she had definitely seen something.

"This seems a touch uncouth." Lache arranged herself on a lounge chair. Comfortable. Composed. Spouting irritating vocabulary like *uncouth*.

Enzi plopped his head in her lap.

"Leo's sweatshirt is grey," Natalie muttered more to herself than anyone else.

Lache leaned forward, robes rippling over her feet. "Are you alright, Nat?"

She's concerned.

No, that couldn't be right.

Natalie's breath quickened into frigid blasts that stung her lungs. Lache wouldn't be concerned, not about her. Not about anyone but her sisters.

And where are they? Natalie wondered, suddenly uncertain if she had ever seen the three apart. Though perhaps she had. Surely she had…

Though the room felt stiflingly hot, cold sweat slicked her brow.

"Edwin's hoodie," Natalie meant to shout, to accuse, but barely managed a mumble. "I saw it…I saw it *here*. At least I thought," she tried to swallow. Her mouth was dry. "I thought I did…"

"She is unwell." Lache sounded an ocean away, a siren's whisper on the sea. "Has AJ seen her?"

The familiar hum of Leo's voice reverberated against her, within her, but she couldn't *hear* it. She was slipping. The room tilted. She reached for him, for her anchor, for her something real–

"Nat."

Her name beckoned like the first morning's tide: quiet and gentle. But she was comfortable in the dark. She folded into it, content to sleep.

Her cheek smarted.

"Nat."

No.

"Wake up, Natalie."

The words tickled a memory. She'd heard them before.

"Leave me alone," she grumbled, her tongue thick and heavy.

"We need to take her somewhere," someone said near her head. Her someone. Leo. "A hospital. Something."

"Wouldn't recommend it," another voice echoed by her feet. How were they beneath her? "Unless you want them to never let her out."

Natalie stirred. No one would put her in another cage. Not another prison without sun. Not while she was still breathing. She rolled to her side, sluggishly propping herself up on one elbow.

She was on the ground. In Lache's apartment.

The Moirai hovered over her like an angel, haloed by the afternoon sun. She pressed a deliciously cool cloth against Natalie's face.

It came away red.

Natalie's heart hammered in her chest. She sat up, wiping away the blood that trickled from her nose, her ears. The room spun. Something was *wrong*.

Leo pressed against her back. Or maybe she leaned against him. Either way, he held her up as her world fell apart.

"I didn't travel," the fact came out as a whine. "I didn't travel. I didn't."

Leo's touch was firm. No cracks splintered her vision. This was real. So, what made her faint? What made her *bleed?*

"I told you before," Edwin passed her a glass of water, not letting go until convinced she wouldn't drop it. "It's cumulative."

Natalie blinked. He was wearing a hoodie.

"Your sweatshirt's black," she said dully. She'd been right, though at present it brought her little comfort. "Lache's been hiding you here."

"Nice work, Watson. No, don't get up." A quick pat on her shoulder was enough to thwart her efforts. Edwin ruffled her hair for good measure and it made her world spin. "Don't need anymore damage up there than you already have coming."

"If this," Leo gestured to all of her, "is cumulative, then how do we stop it?"

Squatting so he was eye-level with Natalie, Edwin stilled. No rifling in his pockets for sweets. No adjusting the three hoops on his ear. His coal eyes tightened at the edges and Natalie stopped waiting for him to respond. She was grateful, at the very least, that he wouldn't lie. That he wouldn't give them false hope.

Natalie knew they couldn't stop it. Now Leo did, too.

Leo's touch dropped away as he started to pace, spearing Edwin with glares as though sheer power of will could change her fate.

Meanwhile, Lache found her hand and squeezed. She was marble: cold and solid. A relief against the fever that burned in Natalie's skin.

"Nautilus is here," Natalie changed the subject, eager to focus on something that wasn't her. Something they could fix.

"I know." Edwin tugged at his hair, his cheeks gauntly pale. His contract with Aislinn had been broken. The devils were inside the walls.

"Regent Aislinn blames you."

Instead of rising to his own defense, Edwin merely inclined his head. "Naturally."

By the promise he'd made the Curia on their admission into the city, Edwin's life would serve as payment. It seemed as excessive to Natalie now as it did then.

"They're going to kill you," she whispered.

Edwin gave her a one-sided grin. "Not yet, they're not. First, they have to catch me. Then, they have to try me. And between those two things, they have to deal with Nautilus, no matter how much our lady Regent would prefer not to."

Natalie wiped a stray trickle of blood from her upper lip. "Why does Aislinn hate you?"

Edwin glanced out the window where Archimedes' sun hung low in the sky. "I'm not certain we have time for that."

"Make time," Leo countered.

Edwin's mischievous smile transformed him back to the rebel Natalie discovered plotting against the Ward within his own Helix. "Aislinn doesn't hate me," he explained. "She's afraid of me. Reason makes people powerful. Fear makes them dangerous."

"You are not scary." Clo peeked in from the hall, a potted eucalyptus hugged against her chest.

"Not now," Edwin agreed. "But when the Atlantean Curia named me Regent four years ago, I was Aislinn's worst nightmare."

"You?" Natalie blurted. "Regent? But you're so..."

Edwin's smile soured. "If you say *young*–"

"Progressive," Natalie finished. She recalled the careful composure of the Curia. They were bricks and mortar where Edwin was rocket fuel. That he'd come close to Regent was improbable, to have been chosen bordered on impossible.

"Ah," Edwin softened. "Atlantis is a pillar of invention, of progress, but that was a sticking point." He met Natalie's gaze head on. "And though they'd never admit it out loud, the fact I cannot tack didn't help my case either. But the real problem was that as Regent I planned to bring Atlantis to the surface. I wanted us to rejoin the world, to lead an era of progress. I wanted us to rise." Edwin paused. "I called it the Coelacanth Project."

CHAPTER 24

Natalie felt as though all the air had been sucked from the room. It couldn't be a coincidence. Yet she could see no connection between Edwin's Coelacanth Project and Christopher's beyond the band of aurichalcum on her wrist.

"The Coelacanth Project?" Leo repeated. "Are you sure?"

"Of course, I'm sure," Edwin snapped. "It was my bloody plan! Your uncle just seems to have thought of it first. And a right foul mess he made of it, too," he scoffed. "Bringing Atlantis to the surface by taking its people out of it. Absurd! No offense," Edwin added quickly. "I know you loved your uncle. But you have to wonder what his intentions were, and who was meant to benefit from them. I never even met the man and he's kept me up more nights than I care to admit."

Natalie and Leo exchanged a loaded glance. They'd known Christopher their entire lives and never managed to figure him out. It was hardly a surprise Edwin couldn't either.

"Regardless," Edwin went on, "my plans were too bold for the

Curia, so Aislinn convinced them to overturn the vote. She told them I wasn't ready." The muscles of his jaw tightened. "She argued that a tacking Atlantean should lead. That youth equates to ignorance." He snorted. "A primeval concept."

"Then she's holding a grudge?" Leo asked skeptically.

"Hardly," Edwin's grin returned, brighter than before. "Though she is afraid of me being here. Afraid the Curia may change their minds again when they discover exactly what I've brought into their city."

"Nautilus," Lache supplied.

Edwin rolled his eyes. "Aislinn fears them far less than she should. She believed us invincible until her Patrol discovered those two Legates by the cliff. No," he touched Natalie's wrist, studying her spark before lifting his gaze to hers. "Aislinn may be wary of me, but she is outright terrified of you."

"Me?" Natalie balked.

"Do you know what a regent does, Miss Morrigan?" Edwin dragged out the name, as though he knew it grated like sandpaper on her soul.

"They rule in a leader's absence." Natalie realized she'd never given Aislinn's title any thought. "It's temporary."

"Outside of Atlantis, yes, but here," he pointed to the city outside the window. "Here, the Regent often rules for life. True kings are…rare," Edwin tapped the spark. "As rare as traveling through time."

Natalie's body stitched together his implications ahead of her mind. Her gut twisted, making her mouth water in a way that made her feel sick. She didn't like what he was saying.

She didn't like it at all.

"Aislinn is desperate to silence me by any means necessary because she rightly suspects you don't know your own legacy."

Edwin wiped the last bit of blood from her ear and cradled her hands, smearing them in crimson. "She's afraid I'm going to tell you the truth about your name. She's afraid I'm going to tell you that an Atlas is the rightful leader of this city. And most of all," Edwin's voice dropped to a devious whisper. "She's terrified you're strong enough to do it."

The color drained from Natalie's face. If it wasn't for Leo's firm hand at her back, she'd be on the floor again.

"You're saying," Leo pulled at his hair. "You're saying…what exactly?"

A commotion outside made Edwin tense. His knees bent to run but he didn't. He held his ground. "I think you know what I'm saying."

Natalie didn't want to believe him. It was crazy. It was madness. Yet the more she thought about it, the more it started to make sense.

Why else would Aislinn downplay her ability to travel through time? Why else would she squirrel Natalie away while parading the Moirai as champions of scientific achievement, distracting the city with silver and scars? Was she afraid Natalie would erase her rule as Regent? Take the city? Or, worse, put Edwin in charge?

Natalie had to admit, that last bit held merit. Aislinn was respectful and level-headed; she had the countenance and composure of a leader. Just not the leader Atlantis needed. And with Nautilus slipping through the cracks, Atlantis needed someone willing to take risks. Someone passionate and courageous and strong.

And that was Edwin.

Something slammed against Lache's door, making everyone but Edwin jump. Enzi's hackles rose as he growled at the shadows shifting beneath the doorframe.

Their time was up.

"It's you," Natalie gripped Edwin's wrists. "Atlantis needs *you.*

Nautilus is here and the Ward is after something and—"

"Every time Atlantis steps out of the picture, the world goes to war," Edwin's words silenced her. "The Trojan War. The Taiping Rebellion. The Punic Wars. The World Wars." He cringed as Lache's door took another beating. "Atlantis must stay relevant in global affairs, even if only behind the scenes. You cannot let this city fall. If the Ward wants what I think he does, if he gets his hands on it—" hinges cracked, the paneled wood bowed "—there won't be an Atlantis left. And the world will be left to chance."

Enzi snapped and snarled as the Patrol muscled their way inside. Edwin pinched Natalie's chin, forcing her attention back to him.

"There are a thousand causes to die for," he said quietly. "But something to live for is rare. Natalie Atlas, this city needs you to live. *I* need you to live."

Edwin didn't run. He surrendered in silence, allowing the Patrol to bind his wrists behind his back. As they yanked him away, he stared back at Natalie with the same dangerous glint in his eyes she'd seen when they first met.

Hope.

"Wait!" Natalie broke away from Leo, tugging on the sleeve of a Patrol officer like a child. "Where are you taking him?"

They didn't answer. Edwin, who fought a bridge full of Nautilus, who would give his life to keep the Ward's hands off the world, went without a single word of protest. Meanwhile, Enzi protested enough for them all, barking so loud Natalie couldn't hear herself think.

"Why are you doing this?" Natalie shouted to make herself heard.

"Orders," one officer grunted before turning to Lache. "You have the Regent's gratitude, Lachesis," he nodded at the Moirai. "The Curia will remember your loyalty to our city."

"Of course." She bowed slightly, silencing the protest in Natalie's throat with an icy glare.

And as quickly as the Patrol arrived, they left. She stumbled over the broken door after them, desperate to know where they were taking Edwin, where she could find him. But by the time she navigated the debris, they were gone.

Natalie stood for three full breaths at the place Edwin had been. Her chest heaved. Her temples throbbed. Then she stepped over the fractured door, crossed the room, and pinned the silver haired Moirai against the farthest wall.

"Why?" Natalie seethed. "Why would you shelter Edwin here just to turn him in? What could they have possibly offered to make you betray him? He. Saved. Your. Life." Natalie jolted her against the wall with every syllable. "*Twice!*"

She wished Lache would shout back, that she would hit her, because Natalie desperately wanted an excuse to hit back. A reason to pummel that perfect silver head of hair into the ground.

But Lache didn't fight. She sank against Natalie's arm until she held Lache up as much as she pinned her down.

"Why do you think?" Lache sighed.

"Because," Leo pried Natalie off of her. "Edwin asked you to."

Clo sat cross legged on the floor, her plant in her lap as she massaged her forehead. "You all are exhausting."

Ignoring Clo, Natalie frowned, all the gears in her brain turning at once. "He asked you to," she looked at Lache. "No. He couldn't possibly want to get caught. He couldn't want–" She stopped. Of course Edwin didn't *want* to get caught. But since he refused to leave the city, it was only a matter of time before the Regent found him. And when she did, he didn't want them going down with him.

He was saving them. Again.

"If any of us were found protecting Edwin, we would all be punished," Lache said quietly. "We are no good against Nautilus locked away in a cell."

"Clo! Atro!" Owen ran in off the street, leaping ungracefully over the splintered remnants of the door, spectacles spilling from his face. "Lachesis!"

Clo fetched his glasses and Owen latched onto her shoulders, making the potted eucalyptus she hugged tremble.

"You're okay?" He scanned her head to toe before looking to Lache, and, finally, to Leo and Natalie.

Natalie nodded, her fists still undecidedly clenching and unclenching at her sides. "Where's Tawney?"

"Chores," he said automatically. "Where's Atro?"

"Elsewhere," Clo scowled.

Owen dragged through his fire-red hair and nudged a splinter of Lache's door with his sneaker. "What happened here?"

"The Curia took Edwin," Leo summarized.

"What does that mean?"

"We do not know," Clo shrugged.

Owen's freckles appeared to darken as he blanched. "How long do we have before...before they..."

Lache cleared her throat. "Edwin assured me that until the Curia has dealt with Nautilus, he will not be touched." She fiddled nervously with the hem of her robes. "However, with Nautilus in the city and the Regent so distressed," the Moirai lifted a porcelain hand and let it fall. "I am not certain we can be certain of anything."

"Then we need to get him out," Leo rubbed his palms together. "We'll find out where they've taken him and–"

"No." The protest was out of Natalie's mouth before she could stop it.

Leo turned to her. "No?"

Natalie Atlas, Edwin had said. *I need you to live.*

Natalie swallowed hard. "Edwin doesn't want us to find him. He asked Lache to turn him in so we'd be clear to do what we need to, to focus on the problems the Regent won't." She took a steadying breath. "Nautilus."

Edwin put himself in chains so they'd have a shadow of a chance of saving their city. Natalie didn't know how to help Edwin or how to solve his endless riddles. but she did know that Nautilus was inside their walls. And that was more important than uncovering her history. They couldn't let Nautilus win.

All of her questions could come after.

Leo crumbled against the wall, his stare glazed over and distant. "We can't lose him, Natalie. Not like…"

She didn't need him to finish.

Like Christopher. Mom. Dad. Angie. Chef. Brant.

All of their names could have filled that blank space.

"Natalie is right," Lache acknowledged her with a modest nod. "Our best chance of saving Edwin is to stop Nautilus."

"How are we supposed to do that?" Owen huffed. "Do you want me to calculate the odds for you? Because they are most certainly not in our favor."

"Edwin said the Ward is after something in the city," Leo fiddled with the spark on his wrist, rolling the stone beneath his thumb. "Something dangerous." He folded his arms, turning to Natalie. "What's more dangerous than you?"

The thought made her stomach churn. Natalie had no idea. But if anyone knew what the Ward was after, it would be his son.

And he'd left them a motorcycle.

"Remember what I said about dinner with your dad?"

Leo looked sideways at her.

"Turns out I'm starving."

To her relief, he didn't press for details.

She followed him blindly through the streets, the blue and green tiles a blur underfoot. Edwin at least suspected what the Ward wanted, yet in their final moments together he neglected to share it. After all this time, did he not trust her? Or was it like the city's synapse block? Something he couldn't share even if he wanted to?

Perplexed, her thoughts snagged on one of Edwin's clearer points. A warning.

Every time Atlantis steps out of the picture, the world goes to war.

If the Ward wants what I think he does…there won't be an Atlantis left.

CHAPTER 25

Failure demands grace.

Not the kind Tawney's parents wanted her to learn in ballet, or how years of soccer made Leo light on his feet. But the kind Christopher tried to teach them. The kind that treats defeat as an opportunity instead of an ending. The kind that meets *no* with a lifted chin and tenacious mind.

Natalie forced her head high as she waited on Mr. Merrick's stoop, yet she felt anything but graceful.

Her failures were heavy. It was more than a forgotten dance step or a missed goal. Every warning she'd dismissed, every moment she assumed she knew better than Nautilus had led her parents and many of their friends to their deaths.

And that kind of failure was permanent. One that could not be conquered or redeemed, only accepted. A grief she must learn to carry. A demon she had to embrace but she wasn't sure she was ready. She wasn't sure she could look Mr. Merrick or Mrs. Davis in the eyes, the only two survivors of their parents, and endure that misery again.

She certainly didn't have the grace for it.

"Coming?" Leo peeked back at her through the open door, Enzi an island of white between them.

How long had she stood there, staring at the iridescent sheen of light on the building? A minute? An hour?

Tick-tock.

"Hey," Leo untangled her fists from her shirt. "It took me a while, too, but he's the same man he was before."

Before. Natalie grimaced.

Before they learned Merrick wasn't his name any more than Morrigan was hers. Before Brant and his father had betrayed them. Before she slipped into the Ward's trap and killed nearly everyone they loved, including this man's wife. Including her own parents. Including any residual delusion they'd had of returning to a normal life, to the before.

Yet it wasn't until she conquered the threshold that Natalie realized she hadn't been avoiding seeing Mr. Merrick at all. She'd been avoiding *him* seeing *her.* Avoiding the outpour of blame and contempt and shame. For a tense moment, she blinked in the dimly lit interior, her sight adjusting away from the brightness of Archimedes' sun. She waited, a breath trapped painfully in her chest, and Leo never let go of her hand. He remained her anchor, holding her in his gravity.

"Nat, my dear!"

A kiss landed on the top of her head as strong arms enveloped her. Her vision cleared enough to make out the flecks of grey in Mr. Merrick's hair and the rosy round cheeks of the woman behind him.

She could have been back in Williamsburg. Those strong arms could have been her father's, and that brilliant smile her mother's, and something between a laugh and a wail squeaked from her throat. The impossible vision stretched and warped and Natalie closed her eyes to hold it, to live as long as the universe would allow in that glimpse of another life. Of the before she could never have back.

"We are so happy to see you, dear!"

The illusion shattered. Because that was all it could ever be: a vision, a dream. When Natalie opened her eyes, she clung to what was real.

Mrs. Davis tidied her hair and pinched her waist, insisting Natalie stop scurrying around the city long enough to eat a proper meal. Meanwhile, Mr. Merrick dove headfirst into a detailed description of the Ancient City, dating back to before recorded history (at least what's recorded beyond Atlantis, he clarified). It was more than she could have asked for. No resentment. No blame. No simmering hatred in their stares. Instead they fussed over Natalie like she'd barely been gone a day. Like their entire world hadn't been upended.

She sucked her bottom lip to stop it from quivering.

"I have some potato hash in the fridge, honey," Mrs. Davis patted her back. "I'll have it ready in a jiffy."

"Now, have you actually seen the Ancient City yet?" Mr. Merrick's stubbled cheeks wrinkled with his grin. "AJ gave us a tour on our first day and I swear you can *feel* the history wicking up off the ground!"

They circled her like bees over a flower, like a cat around a—

Something soft and warm vibrated against Natalie's ankle and she jumped. A ball of grey fluff with tiny, black-tipped ears batted ferociously at her shoelace. Natalie scooped the kitten up, letting the creature rest in her palm. Round topaz eyes blinked back at her.

"You're lucky Enzi didn't find you first," Natalie said.

"Actually—" Leo was cut off as Enzi bounded past him.

He planted two giant paws on Natalie's shoulders and promptly licked the kitten from tail to nose. Fur spiked and damp, it hissed indignantly, its jaws full of tiny white teeth.

"They've met," Leo finished. "Enzi loves her, but so far the relationship is a bit ah…one-sided."

The kitten hissed again. Enzi cocked his head at it.

"Oh," Mrs. Davis rubbed a flour-dusted thumb under the kitten's chin. "Tofu will come around."

"Tofu?"

"Tawney," Mrs. Davis made a face. "My girl dropped her off a few days ago with nothing but a bag of cat food and her name."

A stolen bag of cat food, Natalie suspected silently.

"Where did she find you?" Natalie asked Tofu, allowing the kitten to snuggle the crook of her neck. She had seen plenty of wildlife in the Atlantean gardens, squirrels and various species of birds, but never any cats.

"Oh, who knows?" Mrs. Davis's smile faltered and a bit of the warmth drained from the room.

Natalie tensed. Here it was: the fallout. The rifts in their family motif laid bare. Natalie called upon to answer for the damage done, the lives lost.

"She's at Contributions, Mrs. Davis," Owen dipped around Natalie to embrace Tawney's mother, whose head barely brushed his chest. "She'll be along soon."

"I've known you long enough to know when you're lying," she scolded him lightly. "Tawney has her own wants and needs, her own responsibilities that expand far from me no matter how much I wish it wasn't so. Though your heart's in the right place, dear," Mrs. Davis patted Owen's cheek, as determinedly bright as her daughter was fierce. "At any rate, Leonidas says you need our help."

"Yes," Natalie cleared her throat. "It's a little…complicated."

"Trust me," Mr. Merrick snorted. "It can't be as complicated as Leo's aqueduct blueprints."

Natalie glanced in Leo's direction.

194

He shrugged.

"Perhaps not in technical terms," Natalie sat on the plush couch and settled Tofu in her lap. Enzi rested his muzzle on her knee, whining occasionally at the creature. "It's about your motorcycle."

"My motorcycle?" Mr. Merrick occupied the armchair opposite her. "I'm afraid I haven't seen it since–"

"I know," Natalie could feel the tension radiating from Leo across the room. "Just…what can you tell me about it?"

"What do you want to know?"

"Well," she rubbed Tofu's fluffy belly, hoping the kitten's purr would calm her. It didn't. "Everything."

Leo's stare bore into her. She avoided it, waiting patiently for any information Mr. Merrick was willing to give.

"I'm afraid there isn't much to tell." He ran a hand through his hair, a motion so like Leo's that Natalie was reminded their familial bonds went deeper than DNA. "The motorcycle was a gift, received after *someone* wrecked my first one."

Leo was suddenly captivated by some spot on the ceiling.

"A gift from who, exactly? Christopher?" Natalie tried to swallow but her mouth was dry as cotton. "Or…or Mr. Smith?"

The Ward's name landed like a boulder in a pond. Mr. Merrick turned a sickly shade of green. Mrs. Davis spilled tea in the kitchen. And Leo and Owen shifted uncomfortably on their feet. Only Lache and Clo remained unphased. They'd known the Ward in his true form from the beginning.

"Christopher," Mr. Merrick answered quietly.

"Why does it matter?" Leo probed. "The bike has been at the marina for months. It's irrelevant."

"Wrong!" Tawney burst through the front door. Hugging her arm to her chest, she beelined for the kitchen sink, cursing colorfully as the water hit her. She bounced from foot to foot for a moment before finally leaning against the counter with a groan.

"Tawney–" Her daughter didn't let Mrs. Davis finish.

"Children are disgusting! I swear, as soon as I can choose another Chore, I'm out. The entire Atlantean Academy is covered in spit and snot, and they put *everything* in their mouths." She held up her bleeding forearm. "Myself included."

"They're just kids, Tawney," Mr. Merrick stifled a laugh.

She rounded on him, folding her wet hands behind her back. "No. No, sir. They are gremlins. Those chubby little cheeks are a distraction from their plot to overthrow all things sanitary and sane. And *you*," Tawney advanced on Leo who took a pointed step back. "Still assuming you're the smartest in the room." She clicked her tongue. "Arrogant."

"Adorable," he grinned.

"Ohh." She clenched her fists, the soapy sheen on her skin streaked with blood. "Watch yourself, Merrick."

"What does it matter if a motorcycle is or is not at a marina?"

Natalie hadn't noticed Atro follow in Tawney's chaotic wake and, judging by the quick turn of heads, neither had anyone else. Sweat sprinkled across the Moirai's bald scalp.

"It doesn't," Tawney boasted. "Not anymore."

Clo's stare flicked between Atro and Tawney with the agitation of a cat's tail. Natalie studied them too, remembering Atro's hold on Tawney's wrist and wondering if perhaps…

"You left Atlantis." Leo accused only Tawney at first, but the flush of Natalie's cheeks quickly gave her away.

She forced herself to look at him. She'd made her choice, knowing he would disapprove. Knowing he would be angry.

"Three times," Natalie confessed. "So far."

"Why?" Mrs. Davis marveled.

Natalie didn't answer right away. She worked her jaw, searching for the right words to explain why she'd needed to reach out to Brant. That she had to know if his betrayal had truly been his choice, even if there was no chance he could ever come back to them.

In the end, Mr. Merrick answered for her.

"I think we all know why," he said slowly.

Leo's expression darkened.

"Did you find him?" Mrs. Davis asked.

It was the hope in her question that reminded Natalie she wasn't the only one who had loved Brant. Who somehow still did.

"Yes," she sighed. "In a way."

"Is he alright?" Mr. Merrick asked.

"I don't know," Natalie fished his note from her pocket. "But he left me this."

Leo stepped just close enough to take Brant's message from her. "Who is going to keep them safe?"

"It's what I asked Christopher," Owen explained, his ears burning. "When we first arrived at the marina that night."

"I remember," Leo frowned. "What does this have to do with the bike?"

"When we went back, the motorcycle had been cleaned. It was completely spotless," Owen went on. "And when we couldn't figure out the clue, we brought it back here."

Leo turned the note over, inspecting both sides. "I don't like this, Natalie."

"That's why I didn't tell you."

His mouth clamped tight around whatever he wanted to say.

"Am I to understand that you brought the bike here?" Mr. Merrick peered out the round windows to the street.

"Sort of," Owen stumbled through the answer. "Rolling a motorcycle through Atlantis would have drawn too much attention."

With an extensive network of walking paths and tacking streams,

Atlanteans had no need for cars, let alone motorcycles.

"It's by the beach," Tawney elaborated. "We were hoping you might know something about it. Something no one else would."

"Afraid not," Mr. Merrick offered an apologetic shrug.

Leo shoved his hands in his pockets and studied his shoes. A vein in his temple pulsed.

"But you do." Natalie knew she was right, even before his gaze flicked up to hers. "And you're angry with me."

"I'm not angry you've been hiding things," Leo kept his voice low and controlled. "I'm not mad you didn't let me in. Hurt, yes, but not angry. Even if I don't like the play you're making, I'm always on your team. Always. But you're not letting me help you, defend you." He paused. "If you want to talk to Brant, if you insist on picking at this wound, then I want to help you. You, not him." He rubbed through his shirt at the scar left by Brant's bullet. "He's not who he was, Natalie. Some things can't be forgiven."

Natalie knew that. Natalie knew that better than anyone.

"I'm not looking for forgiveness," she assured him. "I'm looking for answers. If anyone knows what the Ward is up to, it'll be his son. He's trying to tell us something," Natalie pointed at the note in his hands. "And I'll look under every stupid rock he points us to until I can figure it out."

Leo shook his head. "It's not a rock you need to look under," the words tore from his throat as though it pained him to let them go. "It's the frame."

CHAPTER 26

"Tofu?" Natalie kept pace at Tawney's side, jogging in lockstep towards the beach.

"If the name fits," Tawney slipped her a sideways grin. "The cat was a sopping grey mess when I found her."

"Which was where, exactly?"

"In a dumpster." Blood seeped through the cloth Tawney had wrapped around the cut on her arm. Enzi sniffed at it until she booped his snout away.

"What happened?" Natalie pressed.

"I told you," Tawney pulled ahead, pointedly putting herself between Owen and Clo. "Toddlers bite."

"Uh huh."

Whatever Tawney had been doing, it wasn't her Contributions. And as for Tofu, her friend was keeping secrets. Just like Leo and Lache. Just like Edwin.

Just like her.

Slipping over rocks coated in algae and sea spray, Owen reached the alcove at the cliff's base first. He dragged away the foliage covering the entrance and Natalie watched the tension melt off his shoulders. The motorcycle was still there.

"You said there's a cubby?" Owen frisked the bike, deftly skimming every surface for a catch or lever while Enzi pranced around him. The dog might not know what Owen was doing, but the chance for treats was rarely zero.

"More like a compartment." Leo spoke over the crash of waves on the shore. He watched Owen's frustration mount a moment more before finally pointing to an unremarkable length of matte black chrome.

It slid open and Owen whistled, wiping sea mist from his glasses to better inspect the hidden hinge.

"Wow." He toyed with the mechanism, far more interested in the compartment than its contents.

Tawney, on the other hand, was not. She slipped between the two boys and emerged with something small enough to fit in her fist. Two somethings, to be exact.

"What are they?" Atro peered over Tawney's shoulder.

"Well," Tawney passed the contents to Natalie. "It's not a note."

Natalie's throat tightened.

It was Brant's red cap.

She'd risked her life more than once to give Brant an opening, to find a way to talk to him, and he used it to give her his most prized possession: the last thing his mother ever made him. If Natalie had any doubt left for why Brant aligned himself with the Ward, it evaporated. Everything pointed back to Mrs. Smith.

Everything pointed back to his mother.

The worn stitching threaded through her fingers until, inside, she skimmed over something else. A black paper bird tumbled into her palm and Natalie discovered Tawney was wrong. It *was* a note.

I'm sorry.

She read it again, blinking at the dried ink as though more might suddenly appear. An explanation. A reason. Anything. Instead, there was only an apology.

But what was he apologizing for? Shooting Christopher? Leaving them? Starting the fire that killed Angie?

He'd have to be more specific.

Unsatisfied, Natalie stuffed the cap and note into her pocket and focused on the other object Tawney had plucked from the compartment: a tangled knot of wood, metal, and glass. Natalie's heart skipped.

It was a puzzle.

"Is that supposed to mean something?" Lache asked.

"No," Leo crossed his arms. "It's just another distraction. He's aiming to waste our time."

Time.

How long did they have before the Curia decided to deal with Edwin?

Tick-tock.

How long before the two Nautilus Legates welcomed every other Legate, Curtana, Dove, and Artisan to take up residence in Atlantis?

Tick-tock.

Natalie set to work on the puzzle.

"How did you know about this?" She questioned Leo as she felt for levers and grooves, loose ends and moving parts. A chill worked up her spine that had nothing to do with the ocean breeze. The design was nearly identical to the puzzles in AJ's office.

"Uncle Chris showed us that night." Leo flipped the chrome compartment shut. "It's where he stashed the key to Brant's truck."

"And this wasn't there?"

"No." He moved as though to take the puzzle from her and Natalie clutched it close to her chest.

"I can solve it," she insisted. "Just give me a minute."

Tick-tock.

"There's no point in solving it!" Leo's face flushed hot with frustration. "We need to let this whole thing go."

"Do you not want the next clue?" Clo cocked her head.

"No," he barked out a hollow laugh. "I don't. He's playing with us, baiting us."

"That doesn't sound like Christopher," Tawney argued.

"But it sure sounds like Brant," Leo shot back. "This is all a joke to him. A game."

"Maybe you're right." Owen pushed up his glasses and rubbed his eyes. "Maybe this is a wild goose chase."

Tick-tock.

Wake up, Natalie.

"No," Natalie argued. "This means something. Brant may have led us here but this," she held up the puzzle, turning the first piece as it slid loose. "This is Christopher."

"Fine," Leo caved, "even if it is from Christopher, Brant must have seen it to lead us here."

"What if he did? Maybe he's helping us. Maybe Brant's trying to tell us something. Maybe–"

"Maybe this isn't real, Natalie."

She flinched. The blow hurt more than it should have because it came from Leo. Because he knew exactly where the pressure would break her.

"You have too much faith in him," he said gently.

Natalie disagreed. "He'd have the same in us." She held up the red cap. "He still does."

A final twist freed the metal hoop from the glass and Natalie laid the pieces out in the order she'd freed them.

"Do they look like anything to you?" Owen cocked his head to view the set from another angle.

"They're squiggles," Tawney tugged on a curl. "They could be anything."

"They feel strange," Clo traced each piece. "Rough, like…like mint leaves."

Lache shook her head. "That is nonsense."

"No…she's right!" Owen held them towards the light. "Look."

Where the three loops locked together, a series of numbers had been etched into the heart of the puzzle. Natalie squinted to make them out.

"48.852524 and 2.347130."

"What is that?" Atro's silver brows furrowed. "A cypher?"

"No," Leo's frown deepened. "They're coordinates."

CHAPTER 27

Natalie scowled at the etched coordinates. Somehow, she'd let herself believe Brant's message would give her answers. Or, at the very least, closure. Instead, she held another question, another mystery shrouded in ambiguous clues and maddening switchbacks. She'd been foolish to think death would stop Christopher's riddles.

"We need a map," Leo said pointedly.

"We have one." Owen dug a silver disk from his pocket. It balanced on a paper-thin edge and, with a deft flick of his wrist, projected a translucent globe as tall as Natalie's hip.

"Woah," Atro gaped.

The sphere reminded Natalie of satellite images of the Earth at night. Pinpoints of light marked cities and towns against an inky blue canvas.

"Where did you get this?" Lache asked.

"Contributions. Everyone in the Tech Unit has one." Owen's smile fell as he entered the coordinates. "Are you sure those numbers are right?"

"Yeah," Natalie scanned the puzzle pieces again. "Yes, I'm

positive. Wh–"

The question died on her lips as the hologram zoomed in on a storefront. It sat on the banks of the Seine, overlooking the charred buttresses of Notre-Dame with its iconic green and yellow sign.

"Shakespeare and Company." Leo's gaze met Natalie's for the span of a breath before he began to pace.

She couldn't blame him. To Leo, Shakespeare and Company was the place she was almost killed. Where, after months of searching, he'd had to let her go. But to Natalie it was still a refuge of shelves, cat naps, and coffee, worked by two of the nicest bookkeepers she'd ever met.

It was also where Christopher had left her a book.

"This is about *The Sceptical Chymist*." Natalie was so close to the projection the blue and green shimmer drowned her vision. "Christopher left it for me there. What if there's more in that book? What if there's something we missed?"

"We've scoured *The Sceptical Chymist* cover to cover a hundred times over." Owen chewed on the edge of his thumb. "What else could there be?"

"I don't know," Natalie confessed. "Maybe nothing."

"Do you still have it?" Lache asked.

Tawney snorted. "It's a book. She still has it."

Natalie was already moving. She pulled Leo away from the cliffside and towards the city.

"Where are you going?" Clo asked as Tawney blocked her path and pointed up the cliff.

"Isn't *The Sceptical Chymist* in your apartment?"

Natalie moved past her. "I need to talk to someone first."

"*We* need to talk to someone," Leo corrected.

"Right." Natalie flashed him a smile, still squeezing the pieces of the puzzle tight in her fist. The puzzle identical to the ones she'd solved in Counseling.

Tell me when you solve the fifth.

Yet when they reached the stoop outside AJ's office, Natalie stalled. The last time she'd passed between those columns, AJ had given her a name.

Not Natalie Morrigan.

Not Natalie Alone.

But she wasn't sure she wanted to be Natalie Atlas.

"Are we pausing for dramatic effect?" Tawney peered around the group. "No? Okay then." She forced her way inside the Counselor's chamber without bothering to knock.

"AJ?" Natalie called. Her search skipped over stacks of books and lavish chairs. The once impeccably organized desk was a wreck of flickering holograms and puzzle pieces.

And the Counselor's body laid strewn over all of it.

"AJ!" Tawney shouted.

AJ jolted upright and Natalie's stomach dropped back where it should be. The Counselor's alarm crumbled to anguish as she took in the sight of them. Her hair frizzed out to the side, her eyes were bloodshot and puffy.

"Are you alright?" Owen asked.

"No." AJ steadied herself with both hands planted flat on her desk. "Where would you like to start?"

Natalie figured they didn't exactly have time to beat around the bush. She laid the logic puzzle out for AJ to see. "You said to tell you when I solved the fifth."

The Counselor studied each piece. "What is this?"

"The fifth puzzle," Natalie answered, feeling less and less certain. "It's just like your others."

"It is," AJ folded her arms. "But this is not one of mine."

"Then what's the fifth puzzle?"

"It's you!" AJ nearly shouted. "It's you deciding who you are going to be!" She leaned forward over the desk. "Though based on your visit here, I don't suppose you've solved that one?"

Natalie glared at her.

AJ crumbled back in her chair, all poised composure lost. "Do you know why Atlanteans, born and immigrated, are required to attend Counseling?"

"To find their purpose," Lache answered.

"To gain perspective," AJ corrected. "Because sometimes shining new light on an old problem can give us all the answers we need." The Counselor sighed and studied the puzzle pieces again. "These are coordinates." It wasn't a question.

"Yes," Owen cleared his throat. "It's kind of a long story but it points to a book. *The Sceptical Chymist.*"

AJ's lips parted, the reaction so subtle Natalie almost missed it. The puzzle might not mean anything to the Counselor, but the book certainly did.

"Where did you get this?" AJ's voice was strained.

Natalie chose her answer carefully. "A friend."

"We think," Leo added dryly.

"You think?" The Counselor's tone turned cold. "The Regent has her head in the sand, Edwin's in prison, and every minute Nautilus creeps closer to this city. You're going to need to do more than *think.*"

"I've read *The Sceptical Chymist* fifty times," Natalie snapped. "Someone very dear to me–someone I loved very much–left me that book. I thought it served its purpose by leading me here, by helping me enter Atlantis, but now," Natalie approached the desk until she was close enough to smell the citrus blend of AJ's perfume. "I can't do anything unless you tell me what I'm missing."

Natalie sucked in a breath. She was sick of smoke and mirrors.

She would have demanded clarity, she would have stood her ground and waited for a straight answer.

But the earth rumbled above their heads.

It was low at first, like a deep growl from Enzi's chest, resonating out until the ceiling, the walls, the floor trembled with it. Until chunks of the dolphin mural behind AJ's desk broke away, shards scattering over the tile.

Instinctively, Natalie's fingers found Leo's. Enzi cowered under AJ's desk, and the Moirai huddled together as Tawney and Owen locked stares on either side of them. The shaking continued, the rumble mounting to a roar, moving under their feet into the earth.

For a long moment, no one said a word. Natalie wished it was an earthquake. Or construction. Or an Atlantean experiment gone awry. Yet she knew it was something far worse.

"Is that…" Tawney's mouth pressed closed in a thin line.

"Nautilus," Owen finished for her. "They're coming."

"They are here," Lache corrected.

"You have the book, yes?" AJ rummaged through her desk, pulling out binders overflowing with notes. More paper spilled from that single drawer than Natalie had thought existed in the entire city.

"Not with me but yeah…yes, I have it."

"Good. Get it." AJ struck a matchstick and sparks danced over her palm. "Meet me at the Curia." She dropped the tiny flare and set her pile of records aflame. "Our Regent is about to need all the help she can get."

CHAPTER 28

Natalie had never been good at running. Not the spring her parents signed her up for softball. Not in gym class when she had to conquer a mile. Not even when Nautilus was on her heels on the Chesapeake Bay Bridge.

Running in Atlantis proved no different. Her lungs couldn't get enough air, her muscles outright rejected the concept of stamina, and a cramp stabbed savagely beneath her lowest rib. But she couldn't stop. She wasn't there yet.

Natalie focused on her breathing.

In, two, three, four. Out, two, three, four.

Mom, Dad, Angie, Chris. Chef, Eleanor, Nora, Brant.

Their names kept her moving, kept her focused on something other than the fact her body was simply not made to run. And they distracted her from Tawney's complaints that she didn't know the plan. Or at least mostly distracted, because the truth was Natalie didn't have a plan. Her only option was to follow without question the same uncle who'd told her again and again to question everything.

And she wasn't ready to admit that. Not to her friends. Not to herself.

She'd actually rather run.

The apartments stuck out from the basalt wall as the main stretch of Atlantis dissolved behind her. Sprinting through the familiar corridors, Enzi bounded at her side, pink tongue lolling.

"We're nearly there." Leo glanced over his shoulder, nodding curtly once, twice, five times. A headcount. "Don't worry about anything else," he told her as they reached her door. "Let's get the book and go."

Inside her apartment, Natalie dug through her nightstand and stuffed *The Sceptical Chymist* into her bag. Her hand hovered over *Jurassic Park* and *Oh! The Places You'll Go*, before she finally pushed them aside. As much as the titles meant to her, as badly as she wanted to carry them, she didn't need them anymore.

But the family photograph was another story. One much denser than it appeared. The picture was all Natalie had left of her parents, of her life before tacking and time-travel.

Tick-tock.

Natalie grabbed the picture and the Coelacanth Project document and kicked the drawer shut.

"Done," she straightened. "Now we have to get—"

The world rumbled around them, violent enough to send Enzi's ears flat against his head and the bedside lamp crashing to the floor. Exchanging nervous glances with her friends, Natalie knew they were all thinking the same thing. It wouldn't take long for Nautilus to force its way into the city.

Without a word, they made for the exit.

Running as fast as they dared, Natalie watched Atro hip check Tawney into the next passage.

"That way," the Moirai snorted. "You will get us lost just like last—"

"Shh!" Lache pointed down the corridor.

Five Nautilus fighters marched at the far end of the hall. Bolts at their sides, pistols on their hips, they were a wall of navy blue that shouldn't exist in the city.

Natalie squeezed her eyes shut and opened them again. The Curtanas were still there, impossibly real.

"That was too fast," Owen muttered somewhere behind her, fear leaking into his voice. "How did they get into the city already? How are they—"

"One thing at a time," Leo cut off his spiral. "First, we need to get out of here."

Natalie hugged her pack to her chest. Leo was right: in that moment, the *how* hardly mattered. The fact was Nautilus was right where they shouldn't be. Their presence was outright odious, demons tainting hallowed ground, and the sight of them made Natalie's blood boil.

This was her home. Nautilus had no place in it.

"Turn around," Leo tugged at her. "Try the other—"

Turning the opposite direction down the corridor, Natalie's breath lodged in her throat.

Brant.

It was him.

Or at least the ghost of him. The brown curls spilling into his eyes were the same, though the sick pallor of his skin wasn't. His cheeks sunk in places that had been full and bright. Wide, strong shoulders now slumped beneath an invisible weight.

After weeks of ceaseless worrying, nights reliving his betrayal on the bridge, days wondering if he wanted forgiveness or if she'd ever be willing to give it, he was just *there*.

"Brant." She said his name for no other reason than to solidify his existence in the room. Enzi pawed hesitantly towards him and moved back.

"Hey." Brant's hands buried deep in the pockets of his suit. His chestnut curls hung loose, spine stacked straight.

"Hey?" Tawney gawked. "That's it? *Hey?*" She marched towards him, fists clenched. "Allow me to jumpstart your vocabulary."

"Don't," Leo caught her arm. "He's not worth it."

"I thought you were—" Natalie bit back the sob in her throat. "I thought…"

What had she thought? That because Brant hid a few notes, he had missed them? That he helped her find Christopher's last clue because he was on their side? That he regretted all of the wrong he'd done? That he'd changed?

Yet instead of remorse and regret, he'd arrived with a fleet of Curtanas, and Natalie knew he hadn't changed at all. She couldn't let him be the reason she hesitated to defend her city. She refused to.

"You received my letters?" Brant barely met her gaze.

"Yeah," Natalie folded her arms. "I got them."

"How did you get into the city?" Lache asked, pulling her sisters closer. "The boundaries still stand."

Brant ignored her, nodding pointedly to Natalie's pack. "I trust you still have Boyle's book?"

With nowhere to run, Natalie saw no point in lying. "I have it."

"Good. Follow me." Brant started walking, pausing only when he realized no one had moved.

"You really think we're going to follow you anywhere?" Tawney snipped. "You're lucky I'm still allowing you the privilege of breathing let alone—"

"You can walk," Brant interrupted, gesturing to the Curtanas at their backs. "Or you can be moved."

A muscle ticked in Leo's jaw, every line of his body rigid. He knew as well as she did, they didn't have a choice.

"Where are we going?" Owen asked.

Leo pulled Natalie to him as Brant stepped forward, but he reached for Enzi instead. His eyes tightened when the dog's hackles lifted, making Natalie wonder if he was thinking of Angie, of the fire he set that killed her. Ignoring Enzi's warnings, Brant gently scratched behind one ear before smoothing the fur down his back.

Enzi grumbled but relented, leaning into the affection with a swish of his tail, and Natalie knew then that, in spite of everything, she'd follow him.

"Where are we going, Brant?" she repeated Owen's question.

"Somewhere quiet," his brown eyes flicked up to hers for the first time. "To solve Christopher's last puzzle."

CHAPTER 29

S ilence has weight.

There was the buoyant quiet of fishing on Christopher's boat. Or the airy hush of libraries, light with whispers and the hum of thought. There was the dense stillness of a cemetery, of loved ones laid to rest between strangers and amongst friends.

But the silence that filled the Atlantean passage was leaden. It pushed on Natalie's shoulders, rivaling the ocean depths where all was shadow and strain, until it became so thick she could barely breathe. Yet no matter how heavy, all silence remains fragile.

"Leo–"

"I'm not one to say I told you so–"

"Then don't."

"But I told you, Natalie. I *told* you. He doesn't care about us," Leo's stare bore into Brant's back. "He never did."

Natalie could have imagined it, but she thought Brant cocked an ear in their direction. Regardless, he said nothing.

"Nat," Owen slipped in beside her, eyeing the Curtanas behind them and keeping his voice low. "Nat, I've been thinking about what

AJ said, about problems and new light–"

"Shh," Lache elbowed him. "Not now."

She nodded pointedly at Brant, but as the entrance to the Temple of Thoughts loomed over them, Natalie guessed it was already too late. The doors hung awkwardly from their hinges, charred and splintered.

Clo gaped. "Nautilus cannot know about the Temple of Thoughts."

"We assumed." Atro frowned. "They did find an unfindable city."

Though his steps fell with surety, Brant's mouth dropped open as they entered the Temple. He followed the twin stagnant rivers, in awe of the history preserved within them. Nautilus may have known of the Temple of Thoughts, may have read of its purpose or heard rumor of its grandeur, but that wasn't the same as living it.

Natalie knew that feeling. She'd experienced something similar when visiting the bookshop in Paris. It was familiarity and fascination; the difference between seeing the riverbank in photographs versus drinking the breeze off the Seine.

Brant may not have been surprised by the Temple of Thoughts, but he was still enchanted by it.

"What are you playing at?" One of Brant's men complained. "We are supposed to bring them to the Curia."

The voice caught hold of Natalie's insides and squeezed. She'd heard it before at Lighthouse Market, at Ancora, and in her nightmares a hundred times since.

"Tanaka," Tawney rolled her eyes. "What are you, Brant's babysitter?"

The Legate coiled like a snake, his oil-black hair a slick knot at the crown of his head. "You're wasting our time," he seethed at Brant.

"Your time is mine," he silenced Tanaka with a look that chilled Natalie to the bone. This wasn't the Brant she'd split a sampler tray with at Colonial Custards or who threw her in the pool when she was trying to read. This was the Brant who'd held her at gunpoint on the bridge. "And you haven't done your homework; the fastest route to the Curia is through here."

He pressed forward but Owen lagged behind, lingering alongside one of the rivers.

A Curtana nudged him. "Move it."

Owen stared into the water and didn't budge.

"I said *move!*"

"Edison's bulb." Owen's gaze flicked up to Natalie, eyes wide with clarity. "A new light."

She straightened.

Sometimes shining new light on an old problem can give us all the answers we need.

He'd figured out AJ's clue. The last thing they needed was for Nautilus to figure it out too. She gave a subtle shake of her head and Owen looked to his feet.

"What is it?" Brant studied the two of them, and Owen shifted under the scrutiny.

"Nothing."

"I've known you my entire life, Owen. It's never nothing."

"I was just admiring the light in the water. The bulb, I mean. It's Edison's."

Brant's stare narrowed. "And that's significant?"

"I would presume that all of the items here are of significance," sweat beaded on Owen's forehead. "If not to us than to someone."

Natalie tried to keep her expression vacant, but Owen's voice was too high, his words too fast. Brant turned to her.

"Give me the book."

"I'm not sure what you–"

"The book, Nat." He drew his pistol and pointed it at Owen. "Now."

Tawney jolted and Atro held her back. Natalie didn't blame her, but from where she was standing, Tawney couldn't see what she could. She couldn't see that though Brant aimed for Owen pointblank, his finger wasn't on the trigger.

Natalie's heart slammed against her ribs, half terror, half hope.

"Okay! Okay," Natalie dug Boyle's book from her pack and pushed it against Brant's chest. "Happy?"

He didn't answer but he lowered the gun. Carrying *The Sceptical Chymist* to the water's edge, Brant knelt until the filament bulb's amber glow bathed the parchment.

Enzi kept tight to her side as she peered over Brant's shoulder. He fanned through the pages twice, but the book offered nothing new. Artificial light was a technological breakthrough; it changed the course of history. Yet when projected onto *The Sceptical Chymist*, it only illuminated what Natalie already knew, gilding the old English text she'd read a hundred times over.

Disappointed, she folded her arms. She couldn't imagine a better answer to AJ's cryptic clue. Unless perhaps the counselor never meant a literal light at all.

"Chris left this for you in that bookstore in Paris," Brant fanned the pages. "And left those coordinates in the motorcycle to be sure you'd find it. But," he tapped a filigreed page at random, "we never found out why."

"We didn't," Owen gestured to all of them, "but *we*," he excluded Brant, "did."

Natalie bit her cheek to keep her emotions off her face. Owen was trying to mislead him, to make him think Boyle's book had already shared all its secrets. And if that was the only advantage they had, she wasn't going to ruin it.

Brant snapped the book closed. "I don't have time for games, Owen."

"He's not the one playing games," Natalie argued. "*The Sceptical Chymist* has a password inside. The answer to a riddle that got us into Atlantis. You just weren't around to see it."

He frowned, thumb tracing the unevenly cut pages. "This was never a game to me."

"Then what was it?" Leo's expression was cold, every syllable dripping with venom.

Without offering a clear answer, Brant marched on, tucking Boyle's book under his arm and leading them clear across the hall.

"Right now, Nautilus is securing the streets," he said quietly. "My father has the Curia and their Regent and is enroute to the Archives."

Natalie's head spun. Edwin had told her Atlanteans weren't used to fighting, but for the Ward to have conquered the Curia so swiftly was unthinkable. It had to have been an ambush. But how had Nautilus entered the city so fast and so smoothly? How had they bypassed every defense system that kept Atlantis safe for millennia? It didn't make sense. It was almost as if they had–

Every hair on Natalie's neck stood on end. She'd been sneaking in and out of Atlantis for days. It didn't make sense for the Curia to waste resources monitoring their own Atlantean Sea. They had expected attacks from outsiders, but not someone who could tack. Not one of their own.

Natalie's escape route *was* the breach.

"It was you," angry tears pricked her eyes. "You tacked Nautilus into the city. You did this, this is *your* fault!"

Brant halted before a gaping passageway, rounding on her so violently Natalie took half a step back.

"No," he said firmly. "The Atlantean Curia brought this on

themselves. I just found the door."

"Traitor," Tawney spat.

"You can't see the big picture."

"It's worse," Owen frowned. "We see you."

Pain flashed over Brant's face, dissipating as quickly as it appeared. He marched into the passage, talking over his shoulder as they walked.

"The city is going to fall," he explained, his tone lifeless and flat. "If you intervene…you'll fall with it."

After a few winding turns, the tunnel dumped them out onto a wide boulevard with the turquoise dome of the Curia straight ahead.

Another rumble threw Natalie to her knees. Pebbles rained from the flickering sky, columns cracked, and in the distance, the Atlantean Academy's clock face shattered.

Strong hands yanked her back beneath the outcrop of the passage.

"Look." Leo pointed into the city, beyond the sprawl of gardens to a knotted intersection of boulevards flooded with Nautilus blue. Curtana after Curtana filled the streets, the glint of their bolts at the ready, but that wasn't what Leo was pointing to.

Tawney was halfway to the Atlantean Academy.

"Argh!" Tanaka whipped the bolt from his back, spinning the weapon to life at his side as he made to run her down.

Brant's arm landed hard across Tanaka's chest. "Don't waste your time," he warned. "You'll never catch up. Besides, she has nowhere to go; the other patrols will catch her soon enough." His stare lingered after her a moment longer, his expression guarded. "We go on as ordered. The Ward wants them locked away before the Regent unlocks the Archives."

Brant held Natalie's bicep but his touch was light, guiding more than forcing her towards the damaged dome.

"I know this is about your mom," Natalie whispered. It wasn't a conversation anyone else needed to hear. "But whatever the Ward," she caught herself, "whatever your father has promised you, I can't do it. A change like that, after so much time, it's not likely I'd even survive the attempt."

Brant listened without comment, his gait stiff and eyes averted.

"And if by some miracle I did, the consequences would be innumerable. I'm not even sure we could—"

"Nat," Brant cut her off. "That big brain of yours is going to burst if you don't give it a break one of these days." A smirk slid up his mouth and he was there again.

She was so relieved she almost forgave him on that alone. Almost.

"You can still stop this."

His smile faded and as they neared the Curia, he addressed his Curtanas instead. "Stay alert," he warned.

For what? Natalie scoffed silently. *Some defenseless Atlantean councilmembers?*

But clearing the Curia steps, she saw what he meant. The iron door pitched off its axis. Water glinted on the pearlescent green tiles. Cautiously, they stepped inside. Bolt aloft and eyes ahead, every muscle in Brant's body drew taut as Natalie's own heart thudded louder with every flicker of the failing lights.

The Curia was abandoned. Some part of her registered the overturned pews and split podium, but all she truly saw were the holograms. Projections stretched from floor to ceiling, each exhibiting a Tertian of the city.

The Atlanteans scattered. Smoke billowed where a building had been. More than one figure sprawled unmoving in the street. And through it all was the blur of Nautilus blue.

Natalie clutched Brant's arm to stay standing.

"He'll fix this," Brant muttered, the destruction reflected in his eyes. "My father will fix–"

A roar shook the Curia. Dust thickened the air as what remained of the stained-glass ceiling shattered, sending a rain of turquoise glass skittering over stone.

She should have ducked for cover, but as Natalie yanked out of Brant's shock-slack hold, she fought for a clearer view of the projections.

She instantly wished she hadn't.

Curtanas trapped Atlanteans in the streets and around them, their city crumbled. Large chunks of the sky flickered out and broke free, dropping like asteroids on ancient architecture. Buildings sagged. Walls collapsed.

The Ward would never be satisfied for Atlantis to merely bow. He wanted it to break.

Frantic, Natalie scanned the holograms for the clock tower, for any sign of the Academy, but Owen found it first.

Pale, he pointed at the farthest screen. Dust fogged the image, shrouding the figure racing down the corridor, but there was no mistaking her.

Tawney sprinted full pelt into the frame. Ahead of her a small boy stood frozen, mouth wide in a silent scream. He reached for her, tiny fingers splayed, and as the earth shook again Tawney dropped. Curls haloed her head as she turned mid-slide, shoving the boy behind the camera's range. She was on her feet in an instant, but for the first time in Natalie's memory, Tawney wasn't fast enough. With an aching gasp, the ceiling collapsed. Trapping her.

Burying her.

The rumbling stopped. The ground stilled. And the entire world fell silent save for the whisper of her name, a desperate prayer from Owen's lips.

"Tawney."

CHAPTER 30

Someone screamed in the Atlantean Curia.

The sound splintered the room, bouncing off shattered glass and crashing back on Natalie's ears. She'd heard that scream before. It was her own.

The Atlantean Academy settled in slow motion. Dust billowed. Pebbles shifted and stilled.

She got out, Natalie stared unblinking at the screen. *There was a pocket. A tunnel. Something. Tawney always thinks of* something.

Hot tears slicked her cheeks as, for once, Natalie told herself it wasn't real. It couldn't be. Not Tawney.

"She got out, right?" Atro leaned towards the projection as though it would help her see through the plume of dust. "Right?"

Natalie couldn't answer. Her throat closed. She couldn't breathe. She couldn't think. A Curtana urged her forward but she sank, fingers clawing the earth, trembling too violently to stand.

Tawney was in the Atlantean Academy, and the Academy was in the dirt.

"No," Owen shook his head. "That wasn't her. I was wrong. That wasn't…it couldn't have been…" He turned to Leo, green eyes wide and empty behind cracked lenses. "Did we just lose her?" his chest hitched. "Did I just lose her?"

Leo moved to console him, but Owen backed away, shaking his head. Snapping the bolt off the nearest Curtana, he lunged for Brant.

Tanaka caught the blow outright and yanked the weapon from Owen, cracking the uncharged metal clear across his jaw.

Owen dropped in a heap.

And Brant never even flinched. "He'll fix this," he repeated quietly. "My father will fix this."

Natalie suspected he spoke more to himself than to her, but it didn't matter. Nothing mattered.

Tawney was dead.

Tawney was *dead*.

And Brant might not have been the one to kill her, but he helped. He brought Nautilus to Atlantis. He chose to listen to the Ward because he said what Brant wanted to hear, even if it wasn't the truth.

"I hate you," Natalie breathed.

He didn't respond. She wasn't even certain he heard her.

Someone's fingers laced briefly between her own, squeezing before they were pulled apart.

Leo.

He was deathly pale, cheeks slick with tears, yet he offered her a single slow blink. Whatever they were in, they were in it together. And this pain, they were in that together too.

Enzi growled as the Curtanas forced them across the Curia. Shuffling through broken shards of the turquoise glass dome, Owen's limp form dragged behind them as Tanaka hoisted him under his arms. Brant shook himself and nodded Natalie forward.

She descended a narrow staircase with leaden feet. She heard the breath in her chest but couldn't feel it. She couldn't feel anything. She was numb and Tawney was dead and for all Natalie cared, the world could burn.

"He's going to fix it," Brant's promise fell on deaf ears. "He's going to fix everything."

Natalie punched him in the mouth.

The Curtanas were on her faster than Brant could nurse his busted lip. They locked her arms behind her back and put a sparking bolt beneath her chin. The heat of it singed her skin and part of her reveled in it. She could hurt if it meant hurting them.

"Natalie!" Leo rushed for her and they pinned him down.

"Stop!" Brant spat blood and pressed his sleeve to his mouth. "Stop. Release her."

"But sir—"

"I said release her," he grunted. "What is she going to do? Run for it?"

"Hit you," Tanaka suggested smugly. "Again."

"Not likely," Brant glared at her. "Walk."

Begrudgingly, the Curtanas dropped their hold, but every bolt remained trained in her direction.

The stairwell leveled out before a solid wall of stone. Brant pressed a holographic card against the wall and it dissolved with a subtle *hiss*.

The Moirai were hauled by, followed quickly by Leo who touched her arm with one hand while the other held tight to Enzi's raised hackles. She caught Owen take a breath, but his eyes stayed closed behind skewed frames as the Curtanas dragged him through.

Anger burned like venom in her veins.

Fishing his faded cap from her pocket, Natalie shoved it against Brant's chest. "The Ward is a liar," she seethed. "And you're a coward."

Brant stared at the worn fabric. "It's not his fault."

"Not his fault?" Natalie barked a manic laugh. "And I'm supposed to be insane." He gave her a curious look but she didn't pause long enough for him to speak. "He's a monster, Brant. He's manipulating you and everyone behind you. He's killing people." She shoved him. He fell away and she shoved him again. "He's killing our family!" Natalie twisted her quivering lip into a snarl to keep from crying. "And you're helping him."

Brant's back hit the wall and he stayed there. He made no move to defend himself and Natalie made no move to run. There was no point. If Brant didn't stop her, the Curtanas would.

"He wanted to leave the Coelacanth Project," Brant said. "He wanted to take me and my mother and go."

"He did," Natalie croaked. "Straight into Nautilus."

"No," Brant's expression was pained. "He stayed. He stayed until the end because she wanted to. Because he loves her."

Loves. The word bounced around Natalie's skull. Present tense. Out of place, out of time.

"I can't bring her back," Natalie whispered. She hated him. She hated him for fracturing their family. She hated him for Christopher, for Angie, for Tawney. And most of all she hated how she itched to hug him, to pull him to her and squeeze the sense back into him. "I can't do it, Brant, no one can. The cost is too great—"

"You're wrong," Brant drew himself up. "He's going to fix everything. He's going to make it right. All the pain will end because he's going to make sure it never existed at all."

Natalie pressed her fists against her forehead. "Just stop and think for a second, would you?" she begged. "Your father is the *Ward*. He experimented on the Moirai before commissioning their execution. He hunted us, he hunted *me*. And because I refused to help him, he's torn half the world apart. People are dying, Brant. My parents. Christopher. Angie." Her breath caught in her throat, knife sharp. "Tawney…"

Brant didn't look at her. He fingered his cap, the last thing his mother ever gave him.

"Even if I could do it," Natalie went on. "Even if by some miracle I could bring your mother back, seeing this," she gestured to the ruined streets somewhere above their heads, "would kill her."

Brant's gaze flicked up, his expression steely cold. "Atlantis already killed her. They had a vaccine against the cancer. Did you know that? And they released it seven years too late."

"Brant—"

But he was done listening. He forced her out of the stairwell and into a wide cavern. There was just enough light to carve silhouettes in the darkness, and muffled weeping echoed from every direction.

They stopped before a nondescript square, remarkable only by a familiar iridescent glow. It was the same kind of force field that had confined Max and her accomplice in the Curia. The same kind of prison Natalie had suffered in Nautilus's cells, trapped beneath the earth with no light.

The memory prickled sharp and real and panic seized her. She bucked against Brant's hold.

"Don't do this. Brant, don't do this."

He flattened the keycard against the transparent wall and Natalie felt the space open up before her. Brant shoved *The Sceptical Chymist* against her chest and pushed her inside.

"You're putting me in a cage." She only said it out loud to make it real. To solidify the ground that tilted under her feet because the fact that Brant was choosing Nautilus again was enough to rock the entire Earth off its axis.

The force field snapped back to life, a near invisible barrier between them. Brant drummed his fingers across it.

"This is to keep you safe."

"Safe?" Natalie croaked. "What does that even matter? What does it matter what happens to me now?"

"I guess it doesn't," Brant admitted. "But I don't want to carry it."

"What about Tawney?" Natalie's voice broke. "Will you carry her?"

Brant flinched. "He's going to fix it."

"No." Natalie squeezed Boyle's book against her, watching Brant's face in the shifting light. His bleeding mouth was downturned but set, his attention focused straight ahead. "I won't do it. I love you, and I loved your mom, but I won't do it. No matter what the Ward does, I won't time-travel for him. There's always a cost, Brant. And after so much time, after so much has happened, it would be more than me that has to pay."

"It doesn't matter," Brant turned to leave. "He doesn't need you anymore."

Natalie stared dumbfounded at the rigid line of his back. "It doesn't matter…" She'd been wrong.

Her Brant wasn't in there at all.

Natalie dropped her head back, listening to his footsteps fade as she envisioned the ruined streets overhead. In the end, Atlantis was just another Ancora doomed to burn. She'd been foolish to hope for anything else.

Sagging to the floor, the sob she'd been biting back bubbled up with a vengeance. It rocked her, choked her, until her breath came in gasps and hot tears soaked her collar.

"What about Tawney?" Natalie whispered into the dark.

But Brant was long gone, and his absence was answer enough.

CHAPTER 31

What about Tawney?

Natalie's vision swam with tears. In the dim light of the holding cell, all of the shadows had ringlet curls. Every echo whispered her laughter. And when Natalie blinked, she saw the whole scene again.

The Academy. The boy. The cave in.

Tawney.

And Natalie wasn't there.

She threw *The Sceptical Chymist* across her cell and tucked her knees under her chin. She wanted to question what she'd seen. She wanted to believe that Tawney got out. That she found a passage to dart into or a crevice to cower in. Natalie wanted to believe the rocks never touched her.

Yet the scene replayed again and again. Never changing.

The Academy. The boy. The cave in.

Tawney.

And Natalie wasn't there.

What about Tawney?

What about Tawney?

She had no idea when she stopped thinking the question and started hearing it.

"What about Tawney?"

Natalie jumped to her feet. "*Edwin?*"

"What. About. Tawney."

It was him. He was there, somewhere, trapped between the violet force fields that shimmered through the dusk.

"Edwin!" Natalie traced the length of her cell, testing every solid inch of it and squinting through the glare. In the prison next to hers, Enzi whined and yipped, following Leo who turned in a slow circle, searching for–

"Edwin!" Natalie sucked in a breath at the sight of him. His cheeks were sunken and hollow, his brows drawn tight. Blood coated the hard line of his jaw as though he'd been struck there. Repeatedly. But by the hunger in his eyes, Natalie knew it wasn't the confinement doing him in; it was the ignorance.

"You're alright," she said. And then, less certain, "Are you alright?"

"Am I *alright?*" Edwin's shout echoed. "What are you doing here? You should be out there!"

"We were–"

"You should be fighting!" His palm smacked the barrier, sending violet ripples to the edges of his cell. "I put myself in this Atlas-forsaken-hole to get the Regent off your back. Not for you to get locked in here with me!"

"Edwin." Leo said it like a warning, voice low and gravelly.

"What is going on out there?" Edwin pressed on as though he hadn't heard him. "What about Tawney?"

As Natalie steeled herself to answer, muffled sounds filled the shadows. Sobbing interrupted the reassurance of a sister. A distant groan overlayed the nearby pacing of feet. Her friends were there in the darkness. Broken. Listening.

Edwin pressed against the cell wall and a purple glow haloed his palms. "Please," he begged. "What's happening?"

Natalie shifted. She didn't know how to put the destruction of Atlantis into words. How to tell Edwin that the city he'd fought so hard to protect fractured at the edges, crumbled into the streets.

"That bad?"

Natalie sighed. "Nautilus has taken the Curia."

Any color left in Edwin's face blanched.

"Regent Aislinn is weak," Atro's voice rose out of the dark, angry and hurt. "She would rather surrender her city than fight for it. She has forsaken her people—"

"Aislinn isn't weak," Edwin argued. "I don't agree with half of the ways she leads our city, but she isn't weak. She isn't the enemy."

"That doesn't make her a friend," Leo countered. "She made you offer your life as collateral just to allow us into Atlantis in the first place."

"Yet I'm alive, aren't I?" Edwin dragged through his hair, making the ends stick up at odd angles. "She's doing the best she knows how."

"But you know better," Natalie said. It wasn't a question or a challenge. Edwin had been the original choice for Regent. He was innovative, curious, and most of all he lived and breathed for Atlantis. For its people.

"Yeah," Edwin slid her a sidelong glance. "I know you."

Natalie stared at him, his image warped by the force field. She didn't like what he was implying.

"Now, *please*, what's happened to Tawney?"

"She's dead," Owen croaked, his words groggy and slurred as he clung to consciousness.

Dead.

The word slammed against her chest. Natalie's ribs folded in, piercing her heart, expelling her breath.

"Bloody hell," Edwin leaned against the light barrier until only his forehead propped him up. "How?" The question dredged the back of his throat, gravelly and thick.

Natalie tried to answer, yet when she opened her mouth the words stuck there. Tawney had been her best friend for longer than she could remember. She was a spitfire tongue and stubborn confidence, even as a toddler. She made Natalie bolder, stronger, braver than she ever believed she could be. The idea that Tawney was gone…

Natalie couldn't bear it.

"Fighting," Atro answered for her. "She died fighting."

"Yeah. Yeah, of course she did." Edwin was quiet a long time before he spoke again. "We can't stay in here if she's dead out there."

"How do you suggest we get out?" Lache asked from somewhere Natalie couldn't see.

"Not sure yet. How did Nautilus get inside the city?"

"Brant had to of tacked them in," Natalie scuffed the floor in frustration. "There's no other explanation that fits. They got here too fast."

"She's right," Owen groaned, reality pulling him from his stupor. "The surface bombings are a diversion. This had to have been Brant's plan from the beginning."

Edwin tugged at the hoops on his ear. "He'd do that?"

"Apparently," Leo grumbled.

Natalie's eyes slid to the silhouette of Boyle's book on the floor of her cell. Something Brant had said tickled the back of her mind. "Edwin?"

"Hmm?"

"What are the Archives?"

The lines on Edwin's face deepened. "It's like the Temple of Thoughts, only the inventions housed there have never breached the surface. They're unfinished, or dangerous, or both."

Brant's words echoed in her mind. *He doesn't need you anymore.*

Natalie's stomach sank. There was only one reason the Ward would no longer require her power. Only one thing that would render her irrelevant.

"There's something in the Archives that can manipulate time."

It wasn't a question, but Edwin answered anyway.

"Yes," he said slowly, "and no."

"You'd better decide which it is," Natalie warned. "Because the Ward is headed there with Aislinn right now."

CHAPTER 32

Edwin went deadly still. "You're certain?"

"Brant said it so…no," Natalie shrugged.

Leo pushed against the force field, testing its strength. "Edwin?"

"Fantastic," Edwin hissed between his teeth. "Fan-*bloody*-tastic."

"Natalie is right, then?" Lache asked from the dark. "There is something in the Archives that can travel through time?"

"Not exactly," Edwin paced the length of his cell. "The Reverie is there, but it doesn't work. It never has."

Owen managed to sit up straighter. "Reverie?"

"That's promising," Leo muttered.

"Well, Brant's under the impression that the Ward can undo…*this*," Natalie gestured at everything. "Starting with the death of his mother."

Edwin let loose a string of curses Tawney would have been proud of. "But the Reverie can't fix anything! Nothing in the Archives will. It's folly. It's fallible. The Reverie is bloody *fallible*."

Leo knelt, finally complying to Enzi's relentless demand for pets. "What kind of fallible?"

"The turning-cities-into-craters kind."

"Well then," a familiar voice radiated through the dusk. "We'd better move quickly."

"AJ!" Edwin stood tall on his toes, craning to see her in the dark. "Over here, you brilliant, beautiful guru!"

"For the last time, I am a *counselor*." AJ produced a glass square from her pocket and pressed it to his cell. The force field dissipated. "Call me a guru again and I swear I'll–"

"Stop," Leo interrupted as AJ freed him. "Explain."

Edwin shrugged. "She loves me."

"No, you idiot." Leo borrowed the key from AJ and let Natalie out. "What makes the Reverie fallible?"

Freed, Enzi threw his front paws over Natalie's shoulders. She buried her face in his fur, half to embrace him and half to dodge the kisses he slathered on her cheeks.

"We don't have time." AJ moved quickly, releasing the Moirai before moving on to Owen.

"Make time," Leo countered. "We can't make a play if we don't understand the game. Now, one of you, *explain*."

"Right. Fine," Edwin paced as he spoke, knotting a thread he yanked from his jacket. "The Archives are full of unpolished inventions. Daring new realms of thought. Ideas unfit for use." He snorted. "There are a hundred deadly things in that vault, and the Ward wants the only one that bloody *explodes*."

Natalie felt sick. "The Reverie is a bomb?"

"It wasn't designed to be," Edwin defended. "It just acts like one when it...when it fails."

Owen slouched on the fringe of the group, nursing the bruise budding along his jaw. "How often does it fail?"

"Every time," Edwin stopped pacing. "Every single time."

"Then why create it?" Atro snapped.

"That's not important," Leo waved away her question. "What we need to know is how to stop it."

"You don't." Edwin spoke to the floor. "You can't get into the Archives without the Regent. I don't know what Aislinn's thinking letting him in. She won't save the city." His fists clenched and unclenched at his sides. "She'll sink it. It's madness."

Madness. The word knotted Natalie's gut.

"She has given up," Clo accused.

AJ twirled the glass key between her fingers. "I don't think the Regent would have given me this if she's given up. I knew you must have been captured when Nautilus appeared in the Curia and you didn't. I told her you were the answer. She agreed."

Edwin scoffed. "The last thing Aislinn would want is me out of this box."

"Not you," she turned to Natalie. "Her."

"Me?" Natalie balked. "Why on Earth did you want *me*?"

"An Atlas won't do us any good locked away down here."

"Do us any… No," Natalie's pulse throbbed in her throat.

The whole point of coming to Atlantis was to find someone to lead them, protect them, to get away from Nautilus. Regent Aislinn was supposed to be in control. That's why Christopher sent them there in the first place.

Natalie had confronted Nautilus because they'd made her, because they had her parents. Did she want to help take them down? Absolutely. But she'd never wanted to lead the fight. She couldn't.

"No," Natalie folded her arms. "Me – I, I can't do anything! It's the Regent's responsibility to keep us safe. Protecting Atlantis, protecting *the world*, is literally her job. It's what the Curia elected her to do!"

Silent, AJ and Edwin exchanged a look. They knew more than they were saying, which meant Natalie was missing something.

She was sick of missing something.

"I'm sorry, what exactly do you expect me to do? What does anyone expect me to do? If you think I have some magic plan, I don't. *This* was the plan. The Regent was the plan. She promised that the Curia had everything under control."

The world started shaking again and Natalie watched the ceiling. She expected another shower of pebbles and dust, but the rocks were still. The only thing trembling was her.

Tawney was gone, Atlantis all but belonged to Nautilus, and now the Regent wanted her to do something about it, but she had nothing. Everything that anyone had ever sacrificed to save her, to save the city, was a waste. It wasn't fair. It wasn't right.

"I don't know what you want from me."

Cracks splintered the corners of Natalie's vision and she blinked against them. She wrapped her arms around her chest, holding herself together with relentless, stubborn pride. They couldn't let everything Christopher and her parents worked for die with them in those cells.

"I might have a plan," Atro spoke up. "It would at least buy us some time."

Edwin folded his arms as Enzi made his way around the others, booping open palms and rubbing their knees. "That sounds like a bandage, not a solution."

"I did not say it was a good plan," she clarified.

Regardless, hope crept up Natalie's chest like a weed. Buying the Regent time sounded perfect. "It's better than nothing."

"I do not know," Atro rubbed the back of her neck. "You are not going to like it."

"Why's that?"

"Do you remember when Tawney said she hurt her arm at Contributions?"

"Yeah." The image of Tawney's bloody arm in Mr. Merrick's

apartment quickly came to mind.

"Well," Atro picked at her fingernails. "That was not exactly how it happened."

CHAPTER 33

Atro stood by the broken door of the Atlantean Curia. "We must head straight for the beach."

"There will be Nautilus covering every inch of the city." AJ warned. "We'll have to rely on stealth and speed."

"Meaning?" Clo bobbed behind Lache.

"Don't stop," Edwin paraphrased. "And don't get caught."

Atro braced against the door. "Ready?"

"Ready." Natalie slipped outside and crouched behind the nearest column. She pressed her spine against the marble, listening, waiting. Until, finally peeking out at the street, she saw…nothing. No Nautilus. No Patrols. Other than Enzi weaving between columns, the square was empty.

"There's no one here."

"If Nautilus is not guarding the streets," Lache pulled her silver hair over one shoulder. "Then where are they?"

"With the Ward." Leo rubbed his side, and Natalie wondered if it was the scar or the memory that bothered him. "He's not risking any mistakes this time."

Edwin scanned the streets again. "We'll be on borrowed time once he makes it to the Archives."

"Then let's move." Leo held Natalie's hand and broke into a flat-out sprint.

Beyond the steady rhythm of their footfalls, Atlantis was unnaturally quiet. Windows were shuttered. Corner parks sat abandoned. Even the birds had silenced their songs, put off by the quaking of the earth or flickering ceiling-sky that threatened to give way.

Eerie was an understatement. Natalie kept her head on a swivel.

"Alright, Atlas." Edwin sidled up beside her once their feet hit sand. "You know this isn't going to be enough."

"Don't call me that," Natalie put her elbows on her knees, catching her breath. "And anything is better than nothing."

"And you're better than anything."

She glared at him. "What am I supposed to do, Edwin? Travel back and make it so the Ward never existed? So that he never finds Atlantis?"

"Not exactly," he shrugged. "But you're on the right track."

Natalie cursed under her breath. Edwin had to be wrong, because traveling back in time to stop the Ward was a terrible idea. If she didn't go back far enough, the trip would be pointless. But go too far and she'd die paying the cost without changing anything. Not to mention that stopping Nautilus from finding the city would only stall them. The Ward could be delayed but not deterred.

No, her best chance was to stop the Ward here and now.

"Atro's plan is solid."

"You don't even know what it is," Edwin balked.

"Well, it's more than I have."

Atro paused at the water's edge long enough for Natalie to catch her.

"What exactly are you going to do?"

"Plan D," Atro answered seriously.

"D?" Leo huffed out a laugh. "Did we already pass A, B, and C?"

"It is not so much a matter of progression," Atro explained, "as it is desperation."

Natalie frowned. "That's reassuring."

Behind them, Owen fidgeted so much Leo finally called him out. "You know about this?"

His cheeks splotched burgundy. "I might."

"I will not be long," Atro promised. Adjusting the five-sided spark on her wrist, a generous gift from the Curia, she turned towards the waves. "I will be back with more Tofu."

"We are going to fight the Ward with an army of kittens?" Clo blanched.

Edwin cut his eyes at Natalie. "We're doomed."

Before anyone could ask more questions, Atro tacked away in a burst of white light.

Natalie stared at the space where the Moirai disappeared. Wave after wave rolled up the shore and, tracing the tips of Enzi's ears, Natalie waited.

Owen stood vigil with her, his sage stare fixed on the ocean. "Give her a minute."

"It's been a minute."

Two minutes.

Three.

Tick-tock.

Clo's toes curled carefully out of reach of the surf. "How long do we wait?"

"As long as it takes." Lache's calm veneer was betrayed by the lock of hair she knotted around her fingers.

"Maybe we should–" Clo gasped.

The flash came and went faster than Natalie could blink. She squeezed her eyes shut, fighting the dazzled spots in her vision because it wasn't some*thing* that tacked back with Atro, but some*one*. Many someones.

A river of blue jumpsuits flowed from the sea and Natalie instinctively took a step back.

"It is alright," Atro assured her, though the words provided little comfort as the tide of Nautilus swelled at her back. The Moirai beckoned Natalie closer. "They are not what they seem."

Settled on the shoreline, the crowd removed their navy jackets, turning them inside out so blue fabric turned to black. Most were strangers, though some faces Natalie recognized from the Helix, and others–

"I believe you have met," Atro introduced her nearest guest.

She looked exactly the same as the last time Natalie saw her, standing alone on the hill by Christopher's grave. The same towering height and willowy build, yet she was entirely different. Her auburn hair was plaited down her back, exposing violet-yellow bruises on her neck and jaw. There was an intensity she lacked before. A fire. One that squared her shoulders and lifted her chin.

Nora beamed at her. "Hiya Nat."

"What are you doing here?" Natalie blurted. "Where is your mom?" Her thoughts darted to Mrs. King, who had selflessly supported Natalie through Christopher's injuries and death. Who had been taken by Nautilus. Who Natalie hadn't been able to save.

My fault.

Nora might have answered, but more questions fumbled out of Natalie's mouth before she could stop them.

"Why are you still wearing Nautilus navy?" Natalie tugged at the familiar jumpsuit as Nora flipped her own jacket, turning it inside out until a flat black fabric replaced the blue. "Ignis was supposed to get you out. She was a recruit. She promised–"

"Take a breath," Nora squeezed Natalie into a hug. "Ignis found us. She got my mom out and then she gave me a choice. I could run and hide, or…" She nodded towards the others that had tacked back with Atro, their dark blazers dotting shadows across the shore. "I chose the *or*."

"A choice," Natalie repeated dumbly, turning on Atro as the pieces clicked into place. "A choice? *This* is what you've been doing? Finding people to fight Nautilus? The people we're supposed to be saving?"

"Not everyone needs saving," Atro drew herself up as though she had steel in her spine. "Nora wanted to help herself, just like the others." She gestured at the crowd. "Just like Tawney."

Her name seared over Natalie's skin. But before she could protest further, Leo pointed out a petite girl with sleek black braids.

"Ignis!" Natalie called her over.

"Raven." Ignis's accent lilted around the name Natalie used in the Helix. "I knew I would see you again."

"This is why you stayed behind?" Natalie tugged on the end of Ignis's braid. There was a wicked bruise on her arm, yet the black coals of her eyes had lost none of their intensity.

"The show Nautilus put on for Graduation mostly worked as they intended. Nearly every Curtana, Dove, and Artisan were tripping over themselves to lend aid to the Ward." Ignis's grin was mutinous. "I took note of every one that was not.

"Some just wanted out but others…others wanted to do more." Ignis nodded to Atro and Nora. "How do you like our Ravens?"

"Ravens." Natalie scanned the mass of strangers, the swell of Nautilus navy turned black, and her chest ached with a mix of pride and fear.

If what Ignis said was true, every single one of them had had the opportunity to escape Nautilus. To run. Yet all of them had chosen to stay. Not for themselves, but for each other. For a chance of freedom, of true peace.

"Do they know what we're up against?" Leo asked quietly.

Ignis cut him a look. "This is not their first fight."

Natalie thought of every time Tawney had been missing since they'd arrived in Atlantis. Of the cut on her arm she'd haphazardly bandaged. Of the stolen glances and half-hidden smirks between her and Atro.

Natalie had hidden herself away in Atlantis to hide and forget Nautilus. Meanwhile, Tawney never stopped fighting back.

She swallowed down the lump in her throat.

"You and Tawney were sneaking back to the Helix to do what?" Natalie asked Atro. "Raid and pillage?"

"We have been assembling the Ravens at Nautilus missions, using their intel to disrupt the Ward's plans. Leo saving you in Paris actually gave us the idea." Atro's gaze dropped to her hands. "Ignis established the Ravens, but Tawney…Tawney gave us heart. No mission was too small to matter."

"It's nothing substantial enough to take the Ward down, but," Ignis smiled, "a little chaos could not hurt."

"I am sorry we did not tell you." Atro put herself next to Clo, twining fingers and arms. It was as though Atro's secrets didn't matter. As though the entire world wasn't crumbling overhead or underfoot.

"Atlantis just wasn't enough?" Leo teased.

"Tawney never felt like she belonged in Atlantis," Natalie confessed. "Or the Coelacanth Project. But this," her voice shrank to a whisper, "this is her."

"This is her," Owen agreed, fresh tears spilling down his cheeks.

"So," Nora gestured at the Ravens. "Where do we start?"

"Nautilus is here and Atlantis isn't ready," Leo summarized the situation in a breath.

"Alright," Ignis nodded, her braid swishing down her back. "What do you need from us?"

"Our people don't know how to fight." AJ found her voice for the first time since the Ravens tacked ashore. "Can you get them off the streets? Into the basalt tunnels?"

"Sure thing." Nora called a group of Ravens to her and they began dividing themselves into teams.

"It's not enough," Edwin said just loud enough for their small group to hear. "Nat, you know it's not enough."

"Stop."

"Be reasonable—"

"I said *stop*."

"Nat," Edwin caught her pack and when she tugged it back the zipper ripped, exposing the book and papers stashed inside. "If you're going to do something you need to do it now. You're running out of time."

Natalie threw the bag down in the sand. "We are doing something."

"Natalie," Leo's voice frisked the edge of her enraged consciousness.

"You know what I mean," Edwin stared her down. "You are an Atlas, Nat, and I told you I need you to live for Atlantis."

"Natalie…"

"Haven't I done enough?" Natalie's frustration and grief overflowed. "Haven't I *failed* enough? I don't even know what being an Atlas means! And I didn't ask to be one. So why are you turning to me when there's a perfectly capable Regent ready and willing to protect this city?"

"The Curia chose Aislinn," Edwin yelled back, "but the city chose you."

"Natalie!"

"What?" Natalie and Edwin both turned on Leo.

He stood over Natalie's ripped pack, pointing at *The Sceptical Chymist*. In the glow of the setting sun, its deckled edges shimmered.

CHAPTER 34

Leo presented Boyle's book to Natalie, but she made no move to take it from him.

"Has it done that before?" Owen asked, his glassy eyes wide.

Natalie shook her head.

"I told you," AJ shifted, avoiding Edwin's gaze as she tangled her hands behind her back. "You needed a new light."

Perplexed, Natalie studied the projected sky. Flickering clouds dotted a lofty stone ceiling where huge fissures left defects in the imagery. Real cracks that stayed no matter how hard she squeezed Leo's hand. Sunlight gilded every inch of damage Nautilus's explosions had already dealt.

Sunlight.

"Owen?"

"Hmm?"

"Who came before Einstein?"

"Well," he took off his glasses and rubbed his eyes. "There was Humphry Davy with the arc lamp. Alexander Lodygin with the bulb."

"Before them."

Owen shrugged. "Nothing that I know of. Nothing proven, anyway."

"What if it was never proven?" Natalie's pulse slowed, steady and sure. "What if it was an invention that never left Atlantis as more than scribbles on parchment?"

"I don't follow…"

"What if the light was so advanced, people would have panicked? What if they wouldn't call it a light at all, but a—"

Owen snapped his fingers. "Death ray!"

Natalie finally looked at him. His smile was small, the dissatisfied grin of someone who'd solved an impossible puzzle with a broken heart.

"Archimedes," they said together.

Natalie took *The Sceptical Chymist* with trembling hands and knelt in the sand, laying the book in front of her.

"If you're right…this is genius." Owen's fingers drummed on his knees. "If there really is light reactive ink in there, and this is really Archimedes' design," he whistled out a breath. "Then whatever's written inside that book can only be read right here in Atlantis."

Natalie's thumb rested beneath the cover. The pages were worn and velvet soft, curving at the edges and sparkling in the waning light. They begged to be opened.

Her gaze flicked up to Edwin. His lips were pinched tight, face pale, fingers toying with the rings on his right ear.

Natalie flipped the book open to familiar elegant print. The first page looked exactly the same as it always did: a lengthy title in blocky red lettering, all credited to *the honourable* Robert Boyle.

But the inside cover glittered.

Natalie traced over newly exposed text: a list of names and dates blurred in iridescent shades of blue, and above them all, at the very top, were three impossible words.

The Atlas Atlas.

Her heart pounded harder than a war drum in her chest as time seemed to stutter.

Tick…tock.

The Sceptical Chymist held record of the Atlas name. Her name.

Avoiding *The Atlas Atlas,* Natalie perused the rest of the book. She examined the margins, the narrow chasms between paragraphs. Slowly. Deliberately. Inspecting every inch of every page until it was clear *The Sceptical Chymist* had no other secrets to hide. All that was revealed by Archimedes' light was etched on that inside cover.

Her hands shook.

"What are you looking for?" Lache asked finally.

"There has to be something else," Natalie's voice was strained. "This is supposed to give us answers." She slammed the book shut and started again. "There has to be something else…"

"There isn't." AJ knelt beside her, her charcoal robes gathered carelessly over one arm. She eased Boyle's book open and traced the shining text with reverence.

The Atlas Atlas
Those who have borne the weight of time.

Kitar Atlas: 561 BCE - 539 BCE. Salvaged Babylonian cuneiform from northern invaders. Succumbed to terminal delirium.

Cleopatra Atlas: 69 BCE - 30 BCE. Ended Roman Civil War. Succumbed to terminal delirium.

Einar Atlas: 90 CE - 117 CE. Halted expansion of the Roman Empire via assassination of Emperor Trajan. Succumbed to cerebral aneurysm.

Alice Atlas: 1321 CE - 1351 CE. Reversed extinction-level spread of plague through redistribution of trade. Succumbed to cerebral aneurysm.

Perseus Atlas: 1900 CE - 1918 CE. Ended the First World War by simultaneously leading numerous revolts in Germany. Succumbed to terminal delirium.

Reverie. August 9th, 1945.

Reymond Atlas: 1960 CE - 1978 CE. Reversed bombing of Cuba, diverted the Third World War. Succumbed to cerebral aneurysm.

Natalie Atlas…

Delirium.
Madness.
Death.
Over and over that was the cost, the fate every Atlas suffered, every person burdened with the ability to slip through the gossamer veil of time.

And Natalie had been named among them.

CHAPTER 35

Leo's stare weighed on her and Natalie didn't dare look at him. Not yet. She wasn't ready to face his questions. Not before she answered some of her own.

When she spoke, Natalie's throat was grave-dirt dry. "My name is in this book." She looked up at Edwin. "And you knew it."

"No," Edwin said quickly. "I wasn't certain, but...but I suspected."

"For how long?"

"Since the night you saved Lachesis on the Chesapeake Bay Bridge-Tunnel," he carefully avoided her gaze. "Time-travel leaves no question."

Natalie's vision swam. *Leaves no question...*

Which meant Christopher had known. How could he not have? He knew about time-travel and the city for *years*. He'd left *The Sceptical Chymist* for her in Paris. He'd organized the Coelacanth Project to protect her power, to nurture it all the while knowing it could *kill* her.

Meanwhile, Edwin brought her to Atlantis only to take her

straight to the sea. He offered an escape. Though she felt foolish for ever thinking it was because he'd actually cared. The fact was Edwin wanted what Christopher wanted: for her to assume her Atlas name. He just wanted her to choose it for herself.

He wanted her fate off his conscience.

Their mutual betrayal sliced through her like a double-edged sword. Natalie held her breath until the burning in her lungs won out over the stinging in her eyes.

Edwin let out a sigh. "Nat–"

"I didn't ask for this." She shut the book and glared at its cover. "I don't want it. Any of it."

"This doesn't mean anything. It's just words on a page." Leo's thumb traced the blanched ridges of Natalie's knuckles, easing her grip on the book's spine.

AJ crouched in front of her. "The Reverie was a mistake," she explained. "Atlantis could never be satisfied relying on the chance an Atlas would always be around when events needed fixing. What if there was a disaster and no Atlas ever came? What if one day an Atlas alone wasn't enough?" The Counselor shook her head. "Atlantis is built on the question *'what if?'* by masons who are not content to wait."

"A Regent is chosen by the Council when there is no current Atlas to oversee the city," Edwin watched her closely, the corners of his mouth turned down. "I told you before, time-travel is a genetic slip we can't replicate. The Curia chose Aislinn, but Atlantis chose you."

Panic seized Natalie's heart in a vice. Her breaths were thready and thin.

"But every Atlas in this record," Clo paused, wide eyes locked on *The Sceptical Chymist*, "they…they *died*."

AJ nodded. "Death is not exceptional. All that exists dies. We can only hope to be worthy of the time we are given, and you," she eased the book from Natalie, "have been given more than most." She turned again to *The Atlas Atlas*, the text shimmering teal and blue against the sinking sun. "Do you know the difference between fate and destiny?"

Natalie didn't answer. She stared down at the *Atlas*, lost in the blank space that followed her name.

"Fate is a future we meet as it comes. Destiny is the future we choose."

Edwin's eyes caught on hers.

There are a thousand causes to die for, but something to live for is rare.

Christopher had lived for the Coelacanth Project. Her parents had lived for her. What did Natalie live for?

She eyed *The Sceptical Chymist* that sat open in AJ's lap. There were no more clues. No more cryptic messages. No one else to help them.

Reverie. August 9th, 1945.

The date snagged in her mind. Nagasaki. The bombing that ended the second World War.

"Like I said, it was never meant to be a bomb," Edwin explained, as though reading her thoughts. "An Atlas emerges once in a generation if we're lucky, but when the world was devastated after World War I, no Atlas ever came," he dragged a hand over his face. "Atlantis needed a back-up plan. Hell, *humanity* needed a back-up plan. What if the Atlas line stopped altogether? What if we could bypass natural selection and think of a way to save ourselves?" He half lifted one shoulder. "A way to artificially manipulate time had to be attempted. It's human nature. We are cursed to try even when we are doomed to fail. When no Atlas emerged to undo the devastation of Hiroshima, the Atlantean Curia deployed the Reverie, giving us Nagasaki."

Edwin shook his head, weariness etching hard lines on his face.

"The Ward knows what the Reverie can do and he's choosing to use it anyway. What about you, Nat? What do you choose?"

The idea of leaving, of walking away, was impossible. And not because of fate, or destiny, or a few damning lines of invisible ink. Atlantis was her home. Natalie felt it in her bones. And she would not let it burn.

She was done letting Nautilus reign over her life. She was finished with the Ward's destructive campaign to sate his own heartache. But most of all, Natalie was done running.

She'd never been good at it anyway.

Edwin saw the decision in her eyes and his mouth ticked up in a sly grin. "Ready to fight dirty?"

"Lucky for you, Tawney taught me no other way."

Leo turned her to face him. "If you want this, I'm with you. But you are more than a dash between dates. You can live like an Atlas without dying like one." His forehead pressed to hers, voice dropping to a whisper meant just for them. "I will not lose you. Never again. Do you understand?"

Natalie grabbed Leo's collar and kissed him. His lips crushed against hers, sure and fierce. Maybe he was right. Maybe she didn't have to die like an Atlas to live like one. After all, she had help. Broken and bruised, they were still a family.

Sieged and splintered, Atlantis was still their home.

CHAPTER 36

Decided, Natalie stood. "Nora! Ignis!"

They hurried to her, a confused expression passing between them.

"AJ told you to clear the streets?"

"Yes," Nora pointed back at the Ravens. "We were just–"

"Do as she said," Natalie interrupted. "Evacuate everyone who wants to go. But those who don't," she hesitated, knowing there was no going back once she gave the word. "Those who want to fight…let them."

"No," AJ bristled. "Our people know nothing of combat. Asking them to fight would be a massacre."

"I'm not asking anything," Natalie countered. "But this is their home, and if they want to fight for it, I won't deny them the chance." She turned back to Nora and Ignis. "Follow the Curtanas; they'll go where the Ward goes."

"What about you?" Ignis asked.

"If what I'm about to do works," Natalie wiped the sweat from her palms. "Hopefully, we won't need you."

"You're going back?" Owen gaped, something between hope and fear shone in his eyes.

"I'm going back."

"This is not like when you saved me," Lache warned her. "That changed nothing. Going back now…" Her ice-blue stare only made Natalie more nervous. "This is dangerous."

Natalie glanced at Leo, hoping he missed Lache's ominous tone. He didn't.

"Why is this different than last time?" His question was directed at Edwin, but Natalie felt obligated to answer.

"Before, Lache's fate was hers alone," she said the words quickly, as though the faster she got them out the less weight they would carry. "Not enough time had passed for her death on that bridge to affect anyone beyond herself. I was able to reverse it quickly. Almost immediately." Natalie paused. "But Atlantis…"

"Atlantis has been dying for hours," Clo finished for her.

Natalie dug her sneakers in the sand. The truth was she wasn't sure she'd survive changing anything before Nautilus's assault on Atlantis began. Too much had happened.

"You can do this," Edwin assured her.

"We can do this," Leo pressed his lips to her hair. "Together."

Natalie's heart skipped. "Together."

"Is that possible?" Lache asked.

"I think so," she nodded. "I took Edwin and Leo back to save you. The hard part isn't getting us there. It's what we do after."

"I will stay with the Ravens and AJ," Atro chimed in. "My place is with them."

"And ours is with you," Lache and Clo stood with their sister.

"Good," Natalie offered a smile that she hoped came off braver than she felt. "They'll need your help."

She moved towards the water's edge, the wind whipping at her hair. She knew what was at stake: her life, her home. But when the black water of the incoming wave rushed up, Natalie stepped back.

"We don't really have time for second thoughts here, Nat," Edwin warned.

"I have all the time we need," Natalie muttered, scanning the crowded beach. Someone was missing. She made it past Edwin and the Moirai before Leo caught up with her.

"Where are you going?"

"Owen," she craned her neck, searching the crowd of Ravens for his telltale flash of red. She was done leaving people behind. And she wasn't sure her plan would work without him. "Wait with the others."

"You're crazy."

"I think the correct term is *mad*."

"Not funny," Leo chided her. "You're not going alone."

"It's only Owen–"

"A month ago we would have said the same about Brant."

He had a point.

"Fine," she relented. "Stay close, but let me talk to him alone."

Leo snagged her arm as Enzi stubbornly wedged between them. "Why don't you want me to go with you?"

"Because," Natalie dropped her voice. "He hates me right now. He blames me for…" Tawney's name lodged in her throat. "He needs to say so, and he'll never do that in front of you."

Leo stared at her, all green eyes and concern.

"Give me two minutes."

She watched the argument build behind the muscle that ticked in his jaw, but ultimately, he relented. "Sixty seconds."

Determined not to waste any of them, Natalie made her way towards Owen. She found him among a tight knit group of Ravens, slouched against a boulder with his head in his hands. He ignored her approach, declining to look up even as she eased herself beside him.

"You aren't coming with us." His actions, or lack thereof, were clear. Owen wanted to sit on that beach and wait for the end.

"No," he croaked. "I'm done."

Natalie forced herself to fully look at him. Rage simmered behind bloodshot eyes while every ragged breath wavered between a sob and a snarl. And beneath that pain and anger, he looked hollow. Carved out. A void had opened where love had been.

Natalie found Owen's hands with her own. He swatted her off but she persisted, closing sure fingers over desperate ones. Brant had once told her that grief was a constant weight to bear. A suffering that never eased, no matter the sympathy of others or the passage of time. It was a backpack full of books that never lightened, but the longer you carried it, the stronger you became.

So Natalie offered no cardboard comforts. Every sentiment would wither in the reality that Tawney was gone.

"You blame me," Natalie said softly.

"I do," Owen admitted. "It's your fault. She's gone because of you, because of what you can do." Yet even as he said it, anger succumbed to ache. "That's why we're here at all. And, honestly, Nat," his voice fractured at the edges. "I hate you for it."

She'd known that truth was coming. She'd felt it boring into her the moment Tawney disappeared on that screen and she'd thought herself prepared. But the sting of it sent her gut coiling beneath her ribs.

Guilt wrecked her, wild and savage. She blamed Brant. Brant blamed his father. Owen blamed her. The circle was endless and the result the same. All that really mattered was that Tawney was gone.

"I can't do this without her," Owen's shoulders shook. Tears dotted his glasses. "I can't, Nat, I can't–"

"Neither can I." She moved to sit in front of him, forcing him to look at her. "So…let's go get her."

Owen blinked. His expression morphed from anger to disbelief, before finally settling on a desperate pinched hope. "But…but you can't–"

"I need her, too."

He stared at her, his face unreadable, and she waited. Finally, he pushed himself to his feet. "She's going to be pissed, you know."

"Yeah," Natalie smiled. "Yeah, I know."

They moved back towards the water and Leo's gaze darted from Natalie to Owen and back again, one eyebrow raised in silent question.

Natalie answered with a tentative smile. She'd given Owen a dangerous motive: hope. And she wasn't certain she could deliver. She wasn't certain about anything.

But if she started with Tawney, if she saved her best friend's life first and they went to the Archives together, they could still head off the Ward. They could still save the city. It was a big *if*. One she wasn't ready to share because failure meant Atlantis would follow Tawney to the grave, and Nautilus would bury the world with them.

Edwin sidled up close. "This is going to cost you."

"Everything has a cost," Natalie rocked on her heels, nervous energy making her fingers itch. "I can do this."

"Good," he beamed. "Let's save a damned city."

The incoming wave rushed up, and Natalie leaned in.

CHAPTER 37

Traveling through time felt like breathing backwards.

Ocean water rushed to meet her, sliding over shoes and ankles without ever touching skin. The water disappeared, replaced by light and weightlessness, and, once upon a time, Natalie wished to stay there. She would dream to leave the pain and questions on the shore, to remain trapped in an infinite abyss.

But now Tawney waited on the other side.

Air was dredged from her lungs as though the universe inhaled as she stepped between its folds, emptying her when she already had nothing to give. It lasted an instant. Weightless. Breathless. Hollow.

Then with gravity came air.

Natalie knelt, gasping. Trembling fingers trailed sand over her face, checking for blood she knew shouldn't be there. Not yet.

It was one thing to visit the past. It was another to change it.

Enzi nuzzled her as she rose. The ceiling-sky was still whole, no debris clogged the street, and in the distance, she caught the glint of brightly colored robes as Atlanteans went about their day.

"Nat," Edwin squinted up at the manufactured sky. "When are

we?"

"Should be a few minutes before Nautilus is in the city."

"Should be?" Owen peered at her through cracked frames.

"It's not really an exact science."

"Right," he rubbed his neck. "Of course not."

Edwin's stare narrowed on her. "This is the farthest you could go?"

Natalie didn't answer.

"Come on," Leo cut in, focused on the play at hand. "If we hurry we can still get in and out of the Archives before anyone knows we're–"

"No," Natalie stopped him. "Tawney first."

Leo smiled at her. Edwin cursed.

"Tawney first," she insisted. "My cost, my choice."

A flush crept up Edwin's neck, but to his credit he didn't argue. At least not out loud. He pursed his lips and gestured towards the central city. "Best not dally then."

Dallying, it turned out, wasn't the problem. Rushing was.

When they'd sprinted from the Curia to the beach only minutes before, the streets had been empty. But now, before Nautilus invades the city, Atlanteans were everywhere. Natalie followed Enzi's lead as he wound his way through the anxious crowd, white tail waving like a flag.

"They don't know what's coming," Owen marveled at the crowd. "We have to warn them. We have to get them off the–"

"No," Leo and Edwin said together.

"It will be harder to save them if everyone's in a panic." Leo went on. "Individuals are smart, but crowds are…"

"Stupid," Edwin finished.

Owen might have argued more, but the opal face of the Academy's clock tower loomed ahead. "There," he pointed. "It's still standing!"

Natalie grinned in spite of herself. She'd really done it. She'd taken them back. She was going to save her best friend. Natalie started to rush through the crowd when the ground rumbled under her feet.

On instinct, she faltered. Enzi's ears went flat. The leaves on the garden trees quivered as a shower of dust smudged the late afternoon sky.

Natalie doubled her pace.

Dodging stalled Atlanteans, she beelined for the clock tower, darting into the Atlantean Academy as it happened again.

The roar started low and steady, a thunder that rippled out from the sky to consume the earth. Natalie braced against the wall, feeling the marble shift beneath her palms. It lasted only seconds, but it was long enough for Enzi to cower against her knees. Long enough for Leo's grip to blanch her fingers white, for the cries of nearby children to puncture the sound of shifting stone.

Natalie couldn't wait for the quaking to stop.

Her shoes smacked against the pearlescent floors as she sprinted down the halls. The school was massive: a labyrinth of unmarked passages and countless chambers, including the Atlantean Article and Genesis Room.

And she had no idea where to start.

Another explosion nearly sent Natalie tumbling. She stumbled, managing to stay upright as she refused to slow her pace.

Doors opened as they passed, their archways filled with anxious teachers after reassurance. Edwin wasted no time with lies.

"Get out!" He shouted without stopping. "Evacuate the halls!"

Inspired, Natalie adopted his tactic.

"Tawney!" she screamed her throat raw. "Tawney Davis where are—"

A massive blast put Natalie on the ground. She hit the tile hard, instinctively covering her head even as Enzi's thick fur threatened to smother her.

"Nat," Edwin coughed out dust as the world stilled. "We're running out of time. The Archives—"

Tick-tock.

Natalie pushed herself up and took off again.

"Tawney!" Her name tore from her chest, threatened to rip out her heart. "Tawney-Freaking-Davis, I swear if you don't come out this second—"

Rounding a corner, Natalie felt as though she was traveling through time all over again. The breath bled from her lungs while every atom of her being felt charged and alive.

Tawney was right *there*. Spiral curls framed a stubborn pout. Thick brows met over her suspicious glare. Tawney looked as fierce and strong and alive as ever.

"Nat?" she gawked. "Owen? What are you—"

Owen silenced her with his mouth. Bursts of relieved laughter escaped between kisses, and he broke away only to push back the hair from her face, to be certain it was her. Enzi pawed at them both, yipping and nosing the back of Tawney's knees.

"Uh, hello," Tawney's cheeks turned a rare shade of pink. "What's going on? Why are you…" Her thumb brushed at the tears that dampened Owen's scruff. "Crying," she finished, deadpan, the words no longer a question.

Natalie moved closer, touching Tawney tentatively at arm's length. She looked real. And, bouncing one perfect curl, she certainly felt real.

Tawney studied each of them in turn, and Natalie watched the unspoken questions flit over her expression: *What happened? Why are you here?* But Natalie couldn't bring herself to answer them any easier than Tawney could bring herself to ask.

"You're…you're supposed to be in the Curia." Tawney sounded small, her voice tainted with something Natalie had never heard from her before. Fear.

"I am," Natalie said slowly. "I'm in the Atlantean Curia. Right now."

Tawney's eyes went wide with understanding. "No," she backed away. "No…you wouldn't come back. You wouldn't, Nat, you *wouldn't.*"

"I had to."

Tawney's chest heaved and she paced. Two steps to Natalie, Owen, and back again.

"When?" She adjusted the neckline of her shirt, tugging as though it was suddenly suffocating. "When does it happen?"

"Minutes," Natalie whispered. "Maybe more…likely less."

"Son of a–" Tawney bit her fist. "And you came back to…to what? Change it?" Disbelief colored her tone. "Why? You never would before, not with Christopher or Angie, so why now? Why me?"

Natalie pulled Tawney to her, squeezing so tight her friend's breath came out in a huff. She thought of Brant and his mother. Of Christopher. Of Angie, and Mom, and Dad, and Chef, and she knew the truth of it was selfish. The truth was there was only so much she could bear.

"Because I couldn't carry it," Natalie confessed.

"What about the cost?" The question was so quiet Natalie hardly heard her. "What about you?"

"My destiny is my choice," Natalie blinked away tears. "And I'll choose you every time. No matter the cost."

The tension coiled between Tawney's shoulders dissolved, and Natalie squeezed her tighter.

"I won't let anything happen to you."

"Honestly, I'm quite fond of you myself," Edwin bounced impatiently. "However, this Lost City is going to become the Lost Crater if we don't get moving."

Tawney pulled away, cheeks dry, mouth set, brown eyes sharp as steel. "What do we need to–"

BOOM.

The force of the explosion radiated through Natalie's body. Vibrations rattled the walls, shaking more than pebbles from the ceiling. Chunks of rock fell and split, panicked cries echoed from classrooms. Every instinct told Natalie to take cover.

Another told her Tawney would run.

Using the wall to stay upright, Natalie chased after her. She ignored the ache in her bones and the ringing in her ears. She had to reach her. They had to get to the Archives together. They had to stop the Ward *together*.

But it wasn't until Tawney hit a full sprint that Natalie realized it wasn't a ringing in her ears at all.

It was a scream.

Tick-tock.

Natalie's time was up.

CHAPTER 38

Arms pumping, lungs burning, Natalie careened down the corridor. A few more paces and she'd have her. A few more paces and she'd reach the back of Tawney's shirt.

Then she saw the kids.

The group rushed towards her and Natalie skidded to a stop as they blurred past. Not yet waist-high, they couldn't have been more than a few years old. And, more importantly, they couldn't be in the halls. Not when the ceiling was about to cave.

But she had to catch up to Tawney.

"Help them!" Natalie yelled to her friends behind her.

"On it!" Edwin shouted, already running after them.

Natalie turned her attention back to Tawney, but what she saw made her heart seize.

A boy stood ahead of them, his cheeks tomato red and fists clenched. Natalie had seen him before on a screen in the Atlantean Curia, but that wasn't what rooted her feet to the ground.

Above him, the ceiling cracked. It was the same branching fissure that plagued her visions. It had the same twists and turns, the same ink-black fractures. Only now when Natalie blinked it didn't go away. It was there.

It was real.

The tattered threads of Natalie's thoughts wove together and pulled taught. She was falling, falling, falling down the rabbit hole and, for once, she let herself go. She didn't fight or struggle, made no effort to cling to the rocks of reality. Instead, she got swept away, she lost her hold and sank.

Curiouser and curiouser…

Reality left a bitter taste in the mouth. Madness, perhaps, was sweet.

No, not madness, she realized. *Memory.*

She felt it, somewhere in her depths, but couldn't spare the seconds needed to dredge the image to the surface. In a desperate lurch, she threw herself forward, catching Tawney by the fringe of her shirt.

"Stop!" Natalie cried. "You can't do this."

Tawney turned to her, eyes blazing. "Nat," her certainty turned Natalie's blood to concrete. "Owen gets Tofu. And tell my mom," she winced. "Tell her…tell her I'm sorry."

"Shut up," Natalie's voice shook. "Shut up you obstinate, stubborn, pain in the–"

"Nat."

"–obnoxious, reckless–"

"If we win, don't you dare come back for me."

"I *can't*, Tawney! If this doesn't work, I can't try again. There won't be enough of me left. And if it does…" Natalie choked on a sob, unable to voice the rest. Unable to imagine a world without her best friend. "What if we go?" she begged. "What if we leave? Right now. You and me."

Tawney gave a rebellious smile. "What if we don't?"

"You can't do this. Don't do this. *Please.*"

"Love you, Nat." Tawney kissed her cheek and, in one swift motion, swept Natalie's legs out from under her.

She hit the ground flat on her back and Enzi's fur blinded her. He was everywhere, whining and sniffing and nudging. When Natalie finally managed to scramble to her knees, she knew it would be too late. She knew what she'd see when she looked up.

"Tawney!" Owen's desperate shout ripped open Natalie's heart.

Down the hall, big brown eyes locked on hers before the small boy filled her vision. Natalie caught him, clutching him to her chest as the ceiling gave a final *crack* and collapsed in a roar. Turning her back on the cave-in, Natalie wrapped around the boy as rocks dropped behind them.

Natalie's vision blurred and dust choked her. Her arms burned as tiny fingers dug into them, trying to claw their way free. She didn't realize she was screaming until Leo knelt in front of her, cupping her cheeks and closing her mouth.

She yanked away. There was no comfort in his touch, only truth. And she wasn't ready for it.

"Don't," she sobbed. "Don't touch me, don't touch me…"

"…her choice," Leo's words floated in the sea of white noise. They parted around her, leaving her drifting and alone. "It was her choice, Natalie." Tears streaked his face. "Her choice, her cost."

Her choice. Her choice to leave us.

Her choice to die.

A knife twisted in Natalie's gut.

Somewhere behind them, Owen slammed against the rubble.

"Tawney!" he screamed. "Tawney!" But the boulders wouldn't budge. Not as he threw his body against them. Not as his palms split open and streaked them red.

It was finally Edwin who pulled him away. "She's gone, Owen."

Owen's expression contorted with rage. He wrenched himself from Edwin and rounded on Natalie.

She had just enough sense to put down the boy in her arms before Owen's shove sent her sprawling.

"Owen," Leo growled, stepping between them. "Watch yourself."

Owen stared past him, glaring at Natalie with red rimmed eyes. He stiffened, ready to strike her again, and she made no move to defend herself. Part of her wanted it. Part of her knew she deserved it.

He swung and Leo moved to block him, but the blow never landed. In a blur of white, Owen was gone.

Enzi pinned him with two massive paws on his chest. A snarl exposed jaws of pearly white teeth.

Owen blanched. "I…I–"

Slowly, Enzi's hackles lowered. He backed off of Owen with a final threatening grumble.

"Nat…"

"Forget it," Natalie mumbled.

Leo stared down at Owen, every ridge of him taut. "Get up," his voice was low and heavy, but not without sympathy.

Natalie's gaze slid unbidden to the pile of rubble. She meant what she'd said to Tawney. She wouldn't be able to save her. She wouldn't survive the cost.

Not again.

"Nat," Edwin plucked up the boy that still cried at her feet and swung him onto his back. The kid sniffled, locking small arms around Edwin's neck. "I'm sorry." His black eyes were glassy. "Truly, I am. But we've got to move."

Natalie gulped in air and coughed out dust. He was right. She knew he was right. Any chance to save Tawney was over. No matter what happened, no matter who won, Tawney was gone. No amount of time-travel would ever bring her back.

"She'd want us to keep going," Leo frowned at the unmoving pile of rock.

"I know," Natalie's voice shook. She cleared her throat and tried again. It didn't help. "I know."

"I am sorry." Edwin's expression pinched with genuine sympathy. Sympathy for Tawney. Sympathy for the fact they had no time to grieve.

Natalie gave no more response than a nod. She couldn't think about Tawney now. Not when they still stood any kind of a chance against the Ward.

She scanned the group, checking them over and catching her breath. Edwin hovered near Owen, muttering something too low to hear. Enzi herded together the small group of kids Edwin saved, his fur more dusty grey than white. Though the children hardly seemed to care, digging small hands deep into his coat as he licked them from chin to forehead. And Leo planted himself at Natalie's side, close enough that she could reach out if she needed to. If she wanted to.

She didn't.

Natalie focused on the next impossible problem: the kids. Five sets of wide eyes looked to her, five downturned mouths silently questioning what came next. Natalie envied them having someone to ask.

"We need to get this lot somewhere safe," Edwin voiced her thoughts. "And quickly. Any ideas?"

"Safe?" Leo dragged through his hair. "Nowhere is safe in this city. It's only going to get worse."

Natalie clung to the issue in front of her as she tried to hold her sharp edges together. She couldn't leave a bunch of children in the middle of a collapsing building, and they certainly couldn't come to the Archives. Tawney had trusted her to do something; she'd given her life for those kids. Letting her down was not an option.

The boy on Edwin's back finally stopped crying. Fascinated by the three hoops capping his carrier's ear, stubby fingers fumbled over the metal. Flashes of silver glinted through Edwin's charcoal hair, making him look…

Natalie's stomach flipped as though she missed a step.

It was just like the crack that had haunted her since she'd set foot in Atlantis. The fissure that split dreams and reality until it manifested directly over Tawney's head, deadly and real.

Realization mineralized cold and hard in her bones. The *Atlas Atlas* had it all wrong. It wasn't madness that killed the time-travelers.

It was memory.

CHAPTER 39

Natalie tumbled the idea through her mind in the few seconds she had. It was improbable, near impossible; a puzzle that only made sense from the inside out. She knew then why the other Atlas must have seemed mad. If she tried to explain it, she would sound insane.

So she didn't.

Natalie picked up the child closest to her and hurried back towards the exit of the Academy.

"Nat!" Her friends shouted after her.

"Come on," she answered. "Bring the kids!"

Without waiting to see if they listened, Natalie navigated around fallen chunks of ceiling and fractured floor. It wasn't until she reached the entryway that a familiar sound stopped her. The others caught up, Edwin and Owen each with a child on their backs and Leo balancing one on each hip.

"Is that," Leo cocked his head, listening. "Water?"

Outside, a snaking track of stone curved above them. It was the same funnel they'd raced on Edwin's DartFrogs only days before, but now it channeled a rushing flood of water.

"Woah," Leo stood directly beneath the aqueduct. The children he carried dodged droplets raining from the stonework. "The aqueducts…they're running!"

"Aislinn," Edwin nodded. "I knew she hadn't given up. It's a shortcut to the Ancient City."

But Natalie had other ideas. She shifted the increasingly heavy boy to her other hip. "Do all the aqueducts lead to the sea?"

Edwin squinted at her, his mouth clamped shut.

"Please, Edwin—"

"You're running away." The accusation was laced with warning.

"What?" Natalie balked. "No, I'm—"

"We are not leaving this city to burn. We're staying. *You're* staying."

"I have to leave." She couldn't find the words to explain everything, but she knew Edwin would never budge unless she gave him something. "I'll come right back."

"And I'm supposed to believe you?"

"Yes."

"Well, I don't," his lips pursed.

"Damn it, Edwin." The boy Natalie carried tugged on a lock of her hair. She winced, prying the strands from his grasp. "Look," she searched for the simplest explanation that would get him on her side. "It's not madness that kills the Atlas."

He stilled, suspicion faltering to curiosity.

"Come on," Natalie begged. "Don't you trust me?"

He was quiet a painfully long moment as many answers to her question rolled over his face. *Yes. No. I'm not sure. I want to.* Finally, Edwin set his jaw.

"They lead to the sea," he conceded. "Every aqueduct is connected to the Atlantean Sea."

Natalie's pulse ticked up. They didn't have time to make it all the way back to the beach and then the Archives on foot. But with the aqueducts…

"How do we get up there?" she asked, eyeing the stone structure overhead.

In answer, Leo led them into the nearest garden. The aqueduct curved lower and lower until the cement dipped just higher than her waist. The water rushed furiously past, pulled by the weight of its own fate.

"Nat," Edwin delayed her at the water's edge. "Are you sure about this?"

"We have to get them somewhere safe." She wasn't sure if she was convincing him or herself. "I…know a place. And if we win," she chose her words carefully. "If we win, they can come home."

Turning her back on him, she fastened the boy's tiny hands around her neck.

Somewhere safe. Natalie fought the panic tightening her insides as Enzi whined, pressing himself between the aqueduct and her knees.

She flicked a nervous glance back at Edwin, the motion so fast his features never focused. So fast that he was a smudge of dark hair and a stubborn jaw.

The crack.

The madness.

The memory.

Curiouser and curiouser.

Wake up, Natalie.

She climbed onto the aqueduct's thick rim and the others followed suit, fanning out as they lined up on the edge. Leo laced his fingers between hers and gave a gentle squeeze.

The issue wasn't where Natalie wanted to go but when. The memory was slippery, as difficult to summon as it was to catch. So she clung to the feeling instead, to the first time she felt safe.

She recalled the warm wind carrying a cricket's song. The security of her hand held tight in another's. She remembered the first time she'd truly seen the sky, that vast expanse of stars, and she hoped it was enough.

Atlas, let it be enough.

Before she lost her nerve, Natalie dropped over the edge.

Atlantis vanished. Weightlessness engulfed her as she drifted, the breath pulled from her chest and a tingling seeded her limbs until she landed on solid ground.

Enzi darted from her side, but Natalie kept her eyes closed. Her senses filled with the scent of pine, of muddied sand at low tide. And somewhere in the reeds, a brave cricket resumed its song. She smiled.

"Natalie," Leo said warily. "Where are we?"

"*When* are we?" Owen clarified, his voice hoarse.

Natalie put the child she carried on his feet, tousling his hair before squaring her shoulders to Edwin. "You've been obsessed with my name since we met," she said. "But I never asked yours."

"You know my name." He waved her off, scanning the nearby forest where fireflies blinked in the gathering dusk. "It's Edwin."

"Your full name," Natalie lowered her voice to keep it from breaking. Tears pricked her eyes but she hardly cared. He'd see her cry plenty of times before the end. Before his end. "Please."

Swinging the child from his back, he fished a saltwater taffy from his pocket. "Edwin Christopher Reyes." He popped the candy into his cheek. "Why do you ask?"

CHAPTER 40

It's said laughter heals the soul.

Natalie once thought the concept ridiculous. Yet as delirious giggles bubbled out of her, she could have sworn she felt her rough edges soften. Pieces once lost finally falling together.

Owen placed the child he carried on the sand before promptly seating himself. He leaned back, gazing up at Edwin, at *Christopher*, with a mixture of admiration and hatred and something else Natalie couldn't place.

"Well," he sighed. "That explains a lot."

"No." Leo clutched Natalie's hand so hard her fingers throbbed. "No, I don't think it does. What are you saying?" His green eyes snapped between Edwin and Natalie. "That he's… That you're…"

Edwin opened his mouth but before he could formulate a question into words, one of the children began to cry. Enzi immediately came to investigate, however the giant dog only aggravated her more. Scooping up the girl, Edwin bounced her on his hip. Her ringlet curls sprang with every jolt.

Natalie's laughter died in her throat.

"If he's…then that's…Tawney?" Leo breathed, voicing the truth Natalie couldn't.

The girl quieted at the sound of her name, her big brown eyes scrutinizing them. Leo drifted towards her, smoothing her pouty lip with his thumb before taking her from Edwin. He cradled her against his chest and, slowly, her arms wrapped around Leo's neck.

Beside them, Owen went deathly still. He stared at tiny Tawney, neither reaching out or pulling away, silent tears tracking down his cheeks.

Stubby legs capped with a mop of chestnut curls darted over to Leo and clung tight to his calf, reaching for the girl. Amused, Leo ruffled the boy's hair.

Brant's hair, Natalie realized.

"Do others go mad besides the Atlas?" Leo asked through a cautious smile. "Because this…this can't be real. They can't be…they *can't* be…"

"Us," Natalie finished. She scanned the rest of the kids, simultaneously fascinated and afraid to look too close. The redhead already digging for shells left no question, and the round-faced boy climbing Edwin's legs was undoubtedly Leo. Which only left…

"Hello." Natalie knelt by the girl toeing the line where grass met sand. Her hazel eyes lifted and a flicker of memory dripped down Natalie's spine.

She *remembered* this.

She remembered standing on the shore with fireflies by the sea. She remembered being relieved. She remembered feeling *safe*.

"You're going to be okay," Natalie promised. "You and your family…everything's going to be fine."

The girl shrugged her shoulders in the dramatic way kids do before following Enzi to join the growing petition for Leo to put Tawney down.

"This was your plan?" Edwin gestured around the clearing. "We can't leave them here! They'll get eaten by a bear. Or kidnapped by bandits. They'll get lost and drown!"

"They'll be fine," Natalie sighed out the words, all of her strength gone.

"Nat, this," he shook his head. "This is *mad.*"

"On the outside, it looks like madness, but it's not," she shifted until she was right in front of him. Until she could see nothing else. "It's memory. It's guilt. It's knowing what could have been. Not imagining or wondering, but actually *knowing.* Remembering. Seeing it with your own eyes. That's the true cost: memory." She blinked back the sting in her eyes. "Madness would have been kinder. And I have nothing kind to ask of you."

Edwin stepped back. "You—you don't mean for me to stay *here?* With, with," he gestured with mild panic at the kids.

"You were once chosen to be Regent," she reminded him. "Do you still want to serve?"

"Not by babysitting!"

Leo shouldered him. "Do you truly not see it?"

Frowning, Edwin looked at each child, then back to Natalie. To Leo. To Owen. And slowly, frustration gave way to awe. "But that...that can't be."

Natalie almost smiled. Almost.

"This is why I keep seeing the cracks," she explained. "I *remember.* I remember the crack in the Academy's ceiling and the cave in, but I couldn't place it before now." She shrugged. "Memory is fallible. Memory is madness."

"It's a circle," Owen's voice broke, his stare still locked on little Tawney. "It's a loop. All this time...we've been in a *loop.*"

"One we're about to exit, I think," Natalie agreed. Turning back to Edwin she added, "If you will still serve."

He stared at her, mouth open and eyes wide. She knew what he would say, what he *had* said, for the circle to complete itself, but she needed it to be his choice. It had to be his choice because it was his cost. It wouldn't work any other way.

Edwin dragged a hand over his face. "Of course I will."

Natalie closed her eyes, her emotions a mixture of dread and relief. "There's a cost—"

"There's always a cost."

"You won't go back."

Edwin tensed. "You can't know that."

"I do," she promised. "If you choose to stay, you will never go back. You'll have friends, a family, you'll have us, but—" the city stuck on her tongue, the synapse block preventing her from speaking its name beyond its walls. "This will be your home."

He looked away, fidgeting with the hem of his shirt.

"And there's something else." Natalie hated herself for telling him the truth, all the while knowing he deserved more than anyone to hear it. "You will never know how this ends."

Edwin stepped back as though she'd slapped him. His chest swelled and he turned his back to her, pulling his hair up at odd angles. When he finally faced her again, his eyes were red.

"Your uncle," he pointed at the sand, at his own feet. "Chris," his mouth grimaced over the name. "Christopher. He died before I met you."

It wasn't a question, so Natalie didn't answer.

He stared at her, expressionless. She waited for him to demand why she'd ask so much of him. Why he'd have to forsake his home to save it, why he should give his life for a plan that may never work. Like her parents. Like Chef. Like Tawney.

A large part of Natalie hoped he'd say no. Because he deserved better. Because he deserved the world.

But of course, he didn't.

"Well," Edwin hooked his thumbs in his pockets in a manner so Christopher-like Natalie's heart lodged in her throat. "If this is going to cost me everything, you'd better give me all you've got."

Natalie dug through her pockets and dropped two coins into his palm.

"A nickel and a penny?" He snorted. "That's it?"

"Fate's a wicked beastie."

His response came quickly. "I don't believe in fate."

Natalie thought of every sacrifice that had brought her to that beach. Every selfless choice made by family and loved ones and strangers had been exactly that: a *choice*. A choice made in spite of the cost.

The corner of her mouth curved up. "Neither do I."

"Good," Edwin nodded. The next time he spoke, his voice shook. "Will you do something for me?"

Natalie's stomach muscles tightened. He was giving up his life in more ways than one to save her, to save her friends, to roll the dice for a chance at saving their city. Natalie would go to the ends of the Earth and back for him.

"Anything."

"Tell AJ I'm dead."

Natalie's lips parted. "What?"

He grinned, and she wondered if it was Christopher who taught Brant to mask pain with a smile. "You said I'm never going back," he shrugged. "She deserves better than false hope."

Maybe I'm wrong, the omission stuck on her tongue. *Maybe you do go back. Maybe things will be different—*

She couldn't say any of it. Because things wouldn't be different. They couldn't be. And he knew it.

"It's kinder not to wonder," Edwin gave a wry smile. "Don't you think?"

Edwin would find ignorance the cruelest punishment the universe could offer. Never knowing the end, never being sure. He wouldn't want to inflict that suffering on someone else when there was any other option. Especially for AJ.

Without waiting for her answer, he gestured grandly about the coastal woodland of Virginia's Eastern Shore. "So, here begins the Coelacanth Project." He flashed a wicked grin. "Our city rising from the sea."

Owen rushed up to him, his expression wild. "You can change it," he shook Edwin's arms, his knuckles white. "You can choose the right people. You can fix *all* of this."

Natalie made to pry him away, but Leo reached him first.

"He does pick the right people."

"No!" Owen's shout silenced the crickets in the reeds. "We can save her! We can make it better."

Natalie resisted the urge to explain that every step Edwin would take beyond that beach would help shape who they became. She didn't explain how hard it was to shift a timeline, or how Edwin would have no means of paying the cost. She subdued every fact and explanation that her rational friend would normally welcome because it wouldn't be heard. Grief boxed his ears.

She gave the only explanation he would take. "This is why she saved us."

Owen withered at her words, folding in on himself.

"Nat's right," Edwin said quietly.

"Yeah," he shrugged. "Yeah…I know."

Leo extended his hand to Edwin. "I guess this is goodbye."

"Goodbye?" He threw an arm over Leo's shoulders and nodded towards the kids. "Seems to me we're going to have a lifetime of fun together! Meanwhile, be careful with that one." He winked at Natalie.

"She's too clever for you."

"Your doing," Leo accused.

Edwin gave a less than modest shrug. "Now," he rubbed his palms together. "I distinctly remember you stating your uncle hailed from the land of saltwater taffy."

Leo laughed. "You're going to be just fine."

Edwin grinned and even Owen seemed to briefly brighten, but before Natalie could join them, she remembered Leo was wrong. Edwin wouldn't be fine. He'd die for them, and he knew it.

Natalie threw her arms around him, pulling him close. "Thank you," she whispered.

As they parted, he pressed something metallic into her hand. The silver hoops that always capped his ear unfolded in her palm. Linked, they formed a perfect triquetra.

"Don't let Atlantis sink," Edwin reminded her. "You know what follows when it does."

Natalie did know. *War.*

"Live for our city," he kissed her firmly on the forehead. "There's never been a stronger Atlas for the job." Edwin paused, then added, "Do you know how to get to the Archives?"

Unable to speak past the lump in her throat, Natalie shook her head.

"The most sacred secrets lie beneath the oldest stones."

"Seriously?" Natalie blurted. "A puzzle? Now? You want to play games, *now*?"

Edwin smiled. "What's the oldest building in Atlantis?"

"The Library." The answer came from Leo. "It's the Library."

Natalie blinked. She should have known. It was the same reason a pilgrim would erect their village after their church. Atlantis was a culture built on intellect; a house of knowledge would come first. And the desolation of the Ancient City only served to further disguise what hid there.

Edwin hoisted the red-haired boy up onto his hip. "Uncle Edwin doesn't feel quite right, does it? Doesn't flow off the tongue." Little Owen tugged on his collar. "Uncle Chris it is then, eh?"

Natalie backed towards the water, knowing no amount of waiting would make leaving any easier. Owen and Leo took her hands, one of them seizing Enzi by his scruff. She sensed more than saw the wave rippling up behind them, and just before it reached her, she gave Edwin her bravest smile.

"See you."

His black stare locked on her. There was sadness in them, and pain, but mostly a gut-wrenching wealth of pride.

"No," he winked. "You won't."

CHAPTER 41

Tacking had become as natural as walking. Intention, seawater, weightlessness, gravity. The tingling hit Natalie like the first plunge in the pool midsummer: a shock of sensation and then it was over. All faster than she could blink.

Time-travel was different. There was a price. And after leaving Edwin stranded in the past with five kids, with *them*, Natalie's cost rushed up to claim her.

Intention, seawater, weightlessness–

Dark.

Quiet.

Painless.

Natalie knew she was dead. She must be. How else could she have achieved a state of such pure peace?

Eleanor had promised she'd find peace.

Her thoughts fragmented, her senses dulled. Time was inconsequential; an hour or an eternity made no difference. She was content.

Bump.

Something skimmed the surface of Natalie's mind. She ignored it. She had earned her peace and she would keep it.

Bump… Bump… Bump…

Annoyed, Natalie groaned. The sound scratched against the back of her throat, settling thick as concrete in her gut. It *hurt*. Things shouldn't hurt when you're dead. It wasn't fair. It wasn't right. Which left only one other insufferable conclusion.

She wasn't dead.

Not yet.

Natalie's eyelids drooped, stubborn and heavy. Ripples of sound radiated around her as light beams and shadows flickered. And everything was underlined by that incessant *bump… bump… bump.*

She tested her fingers and toes. They wiggled. But when she attempted to straighten, pain shot through her like lightning. It lanced across every muscle, electricity turned to fire, but she didn't stop. Forcing herself upright, she let the pain wake her up.

Bump… bump… bump.

Other sensations washed over her. Wind blew through her hair. Her shirt was soaked through with sweat. Goosebumps tickled her skin, blood dribbled from her nose, and, beneath it all, the world moved.

No. The crumbled remains of buildings zipped by. She swerved around piles of rubble clogging once beautiful Atlantean avenues. *The world isn't moving. I'm moving.*

With another jolting *bump* the final piece slid into place.

Natalie wasn't moving; Leo was. She was just along for the ride. Draped over Leo's back, her arms hung around his neck and her legs hooked over his waist.

"Let me down," she said groggily.

Leo tripped and caught himself. "Natalie," he tried to make light of it, but his voice was thick. She actually felt the tension melt out of his shoulders. "Nice of you to join us."

"Let me down."

"I don't think–"

"Leo."

He did as she asked, but when her feet hit the tiled street she sagged. Atlantis tilted like a sinking ship and Natalie battled the nausea churning her stomach. Enzi nudged her, his cold nose inspecting every inch of her he could reach.

"Ugh," Natalie clutched her head, batting him away. "Pick me up, pick me up."

Leo scooped her up again and there was a blur of red as Owen looped around them, securing her arms and legs.

"Hey," she murmured, grateful to see him.

His complexion turned a sickly green. "Don't fall," he patted her, never meeting her eye.

Not trusting only words to escape her throat, Natalie responded with a feeble thumbs-up. She sank into the hollow between Leo's shoulders, not rousing again until he banked a turn so sharp her stomach flipped.

She smacked his bicep. "Sick."

"We're almost–"

"*Sick.*"

Leo dropped her on the spot. Enzi bounded for her again only to prance backwards as the contents of her stomach poured over the pavement. She rocked on her hands and knees, heaving as though everything she'd ever consumed in her life was forcing its way up and out. Finished, she wiped her mouth and cringed. The back of her hand came away wet not with bile, but blood.

Disgusted, she lifted the edge of her shirt to clean herself and stopped. The fabric wasn't sweat drenched at all. Deep burgundy stains seeped across her collar and chest. The copper tang of blood filled her nose and mouth and she tilted her chin to the sky, to clean, fresh air.

Natalie had known there would be payment, that leaving Edwin and their younger selves behind would have a cost. Now she could only hope she'd be done paying it by the time they reached the Ward.

"The visual is effective." Leo wiped a thumb across her forehead, wicking away what, to her relief, really was sweat. "You look outright terrifying."

"Fantastic," Natalie muttered.

With Leo's help she managed to stand. And by the time the mosaic tiles underfoot faded to worn pavestones, she stopped stumbling.

"I don't see anyone," Owen observed, uneasy.

"Neither do—"

Between the ruins of the Ancient City, a flash of movement caught Natalie's eye. She spun, instinctively lifting her arm to defend herself when her assailant caught it outright.

"A traditional 'hello' would have done fine."

"Nora!" Natalie pulled her into a tight hug.

Behind her, Ravens stood crammed into an alley with so many robed Atlanteans not even Enzi attempted to weave between them.

"They came," Nora said proudly. "They want to fight, just like you said."

"Woah," Leo gaped at the mass of people.

The dark jackets of the Ravens dotted a rainbow-robed mob of Atlanteans. Natalie had suspected a few would want to fight, that some would be determined to defend their home even if it was with nothing more than fistfuls of rubble. Yet witnessing their breadth of their bravery with her own eyes made Natalie's chest swell with pride. It gave her strength.

It gave her hope.

"You look terrible," Ignis frowned at her before adding, "Where is Edwin?"

Natalie answered without lifting her gaze from the packed alley. "He's…gone."

The two Ravens shifted, their shoulders slumping even as their spines stacked straighter, as though the news both broke them down and built them up.

"He would want us to keep going," Ignis said quietly. "Tawney, too."

Leo nodded. "That's why we're here."

"We need to get inside the Library," Owen's voice was raw and cracked.

Atro and her sisters joined them, linked arm in arm. "That will not be easy," she warned.

The Moirai guided Natalie through the crowd, the hushed whispers of Ravens and Atlanteans enveloping them like the white noise of the sea. It was empowering to be among them, to feel their resolve reinforcing her own.

And then she saw the army.

There was no other word for it. Natalie stood at the alley's edge, bracing herself against a weathered wall. Wave after wave of Curtana troops guarded the Library. If there were hundreds of Atlanteans behind her, at least a thousand Nautilus waited ahead. Every one of them in her way. Every one of them armed with bolts.

There was only one reason for so much firepower to be gathered in one spot: the Ward was already inside.

"The Archives are somewhere in there," Lache sighed.

"Yeah?" Though Leo's mouth curved in a half grin, his cheeks were pale. "What gave it away?"

Natalie turned her back on the Curtanas, focusing on the Atlanteans and Ravens instead. She wouldn't be able to protect anyone who stood with her. And if any lived long enough to walk away, every one of them would leave scarred. Anyone seeing the breadth of Nautilus's power would know that. And they still refused to run.

Natalie's belly tightened into knots. For the first time, she felt the true weight of her name, and anger poured iron into her spine. She was not afraid. Not anymore. It was one thing to abide her own suffering, it was another to endure her city's, her people's. She would not stand for it.

The Atlanteans had no use for a girl scared of her own destiny. They needed an Atlas ready to seize it. And as she gazed out at them, every single citizen-soldier stared back at her.

"Few of you know me," though quiet, Natalie's words smothered the crowd. "But like you, I am here because Nautilus's Ward will stop at nothing to retrieve the Reverie. Atlantis is accustomed to preserving history," Natalie rested a hand on the ruins that made the alley. "But now we must make it. This city will not fall, not while there is breath in our lungs and fight in our veins. My name is Natalie Atlas," she felt the certainty of it in her bones. "And I will stand with you today and every day until I have nothing left."

Silence. Then, slowly, the man nearest her bowed his head. The motion rippled, and Natalie couldn't have said more if she wanted to. Not past the lump in her throat.

Leo's fingers found hers, and then Owen's, and she clung to them. They stood together. No matter the outcome. No matter the cost.

Natalie squared her shoulders to the Nautilus swell that separated her from the Archives, from the Ward and Brant, and the Reverie. With her first step out of the alley, Archimedes' afternoon sun succumbed to dusk.

With the second it started to rain.

CHAPTER 42

Enzi flattened his ears against the rain, skidding to a full stop in front of Natalie.

"I don't get it," Leo frowned. "Why would Aislinn do this?"

"Wait," Clo gestured to the thickening drops and their dwindling odds. "You think the Regent did this?"

"Of course she did." Owen's neck blotched as red as his hair. "She controls everything: the aqueducts, the media, the Curia. It's not that much of a stretch to know she controls the sky."

Natalie rocked on the balls of her feet. She didn't believe Aislinn would work against her people; at least, not on purpose. Her methods may be off-kilter but in her heart Aislinn loved Atlantis. She led the Ward to the Archives for the same reason she censored what printed in the *Atlantean Article*. She was trying to protect her people, to spare them.

"So why rain?" Natalie whispered to herself.

Thunder rumbled as thick, heavy raindrops pummeled to the earth. She cupped her palm, letting the water puddle in her hand, and where the raindrops met Natalie's skin, they *glowed*.

Natalie huffed out a laugh.

Aislinn wasn't a traitor at all. She was a genius.

"It's saltwater," Natalie watched the silver light fizzle and fade as the rain raced down her arm. "It's *saltwater!*"

Already the pavestones were slick with it. Puddles collected in divots and streams flooded cracks and crevices. Natalie dropped her head back, letting the glowing droplets trail salt over her smile.

When it comes to oceans, size is relative. To an ant, a puddle is a sea. And to the universe, Natalie was no more than an ant. A truth that Christopher, that *Edwin*, would have known and appreciated. Aislinn wasn't putting another obstacle in their way. She was paving their path with aurichalcum.

Rolling the spark against her wrist, Natalie strode into the Regent's saltwater storm. The potential energy of tacking tingled in her veins, trapped in the finite raindrops that glowed and dissipated on her skin.

Still reluctant to get wet, Enzi tucked in close at her side, ears flat and tail tucked. Grabbing a fistful of soaked scruff, Natalie marched into the first trickling stream. There was no splash when she hit it, no sound, no overflow of water to soak her shoes. There was only light.

The first tack took Natalie to the front Nautilus line. She was close enough to see the wrinkles in the Curtana's navy jumpsuits, to see their hair plastered flat by the rain, feel the heat from their charged bolts. And more than close enough to see their surprise.

For a moment, no one moved. Dozens of Curtanas stared at her, still piecing together how she appeared before them in the span of a blink. Collectively, they shifted, holding their bolts and guns before them, but not before Natalie caught the flicker of fear in their eyes.

They were *afraid.* It was all the opening Natalie needed.

Stepping into a small puddle, her next tack put her among them.

Natalie released Enzi's scruff as gravity took her. Emerging from a seawater stream, she fixated on the back of the nearest Curtana. He was blond. Tall. That's all that registered before she was moving again.

"Tawney help me," Natalie hissed under her breath.

The boy never knew what hit him.

Kicking the Curtana's legs out from under him, Natalie yanked the bolt from him. She held the baton with both hands, both relishing and hating its familiar weight. The boy hit the ground with a *huff* and she was gone before she even glimpsed his face.

Strike fast and hard, Tawney's memory echoed in the steady war drum of the rain. *You're doomed if it comes to a hand-to-hand fight. But they can't hurt you if they can't catch you.*

Natalie tacked between two more Curtanas, jabbing her bolt into nearest's gut before he could blink the flash from his eyes. The other swiped at her from behind but she was ready for it. Ducking, Natalie swung her own bolt up, catching the woman under her chin. Her head snapped back as she fell, and Natalie didn't stop to see if either of them rose.

She slid into the nearest puddle and around her, chaos reigned.

Flashes erupted through the crowd like lightning as Leo and Owen chased after her. The Moirai wove between them, keeping Nora and Ignis tight at their sides. Together they followed Natalie closely. Never more than a few Curtanas apart, they appeared just long enough to confront the Nautilus around them while always moving towards the Library.

And the Atlanteans were a tide at their backs. Those capable of tacking deposited Ravens at irregular intervals, splintering the orderly lineup of Curtanas in seconds. No longer attacking a head-on regiment, Nautilus scrambled to defend themselves from within. They'd been waiting, prepared, but it wasn't enough. Not against a legion able to tack behind and between them in a flash.

And a legion they became.

Many Atlanteans fought with bolts brought by the Ravens. Others used holograms to distract the Curtanas, or force fields to redirect them. And some stood their ground with nothing more than their fists.

Around them the Ancient City trembled with all the violence of a storm. And Natalie moved through it as fast as the water would take her.

She sprinted for the next puddle as another Curtana charged her. The woman was all edges and hard lines, her expression lethal as her bolt arced high.

Natalie gritted her teeth and dropped. Her calves screamed as they scraped the ground, but reaching a pool of saltwater, the woman disappeared. Light, weightlessness, gravity. Again and again Natalie tacked among the Curtanas, disarming them between blinding flashes of light.

One managed to lock an arm around her neck but she didn't stop. Dragging them into the next puddle, she tacked to the edge of the fray. The man released her, dazed and disoriented, and Natalie stole his bolt before taking off again, banking towards the Library.

"Enzi!" she called as the weathered columns loomed over her.

A bark answered, lost in the rain and chaos. She turned to search for him and a bolt's heat frisked her spine.

"Look out!" Ignis collided into her, pushing them both away from the Curtana and into another puddle.

Natalie had just enough of her wits about her to tack them away from the Library's main entrance.

"Enzi!" she called again.

"Nat!" Nora shouted from several rows of Nautilus over. She stuck tight to Atro's side, Lache and Clo close behind them. "We're going the wrong way!"

Natalie lacked the breath to explain. She led them around the Library's stone steps and the Nautilus numbers quickly dwindled. As she hoped, their efforts focused on the fight at the front, leaving the side alleyways exposed. She'd be there in twenty paces.

Ten.

Five.

Nora's scream cut between Natalie's ribs like a knife.

She spun, catching sight of her just as Nora hit the pavement. A Curtana stood over her, mouth twisted with fury as he lifted his bolt again. Flat-out and soaked through, Nora neglected to defend herself. She didn't roll away or lift her arms. She didn't move at all.

"Nora!" Sliding into the nearest stream, Natalie redirected towards them. She tacked over Nora, blocking the Curtana's bolt with her own in a shower of sparks.

He stumbled backwards, surprised, and his anger redoubled. In a cry of rage, he launched himself at Natalie. She dropped, tacking behind him and kicking him face-first into the pavestones. She knocked his bolt beyond his reach as he rolled over, propping himself up on his elbows.

"You can't stop the Ward," he sneered, blood painting his teeth. "He's already inside. He's already won. He's going to show you and the rest of the world–"

Natalie snapped her uncharged bold across his cheek. He slumped, silent and unconscious.

"I hope you find peace," Natalie scoffed, breathless.

Looping her arms under Nora's, she tacked to an alleyway alongside the Library.

"Nora?" Kneeling over her, Natalie squeezed Nora's hand. It was limp in her own.

"Is she alright?" Owen ran up behind her, joined quickly by the Moirai.

"I don't know," Natalie answered honestly.

"Is she alive?" Ignis's face was set but Natalie caught the fear in her eyes. Nora was her friend too.

Silent and her eyes closed, Nora's chest still rose and fell with breath.

Natalie nodded. "She's alive."

Sheltered in the Library's shadow, Natalie could no longer see the flood of Atlanteans and Ravens that had followed her, but she could hear them. They were a roar at her back, propelling forward as relentless as the tide. The storm muffled their shouts, the thud of fists on flesh, and constant zing of bolts, but above it all Natalie's heartbeat drummed in her ears. This fight was theirs as much as it had ever been hers.

From the fray, Leo skidded around the corner with Enzi on his heels. The dog barreled into Natalie's chest, whining and whimpering and pawing incessantly.

"You're okay!" She said it to him as much as herself. "You're okay. You're okay, bud."

Enzi whipped his head from side to side, rubbing at his face as he howled. Catching his muzzle in her palm, Natalie's heart wrenched.

His left ear was gone. In its place was a savage line of singed flesh and fur. The dog fussed again, cocking his head towards the wound.

"I'm sorry," Natalie's throat tightened around the words. "I'm so sorry."

"Ouch," Clo winced, cautiously patting Enzi's rump. "You poor thing."

"Poor thing?" Leo scratched Enzi from nose to tail. "You should have seen him. Dog's damn lucky he didn't lose anything else – like his life. No amount of therapy is going to save those Curtanas from Enzi-shaped nightmares."

"You are the best boy," Natalie pressed her forehead to Enzi's, wishing there was more she could do than praise him. Wishing there was more time.

"We'll have to leave Nora here," Leo noted, still rubbing Enzi behind his good ear.

"I will stay with her," Ignis volunteered. "And stop anyone from following you." She clasped forearms with Atro. "Lead the Ravens in surrounding the Library."

"And have the Atlanteans secure as many city streets as they can," Natalie added. "Cut the Nautilus forces off from the sea and their Ward. We're going inside," she looked to Leo, who nodded.

"Together," Owen added.

"And we will see you after," Lache squeezed Natalie's wrist in a rare show of friendship. "When it is done."

"When it is done." Natalie offered a small smile of comfort though her stomach writhed like a bucket of snakes. She turned to Clo. "Will you watch out for him?" Natalie tilted her chin towards Enzi. "Keep him safe for me?"

Clo's icy blue eyes went wide but she nodded. "Of course."

"Enzi," Natalie stroked the damp fur on his nose with her thumb, blinking back the tears that pricked her eyes. He gazed up at her cheerily enough, head tilted towards his missing pinna. "Stay," she said firmly.

He grunted, shaking water from the fur down his back. It was his least favorite request, but she knew he'd listen. She needed him to help the Moirai, to look after Ignis and Nora, and, most of all, she needed him out of the Ward's reach.

"Ready?" Leo grasped the iron ring of the trapdoor they'd used before, waiting for her word to open it.

Natalie kissed the top of Enzi's nose and let out a long breath, exhaling every distracting thought with it. She let go of Tawney and

Edwin, of Nora who still hadn't stirred. She needed to focus and she couldn't carry them where she was going. When all of her air was gone, leaving only a void in her chest, Natalie signaled Leo to lift the hatch.

A pitch-black abyss yawned open at their feet. Natalie hovered on the rim, curling her sneakers over the edge. Every atom in her body begged her to turn around, to flee. As though some ancient part of her knew if she went into the Library, she wasn't coming back out.

There are a thousand causes to die for. Something to live for is rare.

Natalie stepped into open air and dropped into darkness.

CHAPTER 43

The wind whipped Natalie's hair past her ears as she leapt into the Library. She landed hard, crouching with a soft *oof* as Leo and Owen dropped in beside her. They were hardly more than silhouettes in the dark, three solid shadows that adopted the mannerisms of her friends.

Three shadows. Every hair lifted on the back of Natalie's neck.

It was all the warning she had before a bolt sparked to life mere inches from her nose. Dazzled, Natalie leapt back, its heat radiating over her cheeks.

"Hello, little Raven." The shine of Max's bolt made her green eyes glint like emeralds. Her mouth curled into the satisfied smirk of a dragon catching a thief in its hoard.

Max swung at her again and Natalie spun her own bolt to life at her side.

"You're not going to stop us."

In answer, Max lunged. Sparks danced in Natalie's vision as she parried a wild swing of Max's bolt and the Legate didn't stop there. She advanced on Natalie with vicious blows, attacking again and again until every collision of metal radiated up Natalie's arms. She was too slow and Max was too fast and it was all Natalie could do to keep her at arm's length.

The bolts' light was blinding in the dusk of the Library and Natalie blinked against it as Max appeared to be everywhere. Sparks flew from across the room and then so close Natalie could see nothing else.

She retreated, backing into something tall and gangly. Owen grunted, using her as leverage as he whipped his own bolt back and forth before him.

It was then Natalie realized Max wasn't alone. Four more figures in Nautilus blue closed in on them, one trapping Owen alongside her while three others corralled Leo into a corner. Sweat glinted on his brow in the low light as he blocked two jabs but missed a third. It landed hard in his gut and he winced, catching Natalie's eye.

"Nat!"

The slip in Natalie's attention cost her. Max's bolt grazed her forearm and Natalie dropped her bolt. She cried out, clutching her arm to her chest as a red fractal welt blossomed over her skin.

And Max did not relent. She threw her own bolt down, punching Natalie so hard in the side she crumbled.

Every elation of their victory outside evaporated. Without the advantage of tacking, Natalie had ended up exactly as Tawney predicted: doomed. On the ground, panting and writhing, she hissed through her teeth as Max wrenched her up by her collar.

"The Ward thought you might try something clever," Max sneered. "Bring the boys," she ordered the Curtanas. "The Ward would like a word."

Yanked to her feet, one of them buckled the back of Natalie's knees. She shuffled forward, squinting as the amber glow of the Library flickered brighter with every step.

At what appeared to be a dead-end, a bookcase shifted. A stone stairwell opened beneath it and, somewhere nearby, Owen made a small choking sound. Natalie could hardly believe it herself.

It was the Archives. It had to be.

Shoved inside, Natalie followed the passage with her chin lifted. It emptied into a domed chamber, and if Natalie hadn't been wracking her brain for a plan, she might have whistled.

A ring of stained glass married the wall and ceiling, casting a kaleidoscope of colors and shapes over a fractal mosaic floor. Black glass panels lined the walls, as sleek and still as the water in the massive central pool. Leaning over the edge, Natalie eyed the ink dark water.

Salt. She could smell it.

"Ah, Maxine."

Natalie flinched at Legate Shaye's familiar clipped tone. Her navy suit was an assembly of hard edges out of place in the smooth stone chamber. At least a dozen Nautilus flanked her, a toxic combination of Legates and Curtanas judging by their jackets.

"They entered through an evacuation shaft," Max reported proudly.

"So you beat them," Brant stepped out from behind Shaye, his eyes landing anywhere but on Natalie. "Those were not your instructions."

For a breath, all she saw was the little boy clinging to Edwin's leg, a mop of chestnut curls over wide-set brown eyes. The image was gone as quickly as it came.

Max scoffed. "The Ward—"

"Will not be spoken for," the Ward stood alongside his son.

His presence smothered the room. He wore his suit like armor as triumph radiated off of him, his fingers curling over something small and metallic. "Fortunately for you, your sins today will be undone.

Forgotten if not forgiven." Natalie's hope withered as he smiled at her. "Miss Morrigan."

Natalie arched a brow. "I'm certain if you know of this city, and this room, and that device in your hands, then you're well aware that is not my name."

His smile widened. "Miss Atlas," he corrected.

Natalie waited to speak again until she was certain her voice would hold. "That's the Reverie?"

"Indeed, it is." He lifted the orb until it was eye-level between them.

Seeing the Reverie up close sent a chill down Natalie's spine. Notched with frosted ridges, the glass held a swirl of molten aurichalcum and saltwater that glowed silver in the dim light of the Archives. Captivated, she never saw Owen move.

With nothing more than his fists and his anguish, Owen threw himself at the Ward. "You killed Tawney!" Curtanas caught him well before he reached his mark, pulling him back as he kicked and cursed. "You *killed* her!"

A subtle tension coiled between the Ward's shoulders, drawing them back like a spring. A trap ready to snap shut. Yet his composure held strong.

"I have not wept for a single life sacrificed in Nautilus's rise to power," the Ward commented. "I did not weep for your mothers or your fathers, and I will not shed a tear for Tawney. Everything I have worked for, everything I have *bled* for, will come to truth tonight. There is no need for sorrow. I will save them all." His hawkish smile made Natalie's stomach churn. "As soon as I break your precious Regent."

Two Curtanas dragged Aislinn forward. Chin slumped against her chest, blood wept from a gash on her cheek, and her head lolled as they dropped her on her knees. She was conscious, but only just.

"I am here because you have failed." The Ward sneered over her. "You have neglected your duty to lead, to cultivate, to heal. And in your failing, you forfeit your power. It is mine."

Swaying, Aislinn managed to meet his gaze. "You will not have us."

"My dear, Regent." He towered over her. "Everything in this damned city is already mine. Every record, every invention, every artifact you have locked away in your precious Archives." He squeezed her neck, blanching her skin. "You have no city. You have no people. They are *mine* and I will lead them as you could not. I will bring Atlantis's technology to the surface. I will guide humanity into a golden age of peace and prosperity, starting with the Reverie."

The promise hung between them like a guillotine, and Aislinn didn't flinch.

"If only you knew how to use it."

Natalie's heart leapt. She risked a glance at Leo, his lips parted in silent shock. They still had a card to play, and Aislinn was holding it tight to her chest.

Though the Ward's expression remained placid, his grip tightened around the Reverie as it collided with the side of Aislinn's skull.

The blow sent her sprawling. And more disturbing than the sight of her twitching on the stone was the sense of reverence that hummed about the room.

The Ward never bothered to get his own hands dirty. He used Legates to manipulate for him, Curtanas to fight for him, Doves to preach for him, and Artisans to invent for him. That was the truth of his power, a leader no one would question. And seeing him draw blood for his own cause straightened the spine of every Nautilus in the Archives.

"Today, Nautilus ends the Atlantean era of pacifism. The world needs a leader capable of choosing the greatest good. Now," he circled Aislinn, a lion over fresh prey. "Tell me how it works."

Slowly, Aislinn pushed herself up on her hands and knees. "No."

The Ward raised the blood-smeared sphere to strike her again.

"Fate is wicked," Aislinn went on. "But destiny is infinite. And there comes a day when we all must choose." She bared bloodied teeth. "All power has a price. Are you prepared to pay?"

"Ah," the Ward grinned again. "Are you? Tell me what I must know or your people's city becomes their tomb." He held the Reverie between them. "Perhaps I will cut them down one by one, right here in this chamber, until the stones are soaked in their blood. Perhaps I will start with her," he pointed at Natalie, "and end with you."

Aislinn's veneer cracked. Her mouth wobbled. And for the first time since entering the chamber, she looked to Natalie. If Aislinn told the Ward how to work the Reverie, Atlantis would fall. And if she didn't, Natalie would die, followed by Atlas knows how many more before the Ward's bloodlust was satisfied, and he would still use the Reverie in the end. Atlantis lost either way.

One of them had to break and Natalie knew it couldn't be Aislinn.

"I'll do it," Natalie whispered.

She felt Leo's stare on her. He knew she'd never survive the trip. The last thing Natalie wanted was to time-travel for the Ward, but what choice did she have when the Reverie was the alternative? How could she risk the future of Atlantis, of the world, when there was any other option? If the cost was her life alone, she could not live with herself if she didn't pay it.

There comes a day when we all must choose.

Natalie cleared her throat, injecting everything left of her into her surrender. "I'll time-travel for you."

The Ward turned, a satisfied smirk smeared across his face as he uttered a single, impossible word.

    "No."

CHAPTER 44

Natalie blanched. "No?"

She didn't understand. Wasn't this what he wanted? Wasn't this why he chased her halfway around the globe and back? Why he tortured the Moirai to get them to tack? But when she was finally willing to give him what he wanted, he said *no*?

"I... You... *What?*"

"You had your chance." The Ward straightened his suit. "Plenty of them. Now I no longer need you. I have proved the entire Coelacanth endeavor erroneously irrelevant."

Speechless, Natalie gaped as the Ward studied the grooves of the orb, testing them.

"The opportunity for negotiation has long since passed, Miss Morrigan."

"That's not my name."

The Ward's thin lips curled in a wolf's grin. "That hardly matters now, does it?" Polished shoes struck the floor as he stalked around the pool. "After all, not even Shakespeare put much stock in titles. A rose by any other name, yes?"

Shakespeare. Natalie's attention snared again on the sphere between the Ward's palms. What had the quote in the Temple of Thoughts said? The Past is Prologue.

Memory.

Perhaps the Bard had seen the problem centuries ago.

"The Reverie," the Ward lifted the orb before him, "makes you and your name inconsequential."

"And what does it make you? You can't know of all this," Natalie gestured to the chamber, "of Atlantis, of the Archives and the Reverie, without also knowing the cost."

His stare steeled over and she sensed the Ward's resolve stiffen. "Everything in this life costs something," he snarled. "Even your parents knew that. Success is reserved for those willing to pay."

Beside his father, Brant fidgeted, an unspoken question clouding his eyes.

Natalie watched him as she kept up the only plan she could think of: stalling. "History has already proven the Reverie will give you nothing but destruction."

"That isn't true," Brant blurted.

"August 9th, 1945," she recited the date carefully. "Nagasaki *was* the Reverie. A catastrophic failure." Natalie poured every ounce of feeling into the confession, imploring him to see reason. "Do you know why things come to reside in the Archives? Because they aren't finished. Or because humanity isn't ready to receive them. Because the risk of their use so greatly outweighs their benefit."

"Who are you to decide what is ready?" The Ward's expression darkened.

"One of hundreds willing to stand in your way. The Reverie won't take you back to Mrs. Smith." Natalie said firmly. "So let me."

A tenuous silence stretched between them and she was certain the next words she would hear would be her own death sentence. But they weren't.

"What about Mrs. Smith?" Owen asked quietly.

Natalie had no idea how he did it, but all of the anger had leached from his voice. All of the resentment he held about Tawney, all of his hatred for the Ward, he buried deep beneath a veil of empathy.

"Wouldn't she want to see the proof of Natalie's power for herself? That the life she gave up for the Coelacanth Project was worth it? For us and," Owen gritted his teeth, "and for you. For both of you."

The Ward stared at him and Natalie could practically see the gears in his mind turning. Something Owen said hit home.

"I can guarantee you see her again," Natalie coaxed him. "That ball of metal and glass…that guarantees nothing."

"I want Nat to take us." Brant's voice dropped as low as his gaze. "I want her to see Mom, to see why. I want her to see it all fixed."

Natalie bit her cheek to stay quiet. Now was not the time to tell Brant his father couldn't fix anything, that he'd been lied to, cheated, and deceived. Now was not the time to let the truth unravel what might be her only chance to stop the Ward from activating the Reverie.

The Ward brushed off his son's request. "She does not deserve it."

"Don't I?" Brant urged. "This is about more than Mom now," he added quietly. "I've done things…" he stopped, unable to finish. "I need Nat to see it fixed."

The Ward's mouth pressed into a thin line before he finally relented. "One chance," he growled. "For you, she gets *one* chance."

Natalie's knees went weak with relief.

"Legate Shaye," the Ward dropped the Reverie into her outstretched hand. "If Natalie returns without us, break the Regent.

Use the Reverie."

The Legate glowed with pride, clutching the device to her chest. "Peace be with you. It will be done."

"I'm coming with you." Leo spoke up.

"No," Natalie and the Ward said together.

"Natalie."

Her name was a sword. It drove into her chest, cold and unforgiving as Leo's eyebrows pinched together, the crease between them deepening. Her crease.

"I'll be back," she lied. "And I need you here. I need you out there." She gave him a slow, teary blink and hoped he understood what she wasn't saying.

That Legate Shaye was dutiful to a fault. That she needed him to get everyone out of the city. That she loved him.

"Mind them," the Ward instructed Shaye and Max, nodding at the surrounding Curtanas. "And know when I return," he grinned. "It will be to a changed world."

Natalie stepped forward but Leo caught her.

"Do you have a plan?" his whisper brushed the back of her neck.

A lump lodged in her throat and she didn't trust herself to face him. She couldn't be certain her courage would hold if she did. All Natalie gave him was a single, traitorous nod.

"Good." He pressed his forehead to her hair and she leaned into the weight of him. "Don't question it."

"Get them out," she breathed. "Get everyone out before they figure out how to use that thing."

"Shall we?" The Ward gestured impatiently towards the saltwater pool. "Miss Morrigan?"

Natalie didn't move.

Regent Aislinn managed to stand. "That is not her name."

The Ward's smile soured. "Atlas."

Natalie stepped between Brant and his father, her stomach tightening as the Ward's stubby fingers closed over her own. She had no idea if it was his sweat or hers that slicked the space between them, but in her mind it was the blood of everyone he'd ever killed drenching his palms red.

Chef. Angie. Mom. Dad. Mrs. Merrick. Mr. Johnson. Mrs. Johnson. Mr. Davis.

Christopher.

Eleanor.

Tawney.

Any doubt Natalie harbored over what she was about to do disappeared. If the Ward wanted to go to the past, fine. She'd take him. But she wouldn't bring him back.

If she was going to die for his wickedness, she would bury him with her.

CHAPTER 45

Light. Weightless. Breathless. Gravity.

Natalie's memory of Mrs. Smith on the beach was vague and that's exactly why she chose it.

She remembered it was the summer before Brant's mother got sick, her hair long and cheeks forever round with laughter. Natalie knew her own friends were out of sight down the beach, investigating creatures in tidepools with Christopher. And she remembered that Mrs. Smith had lagged behind, content for a moment of solitary peace on the Eastern Shore.

Natalie hoped she had enjoyed it, hoped Mrs. Smith endured the greatest moment of peace the universe had to offer. Because Natalie knew it was the last one she'd ever have.

Brant stopped short when he saw her. Periwinkle gown ruffled in the wind, his mother strolled ankle deep in the surf, picking up shells and casting them away. Even the Ward was speechless, and a full minute passed before either of them did anything more than stare.

Natalie didn't have to guess what they were feeling. She'd

experienced the impossible rush of having again what she'd lost.

"Mom?" Brant's voice cracked, and the sound seemed to wake the Ward from his stupor.

Only he didn't hold himself like the Ward anymore.

"Jennifer." Mr. Smith stumbled through the sand towards his wife, scooping her tight into his arms. She laughed, squirming playfully until she finally caught a good look at him.

Mrs. Smith quieted. Stilled. She traced lines on her husband's face, marks of age that surely weren't there when she'd seen him earlier that day. His hair was thinner, his stomach thicker, and Natalie couldn't help wondering what Mrs. Smith saw in his eyes. Did any of the man she had grown to love still lingered there, or was he truly and wholly gone?

A trickle of blood spilled from Natalie's nose. It had come sooner than she'd expected, and she worried her cost was catching up faster than she could pay it. She sniffled and the metallic tang tainted the back of her throat.

"Robert?" Mrs. Smith shook her head. "Robert, what is…" Her stare trailed to Brant. "Oh!" She dried the tears that spilled down his cheeks. "You are so *grown*! What are you doing here? How are you–" She stopped herself, smile falling as she scanned the beach. When her eyes met Natalie's, she frowned.

"Natalie," Mrs. Smith's expression was set and calculating as she wiped away the blood on Natalie's upper lip. "Oh, Natalie, when are you?"

Her question spurred the flicker of hope in Natalie's chest into a flame.

"It took longer than I expected," Mr. Smith cut in. "But we're here now. We're together."

He's the Ward, Natalie reminded herself. Seeing him on Christopher's beach alongside his wife, inhabiting the life she'd always known, it was too easy to forget what he'd become.

"I'm sorry." He cradled Mrs. Smith's hands. "I'm sorry it took so long. You faded so fast, I…I lost myself. I lost myself when I lost you."

"Lost me," she repeated blankly.

"You get sick, Mom," Brant hovered at her side, looking at his mother as though she could disappear. "But we're going to stop it."

She stared at him, her expression unreadable.

Mr. Smith pulled her close, brushing the windswept hair from her face. "Jennifer, everything Christopher promised is real. I've seen it. I've walked their streets and touched their genius." He pulled a filled syringe from his pocket and Natalie had no doubt in her mind it was the vaccine. A preventative Atlantis released seven years too late to help Mrs. Smith. "It will make you well."

"You came back for me." No emotion colored her words. Not a hint of relief or anger, nothing of joy or sadness. Only the facts.

"Yes," Brant nodded, his mop of brown curls bouncing. "We're here to help you. To save you."

Mrs. Smith studied her son from head to toe and Natalie could only hope they saw the same things. The redness of his eyes and the sunken hollows of his cheeks. The Nautilus suit that hung loose around once strong shoulders.

"Of course you are." Mrs. Smith touched his forehead. Her entire body faced him, but her gaze slipped again to Natalie. "But what does it cost?"

Her husband stiffened. "My love, you are worth every–"

"I wasn't asking you." The correction was firm. "Tell me the truth," she asked Natalie again. "What does it cost?"

Though she managed to keep her chin level, Natalie's bottom lip wobbled. She forced herself to look at Brant when she answered, unloading every ounce of pain she carried into a single, leaded word.

"Everything."

Mrs. Smith eyed the vaccine still clutched in her husband's hands.

"Yes!" Mr. Smith confessed. "Yes, I did *everything* for you. For us!"

"Go home, Brant," Mrs. Smith said quietly to her son. "Go back."

"Wh-What?" Brant looked from his mother to his father. "You have to take this." He pointed to the vaccine. "If you don't, you'll…you'll…" He gaped, unable to finish.

"Or," Mr. Smith gathered his wife in his arms, pressing his forehead to hers. "You can come with us," he pleaded, his expression pained. "Come with us now and one day…one day you'll thank me."

Natalie opened her mouth to argue, but Mrs. Smith beat her to it.

"I'm not going anywhere," she said. "And I don't need you to fix me. Whatever you've done, Robert, I want no part in it. I'll meet my fate on my feet, just as I promised when we started this endeavor." Mrs. Smith sighed. "Can you not do the same?"

His wounded expression hardened and twisted. "I have spent the last decade rewriting our fate." Mr. Smith grabbed her wrist, turning her so he held her back against his chest. "Now you will meet it as I tell you."

"No."

"No? *No?*" He turned her to face Brant. "Don't you want to be with your son? Don't you want this family? I did what was necessary to save you." The syringe glinted as he maneuvered the needle towards her arm. "And I'd do it again a thousand times over because now, now I can *fix* you."

Here was the beast Natalie had come to know; the monster within the man.

"Do you know what I've done to get back here?" the Ward

seethed. "I devoted my life to you, my legacy. I have *killed* for you. And if you say no now, that blood is on *your* hands."

Fear flashed in Mrs. Smith's eyes. She fought to avoid the vaccine and Natalie wasn't the only one who saw it.

"Stop." Brant attempted to step between them, managing to knock the syringe from his father's grasp before getting shoved aside.

"Atlas!" The Ward spat at Natalie, yanking Mrs. Smith towards the water. "Time to go."

Natalie hesitated as Mrs. Smith struggled. The Ward tightened his hold, twisting her wrist up her spine until she gasped in pain.

"I said *stop*." Brant shouted. Blocking his father's path again, he pulled a pistol from his suit, his lips pursed in a bloodless slash as his mother continued to struggle.

Natalie couldn't help wondering if it was the same gun that fired the bullet that tore through Leo's side. With red-rimmed eyes, Brant narrowed his sights on his father.

"Put the gun down, son," the Ward grumbled, his impatience mounting. "You're not going to shoot me."

Natalie agreed with him right up to the moment the bullet clicked into the chamber.

"This was never about Mom, was it?" Brant grated out the words. "This wasn't about her pain or her suffering; it was about yours. You don't want to carry it."

Mr. Smith backhanded Brant so hard the weapon flew free, landing with a soft *thud* in the sand at Natalie's feet.

Without thinking, she picked up the gun. Natalie hated the cool of the metal against her palms. She hated its weight, its finality. But none of that stopped her from taking aim at the Ward.

He's claimed hundreds of lives, ruined thousands.

I can do this, Natalie adjusted her grip. *I can manage one.*

From the corner of her eye, Mrs. Smith gave a single curt nod.

Mortem ante cladem.

Even now, even knowing she faced death, Mrs. Smith put the Coelacanth Project before her husband. Before her family. Before herself.

Could Natalie?

The Ward snarled down the barrel, but his image shimmered out of focus. Thousands of miles away, in another time, Natalie knew the Ravens and the Atlanteans still fought for Atlantis. They trusted her to do her part. She had one job. One purpose.

"Weak," the Ward spat. "Still so *weak.*"

Every question of who Natalie was, of who she was meant to be, who she *wanted* to be, boiled down to her finger on that trigger. No matter her last name, no matter who her parents were or where she came from, Natalie knew if she fired, she would truly lose herself.

Mortem ante cladem.

Death before defeat.

Memory, not madness.

An Atlas went mad because memory haunted what they did and memory haunted what they didn't. Memory forced them to change the past, forced them to change themselves beyond recognition. To load destiny's dice and accept the cost.

All those stars, Christopher's voice echoed. *They're surrounded by an abyss of darkness, but they burn anyway.*

Imagine the courage that takes.

Natalie could imagine it. She could feel it. Edwin chose to stay behind with the kids knowing he'd die for them. Her parents chose to love her as their own knowing they'd lose her. All of their choices had brought her to this moment, and now it was her turn. Atlantis had chosen her to be an Atlas.

But what would she choose?

Natalie's heart slowed to a calm and steady march in her chest.

Decision settled her bones. This wasn't her.

She lowered the gun.

And the Ward's hands closed around her neck.

Panic clawed up her throat as his nails dug in. Heat rushed to her face and pulsed in her cheeks. She couldn't breathe. She couldn't think. And when she scrambled to back away, he followed. Scratching at his arms, her heels sank in the sand. She stumbled until the Ward held her up. Black dots danced in her vision. Fire burned in her lungs.

"Such power is wasted on you," he sneered. "You will not be the reason I fail. You *will* tack us back. *Now.*"

Natalie's body bucked as she fought to breathe. She knew every sense should have locked onto the Ward, should have searched for some way out, some escape. Instead, the world encroached on her.

She felt the mist of sea spray against her back, saw the blur of gulls swooping overhead. The tang of low tide hung thick in the air, filling her nose and mouth. And somewhere behind the Ward, she heard Mrs. Smith muttering to Brant. Natalie couldn't catch the words, but the sentiment was palpable. Love endured. Despite hiding Brant's power to tack, despite a clandestine adoption and almost a decade apart, their bond was unbreakable. A mother and her son.

So Natalie was thoroughly confused when Mrs. Smith shoved Brant away.

He stumbled into the Ward, knocking them all off balance. It was enough to slip the hold he had on Natalie's throat and sweet air flooded her lungs. She gasped and choked, fumbling in the sand, struggling to get away as the means of her escape quickly became her anchor.

Brant clung fast to Natalie's shoulder and his father's flawless suit. He was too heavy, the sand was too soft, and his momentum carried them all towards the sea.

"Take us back!"

Natalie dug her heels in, determined to do precisely anything else. At least until she realized it wasn't the Ward commanding her. It was Brant.

"Take us back!" The shout fractured to a plea.

He wasn't asking her to change the past. He was asking her to leave it.

Natalie stopped fighting Brant's pull towards the ocean. She leaned in and when the wave rushed up, the Eastern Shore and Mrs. Smith were left behind, lost in light.

CHAPTER 46

The moment Natalie returned to the Atlantean Archives three things became painfully clear.

First, she was alive. Traveling back in time with Brant and the Ward should have cost her everything. Especially after what she'd already done with Tawney and Edwin. Instead, she had a splitting headache and the tang of blood in her throat, but she was undoubtedly, impossibly, *alive*.

Second, Leo and Owen were gone. Aislinn knelt surrounded by a handful of Nautilus as they waited shoulder to shoulder for their Ward's return. Max hovered at Shaye's side, her green hair slicked back.

And third, whatever fragile hope had anchored the Ward's sanity finally snapped.

"Argh!" He spun like a rabid creature, eyes wide and wild and searching for– "Give it to me!" He bellowed at Shaye. "Give me the Reverie *NOW*."

Shaye blinked, put off by his flawed composure, then shook herself and did as ordered. Palms cupped, she lifted the Reverie to the Ward.

"It's alright, Dad," Brant soothed his father. Moving swiftly around him, he placed one hand on the Ward's shoulder as the other scooped the sphere from Shaye. "It's just like you said: we can still fix this."

The Ward's snarl eased, his chest rose and fell as he caught his breath.

Behind them, Natalie's mind raced.

She was outnumbered, unarmed, and the Ward was about to get his deranged hands on the Reverie. She had to trust that Leo and Owen were evacuating whoever remained in the city. She had to trust that her friends would make it out. She had to do something but knew that anything would be stopped in seconds. There were too many Nautilus. She wasn't enough.

But she had to try.

All eyes were on the Ward as Natalie drifted towards him.

"We can still fix this," Brant said again. "If you still want to."

"I've given my entire life to fix this," the Ward growled. "I'm ready."

Something flashed in Brant's eyes akin to pain or regret but it passed too quickly for Natalie to catch. Brant reached for the Ward the same time Natalie did. She lunged, her arms outstretched, desperate to pull the Ward as far from the Reverie for as long as she could manage.

Instead, Brant yanked his father forward, out of her reach, pulling him into a tight embrace.

And dropped the Reverie into Natalie's open palm.

Molten aurichalcum swirled in the glass sphere, golden bands streaked through with silver seawater. It was a sparkling twist of light and dark, of fate and destiny, an ebb and flow like the swell of the tides. Her fingertips skipped over a belt of frosted notches across the surface. It felt so delicate. Not fragile like flowers or promises.

Fragile like a bomb.

"Go," Brant urged. He locked his father against his chest with vice-like strength, veins roping across his arms as the Ward began to struggle, as he pieced together his son's betrayal. Brant held him tighter. The stubborn set of his jaw matched the fire in his eyes.

And Natalie knew what Brant wanted her to do.

He wanted her to carry it. To leap into the salty pool and tack somewhere far away. Somewhere beyond the Ward's reach and Brant's own desperation to be reunited with his mother. He wanted Natalie to take temptation from their path.

Her own feet itched to move. To give in and flee with the Reverie. To find somewhere safe to hide.

But Natalie could no longer deny the bitter truth of reality. The Ward would never stop searching for her, he'd never stop hunting the Reverie. Nowhere would ever truly be safe with Nautilus in the world. Not while the Ward lived and breathed and preyed on the malleable for his own selfish needs.

The truth was, there was no one else to take the Reverie, to take time-travel off of her shoulders. It was her weight to bear. Her responsibility. Not because of a name she was given by her parents or a book, but because she chose it. And in her heart, in her soul, Natalie knew she'd choose her city, her name, her family again and again.

She didn't have the power to wipe the slate clean, to undo all the suffering that came of the Ward's endeavors. But she did have the strength to end the game, to let the world start fresh, to get rid of the slate entirely.

"*Go*," Brant urged.

Natalie hardly heard him. She had seconds at most before his father broke free, before the Legates realized their infallible Ward needed help. Yet time seemed to stretch and bend, warping around Natalie as she turned the Reverie in her fingers.

And then everything sped up.

Max lunged for Natalie but Aislinn blocked her. They tumbled, a blur of emerald and navy until the Regent flattened Max to the ground.

Natalie's fingers worked the frosted ridges of the Reverie, testing it like the puzzles in AJ's office. A moment of fiddling, a quiet *click*, and the orb began to spin.

Above Max, a single tear glistened on Aislinn's cheek.

"Nat…" Brant's brown eyes went wide and Natalie held his stare.

"It's okay," she whispered as much to him as herself. "Everything will be okay." Her voice shook. Her hands trembled. The Reverie hummed in her palm.

The city would fall. Atlantis would sink.

But Edwin was out there. Her people, the Curia, her friends and Enzi were out there. Leo and Owen were evacuating the city with the Ravens. The Atlanteans could get out, even if their buildings would fall. And without the Ward tugging the strings of global politics and hunting her family into every darkened corner, Atlantis could rise again. Would rise again. Stronger. Wiser.

Like a once extinct fish.

"Hey Brant," Natalie sniffled, tears brimming as the Reverie burned hot in her hands. "Want to hear a joke?"

He stared at her, dumbfounded. In her peripherals, Natalie could see the Legates shifting. They sensed something was wrong, but it was too late. Nothing could stop the Reverie now.

"I have a joke about Atlas."

"Natalie–"

"But–"

The Ward wrenched free of his son's hold. He attacked, swift and fierce. His hands flew for her face, his motions feral. Lethal.

Natalie closed her eyes. She didn't want the Ward to be the last thing she saw.

She thought of Christopher. Of her parents and Enzi. She thought of Leo. He'd survive. He'd be safe. Finally, he'd be safe.

Natalie smiled even as the Ward slammed into her. The Reverie flew from her hands, but it didn't matter. The damage was done.

She was still falling when the pulse radiated out.

Every atom in her body vibrated with the force of it. Her teeth clattered, her ears rang, and she floated in a sea of misplaced sensations. She saw stars and light. She drifted into oblivion. Weightless. Peaceful.

Free.

CHAPTER 47

For every sea there is a shore. The ocean stretches desperately, sometimes violently, to taste what lies beyond those first yards of shifting sand. There are glimpses of foreign wilderness. Sips of pavement and forest, of dirt and stone when storms heave waves beyond the dunes.

But they remain only glimpses.

Natalie was the sea. Floating within herself, eternity brushed her consciousness. She glimpsed darkness, a place for rest, for sleep. She tasted death and she yearned for it.

She stretched, reaching blindly for whatever laid beyond that shore, yet something dragged her back. Like the moon pulling the tide, gravity tugged at her until, with a gasp, she surfaced.

Natalie choked. Saltwater seared out of her throat and nose as she sputtered, sucking in breaths between convulsing coughs that wrecked her entire body.

"Bloody hell." Brant hooked his arms under hers and pulled her upright against his chest. His hands were warm against her skin but they shook, and the vibrations made his voice tremble. "You're okay. You're okay."

Natalie groaned. Brant could tell himself whatever he damn well wanted, but she was most definitely *not* okay. She laid as still as she could, soaking in the heat of the sand and as she cataloged her injuries.

Everything hurt. Everything except her toes, which she wiggled with relief. Her head pounded so hard it threatened to split open. Her chest could argue she'd swallowed fire. But the toes, at least, were good.

Beyond the pain and fuzzy ache of her brain, the deep chill in her bones made her skin prickle with unease.

"I'm wet," she croaked. Natalie tugged at her sopping shirt with clumsy fingers. Her hair hung dripping down her neck. It didn't make sense. Alarmed, she tried to sit up. "I'm wet. Brant, why–"

"Nat," Brant's terrified whisper only stoked her panic.

Other than a few stray tears, Brant was *dry*. The sand was dry. And judging from the steady beat of the waves a few feet away, she knew they must have tacked there…wherever *there* was.

"Nat," Brant wiped at her face.

"We tacked, didn't we?" Natalie's mind reeled to catch up. "So why am I wet? Why–"

"Would you shut up about the water already? Nat, you're…you're bleeding." Staring at his blood-soaked palm, Brant blinked away tears. "I'm sorry," he stammered. "I'm so sorry."

"It's not a lot," Natalie brushed away the weak trickle of blood leaking from her nose and ears.

"I'm sorry," he cradled her against his chest. The motion made her head spin.

"This isn't because of you." She pushed herself off of him to stop the horrible rocking motion. "This is the cost."

He gaped at her. "*This*? This is what happens when you travel through time?"

"Yeah," she squinted. It hurt. She relaxed her face and that hurt too. "It's fine."

It struck her then it truly was fine. There was hardly any blood at all. Not nearly enough to pay for all she had done. For Brant's mother. For the Reverie.

The Reverie. Everything came back in a rush.

Aislinn. The Ward. The explosion.

"What the hell is going on?" she blurted. "What happened? I should be dead. *You* should be dead. For the Reverie, for taking you back to your mother and changing–"

Natalie looked up at Brant, realization washing over her like a balm. Yes, she had taken Brant and his father back in time to see his mother, but beyond a rather dramatic conversation, nothing else had happened. In the end, they didn't change anything. In the end, Mrs. Smith chose her own destiny.

"I didn't change anything," Natalie whispered. "Your mom, she…she chose to *stay*." Brant cringed as though reliving the moment again. "And I think," Natalie swallowed. "Brant, I think she saved my life."

He was quiet for a moment, and Natalie wasn't sure how much of her limited explanation he understood until he finally shrugged one shoulder. "I think she saved us both."

Natalie nodded then bit back bile. Nodding was bad. She waited for the meteor shower in her vision to clear.

"I'm sorry, Nat."

For everything was implied, and Natalie sensed genuine regret in the sentiment. Brant's entire body writhed with it. He wrung his hands in his lap, his expression crumpled with shame. Yet Natalie refused to lie to him. She couldn't offer pity or forgiveness. He'd hurt people. He'd hurt her.

She didn't hate him. Not nearly as much as she should. But she wasn't ready to commit to anything more than coexisting on the same stretch of beach. Not yet.

"You couldn't shoot him." Heartache drenched his words. "My Dad." It wasn't a question, but Natalie answered it anyway.

"No," she confessed. "I guess I would rather live as myself than as someone else." Natalie's breath hitched. "But in the end it didn't matter. I suppose…I suppose I killed him anyway." An apology slipped to the tip of her tongue and she closed her lips tight to keep it in.

She did what she had to do. She would do it again.

"It's gone, isn't it?" Natalie stared out to the horizon where grey sky melted into sea. "The city?"

"Yeah, it's gone." He watched her. "Why'd you do it? Why didn't you just leave?"

Natalie's chest ached as she remembered Aislinn's face in the Archives, when she realized that the only way to truly save the city was to sink it. She wasn't ready to relive the defeat out loud.

"We need to find the others," Natalie deflected. "Leo and Owen were going to evacuate the city. I don't know if they got out. I don't know–" She tried to stand but instantly dropped, catching herself on her hands and knees. Blood dripped from her nose, pooling over the sand in a dark puddle between her thumbs.

"Hey," Brant crouched in front of her. "You okay?"

Panic prickled Natalie's skin. The city was drowned, and while she fought vertigo her people might be drowning with it. Leo. Owen. Enzi. The Moirai. *Everyone.*

"Go back," she begged him. "Get out everyone you can. I'll follow as soon as I can stand."

"They got out," Brant pressed against her shoulders to keep her on the ground. "They're around here somewhere."

"You don't know that." Her breath quickened and every ragged draw sent lightning through her skull. He'd lied to her before. Fluidly. Repeatedly. "We have to go back."

"No, I'm sure—hey!" He jumped up, red cap waving in the air. "Over here!"

Following the direction of his shouts, Natalie barely glimpsed the distant outline of Morning Sun Marina before a white blur knocked her into the sand. She reeled, blacking out from the impact and blindly lifting her hands against Enzi's mission to smother her.

"Hi," she greeted him, grinning despite the pain. "Hi. Hello. Everything's fine. I love you, too."

Enzi nosed her chin and shoved his muzzle against her chest, whining and howling before darting off to greet Brant. She managed to prop herself up on one elbow before being hoisted from the ground and set properly on her feet.

The beach spun and snapped into place as Leo cradled her face. He stared at her just long enough for her to blink. Just long enough for him to witness her draw breath.

Then he kissed her like the world was ending.

She clutched at him, fingertips digging into his back. Time slowed and stopped as the universe condensed around them. He was real and whole and warmth raced up her spine as every brush of his lips reminded her so.

"I've never known anyone so brilliantly stupid," he growled against her mouth.

"Well," she winced as he cradled a tender spot on the back of her head. "Someone told me not to question myself."

"They sound like an idiot." Leo kissed her again then, holding her out at arm's length, he frowned. "You're wet?"

Still fluffing Enzi's fur, Brant clicked his tongue. "About that…"

Before he could utter another word, Leo turned and punched Brant clear across the face. He dropped where he stood.

Leo loomed over him, glaring, and Brant made no attempt to stand. Spitting a mouthful of blood into the sand, he kept his gaze on the ground.

A full minute passed before Owen joined them, offering Brant his hand. Brant hesitated, then took it. The moment he was standing Leo charged him again. Brant winced but did not retreat, and when Leo's clenched fist swung past his head to pull Brant into a tight embrace, he stood astonished.

"You're outright ugly in navy," Leo commented.

Owen squinted through cracked glasses. "Probably why he can't get any dates."

Brant stared at them, speechless.

"Where is he?" Lache breathed out the question, jogging to a stop alongside Clo and Atro.

Behind them, at the top of the dunes, a crowd trickled into view. A rainbowed mass of Atlantean robes dotted with Nautilus blue and Raven black made Natalie's breath catch in her chest. She leaned against Enzi for support.

Their city may have fallen, but Atlantis was survived by the people that served it.

When no one answered, Lache folded her arms. "Where is the Ward?"

Brant cleared his throat. "Before the Reverie exploded…well, I couldn't reach them both, him and Nat," he said quietly. "He fell with the city."

Atro nodded. "Good."

Brant winced at the comment and, as Natalie stared at him, pointedly refused to meet her gaze. Their trip back to the Archives was a blur, a tangle of aurichalcum gold and seawater, but she was certain Brant was wrong. The Ward had been between them, right next to her. Brant *chose* not to save his father. He chose her instead.

He was lying, and Natalie let him.

Leo clapped Brant on the shoulder, though whether there was truly any sympathy in the action Natalie couldn't be sure.

"Then why is she all wet?"

Brant flushed. "Well," his brown stare flicked up to Natalie's and away again. "The Reverie exploded maybe an instant after I reached her...I pushed her into the pool and I-I tacked us here but she wasn't...she wasn't," Brant sighed. "Nat, you weren't breathing."

Natalie stared at him. She remembered sinking into that darkness, feeling the ebb and flow of consciousness, the push and pull. She remembered wanting to stay. Instead, she'd blinked awake to Brant hovering over her...

She pressed against her sternum where it ached, where ribs were sore and bruised. Where Brant's fists had compressed her chest again and again, forcing water out and his own breath in. Push and pull. Ebb and flow. Until she surfaced.

Natalie's knees threatened to give and, though she already knew the truth, she reached for Leo's hand.

The explosion in the Archives had been real.

Her glimpse of that distant shore had been real.

"I was dead when I hit the water," Natalie whispered.

Brant nodded slowly. "And dead when I pulled you out."

CHAPTER 48

Christopher once sought the secrets of the universe. He wanted the stars to whisper why they burned, for the sea to share all it had seen. He was hungry for answers until he wasn't. One day curious, the next content. It was his own form of enlightenment, a choice to immerse himself in the world without the need to dissect it.

That's why he named his boat the *Learn'd Astronomer*.

And fixed at the edge of the Atlantic Ocean, gazing out towards the distant home she'd lost, Natalie felt she finally understood.

To the ocean, Natalie was an ant, and to the universe, an atom. It was a fractal existence, circles within circles, and knowing you live within the puzzle, destined to die mostly incomplete and largely irrelevant, was a beautiful kind of freedom.

Perspective was powerful.

But no matter how complex the puzzle, all secrets must surface eventually.

Dawn broke gently over the beach. She'd passed the moonlit hours in silence, savoring the constant hum of the waves, watching chaos give way to order.

Lache and Clo had immediately set to work with what remained of the Curia, organizing the hundreds of Atlantean refugees into groups and getting a sense of who was who and what they could do. Nora, Ignis, and Atro drifted among them, bandaging superficial wounds and stitching up others. Some of the Nautilus who'd fled with them hovered on their own away from the group but, to Natalie's surprise, most made themselves useful. Their navy jumpsuits dotted the crowd, lending aid where they could while Brant kept a watchful eye. And all the while Enzi supervised, obsessively circling Owen with his one good ear perked, still determined to make friends with Tofu who hissed defiantly from Owen's shoulder.

Leo, on the other hand, never left Natalie's side. He cleaned the shallow cuts on her arms, cataloged her bruises, and inspected the lump on the back of her head that still throbbed. She was grateful he didn't make her speak. At least, not until dawn.

"Atlas." A councilmember Natalie recognized from her hearing approached, his voice threading above the breaking waves.

"Natalie works just fine." Her voice grated out, rough against her throat.

The man was one of the youngest members, the lines on his face still shallow, his cheek swelled with a violet bruise. "Natalie," he corrected. "I–"

"I'm ready," Natalie forced herself to her feet, every muscle screaming in protest. "Edwin warned me what happens when the city falls and Nautilus already has the world perched on the edge of a knife. With or without the Ward, war will break if it hasn't already. We need to–"

"Natalie," the man stopped her. "My name is Jon. The Curia would like to show you something, if you are up to it."

"I'm up to it."

"Natalie," Leo's touch found the small of her back.

"I'm alright."

"You are *not* alright."

Natalie pursed her lips. He wasn't wrong. She turned back to Jon. "Is there any time-travel involved?"

"Uh…no."

"Tacking?"

"Preferably."

"Great," Natalie poked Leo's chest. "You can take us."

He squinted at her but relented. "Fine. Where exactly are we going?"

"The city."

Natalie and Leo stared at him. "What?" they blurted together.

Jon gave a pitying look. "You must see it."

Natalie rocked on her heels. She didn't want to see it. She didn't want to see her home, the place her mother and father and Chef and Christopher and Tawney and Aislinn had died to save, reduced to rubble. She wasn't sure she could take it.

"Maybe you're right," she flicked a glance at Leo. "Maybe we should wait…"

"No amount of time will make this easier, Atlas," Jon warned.

Natalie sucked on her bottom lip. It, like most of the rest of her, was bruised and swollen. Deep down, she knew Jon was right. A day or a year would make little difference. Grief could be delayed, never avoided.

Some demons must be carried.

"Right," she said finally. "Alright."

At the waterline, a wave rushed over the sand and as it met Leo's feet, they were gone. Tacking's brilliant light lifted Natalie up, the tingling washed over her, and in less than a second it was over. When Natalie opened her eyes, Virginia's sandy shore had been replaced by

Iceland's dizzying cliffs.

Jon set off at once.

Picking around jagged boulders, Natalie tried to remember the way they'd first come to Atlantis with Edwin. The landscape was familiar, she knew it was close, yet the longer she looked the more every rock appeared the same.

Jon stopped beneath a treacherous outcropping and pointed to a hand's breadth of flat, polished granite. "Your palm, please," he beckoned. "The door will only open for an Atlas."

Natalie obliged. Upon placing her hand on the screen, nothing happened. At least, nothing she could see. But she was certain something must have occurred because a round swath of ground shone bright white and disappeared.

It was a hole.

A rabbit hole, Natalie thought grimly.

Jon lowered himself in first, followed by Leo who hoisted Natalie in by her waist. She followed close behind him, losing sight in complete darkness for several seconds before entering a chamber that glowed.

Spinning in place, Natalie was surrounded by what appeared to be cylinders of pure light. Some were tilted, many laid on their sides, all appearing like giant crystals that had erupted from the earth.

"What is this place?" Natalie asked.

Jon was silent as he moved from cylinder to cylinder, cupping his hands to the surface and peering through. Natalie mimicked him and, peeking into a giant nearby container, a lump caught in her throat. It was the printing press from the newsroom. Gutenberg's printing press.

"How is this possible?" Natalie breathed, inspecting another. And another.

The city collapsed. She'd felt it. She'd collapsed with it. Nothing should have survived.

Not even me.

Jon's shoulders dropped with a motion that relaxed his entire body. "Every artifact, every invention, is coupled with a force field casing," he waved at the cavern. "Should the need arise, the casings are activated and the treasures transported here."

"This is what the Curia was doing," Leo snapped his fingers. "This is why none of them were fighting back."

Jon nodded. "They were fulfilling their purpose," he patted the nearest cylinder. "Preserving our past and assuring our future." He surveyed the room with a sad pride. "Our buildings are gone, yet everything we exist to preserve lives on in this room. And our people live because of you."

"No," Natalie shook her head. "They're alive because of the Ravens. They got the Atlanteans out. They–"

"Our people survived thanks to the actions of your friends," Jon interrupted. "But they will live because of you." He took both of Natalie's hands in his own. "Atlantis has not fallen. Not today."

Natalie looked down at Jon's hands, at the gold and silver bangles that wrapped his wrists. Three of them. Just like the three rings that capped Edwin's ear.

Something to live for is rare.

"Edwin was chosen for Regent," Natalie felt Jon stiffened at her words. "The Curia would have named him so if Aislinn had not challenged him." She met the councilman's guarded gaze. "Why did you do it?"

"Edwin is brilliant," Jon acknowledged easily. "He is an inventor, a scholar, a visionary. But he is also a dreamer, ahead of his time," he paused. "He proposed ideas Aislinn did not believe the world was ready for."

"The Coelacanth Project," Natalie supplemented.

Jon inclined his head. "Yes. He wishes for Atlantis to be brought to the surface, for the world to know what we do so that we may do it better."

"To rise," Natalie nodded.

"Indeed. But he forgets that discretion allows for ingenuity," Jon glanced around the broken remains of their home. "That innovation can be deadly in the wrong hands."

Leo sighed. "A dream he chased to his grave."

Jon turned to him. "Edwin is dead?" he frowned.

Natalie's head throbbed from the question. In a strange way, Edwin had been dead a long time, yet the wound was still fresh. And deep.

"Yes," she whispered.

"I am truly sorry to hear it. To lose him and Aislinn," Jon rubbed his neck. "Atlantis will never shine as bright without them." He fidgeted a moment, his mouth working up the courage to voice what needed to be asked.

Natalie decided to spare him the effort. "On the subject of Atlantis's place in the world," she said. "I agree with Aislinn."

Relief was plain on his face. "You-you do?"

"If Nautilus taught us anything, it's that the world isn't ready for Atlantis. Not yet." Patting the nearest cylinder, Natalie steeled herself for what had to come next. "There are pockets of Nautilus all over the world that need weeding out. If we can organize and dispatch teams quickly, we might still avoid global fallout."

Jon nodded, folding his hands beneath his robe. "And then?"

"And then," Natalie scooped up a chunk of brick and tossed it to Leo.

He grinned, tossing the rock up to catch it again. "We go home."

EPILOGUE

...six months later...

Leo squared his shoulders, a one man wall between her and the sea. "I don't like it."

"I can see that," Natalie tried not to smile. "I told you, you can come with me."

"My going has no impact on my feelings toward you going."

"I have to do this."

"No, you don't."

"Leo–"

"He knew what he was getting into, Natalie. You laid it out clear as glass."

"I owe him this."

Leo softened, uncrossing his arms to pull her against him. "You don't owe anyone anything."

"And what happens if I don't go?" Natalie muttered against his chest. "Alone, Leo. That's what happens. He dies alone."

Enzi whined impatiently at the water's edge and Leo's resolve broke with a huff. "Even the dog's on your side."

"Of course he is."

Victorious, Natalie tugged Leo to the water and, seizing Enzi's scruff, strode into the oncoming wave. Blinding white light enveloped her, lifting her up and away from the Earth as tingles scaled her limbs and time stole her breath. Gravity reclaimed her and she was off before she'd blinked the stars from her vision.

Hospital lights sliced across the night sky, a mountain of glass and steel. Natalie hurried inside, skirting around the nurses' station and taking the stairs two at a time as the bitter sting of antiseptic invaded her nose.

She'd come with Nora and Mrs. King to visit Christopher twice before. First to see him after the surgeons fetched the bullet from his leg. Then to claim him when his body finally failed. She remembered the way to his room whether she wanted to or not.

It wasn't until she reached the door that she paused.

She imagined that goodbyes were never easy. That no matter how much time you had to collect your thoughts, to say everything you wanted to say, it would never be enough. Because in the end it was still farewell. But all of that was just conjecture. Hypothesis and possibility.

This was the first time fate granted her a proper goodbye.

She didn't want to waste it.

Enzi, however, had no such hesitations. He skittered around her and leapt less than gracefully onto the bed.

"Enzi!" a gruff voice greeted him. "What on Earth are ya—"

Christopher stopped short when he saw them. A sickly pallor injected his tanned skin, the truth of his deterioration lurking beneath his salt and pepper stubble. His leg was bandaged and slung, elevated by a network of harnesses that Enzi thoroughly inspected. Monitors beeped. A fluid pump clicked. And whatever haze his medications were intended to induce vanished as he blinked at her.

"By Atlas," Uncle Chris, *Edwin*, grumbled. "It took you lot bloody long enough, didn't it?"

Natalie couldn't help it. She laughed.

"Come here, come here!" He beckoned them forward, wincing and cursing as he fought against the mountain of pillows to sit up.

Natalie rushed over to help him adjust but he stopped her, wiping away the single drop of blood that ran from her right ear.

"You alright, kid?" Christopher probed.

Natalie snorted. He'd suffered a gunshot wound to the leg, intensive surgery, raising five kids as his own, and a lifetime away from home knowing full well death would be his reward.

And he inquired about *her* health.

"I'm more than alright," she promised him.

Satisfied, Christopher reached out to shake Leo's hand. Leo took it, then pulled him into an embrace so tight he chuckled.

"It's damn good to see ya, man. Damn good."

"You got old," Leo grinned.

Christopher shoved him as well as he could manage. "That's what raisin' a bunch of snot-nosed brats will do ya." He beamed and leaned back with a sigh. "I'd do it again, though. You lot gave me more to live for than I'd ever expected."

Natalie blinked back tears, busying herself with the bouquet of saltwater taffy and framed photograph on his bedside table. She would not cry. She refused to waste the precious moments he had left with tears.

Christopher took her hand, his rough calluses grazing her palm. His dark eyes burned with questions, but when he finally spoke, it wasn't the one she was expecting.

"Why are you here?"

Natalie sat gingerly on the edge of the bed as Enzi snuggled up beside them, resting his massive white head on Christopher's gowned chest. He traced the pointed tip of the dog's good ear and the ragged scar where the other had been.

"I'm here," Natalie began slowly, "to tell you how it ends."

Edwin's hunger for answers clawed through Christopher's learned exterior. "Did we win?" he breathed.

"Yes," Leo sated him. "We won."

Chris beamed. "And everyone's alright? AJ? Brant? Aislinn?" He propped himself up on one elbow, plucking a taffy from the candy arrangement. "Tawney?"

Leo stilled. Natalie's mouth opened and she shut it again. Edwin had known Tawney was lost when they left him on that beach. But perhaps hope was stronger than she'd thought. Perhaps time was kinder. Perhaps together they made memory fallible; turned once painful details soft.

And if memory brews madness, perhaps madness is a gift.

Natalie pressed a kiss to the back of Christopher's hand and did the kindest thing she could think of doing. She lied.

"Yes. Everyone's fine."

He sighed, contented, and picked up the photograph Natalie had brought. His hand shook and she supported his wrist to steady him.

"I've always loved this one," he smiled, dark eyes misty.

"You've seen it?" Leo asked, surprised.

"Of course. Lehana took it a few weeks after I recruited her."

"Chef," Natalie recognized the name. She scanned the familiar picture, the parents and children gathered around that giant picnic table in the woods. Their final Formal Friday as a family. "You lied to me, Chris."

He grunted. "You'll have to be more specific, kid."

"In Ancora I, you told me you didn't know who the Ward was. But you did," Natalie swallowed. "You knew."

Christopher put the picture down and settled back into his tower of pillows. His stare flicked between Leo and Natalie, stern and sharp. "I don't know him," he insisted. "Not anymore. The Ward is not the man I recruited for the Coelacanth Project. He's not the man I once called family." Chris smacked his lips. "The fact remains he was the right one for the job. Maybe I hoped things would be different. Maybe I knew they couldn't be. Make no mistake, kid, I've doubted myself a thousand times," he scratched his beard. "But never you."

He wiped another drop of blood from her ear. "You shouldn't have come," he scowled. "Look at ya."

"It's nothing," Natalie insisted. The trip would cost her a few drops of blood and little else. She wasn't there to change his destiny, only to help him meet it. He'd already made his choice. "Besides, what's a little madness between friends?"

Christopher barked out a laugh. "Alright then, on with it. Tell me everything."

Leo seated himself beside her and together they told it all. They talked for hours about the fall of the Ward, the destruction of the city. Leo explained how they'd started to rebuild and established a new Curia, that AJ was elected as Aislinn's successor. Natalie shared that she was going to finish school and had already started classes at the College of William and Mary.

She omitted details about the footholds Nautilus still held across the globe and how Atlantis worked to weed them out. She had hoped the cult would wither away without its leader, yet it turned out there were many willing to adopt the role of Ward.

The fight against their manipulation would be a long one; they'd have to focus on the people, on teaching individuals to question things, to seek truth beyond propaganda and hedged sources. But it was nothing they couldn't handle.

And it was nothing that would ease Christopher's passing from this life.

Natalie talked until her throat hurt, continuing long after Christopher had fallen asleep. Leo's thumb traced circles on the small of her back as their uncle's snores punctuated her sentences. Eventually, his deep breaths turned shallow and thin. The monitor's beeping slowed, but Natalie didn't stop. Not until Christopher's hand fell slack in hers. Not until his chest stilled and Enzi whined.

Whatever adventure waited beyond the shores of death, Christopher had gone to meet it.

"Thank you," Natalie whispered.

Leo tucked a saltwater taffy into Christopher's palm. "For the journey, friend."

They left as the army of nurses rushed in. Leo twined his fingers in hers and the entire walk back to the beach, Natalie expected to break. The pain was agony. The loss was whole and new and ripped open fresh. Yet she was surprised to find she could carry it.

Christopher had given her everything.

And she had finally given him peace.

Natalie found navigating normal life akin to finishing a good book: jarring and mercurial. Attending university had felt pointless at first, especially knowing there was an entire city to rebuild and their people to serve. But with regular visits to the city and their steady march against global Nautilus footholds, she eventually found something of a routine.

"That'll be four dollars and ninety-four cents," the barista said cheerily.

Natalie fished in her pockets, musing that the Atlas of Atlantis could hardly afford her coffee.

"I've got it," Leo sidled in next to her.

"Here you are." His change clicked on the counter.

Natalie grimaced at the worn nickel and penny glinting up at them. "Keep it."

Enzi had reserved their favorite spot on the lawn. Splayed on his back beneath the sprawling oak, he soaked up spring sunshine and enticed belly rubs from passing students.

"Shameless," Leo snubbed.

If Enzi understood the jab, he ignored it.

Natalie dropped her bookbag in the grass as Leo filled her in on all that had happened since the previous weekend. Owen finally finished the blueprints for a new Temple of Thoughts, and the projection systems had synced so the city had normal days and nights again.

His voice threaded harmony through her synapses like music, and she found her mind drifting. She watched a group of students nearby. Two spoke excitedly, their sentences bumbling over one another as they referenced a pile of diagrams held down with rocks and shoes.

"It will work," the girl nearest to Natalie insisted. Amber braids crowned her head. "We just need the material."

"That's a mighty big *just*," the boy across from her frowned.

"Someone will pick this up," another insisted, excitement pulling them up to their hands and knees.

"They won't," the boy argued, "because there's nothing in it for them beyond donating a hoard of cash."

Natalie wasn't sure when she left the spot under the tree, but she found herself standing over their schematics. From what she could tell, it was a trash collector. Solar and wind powered, and as large as a ship, it would filter in plastic and debris from the sea, compact it, and ping a satellite when it was full.

She'd need Owen's assessment to be sure, but Natalie believed the girl was right. It would work.

"Um, hello," the skeptic blinked up at her.

"Who designed this?"

"We did." The braided-haired woman rolled up the blueprints defensively.

"It's genius."

They exchanged glances and one of them asked, "Who are you?"

"My name's Natalie." She produced a holographic puzzle from her pack and handed it to them. "And I have what you need to get that thing working."

The girl turned the sphere over, already toying with the interface. "What is this?"

"An invitation."

"Invitation?" the boy leaned closer. "To what?"

"If you can figure it out, the worst kept secret in history," Natalie smiled. "You're about to question everything."

AUTHOR'S NOTE

I find myself at the end of Natalie's journey and not entirely sure how to let go. A simple *thank you* hardly seems sufficient.

Of all the books in the series, *Regent* was the most difficult and the most important for me to finish. During the writing process, Husband and I had our first child (huzzah). We are overjoyed by our bundle of giggles but finding time (and mental fortitude) to write became difficult. So, while *Regent* marks the end of Natalie's adventure, it signifies a continuation of mine. Of every story I still have to write as an author.

And I never could have done it alone.

First and foremost, a gigantic thank you to my husband Adam. Staying up all night after reading the first draft of *Extant* as I laid out every twist and turn of this story, from the identity of the Ward to the book titles reflecting Christopher's initials, will forever be one of my favorite memories. Thank you for treating my dreams like your own and reminding me daily (sometimes thrice daily) that this is a real book, and I am a real author. I couldn't have snagged a better anchor.

Thank you to Chloe and Autumn for often understanding me better than I understand myself. To my husband's parents for helping me navigate authorhood and motherhood (and the Sunday desserts...let's keep that going). I couldn't dream of concluding this series without a shout out to my dad, who captained the many fishing trips that inspired this story. And dearest mother, who often let me use chores as an excuse to avoid social activities to read...this whole author thing is your fault. Thank you.

And just like Natalie, the family I was born to has expanded to include a unit of authors and readers and booksellers, without whom I would certainly still be too terrified to present any of my work publicly. You helped make my hobby a career, which is truly an amazing feat.

A thousand thanks to the small business and independent bookstores who first found a home for *The Coelacanth Project* on their shelves. Paperbacks Ink, Page After Page Bookstore, Sweet Beans Coffee Shop – your support has meant more than you know.

A whole bag of thanks to the entire team at Biblioboard and the Indie Author Project. Your positivity is infectious, and your work helps so many authors. I am beyond grateful for each of you every single day.

And of course, thank *you* reader for joining me on this adventure. If you find yourself with a moment to spare, an honest review on your favorite bookish platform would be genuinely appreciated. I cannot express how helpful reviews are for authors – they help books find readers, and *The Coelacanth Project* doesn't have an audience without you.

I've spent so long living with Natalie in my head, it's going to be strange closing this chapter and starting a new one. Wherever my next writing adventure takes me, I hope to see you there. Thank you for reading. Until next time…

DISCUSSION QUESTIONS

Level 1

- ⚜ What was your favorite quote or passage from the book?

- ⚜ Who was your favorite character and why?

- ⚜ Which character do you think is the bravest? The most selfless? The most selfish?

- ⚜ Which character do you think is the true hero of the story?

- ⚜ Why were the Moirai more quickly accepted in Atlantean society than Natalie and her friends?

- ⚜ If you were an Atlantean, what would your Contribution be?

- ⚜ What is your favorite part about Newland's Atlantis?

Level 2

- ⚜ What character do you think exhibited the most growth throughout the series?

- ⚜ What were Regent Aislinn's strengths and weaknesses as a leader?

⛄ If you were an Atlas facing the Ward, what might you have done differently than Natalie?

⛄ If the power to tack was prevalent around the world, how might that change war and peace?

⛄ For Natalie, fate and destiny are two separate things. It was her fate to be an Atlas, while it was her destiny to decide how to use it. How do you view fate vs destiny?

⛄ Why wasn't Edwin originally chosen as Regent? Do we see that rationale reflected in our own lives (job qualifications, global politics, etc.)?

⛄ Why did Mr. Smith become the Ward? Do you sympathize with his motives? Do you think he viewed himself as a villain?

Level 3

⛄ Modern science is close to creating something akin to the Atlantean Genesis Room. What is your opinion of the Genesis Room and the Atlantean approach to Progeny?

⛄ Natalie and Edwin argue over the significance of family and what the composition of family looks like. What does family mean to you?

⛄ Compare and contrast the different ways Natalie

and her friends deal with stress and grief.

   △   Brant shows us how far we can lose sight of ourselves when we blindly follow others – even those we love. What do you think finally gave him the courage to make his own choices?

NOW AVAILABLE ON AUDIO

Check out the *Extant* series on Libro.FM – where you can listen AND support your favorite indie bookstores – or wherever you get your audiobooks!

CALLING ALL READERS

Reviews help books find their readers – and they mean so much to authors! If you have a moment to spare, please consider leaving an honest review on your favorite bookish platform.

Connect with Newland on Goodreads, BookBub, and Instagram, and don't forget to join her newsletter at www.SarahNewlandBooks.com for exclusive content and thrilling updates on her cats. They're more mischievous than you think.

9 781733 345880